Available in May 2010
from Mills & Boon® Intrigue

D1424952

MORE THAN A MAN

"This is the second time someone's attacked me in the past few days."

Olivia looked up at Noah as he closed the door to his suite. "Do you attract trouble?"

"Not usually with such alarming regularity," he answered with a harsh laugh.

Olivia had the feeling he was more shaken by the encounter than he let on. She also thought she'd just experienced something extraordinary – with an extraordinary man. Twenty minutes ago she'd barely known Noah Fielding, but after staring down death at the end of a gun barrel, they'd taken a shortcut to intimacy.

Olivia couldn't deny that something real flared between them. Something more than sexual.

But if she kissed him, she had the sense that nothing in her life would ever be the same…

5 MINUTES TO MARRIAGE

"You told me that you have two strikes against you if push comes to shove over custody of the boys. The first was your past."

He nodded slowly, unsure where she was going with this.

"But you've never been arrested and most of the stories of your legendary antics were in the tabloids, right?" she continued.

"Right," he agreed. "Those tabloid reports were always full of untruths and exaggerations."

"You've kept a very low profile since moving back here to the ranch, and nobody can make a case that you aren't an upstanding citizen now."

He quirked a brow. "Go on…"

"So really the only issue is the fact that you're a single man trying to raise two children alone. We could fix that." She took a deep breath. "We would make sure that their grandfather couldn't use that fact against you."

"And how would we do that?" he asked.

She held his gaze intently. "You could marry me."

First published in Great Britain 2010
Harlequin Mills & Boon Limited,
Eton House, 18-24 Paradise Road, Richmond, Surrey TW9 1SR

More Than a Man © Ruth Glick 2009
5 Minutes to Marriage © Harlequin Books S.A. 2009

Special thanks and acknowledgement are given to Carla Cassidy for her contribution to the LOVE IN 60 SECONDS mini-series.

ISBN: 978 0 263 88222 3

46-0510

Harlequin Mills & Boon policy is to use papers that are natural, renewable and recyclable products and made from wood grown in sustainable forests. The logging and manufacturing processes conform to the legal environmental regulations of the country of origin.

Printed and bound in Spain
by Litografia Rosés S.A., Barcelona

MORE THAN A MAN
BY
REBECCA YORK

5 MINUTES TO MARRIAGE
BY
CARLA CASSIDY

™ MILLS & BOON®

MORE THAN A MAN

BY
REBECCA YORK

Award-winning, bestselling novelist Ruth Glick, who writes as **Rebecca York**, is the author of more than one hundred books, including her popular 43 LIGHT STREET series for Intrigue. Ruth says she has the best job in the world. Not only does she get paid for telling stories; she's also the author of twelve cookbooks. Ruth and her husband, Norman, travel frequently, researching locales for her novels and searching out new dishes for her cookbooks.

Chapter One

"We're too late. They're all dead."

The words drifted toward Noah Fielding as though they were part of a dream. Or a nightmare.

An all-too-familiar nightmare.

Other people spoke around him, the sounds reaching him in a confused babble.

As he hovered in a twilight zone between life and death, paralysis held him in a viselike grip. He couldn't move. Not even twitch a finger. He knew he wasn't breathing because a terrible weight pressed against his chest holding his lungs immobile. His limbs might have been sunk into cement.

Don't panic. You know you can get through this. Don't panic. He repeated the words over and over in his mind, fighting to ground himself.

A commanding voice cut through the shock and confusion around him.

"Get them out of there."

The order came from…

Noah should know the man's name. He tried to call it up, but his mind had turned into a pool of treacle.

He felt hands on his body tug him. Someone grabbed him under the arms and pulled him from the experimental submarine, then laid him on the metal deck of the…

Again, he drew a blank.

He could feel hot sun on his face and the boat rocking under his body. More sensations.

"Get the doc."

"It's too late for that."

His mind struggled to make connections. What language were the men speaking?

Farsi? Eighteenth-century French? Russian?

As they spoke, the words fell into a recognizable pattern. The men were speaking English. Late twentieth century. Or maybe twenty-first.

Twenty-first century. Yes. That was the time period. He remembered that now. And he clutched at the fact.

Were they speaking of a doc or a dock?

A sudden coughing fit shattered his concentration.

All around him he heard excited exclamations.

"Fielding's alive."

Noah's eyes blinked open and he stared up into the face of…Ken Dupont. The doctor. The doc.

When Noah struggled to sit up, the man put a hand on his shoulder. "Don't move."

He tried to speak and was caught in another coughing fit as his lungs struggled to function again.

Someone else spoke. "When we lost communication, we thought you were all dead. How did you get the sub out of there?" Captain Sampson was asking the question, his voice sharp. He was the one who had given the orders before.

Noah focused on him. "I…" Again he started coughing, cutting off his explanation. But the whole picture was coming back to him now.

He was ninety miles off the coast of Grand Cayman Island, on a scientific exploration ship—*Neptune's Promise*. The mission was to test an experimental submarine called *The Fortune*.

This was the second day of diving. He and three other men had gone down into the 25,000-foot trench off the island. Everything had been fine, until Eddie Carlson had gotten over-enthusiastic and maneuvered them into a passage between two rock formations—where the sub had gotten stuck. They'd tried everything they could to get out. But the craft wouldn't budge and they were running out of air.

There was no other submarine in the area that could dive so deeply. Nobody who could rescue them.

When the rest of the crew had passed out from lack of oxygen, Noah had willed himself to stay conscious. He'd staggered to the controls and made one last desperate attempt to free the machine. He remembered silently saying a prayer to any god who would listen as he backed up and rammed forward, like the driver of a car stuck in snow. Apparently the maneuver had freed them.

After that, everything was pretty fuzzy. But he must have set a course for the surface, because the sub had made it up here. Only it sounded like it had been too late for the rest of the crew.

Damn. They were all good men. Dead because he'd dragged them down there with him.

He caught himself up short in the middle of the accusation. They'd jumped at the chance to crew the sub. They simply ignored the risks.

In the background Noah heard people talking. Talking about *him*.

"Something I didn't like about that guy."

"He thinks he can do anything he wants 'cause he's got the big bucks."

"Probably hogged the oxygen."

He understood the need to assign blame. And understood that the rich, handsome adventurer, Noah Fielding, was a convenient target.

Still, he heard himself protesting, "No."

The captain's voice cut through the muttering of the crew, telling them to cool it until they had the full story.

Two men brought a stretcher and lifted Noah onto it. He knew it wasn't easy maneuvering his one hundred seventy pound, six-foot frame down the companionway, but they managed to do it without dropping him.

Below deck, he lay on the exam table in the infirmary, letting Dr. Dupont poke and prod him.

"You're in good shape. It looks like you were damn lucky," the medic said.

Noah pushed himself to a sitting position. "I've got an iron constitution. And that rebreather thing kept me going." His voice caught. "I'm just sorry it didn't save the others."

"Yeah." Dupont walked to the door and stuck out his head. "You can talk to him now."

Captain Sampson came in, his gaze hard. "Do you remember what happened?"

Noah struggled not to tense up. He had nothing to hide. Well, nothing that mattered to Sampson or the rest of the crew of *Neptune's Promise*.

"It got pretty fuzzy at the end. I was functioning on hardly any oxygen, so I don't know if I can be perfectly accurate. *The Fortune* wedged into a rock formation. After Eddie passed out, I was able to shake us free."

"I thought you were just financing the expedition. I didn't realize you could operate the sub."

"I've picked up a lot of skills over the years," he clipped out, hoping that was enough of an explanation—and hoping he wasn't going to have to fight his way out of here. He knew it was natural for the men to resent his miraculous escape and his money. He was alive. The crew who had gone down with him in the sub were dead. But that wasn't his fault. All he'd done was survive.

NEPTUNE'S *Promise* returned to George Town. As soon as the craft docked, Noah left the ship and headed for the luxury B and B where he was staying.

He knew the captain had already informed the men's families of their deaths. After closing the door to his room, he made condolence calls to the widows.

The deaths were like a raw wound in his gut. He couldn't bring the men back, but he could arrange to transfer a million dollars to each of the wives. At least that would make the next few years easier for them and their children.

Guilt gnawed at him. He and the crew had carefully gone over procedures, and the craft should have been safe. Maybe if he'd used another pilot, they would have avoided disaster.

Noah had liked Eddie Carlson, most especially his sense of humor and sense of adventure. Now Noah was second-guessing himself and thinking that the guy was too reckless to have been at the controls. If he'd stayed in open water, everybody would have come back alive.

Live and learn, he told himself.

Twenty minutes after he'd closed the door to his room, a two-man team from the local constabulary showed up. One was a brisk little dark-skinned cop named Inspector Dangerford. In his fifties and balding, he was accompanied by a younger, taller assistant named Sergeant Wilkins, who mostly let his boss do the talking.

Noah knew the inspector's type. Nice and polite—until he thought he had something on you. Then he'd get his sidekick to whip out the handcuffs and march you off to an interrogation room where you might or might not undergo some physical persuasion.

Noah had a lot of practice answering questions—hostile and otherwise. Dangerford asked a lot of them in his soft island accent, approaching each point from several different angles, but he couldn't shake Noah's story that he'd strapped on the rebreather and hoped for the best.

From the first, it was clear the cops were just on a fishing expedition, hoping Noah would make some kind of mistake and incriminate himself in the deaths of the other men.

But he stuck to his guns, repeating the same story over and over. He hadn't done anything illegal or immoral. He didn't know why he was alive and the other men were dead.

Strictly speaking, that was the absolute truth.

At the end of the interview, Dangerford asked him to stay in town until the investigation of the incident was completed.

Noah politely declined, and because he wasn't under arrest for anything, they had to back off.

When they asked for his address, he gave them the condo he owned in San Francisco. He wasn't there often, but he paid the security staff to maintain his privacy.

Although he'd planned to stay on the island for a couple of weeks, he felt a sudden urge to get out of the sun. Picking up the phone, he booked a flight to the West Coast with High Fliers, a company that sold shares in private jet planes to rich passengers who wanted to travel in comfort to various destinations around the world.

As NOAH'S PLANE flew over Las Vegas, an interesting conversation was taking place in a studio apartment in a run-down part of the desert gambling oasis.

"You must be crazy." Olivia Stapler gave her brother a hard stare, struggling not to spit in his face after the hateful suggestion he'd made.

Pearson's response was a nasty smile. "If you don't do this, I'll tell Dad that you're working as a prostitute."

"That's a bald-faced lie!"

"What would you call it?"

"I'm working for an escort service."

His laugh was even nastier than the smile. "You expect him to believe that? An escort service in Las Vegas. He hated the idea of your coming here in the first place. Now he's going to *know* you're wallowing in sin."

A sick feeling rose in her throat. Her dad was in a nursing home back in Paterson, New Jersey. After two strokes he was paralyzed on one side and barely functional, and he'd always favored her brother.

If Pearson said Olivia was a prostitute, her dad would believe it, and it would kill him.

After delivering his threat, Pearson softened his approach. "And there's money in it for you, too. A lot more than you ever saw."

"I earned good money dancing," she shot back.

He made a snorting sound. "In a chorus line?"

"Yes! And I had a featured part."

"Well, you had to kiss all that goodbye. So you might as well get used to being a gimp."

The cruel gibe made her want to rush her brother and beat him with her fists. But he'd only start slapping her around, and she'd be in worse shape than she was now. From where she sat, it was too bad she'd focused all her energy on her dance career, but she'd been young and sure that she had what it took to make it.

While she was still in high school, she'd saved money from her after-school job at Macy's. As soon as she'd graduated, she'd bought a bus ticket to Las Vegas.

With her long legs and years of dance training, she'd been instantly hired by one of the smaller reviews on the strip. Six months later, she'd applied to one of the top shows and gotten in. Her boss had told her she was on the fast track to being offered a starring role.

That was then. Her reality was a lot different now, after a drunk driver had plowed into her in the casino parking lot.

She was still trying to pay off her hospital bills and her physical therapy bills. She'd even reached the point where she knew she should apply for food stamps. Then, at least, she could be sure of eating regular meals.

Pearson must have seen the defeated look on her face, because he visibly relaxed. "It's going to be easy. I got the idea from that guy who ran for president. The one who got caught in a hotel room in L.A. with his mistress."

"That was a longtime affair."

Pearson waved her to silence. "Whatever. The point is, some men have a lot to lose if they get nailed in the wrong bed with a blond looker like you. Let me tell you how we're going to work it."

As she listened, she clenched her fists, her mind scrambling for a way to thwart her brother's plans.

NOAH LANDED at LAX and collected his luggage from the flight crew, then picked up his Lexus hybrid in the private lot. Once he was on the highway, he pulled his cell phone from the glove compartment, plugged it into the cigarette lighter and called home.

His man, Thomas Northrop, answered.

"I've landed. I'm in the car and I'll be there in two or three hours, depending on the traffic."

"We're glad to have you back." Thomas paused. His voice was sober when he began to speak again. "I'm sorry about what happened on *The Fortune*. I know you have to be grieving for those men."

"Yes, thanks," Noah answered. He and Thomas were old friends. Or at least as friendly as a man like Noah could get with *anyone*. "Anything I should know about?" he asked.

"You have four e-mails from that doctor—Sidney Hemmings."

"Is something wrong?"

"He's inviting you to a medical research conference in Las Vegas. He says that would be the perfect opportunity for the two of you to meet. He's holding a complimentary place for you."

"Yeah, he mentioned it a couple of months ago. I'm still thinking about it," Noah answered. He'd been corresponding with Hemmings for fifteen years—first by mail and then by e-mail. The doctor was doing some of the most interesting work in the field of longevity and he was a presenter as well as an organizer of the international conference.

Noah was caught between his innate caution and his desire to meet the brilliant researcher face-to-face.

"I'll think about it," he said. He'd detected a subtle note of disquiet in Thomas's tone. "Anything else?"

His chief of staff cleared his throat, then spoke in a halting voice. "Simon is home."

Noah sucked in a breath. Simon was Thomas's older son. And in following long-standing tradition, he should have been the one to take over from his father. But Simon had never been an easy child to deal with, and in his teen years, he'd exhibited some mental instability that had evolved into paranoid schizophrenic episodes.

Noah had paid for his treatment at a very expensive private mental hospital in the Bay Area. With medication, he'd been able to leave the hospital and had been living in Half Moon Bay, working at one of the many garden centers in the town.

"He quit his job and came home," Thomas said. "I think he might be off his meds."

"Thanks for the heads-up."

"I'm sorry."

"Not your fault. We'll deal with it."

"He's been asking questions about you," Thomas continued. "Questions I won't answer."

"I'm sorry to put you in that position."

"As you said, it's not your fault."

They talked for a few more minutes about the young man as Noah drove north, looking with disgust at the brown haze hanging over the coastline.

By the time he reached Santa Barbara, the sky looked better. Continuing north of town, he turned off on a two-lane road that wound through stands of sycamores, live oaks and mounds of pampas grass.

It was a landscape he liked, a landscape he hoped he wouldn't have to abandon anytime soon.

He had a good chance of realizing that ambition, because the location of his home was secret. When he'd changed his name twenty years ago, he'd made sure that nobody knew where the man named Noah Fielding really lived. His mail came to a post office box. His bank was out of state. And he could handle transactions over the Internet. In fact, there were no clues leading to his current location, and he meant to keep it that way.

GARY Carlson arrived on Grand Cayman just after Noah had checked out of his bed-and-breakfast. Gary was the brother of Eddie Carlson, the man who had been piloting *The Fortune* when it had gone down.

Eddie and Gary had been close, and he was having trouble coping with his brother's death. He was also wondering why Noah Fielding felt compelled to transfer a million dollars to the widows of the men who had been in the submarine with him.

As soon as his plane landed, Gary went directly to the police station and tried to get the straight scoop on what had happened below the turquoise waters of the Caribbean.

The cops were sympathetic, but they wouldn't give him anything beyond basic information because the incident was still under investigation.

Next he talked to the captain and crew of *Neptune's Promise,* which was docked in George Town.

There were mixed reactions from the crew. Some thought

the rich man who had backed the expedition, Noah Fielding, had sacrificed the other men to save himself. Others thought Fielding was just a lucky son of a bitch.

Whichever it was, Gary wanted to talk to him. But nobody seemed to have his address and nobody knew how to get in touch with him.

After thirty-six hours on the island, his anger and frustration building, he knew he wasn't going to get any information on his own. He wasn't a patient man under the best of circumstances, and he suspected his grief was affecting his judgment.

But he wasn't willing to drop the inquiry into his brother's death. Once back in Baltimore he looked up a local outfit he'd heard about—the Light Street Detective Agency—and hired them to tell him where to find Fielding.

PULLING up at the entrance to his walled estate, Noah used his remote control. The gate swung open, then closed behind him as he drove toward the sprawling house.

The landscaping along the winding driveway took advantage of the dry climate, interspersing huge boulders with yuccas, cacti and native plants like manzanita. Rounding a curve, he caught sight of the house which was mostly one story but jutted up to a second floor in several locations.

Home.

It was based on the design of an ancient pueblo village that he'd seen long ago and admired for the simplicity of its lines. He'd drawn up plans and started building the house himself, on acreage he'd acquired years earlier while using a different name. It was the site of an old ranch that the family had never been able to make a go of. They'd been glad to unload it to the eccentric gentleman from San Francisco. Noah had found it the perfect solution to his need for privacy. An estate out in the dry, brown hills.

The first dwelling had consisted of five rooms, but he'd

added on to it over the years, hiring local workmen to help him with the construction. The house wasn't the only building on the grounds. He had a workshop, a lab, a stable, a number of storage buildings and a fully equipped gym spread out around the property.

Thomas must have been waiting for a signal from the gate because he stepped outside the front door and waited for the car to pull to a stop.

Noah slowed, studying the man as he walked toward the Lexus. He'd been with Noah for a long time, and now he was in his sixties. He still stood straight and tall, and his mind was as sharp as ever. But there were little signs that he was getting on in years, like his receding hairline and the sagging skin under his chin. He wouldn't be here forever, and Noah would have to face that sad truth sooner or later.

He pulled to a stop, put the vehicle in park and pressed the button to open the trunk.

Thomas stepped forward. "Let me help you."

"No need."

As Noah walked around to the trunk, he caught a flash of movement and looked up to see Simon appear in the doorway.

Moving slowly and deliberately, he approached Noah and his father.

"I've been waiting for you."

"It's good to see you," Noah answered evenly, as he studied the son of his old friend, trying to figure out how this would go. One thing he knew: he didn't like the look in the young man's eyes or the tone of his voice.

Simon answered with a laugh that made the hair on Noah's scalp prickle. "You can't fool me. You hate me."

"Of course not."

"You and my father. You've always been against me."

"Let's go inside and talk." *And I'll contact the hospital and have them pick you up.*

"You're hiding something from me."

"No. Let's go in and I'll tell you everything."

Hope bloomed in Simon's eyes, and Noah thought he had broken through.

But the moment passed. "It's too late for that."

Simon pulled a gun from under his jacket.

Thomas's eyes widened. "Put that away."

The young man aimed the weapon at his father.

"You don't want to hurt him," Noah called out.

The weapon swung toward Noah who was calculating his chances of disarming the kid before something bad happened.

As the three of them confronted each other, Simon focused on his father again.

"If you won't tell me what I want to know, then you're going to die."

As Simon raised the gun, Noah acted on instinct. Leaping forward, he pushed Thomas out of the way.

He heard an explosion, felt the impact of a bullet slamming into his chest. He crashed to the ground and as he lay in the driveway, another bullet made him jerk.

"Stop. For God's sake, stop." That was Thomas shouting at his son. Then he called out, "Help. Somebody help."

Noah's gaze swung toward his friend's voice, but it was too much effort to keep his eyes focused. Everything around him was dimming.

He heard running footsteps, then scuffling sounds.

"Get the hell off me." That was Simon. He started babbling threats, his voice fading as someone dragged him away from the bloody scene.

Thomas knelt over Noah. "I'm sorry. So sorry."

Chapter Two

Noah felt hands on his body and heard a babble of voices.

"Careful. Get him to his bed."

"He needs a doctor."

"Forget it! He's done for."

"It's not as bad as it looks." That was Thomas, calm and sure as always.

They laid him down.

"Leave me with him. I can take care of this."

The chaos faded into the background. Gently Thomas unbuttoned Noah's shirt. Now that they were alone, his old friend drew in a sharp breath.

Noah could imagine the horrible wounds the man was seeing. He had seen many like them over the years.

His lips moved, but no sound came out. He tried to cling to consciousness, but staying awake was beyond his ability, and he drifted away to another reality. To a time long ago.

He was an eleven- or twelve-year-old boy named Edmond George, crying and wandering through a squalid little village. Everyone else was dead from the great pestilence. That's what they called it then. Not the black death.

He was weak from starvation when a group of friars came through the area, praying for the victims.

"A miracle. It's a miracle that God spared this boy's life," the leader of the group proclaimed as he laid his hands on Edmond's head.

They took him to their monastery and nursed him back to health.

His memories leaped twenty-five years ahead in time. He was a lean-bodied, dark-haired man who never caught the passing illnesses that plagued the rest of the brothers. And he was no longer an uneducated lout. He was a well-read man, versed in all the important disciplines of his time, highly respected by many in the monastery. Except for the ones who whispered that his health and good fortune came from the devil.

Those were violent times, even in the church. He was in line to be the abbot when a rival poisoned him. When he didn't die, the devil whispers became a chorus.

One night he fought off a savage attack and fled, bleeding from a host of stab wounds.

Staggering into an abandoned hut, he prayed to God for a favorable reception into heaven and waited to die. Instead, he awakened in the morning, amazed that he was still breathing and that the holes in his flesh had closed themselves. Another miracle.

He was alive. He didn't know why, but he felt a burning desire to stay that way. The monks had taught him scruples, but they had tried to kill him, too.

Quickly he realized that his situation called for desperate measures. With no money and no place in the world, he stole a horse from the stable at a nearby inn, then robbed the occupants of a coach that was making a rest stop along the road.

While the Earl of Bradford was relieving himself behind a tree, Edmond acquired the man's trunk full of clothing and also enough money to live on while he figured out his next move, which was to one of the Italian city-states.

With his classical education, his dark good looks and the political savvy he'd acquired at the monastery, he set himself up as an expert on religious artifacts, which he exported to England at very advantageous prices. He'd also acquired his first mistress and discovered the pleasures of the flesh.

His mind took another leap—this time skipping a hundred years.

He was Miguel Santana who had made a fortune in the wine trade and was one of the backers of a Spanish expedition to the new world. He'd funded three ships and a crew with the proviso that he traveled with the explorers across the Atlantic and then inland across a vast continent, looking for gold and trading with the natives they met.

The party found no gold and turned around, but Miguel Santana slipped away from the explorers and stayed in the new world, where he eventually set himself up as an apprentice to an Indian shaman.

His mind bridged another wide gap.

He was Justin Glasgow, a rich San Francisco settler who had moved south and bought a piece of backcountry property in the hills north of Santa Barbara, where he'd built himself a comfortable estate. Then Justin had "died" and left the property to "his nephew," William Emerson, who had eventually passed it on to his own nephew, Noah Fielding, the man he was now.

He should have another twenty or thirty years before he had to change his name again.

As that thought settled in his mind, he opened his eyes. When he turned his head, he saw Thomas sitting in a chair beside the bed.

"How are you?" his chief of staff asked.

"I'll live," he answered, then barked out a laugh. "I always live."

"Is that so bad?" Thomas asked in a low voice.

"What's worse, do you think? Dying with everyone else when global warming or some man-made plague kills the population of the planet or still being here?"

Of course, there was no answer to the riddle. Just as there was no answer to the riddle of Edmond George or Miguel Santana or Justin Glasgow.

After seven hundred years on earth and millions of dollars spent on research, he still didn't know why he never got sick and his body was blessed—or cursed—with the ability to heal any injury.

He stopped thinking about himself as he took in Thomas's weary countenance.

"You look like you've been up for days."

"I'm fine."

"What did you tell the gawkers?" he asked.

"That Simon was using blanks. That the wounds looked worse than they really were."

"Did they buy it?"

"If not, they're keeping quiet about it."

Noah thought for a moment. "Maybe it might be a good idea for me to take up Dr. Hemmings on his offer to attend that New Frontiers in Longevity conference in Las Vegas. Getting away from the estate for a week or so might be prudent."

"Yes." Thomas cleared his throat. "Simon is back at Gray-field Sanatorium."

Noah blew out a breath.

Thomas continued with his explanation. "I, uh, bound him and confined him to his room before they got here to pick him up."

"That must have been…difficult for you."

"Yes, but it was necessary. When they got here, I told them the story about the blanks. They have him back in the locked wing and back on medication. He was sounding pretty confused. If we're lucky, maybe *he* will even buy the story that he didn't really want to kill anyone."

Thomas made a frustrated sound. "He's been obsessed with you for a long time. I used to catch him sneaking into the warehouses you have on the estate, looking through your memorabilia."

Noah laughed. "Warehouses packed with stuff I should have thrown out long ago."

"I understand why you want to keep things from your past. They're your continuity."

"Yeah, but someone may get the idea that I've been doing a brisk business in stolen Anasazi pots and Maya stelae. Maybe it's time for some housecleaning and some discreet donations to a couple of deserving museums."

Thomas shrugged. "Do you want some help?"

"I'll leave it until after the conference."

Thomas turned the conversation back to his son. "Simon was always jealous of our relationship. He always knew there was something special about you."

Noah nodded. "I'm sorry you have to go through this."

"Not your fault. The bad genes are just surfacing after all these years."

Noah pushed himself to a sitting position and winced as a healing scar pulled. "Stop. You don't have bad genes. Or at least no worse than anyone else. You've read the articles on what's happening to American kids. Simon's probably just a victim of pesticides or air pollution or heavy metals in the water."

Thomas nodded.

"You've proved you're my friend over and over."

"And you mine," Thomas said. "You've done so much for my family over the years."

The Northrop family had worked for Noah since the seventeenth century. Thomas's ancestor had arrived in the New World as an indentured servant, worked for a time on a plantation in Virginia, then escaped a cruel master. Noah had been on a trip east to find out how civilization was progressing on the coast. He'd been posing as a trapper when he'd saved

Wade Northrop from a slit throat after the master had caught up with him, and he'd had the loyalty of the family ever since.

Thomas had been born right here on the estate. Noah had known him from birth, watched him toddle around the family quarters, tutored him at home until he was ten, then sent him to a top prep school, where he was already ahead of the other pupils. He'd earned a place at Stanford and graduated with honors. And he'd been in charge of Noah's estate ever since his father, Philip, had turned over the reins to him.

"Maybe Jason can take on the responsibility," Noah murmured.

Jason was Thomas's second son. He was still a little young to be trusted with the family secret. They'd have to watch him and see how he shaped up.

Noah reached to adjust the pillows more comfortably behind himself and winced again.

"You should rest," Thomas said.

"I should get out of bed and go down to the lab to prove that story about the blanks."

When he heaved himself up and grabbed the bedpost to keep from falling over, he saw Thomas's lips firm. He knew the man wanted him back in bed. But he had far more experience with his recuperative abilities than his chief of staff. Hundreds of years of experience, and he knew that whether he rested or went back to work, the outcome would be the same. The only difference was in the level of discomfort. Maybe he was after discomfort—as payment for the miracle of his life.

JARRED Bainbridge clenched his fist and waited for the spasm in his rib cage to pass. He had always had a high pain tolerance, which was why he was able to get through most days without a heavy dose of medication. At night, he let himself drift away in a narcotic fog and dream of a cure for the very nasty disease that had its hooks into him.

Multiple myeloma. A cancer of the bone marrow where malignant cells replaced healthy plasma-producing cells and left the patient weak and susceptible to infection.

Thirty years ago, Jarred had inherited the Bainbridge manufacturing fortune and had diversified into a host of other business ventures—from computer software to upscale dog food—to ensure the growth of that wealth.

Unfortunately, money hadn't kept him healthy. He'd done extensive research and he knew there was no cure for multiple myeloma—only stopgap measures, the most drastic of which was bone marrow transplant. Jarred wasn't willing to take that risk yet. He'd be letting himself in for more pain, with no guarantee he'd prolong his life.

He wanted a cure. He wanted to be healthy and vital again—like the eight children he'd fathered. None of them was worth a bucket of warm spit, as far as he was concerned. He was leaving each of them a million dollars, which they'd probably squander away in a couple of years. But he certainly wasn't leaving any of them control of his investments. That was going to various animal organizations, because animals made no claim to intelligence and they were at the mercy of their owners.

But he didn't plan to let his fortune go to the dogs until absolutely necessary and he figured his best hope was some new medical research—or some life-giving secret that only a few people on earth possessed.

When the pain gripping his ribs let him function again, he reached for the folder on his desk. It held worldwide newspaper articles and wire service reports that his clipping service sent him on a regular basis.

Most of it was routine stuff. A boy had been trapped in a storm sewer in Suzhou, China, and suffered hypothermia before rescuers reached him. He was expected to make a full recovery. A sailing ship had gone down in the Pacific, and the two-man crew had been rescued from a rubber raft after drifting for almost a month at sea.

But two articles were of particular interest. A man in Nairobi, Kenya, had been caught in a factory fire and been overcome by smoke. While being prepared for burial, he'd awakened and started asking for his wife and children. That incident was worth investigating.

And so was a story about an experimental submarine that had gotten fouled up in a rock formation at the edge of the Atlantic trough near Grand Cayman.

The research foundation running the operation had kept it as quiet as possible, but a small article had appeared in the local George Town paper.

The sub had been down long enough for everyone to die from lack of oxygen, but when the craft was brought up, one of the expedition members had miraculously revived. A guy named Noah Fielding.

According to the article in the local paper, Fielding had apparently financed the development of the sub, but he'd left the expensive craft on Grand Cayman and headed back to the States. Address unknown.

Jarred reached for his laptop and sent an e-mail to one of his special assistants, asking the man to find out everything he could about Noah Fielding.

Was the guy hiding some secret? A secret that could cure Jarred of his deadly disease.

Jarred had to know. He'd try charm and persuasion first, but if Fielding didn't want to talk to him, there were ways of getting the information out of him.

A man might escape death, but he couldn't escape pain—not at the hands of the right practitioner.

LAS VEGAS REMINDED Noah of the Middle Ages. Of course it smelled a lot better; you didn't have to worry about someone dumping garbage onto your head as you walked down the street, and penicillin was a reliable cure for the surge of syphilis. But life in this desert playground was reduced to basic human emotions. Desperate people risked a fortune on the roll of the dice or the turn of a card. And other people waited to pounce on their vulnerability.

He had encountered every one of these types before and he had experienced all the emotions they displayed. From love and triumph to desperation and despair. He'd tried to kill himself more than once. It had never worked, of course, and finally a French woman named Ramona had made him see the light. Maybe that was too strong a way to put it, but he knew she had changed him. When he'd met her, he'd lived too long and seen too much to feel anything but contempt for the human beings who thought they were better than slugs and worms.

Ramona had convinced him that humans had a core of goodness, and if he helped them expand that core, his generous spirit would be rewarded.

He wasn't sure how well he'd done in changing the equation for humanity. The world was simply too big and too complex for one man to make an enormous difference. At least where good was concerned. Evil was another matter.

Still, over the last two centuries, Noah had poured money into various charities and had reached out to many individuals on a personal level.

He wandered through the casino of the Calvanio Hotel, watching old women with dyed hair, cups of quarters and glazed eyes trained on the spinning symbols of slot machines. He knew the odds on the machines, so he bought five hundred dollars worth of chips and won a thousand at blackjack, then quit while he was ahead.

He strolled toward the bar in the front of the building, where he could watch the dancing waters of a fountain in the artificial lake that fronted the strip.

As soon as he walked into the bar, he spotted a curvy blonde wearing a shimmery gold dress that dipped low over her cleavage. The short skirt revealed long, tanned legs. Her wavy hair brushed her shoulders, and her makeup enhanced her natural attributes.

She was well-proportioned and attractive but not beautiful. Yet something about her features drew him. Her eyes were light and set wide apart. Her face was rectangular, with a jaw that spoke of strength. But the haunted look in her eyes and something about the way she held her full lips told him she was in a world of trouble.

Could he help her? Did she want his help? And would starting something with her count as giving back to Ramona?

He'd loved Ramona and lost her two hundred years ago. She hadn't even lived into old age in normal human terms. She'd died of what he later found out was breast cancer before she reached her fiftieth year.

Her last days had been full of pain. Hers and his, as well. He'd wanted to flee the inevitable, but he'd stayed by her bedside, giving her what comfort he could and taking comfort, too. Since her death, he hadn't gotten close enough to anyone to fall in love.

The blonde sitting at the table looked nothing like Ramona, who had been a striking brunette. Yet some indefinable quality of this woman called to him.

The sudden attraction he felt toward her reminded him that he hadn't taken anyone to bed in a long time. If he got emotionally involved with a woman, leaving her would be painful, and if his emotions weren't engaged, then the sex was meaningless.

Sometimes he was lucky enough to find a middle ground.

While he was debating whether to cross the room, she glanced up and their eyes met. A smile flickered on her lips, only to vanish almost as soon as it appeared, the bleak veil descending again.

Even more intrigued, he started toward her, but the sound of someone calling his name interrupted him.

"Noah Fielding?"

He stopped and turned to find himself facing a portly man with wiry salt-and-pepper hair. He was wearing chinos and a slightly rumpled Hawaiian shirt.

The man's face registered confusion. "Sorry," he said, "I must be mistaken. The concierge said you were Noah Fielding, but you can't be."

"I am," Noah answered.

The other man shook his head. "You're sure?" He laughed and slapped his palm against the side of his head. "What kind of question is that? I'm Sidney Hemmings."

Ah. Hemmings. Actually, the man looked older than the picture he had on his Web site. Apparently vanity had frozen his image.

"We've been corresponding for years," the doctor continued. "I expected you to be my age."

Noah shrugged and called up his most innocent and open look. "I was pretty young when I became interested in your field. And I guess I age well."

"You certainly do. How old are you?"

Noah had a lot of practice in sidestepping that question. "Old enough to know better," he answered lightly.

Hemmings shifted his weight from one foot to the other. "Well, it's wonderful to finally meet you. Can I buy you a drink?"

Noah glanced toward the blonde. He'd come here to meet Hemmings, but at the moment, he would rather have a drink with her, which said something about the pull he was feeling. Still, he had no intention of being rude to a man he'd corresponded with for years.

"Of course," he said, leading the way to a table in the corner of the room.

OLIVIA watched the man who had been standing in the doorway looking at her. He was tall like her, with dark hair and eyes and a trim athletic build. As she'd pretended not to study him, she'd fought off a zing of awareness. That attraction was unnerving, because she hadn't planned on being interested in anyone here.

It wasn't just a sexual pull, although that was certainly part of it. Strange as it might seem, when their eyes had briefly met, she'd thought maybe the guy was going to offer to help her.

Could he? Could anybody get her out of the mess that her brother had cooked up?

What if she went to the police? She sighed. They might believe her, but Pearson's scheme was hardly a big deal in a place like Las Vegas. The cops weren't going to protect her from him.

Her gaze flicked toward her brother, who was as far away from her as he could get in the room, watching the action.

For the hundredth time, she wondered what had turned him into the kind of man he was. They'd been raised by the same parents, yet somehow he hadn't absorbed their middle-class values. Instead, he was completely selfish. Unfortunately, he also knew how to be charming, which fooled a lot of people, including Mom and Dad.

The only ray of hope in her present situation was that since his initial ultimatum, she'd been able to make him alter his plans slightly. When she'd pointed out that getting the escort service involved meant a written record of the men she was meeting, he'd seen the wisdom of working freelance.

So here she was, hating herself as she sat in the Calvanio Fountain Bar dangling herself like a tempting worm in front of a pool full of fish.

A sporty-looking man came in, spotted her and crossed the floor to her table, striking up a conversation.

She decided he didn't appear to be rich enough for Pearson's scheme. Or look like he had enough to lose by having his relationship with her exposed.

Maybe that was what she was going to tell her brother

when he demanded to know why she hadn't gotten "friendly" with anyone this evening.

When the guy started chatting her up, she told him she was waiting for someone else and sent him on his way.

As soon as his back was turned, her gaze flicked to the man who had attracted her. He was still talking to the tubby guy in the rumpled shirt. Her man was dressed casually in jeans and a T-shirt.

As far as she could see, he wasn't wearing a gold chain around his neck. Or an expensive watch. He didn't seem like the type for jewelry. But something about the way he held himself gave the impression that he was well-off enough to fit in with Pearson's plans.

NOAH struggled to focus on the conversation with Hemmings, when he really wanted to talk to the woman sitting half a dozen yards away.

"From what you've said, you're not a trained researcher. What got you interested in longevity research in the first place?" the doctor asked.

Noah went into one of his long-standing explanations. "I was in love with a woman who died very young."

"Oh, sorry."

"It was a tragedy, but she got me wondering about why some people have long lives and others don't. I thought if I got active in the field, that would be a kind of memorial to her."

"Admirable."

"How about you?"

Hemmings spread his hands. "I went to medical school, but I found out I didn't really like working with patients. So I took a job at the National Institutes of Health in Bethesda. And I found out I *did* like research." He tipped his head to the side. "So what do you do when you're not increasing the life span of rats?"

Although Noah had no formal education in the field, he'd had the time to do a lot of reading and experimentation on his own. In a lab building on his estate, he had rats that had outlived their life expectancy by fifty percent. While the experiment was interesting, it had brought him no closer to any answers about what made him different from the rest of humanity.

"I've got a number of businesses scattered around the country. Nothing very interesting," he said. "I'd much rather hear about what you've been doing lately."

It wasn't difficult to keep the researcher talking about himself and his work. Noah already knew most of it, but he sat and listened to Hemmings's stories, anyway.

When the doctor occasionally asked questions about Noah's background, he gave brief answers from the life story he'd written for himself.

According to his fictional biography, he'd lived in San Francisco with his parents who had both been killed in a boating accident. He'd inherited an estate from his uncle and had lived there for the past few years.

He'd situated himself so that he could keep an eye on the blonde. During the course of his conversation with the doctor, several men had come up to her, but she must have discouraged them because they ended up going away.

Noah could see that someone else was watching her, too. A man who'd been sitting along the far wall. He came over and spoke to her in a low tone, his face angry. What was that all about?

The doctor must have noticed he wasn't commanding Noah's rapt attention. Annoyance flashed across his face.

But he quickly recovered. Glancing at his watch, he said, "It's late. I should let you go to bed."

"Sorry," Noah apologized. "I put in a long day in the lab before I came here and I'm a little wiped."

They both stood. Hemmings reached out to shake his hand

again. Noah automatically did the same, then felt a slight prick at the base of his thumb.

"What was that?" he asked.

Hemmings looked embarrassed. "Sorry. This damn ring of mine has a rough edge. It must have slipped around to the inside. Did I hurt you?"

"It's fine," Noah said, looking down at his hand where it was slightly scraped.

Of course, it would be good as new in the next few hours.

"Sorry," the doctor apologized again, then excused himself and hurried out of the bar. Noah stayed in the room, watching the woman still sitting at the table. Before he could stop himself, he picked up his sparkling water and walked across the room.

OLIVIA'S breath caught as the man she'd been watching walked over to her table. This was it, and she wished she knew what "it" was.

"I've noticed you sitting here," he said.

"I was waiting for a friend, but I guess he stood me up," she lied.

The guy looked like he didn't buy it, and she thought he was going to walk away.

Instead, he said, "May I join you?"

"Yes."

"My name's Noah Fielding."

"Olivia…" She hesitated for a moment before adding, "Stapler." She knew he caught the hesitation.

"Can I get you anything?" he asked as he sat down.

Up close he was very handsome and younger than she'd thought. He carried himself with a confidence that usually came from maturity, but his face was unlined and there wasn't any gray in his dark hair. She doubted that a man like him would go to the trouble of dyeing it, although one never knew how much a guy was stuck on himself.

A man like him? She wasn't exactly sure what that meant. When she realized she was waiting a long time to answer his question, she said, "You're drinking soda water?"

He looked at his glass and back at her before nodding.

"That sounds good."

"You don't want champagne?" he asked.

"It's not worth what they charge by the glass here."

He grinned. "I guess you know the ropes better than I do."

"Did you come here to gamble?"

"Everybody comes here to gamble. It's the standard vice. But my excuse is a medical convention in town."

"You're a doctor?" she asked.

"Just a hanger-on."

She tipped her head to the side. "What does that mean?"

"I'm an independent researcher. I like to keep up with the field."

Maybe he was also independently wealthy. She canceled that thought immediately. It didn't matter if he made big bucks, because she wasn't going to play Pearson's game.

"Which field?"

"Longevity."

"Oh," she answered, thinking how easy it would be to fall into the trap Pearson had laid for her and this man.

Suddenly, she felt like the room was closing in around her. "I need some air," she blurted.

"The hotel has a very nice garden out back."

She'd been thinking that she'd go outside alone and incur her brother's wrath later. But when she stood, Noah Fielding did, too, and she didn't protest as he walked beside her toward the back of the hotel.

Outside, the air was hot and dry, and the night sky was filled with a million stars. But no casino relied on nature for outdoor effects. The hedges and flower beds were illuminated by cunningly placed floodlights.

The garden was designed to please the senses. Annual and perennial flowers filled well-tended beds that bordered stone paths. Each plot held a pleasing mix of colors and textures, many of the blooms perfuming the air.

She inhaled deeply, glad to be out of the stale casino atmosphere. Trying to come up with something to say, she murmured, "I love the way they laid out the garden in a pattern. I guess they hired a fancy landscape architect."

"Maybe. But whoever did the design copied it from Versailles."

She tipped her head toward him. "Have you been there?"

"Several times."

No one else was outside, she noticed. The garden apparently wasn't as much of an attraction as the casino.

When she pressed her hands against her sides, he said, "What's bothering you?"

The direct question startled her. In her experience, guys didn't care about an attractive woman's personal problems.

"How do you know something is bothering me?"

"The way you hold your shoulders."

"Really?"

"Maybe I can help."

Could he?

Before she could reply, a man rushed from the shadows. He was holding a gun, which he pointed directly at Noah Fielding.

"I finally found you, you bastard," he growled. "Hold it right there."

Chapter Three

Noah cursed under his breath, and Olivia thought she heard him mumble, "Not again."

At the same time, he thrust her behind himself, putting his body squarely between her and the gunman.

"Move," the attacker said. "Both of you."

"Leave the lady out of this," Noah replied, his voice low and even.

In the part of her mind that still functioned rationally, she marveled at his calm. She had to stiffen her legs to keep from falling over.

"I'm giving the orders," the gunman said. "Hands up. Move to your right."

Somehow, she did what he demanded, but as she raised her hands, she was thinking there must be guards out here and security cameras. If guards came running, though, would they just get her and Noah shot?

"Take it easy," Noah said.

He was talking to the gunman, but his calm, even voice helped steady her as she moved to her right, into a rectangular space formed by a hedge and a wall that enclosed one of the luxury villas for the high rollers.

Noah tried to keep his body between her and the gunman

as they stood facing each other in the little courtyard, but the man maneuvered them so that she was terribly exposed.

She glanced sideways at Noah. He wasn't even breaking a sweat. The other man was breathing heavily. Maybe he'd have a heart attack and drop the gun so they could escape.

"If you do anything to hurt this woman, you will be very sorry," Noah said, punching out the words.

"Her bad luck that she was with a scum like you."

She saw Noah clench the fists held above his head. He looked like he wanted to lunge at the gunman, and to hell with the consequences. Maybe he would have if he'd been alone. Instead, he took a deep breath and let it out slowly.

"Are you after my winnings?" he asked.

The man gave a harsh, nervous laugh that scared her as much as the gun. This guy was on the edge of doing something very foolish.

"You wish. You're going to pay a lot more than any winnings. You're going to pay for what you did to my brother," the attacker bit out.

"Who is your brother?"

"You damn well know."

"Just tell me," Noah said, sounding weary.

"Eddie Carlson."

Noah sighed. "I'm sorry for what happened."

The man snorted. "Oh sure. You killed him."

"No."

"Then why is he dead and you're alive?"

Noah's jaw tightened, and she waited for him to say something devastating to the man. Something that would let him know for all time that his brother's death had been his own fault.

As she watched, Noah's expression changed. When he began to speak, his tone was regretful. "There's always risk with an experimental venture. It was damn bad luck that the sub got stuck in that crevice. I've had a lot of deep-sea training and I've done a lot of exercises that make me able to survive on much less oxygen than normal. It's the same kind of technique that a magician relies on when he's locked in a box underwater. The rest of the crew didn't have that training."

Apparently Carlson still wasn't convinced. "So you say. But if you're not guilty of anything, why did you give each of the widows a million bucks? That's three million dollars you gave away."

Olivia goggled. Three million dollars?

Noah spread his raised hands. "I didn't have to give them the money. But I felt a moral obligation because I funded the expedition and I felt responsible for the safety of the men who went down in the sub with me. Now you have your own moral obligation—to Eddie's children. Their father was taken from them in a tragic accident. You have to be the father he would have been. You have to do that, because he can't. And if you end up in jail for murder, what will happen to them?"

Long, tense seconds passed, then Carlson's expression changed, softened. Moments ago, the guy had been roaring mad, ready to avenge his brother's death. Now, apparently something Noah had said got to him.

When he lowered the gun, Olivia let out the breath she'd been holding.

"Thank you," Noah said.

Carlson answered with a tight nod.

Lowering his hands, Noah said, "Give me the gun."

Carlson hesitated, then handed over the weapon.

Noah took it and shoved it into his pocket. "I know you're grieving, and a grieving man sometimes does things he might regret later."

Carlson nodded again.

"I'm truly sorry. When I was asked to finance the expedition, I thought it was a good idea. I guess I should have planned better."

Carlson looked down at his hands. "I feel like a jerk coming after you. It won't bring Eddie back."

"I understand. You're hurting and you wanted to lash out at me because I'm still alive. I'm curious, how did you find me?" Noah asked.

The man sighed. "The Light Street Detective Agency. They're in Baltimore, my hometown. I couldn't find where you lived, but they saw that you'd registered at this hotel." Carlson swallowed hard. "Eddie always was reckless. Did he do something…that got you in trouble down there?"

Noah answered quickly. "No."

From the way he voiced the word, Olivia thought he was probably lying.

Carlson stepped back. "I'm sorry," he muttered.

"Go back home to Baltimore and stay out of trouble."

"I will. Thanks for keeping me from doing something really stupid." Carlson turned and hurried off, leaving Olivia trembling.

"What just happened?" she asked.

"A man was upset, and I made him realize that if he hurt me, he'd be going against his fundamental values." Noah put a hand on her arm. "I'm sorry you had to get involved in that. Are you okay?"

"I…" She couldn't hold her voice steady.

"Come here." When he pulled her against his body and wrapped his arms around her, she leaned into him as he stroked his hands up and down her bare arms, feeling the goose bumps that had sprung up on her skin. "You're shaking."

"I'll be okay." She was thinking that she'd just witnessed something extraordinary—with an extraordinary man, she silently added, as she closed her eyes and nestled against him.

Twenty minutes ago she'd barely known Noah Fielding,

but they'd just been through the fire together and that was a shortcut to intimacy.

She was still trying to work her way through the terrifying experience. "He was mad as hell, but you talked him down. You've got a knack for reading people."

"Like I said, he was grieving. He just needed someone to point out that he has responsibilities back home."

"But you didn't say that the accident in the sub was his brother's fault."

Noah stiffened. "What makes you think it was?"

"I saw the way you reacted. You were itching to tell him what really happened, but you didn't."

He sighed. "What Eddie Carlson did isn't important now. The fundamental point is that I provided the money that got three guys killed."

"You were taking your chances underwater with them."

His hand on her arm tightened. "I really did have an advantage over them."

"So it was true—about that special training."

"Why do you think it wasn't?"

"Something…"

He looked around, as though he'd just realized they were standing in a public space, embracing and discussing a very private incident from his life.

After a few seconds' hesitation, he said, "Here's an interesting choice. Do you want to come to my room—or get as far away from me as you can get?"

"Why would I do that?"

"This is the second time somebody's attacked me in the past few days."

She caught her breath. "You're kidding."

"I wish I were."

"Do you attract trouble?"

He answered with a harsh laugh. "Not usually with such

alarming regularity. I hope the planets aren't in some horrible alignment."

"You believe in astrology?"

"I've studied it. It's interesting. A way for men—" He stopped and shook his head. "A way for people to make some sense of their lives before modern science offered better explanations."

"A lot of times, modern science wars with superstition. I still cringe when I break a mirror."

He laughed. "You and most other people. Because we're still tied to our roots—to the prehistoric cave dwellers huddled around their fires, warding off the monsters in the darkness."

"Are you an anthropologist?"

"No, it's just another one of my hobbies."

She nodded, fascinated with him and at the same time thinking that walking away from him would be the smart thing to do. But she knew she wasn't going to be smart. Not tonight.

Instead, she walked with him to his room.

It was actually a luxury suite with a plush living room, a well-stocked bar and a bedroom beyond.

When he closed the door, she saw him let out a deep sigh, and she was pretty sure he was more shaken by his encounter with Mr. Carlson than he'd let on. As she looked at him, she wanted to make the hurt go away.

Reaching around him, she snapped the security lock and set down her purse on the long table beside the door. The purse contained a cell phone she was supposed to use to call Pearson just by pressing a button. However, if she didn't use it, he wouldn't even know where she was.

Yet her nerves were still jumping.

Noah Fielding had held her just a few minutes earlier, but that had been outside after the attack. This was in his private suite, where everything was different. Intimate.

Or had the feeling of intimacy come from the shared danger?

He must have understood that she needed a little time to sort out her emotions because he walked to the entertainment unit at the side of the room, put the gun in a drawer and turned on an audio channel of soft, slow music.

The sophisticated arrangement appealed to her. So did the man. When he turned, she gave him a small smile, then walked back into his arms.

They were almost the same height, which made him the perfect dance partner for her.

For just a moment, that made her sad. She would never dance again professionally because her leg no longer had the stamina. But she could dance for fun and she would get through her trouble and make her life over again.

He didn't pull her tightly against his body as he led her around the room in time to the music. His rhythm was flawless. He must be a natural dancer, she thought.

They didn't speak. She just let herself enjoy being with him. Enjoy his subtle scent. His firm touch. His masculinity.

And enjoy the dancing. She hadn't done it in a long time and she knew she'd have trouble with a complicated routine— even in ballroom dancing. But this was relaxed.

By degrees, both of them moved closer together until finally he held her tightly against his body, pressing her breasts against his chest.

Until then she'd felt a slow buildup of sensations. Now they gathered into a jolt of arousal.

She hadn't expected it. No, that was a lie. Noah Fielding was a very sexy man. She would have been surprised if she hadn't reacted so strongly.

With one of his large hands, he pushed back her hair and stroked his lips against her cheek, waiting for her to make the next move. All she had to do was turn her head and her lips would meet his.

It was her choice.

If she kissed him, nothing in her life would ever be the same. But how could that be? She didn't even know if she would see him again after tonight.

Still, something real had flared between them. Something more than sexual.

She sensed that he held his breath, silently waiting for her to make a decision about the two of them. She stayed where she was, her lips slightly parted.

Finally, because it was what she wanted, she turned her face, cupped the back of his head and brought his lips to hers.

The first mouth-to-mouth contact was undemanding, yet it was electric and rich with promise.

She heard herself make a small needy sound. Accepting her invitation, he increased the pressure of his lips on hers, then tipped his head first one way and then the other, changing the angle, changing the pressure and charging the moment with his powerful sexuality.

As the heat of the kiss flared hotter, he slid one hand down her body, pulling her hips against his erection.

The potency she sensed made her moan. When she found it impossible to hold still, she moved against him.

It had been a long time since she'd been with a man this way. A man who turned on every one of her senses. Long before her accident, actually. When she'd first come to Vegas, she'd enjoyed the attention men gave a woman they'd seen up on stage. Then she'd realized it was nothing personal. They wanted to seduce one of the glittering women who were hired for their looks and talent.

The woman would stay in Vegas, and they'd come home feeling like a conquering hero.

This was different. This man didn't see her as a trophy. His focus on her was very personal. She knew it from the delicate way his hands stroked her hips and from the way his mouth moved over hers.

As her insides turned liquid, she pictured the two of them naked on the bed in the next room. Him on top of her, their bodies intimately joined in the age-old dance of love.

The explicit image shocked her. She had met this man less than an hour earlier, yet she was ready to make love with him.

Breaking the kiss, she looked at him, seeing the dazed look in his eyes, and knowing he was affected as deeply as she was herself.

The knowledge should have been reassuring. Instead, to her utter horror, she burst into tears.

Olivia felt Noah stiffen. Leaning back, he stared down at her.

"Sorry. I'm so sorry," she managed to get out between sobs.

She wasn't any kind of delicate little doll a man could easily pick up, but he scooped her into his arms and carried her to the sofa, where he sat down, still cradling her against him.

"I thought…"

"My fault," she said between sobs.

Cradling her tenderly in his arms, he let her cry.

JARRED Bainbridge had learned to trust his hunches. Still, the first report on Noah Fielding startled him.

As far as he could tell, the man didn't exist.

Well, he'd been on that experimental sub. A whole bunch of people had seen him, interacted with him. He'd financed the expedition, and he'd been staying at a bed-and-breakfast in George Town.

But within hours of being pulled from the sub, he'd left the island on a small, private jet. The plane had refueled in Chicago, then gone on to L.A. And that was the last anyone knew of Noah Fielding.

He'd vanished into thin air.

Had he gotten off in Chicago? Or had he gone on to the West Coast? Nobody knew.

Which meant the man had gone to considerable trouble to

hide his whereabouts in a day and age when most people's movements were a matter of record.

If Fielding had his methods, so did Jarred Bainbridge. He picked up the phone and made a call to the security service he used. "I want to know where to find Noah Fielding. And I want to know it now."

NOAH cradled Olivia in his arms, rocking her gently. He'd been right; she was in some kind of trouble. He could tell she'd been holding herself together by strength of will. But she'd been through too much tonight to maintain her composure. That encounter with Carlson had scared her spitless. And her roiling emotions had sent her crashing into Noah's arms.

Well, maybe that wasn't fair. He had felt the powerful attraction between them right from the first, and he'd worried that he was taking advantage of her after the attack. Then he'd let his pleasure of holding her and kissing her take over.

The taste of her had been sweet and heady. So had her response to him. That was the most powerful aphrodisiac of all. He'd thought they were headed for a very stimulating session in the bedroom, until her emotions had taken another wild swing.

He bent to stroke his lips against her beautiful golden hair. He'd been intimate with thousands of women, yet this one stirred him as few of them had.

Once again he thought of how much she reminded him of Ramona, although the two of them looked nothing alike. But there was some innate facet of her personality that was the perfect foil for his own dark view of life. She might be in trouble now, but she would always try to find the good in every situation and every person.

He and Olivia Stapler could mean something important to each other—if he dared to let it happen. And if they did, he would lose her and it would take him years to recover from the loss. That was the risk he faced at this moment.

'Tis better to have loved and lost than never to have loved at all.

Alfred Lord Tennyson had said that in 1850, in a poem called "In Memoriam." Noah wasn't sure it was true. Tennyson had lived a normal life span. How many times had the poet known the pain of lost love?

OLIVIA struggled to conquer the flood of emotions that had swooped down on her without warning. Finally she was able to stifle the tears.

Noah shifted her weight so that he could reach into his pocket and bring out a handkerchief, which he handed to her.

She stared at the folded square of white linen. "What kind of man carries a handkerchief?"

He laughed softly. "It's an old habit."

She blew her nose. "I guess chivalry isn't dead."

He shook his head. "One man can't keep it alive."

"But you try."

"It's too much of a responsibility."

The way he said it made her wonder if he wasn't half serious.

Before she could work her way through that, he asked, "Better?"

"Yes. Thanks."

She tipped her head to the side, studying him. "You're not like anyone I've ever met."

"Is that good or bad?"

"You know it's good."

He shrugged. "Few people have the insight to see the impact they make on others."

She laughed. "I did. When I was working as a dancer. I was talented, but it was pretty obvious men saw me as a sex object."

"They didn't look very far. There's a hell of a lot more to you than a pretty face and a great body."

"Thanks. But how do you know?"

"I'm a good judge of people. Where did you dance?"

"At one of the big hotels on the Strip."

"Why did you stop dancing? Did you get caught in the economic downturn?"

"No. I was on the fast track for a big featured role. Then a drunk driver in the parking lot ended my career."

"Ouch."

"In more ways than one."

"Did they catch him?"

She shook her head.

Noah gave her a considering look. "How do you know he was drunk?"

The question took her by surprise. "I just assumed…you know."

"I've learned not to make assumptions," he said, the words hard-edged.

The way he said it sent a little chill skittering over her skin. Could somebody have hit her on purpose?

But who? And why?

Who would gain from that?

Her brother's smirking face leaped into her mind. But she simply couldn't deal with thoughts of him deliberately setting her up. She shook them away and focused on Noah. "I'm finally back on my feet, but I won't be dancing professionally again. It's just too much strain for someone who injured a leg."

"You got workers' compensation?"

She shrugged one shoulder. "Yes. But it's run out."

He kept his gaze on her. "Before we were so rudely interrupted in the garden, you were going to tell me what's bothering you. I guess it was losing your job?"

She heard the question in his voice. And wondered how she was going to answer.

Chapter Four

Olivia struggled with a surge of emotion. The offer was so tempting. It would be such a relief to tell Noah Fielding the whole truth. Pearson had gotten her into bad trouble. Well, not as bad as it could have been, but bad enough.

She'd seen how Noah handled Eddie Carlson's brother. Maybe he could handle *her* brother, too. Make him back off from his dirty little plot aimed at rich guys who wanted to make sure that what happened in Vegas stayed in Vegas.

But the idea of admitting to Noah that she was involved in a shameful scheme to blackmail men made her chest tighten painfully.

She liked Noah and he liked her. What would he think if she told him that desperation and coercion had driven her to the edge of doing something criminal?

She took a breath and exhaled. Before she could give in to temptation, she said, "It's personal."

"All right."

The flat way he said it made her half wish she had the guts to trust him. But she simply couldn't do it. Maybe because it was too important for him to think well of her.

"I'd better go," she said.

He'd scooped her up as if she was light as a cloud. Now it was awkward climbing out of his lap and she felt even more awkward as she reached to pull down her tight dress and twist the skirt back into place.

He gave her a long look that made her insides quiver. Before she could change her mind, she turned and fled.

NOAH waited until Olivia was out the door. He didn't know why she had become important to him, but she had, in a very short time. Hurrying to the door, he opened it a crack and watched her waiting for the elevator. When it arrived and she stepped inside, he hurried down the hall and pressed the button, hoping the next car would arrive quickly.

As he shifted his weight from foot to foot, he thought about running down the stairs. He was fast, but he wasn't a superhero. From the seventeenth floor, he would never make it before she walked out of the elevator lobby. Then he'd lose her in the crowded casino.

When the next car came, he leaped inside, startling a couple who looked like they'd gotten into something kinky on the rooftop observation deck.

By the time they'd exited on the eighth floor and he'd reached the lobby, Olivia was nowhere in sight.

So where would she go?

He thought about the guy who had been watching her in the Fountain Bar. Maybe he expected her to report in. Maybe she'd oblige him and maybe she wouldn't.

He headed toward the bar, which was also near the hotel's entrance onto the Strip. When he spotted her, he breathed out a sigh of relief. Then he saw that she was talking to the guy in question, who wasn't exactly acting like her best buddy.

Noah's first impulse was to rush over to them and get into the middle of the conversation. He could make sure the man understood it would be dangerous to hurt Olivia. Anybody who did that would have to deal with Noah Fielding.

As his logical mind considered the consequences of such impulsive behavior, he wasn't sure the threat would have the desired effect. Olivia and the guy both presumably lived in Las Vegas, and Noah was only in town for a few days. He might frighten the man in the short-run, but that left a whole lot of time afterward when Olivia would have to deal with any local problems on her own.

Noah had had centuries of practice reading body language. He might have said his life had depended on it, but of course, death was not an option for him.

As he studied the pair, he was sure they knew each other well. Husband and wife? He clenched his fist, hoping that wasn't true. Not when she'd been so responsive in his arms.

Taking a deep breath to settle himself, he studied both their faces and noticed a similarity about their features. There was a definite family resemblance. The guy's face was a masculine version of Olivia's, but while Noah sensed an underlying honesty in her, the man came across as a slime.

It wasn't just his features. From the guy's posture, Noah would bet he wanted to get rough with Olivia, but he couldn't do it in a public place.

Confirming Noah's suspicion, the man looked around the hotel lobby. When nobody appeared to be watching the little drama, he made a grab for her arm. His fingers touched down on her skin, but her reflexes were excellent, and before he could latch on to her, she pulled from his grasp.

The attacker made a low sound as they stood confronting each other.

She raised her chin and met his gaze, although Noah could see she was making an effort to keep her lips from trembling. "Leave me alone."

From where he stood inside the casino, Noah was too far away to actually hear the words, but over the years he'd learned how to read lips.

"Remember what I said about Dad," the guy answered. "The wrong news about you could kill him."

The rejoinder confirmed that they were brother and sister.

She took a step back. "Would you really do that to a sick old man?"

"If I have to. Anything that happens will be on your head."

"You've got that wrong."

Ignoring her, he asked, "What about that guy you left with? Where did you go?"

"None of your business." She gave him a hard look. "As far as I'm concerned, this charade is over."

The brother's look could have withered a whole flower garden. Before he could come back with a retort, Olivia turned and marched out of the building.

She'd given as good as she got in the verbal sparring match, but that didn't solve her basic problem. Now that Noah knew about the hit-and-run accident, he could see the slight hitch in her gait. If she couldn't dance, how was she going to support herself?

And why was that *his* problem? Noah asked himself.

His gaze shot back to the brother. Stapler, if that was his name, slapped his right fist into the palm of his left hand, hard enough for Noah to hear the cracking sound.

Noah waited with his heart pounding while the guy decided what to do. Finally, he shrugged and walked toward the casino, and Noah turned toward a slot machine, pretending that he was going to drop some quarters.

As soon as the man breezed past him, he made for the door and stepped into the humid night air—just in time to see Olivia heading along the front of the casino.

Maybe she was afraid the brother was going to follow her because she stopped and looked behind her, and Noah was glad that he was still in the shadow of the building.

She took a deep breath and let it out, then started down the sidewalk, heading in the direction of downtown.

It was easy to keep out of sight when he joined the crowd of people walking along the Strip, even after midnight. The chase became more difficult when she reached a cross street and turned left onto a route less traveled.

All the casinos along the Strip were relatively new. As soon as one got a little shopworn, a developer tore it down and put up the latest, greatest attraction to pull in the people who liked to gamble in a fantasy environment.

You could take your pick of exotic locales. Paris. New York. Italy. Ancient Egypt. The Arabian Nights. King Arthur's Court. Treasure Island.

But the buildings on the side streets hadn't undergone a similar restoration process. Especially in the older part of town.

As soon as Olivia left the brightly lit casino area, she disappeared into shadow, and Noah didn't know if she was still on the sidewalk. Then she stepped into a pool of light, and he saw her walking into an area of low-rise buildings. Some were motels, others apartments.

He followed her, keeping well back, wondering why he was compelled to stay on her trail. He'd just met her a few hours ago, and they hardly knew each other. But over the years he had learned to trust his hunches, so he kept going.

Las Vegas was a city of contrasts. By the time she was two blocks from the back of the casino, the neighborhood had deteriorated considerably. The buildings were run-down, the cars on the street were older models, many of them banged-up, and the sidewalk was littered with trash.

He was appalled at the idea of her walking in this neighborhood, but all he could do was follow. Finally she reached a set of stucco buildings that might have been called garden apartments if they had had any greenery around them.

When she turned in at one of them, he sped up. From the

open air landing, grimy cement steps led up two stories and down to basement apartments. He didn't know which way Olivia had gone, but he felt a wash of relief when he saw her name on a mailbox. She was in 1A, which must be one of the lower-level units.

As he stood breathing in the dry desert air, he took in his surroundings. The buildings were separated from the sidewalk by a three-foot-wide strip of dark gravel. The doors to the units needed a good coat of paint, some of the treads were off the stairs and kids had spray-painted graffiti on some of the stucco walls.

Not a very attractive place to live, he thought. Probably she'd had a better apartment when she'd been working and she'd been forced to move here after she'd lost her job.

He wanted to knock on her door. And then what? Say that he'd followed her home? In her eyes, that might make him a stalker. Even if she were glad to see him, she'd probably be embarrassed for him to find out where she was living.

He stayed for a few more minutes, debating what to do. Finally he turned and walked back the way he'd come. He was going to be in town for several more days. Maybe Olivia would show up in the hotel bar again.

He knew her brother was trying to involve her in some kind of scheme that she didn't like. And she'd been embarrassed to talk about it with a stranger.

Even as he considered his next move, his saner self told him to back off. She hadn't wanted to involve him, and that should be the end of it.

Shoving his hands into his pockets, he returned to the hotel. He went directly to the conference center, where he registered for the meeting he was here to attend. Days ago when he'd studied the online program, he'd been interested in the lineup of speakers and topics. Now he had to force himself to look through the brochure and decide which sessions to attend.

After checking off some possibilities while he ate in one

of the fancier restaurants, he called Thomas to find out how Simon was doing.

His chief of staff was optimistic, although it was still too early for the medication to have kicked in. At least the boy was where he couldn't get into trouble.

As soon as she'd gotten home, Olivia had drawn the drapes and put the chain on the door—not that either one of those measures would stop Pearson if he wanted to break into her apartment. She knew from experience that her brother could go into a fit of violence without considering the consequences until too late.

When she checked her answering machine, she found a message from the nursing home in New Jersey. Her heart leaped into her throat, and she called back immediately, even though she could hardly afford the charges.

"This is Olivia Stapler. Mrs. Warren left a message about my father."

"Just a moment."

She waited with her tension mounting. Finally the nurse came on the line.

"I'm afraid Mr. Stapler is growing less aware of his surroundings."

"Can I speak to him?"

"I'm sorry. He probably wouldn't know who you are."

They talked for a few more minutes. Then Olivia thanked the nurse for calling and hung up, ashamed that she felt a sense of relief. If her father was losing touch with the world, that made it less likely that Pearson could tell him lies about her.

Which gave her more freedom than she'd thought she had.

As she shuffled through the stack of unpaid bills she'd set on the dining room table, she let her imagination take her into a little fantasy. Noah Fielding would marry her and whisk her off to his castle. And Pearson would be left to stew in his own juices.

What would Noah's house be like? He wasn't one of those guys who showed off his wealth with fancy clothes or fancy jewelry, but he'd quietly given away three million dollars a few days ago, which argued that he wasn't worried about money.

She'd bet he cared about where he lived. Maybe he had a horse farm in Kentucky or a mountain retreat in Colorado. Or he could live on a yacht. Yes, she could picture him sailing from port to port.

Did his accent give her a clue about where he came from? Maybe she could hear British undertones in his speech, but she wasn't sure.

Who were his parents? How had they raised him? Had they given him his old-world sensibility, or had he acquired his polish after he'd left home?

How old was he? Had he been married before? She should have asked him questions about himself.

She pulled herself up short. Why? She'd met him in a casino bar and she wasn't going to see him again.

The idea of his whisking her away like a knight on a white horse was very appealing, but unfortunately not very realistic.

Yet the two of them had seemed so compatible in the time they'd been together.

She made another sound of derision—this one directed at herself. Guys were always willing to take what a woman offered, she reminded herself. Noah would have made love with her if she hadn't gotten up and left his room.

Still, she knew that what had taken place between them was more than sexual. She'd been drawn to him more strongly than she had been to any other man she'd ever met.

Fantasies about Noah Fielding won't do you much good, said an inner voice. *You have to do something for yourself.* She shook her head. As far as she could see, the only solution to her problem was getting out of town.

But how was she going to manage it? She'd already borrowed as much money as she could from some of her friends in the chorus line. But she still had some of her mother's jewelry.

On shaky legs she walked to the tiny bedroom, opened the top dresser drawer and got out the blue velvet jewelry box where she kept the few good pieces that Mom had left her. She carried the box to the bed, sat down and lifted the lid. Inside was a gold ring with a one-carat diamond, a gold charm bracelet and a pearl choker. All of them were precious to her, because they were all she had left of her mother.

Mom had died of a heart condition when she was still young, leaving Olivia and Pearson with their father. Maybe that was what had happened to her brother. He'd lost his footing when Mom had died. She might have, too, but she'd thrown herself into dancing and taking over the mother role in the family.

While Dad had appreciated that, it had seemed like Pearson had resented her trying to hold things together. Nothing she did was good enough.

At least they'd had Mom's insurance policy. Olivia had used her share of the money for dance lessons—until she'd discovered that Pearson was getting money out of Dad to start a retail business, which had gone down the tubes, of course.

She shifted her thoughts away from her brother and back to her own problems. The jewelry was her only source of cash. There were pawnshops all over Vegas. She'd get what she could for the family heirlooms and when she got back on her feet, she'd redeem them.

You're having another fantasy, said that wise inner voice.

Olivia knew that was true. If she pawned these pieces, she'd never see them again. Still, wasn't the important point that she needed to get out of town?

She shuddered. Leaving town was such a big step. Really,

she couldn't take much with her. Maybe she needed to think about it for a few days.

But suppose Pearson came knocking at her door in the meantime?

NOAH managed to stick with the convention for the next day and a half.

Several thousand people, mostly doctors, were attending the meeting. Although it should have been easy for Noah to lose himself in the crowd, Hemmings managed to find him and sit with him at a couple of sessions on brain chemistry and cell regeneration.

"What do you think of the conference?" Hemmings asked as they filed out of the seminar room.

"You've done a great job of setting up the program."

The doctor looked pleased, and Noah found himself sucked into a half-hour conversation about the various professionals who were presenting papers.

The topics *were* interesting, and Noah had attended a number of the sessions, but he wasn't learning more than he'd picked up from the journals he regularly read. He declined Hemmings's invitation to meet some of the speakers for dinner and went to the Fountain Bar. When Olivia wasn't there, he felt a spurt of disappointment—and alarm.

Once again, he told himself that Olivia Stapler's private life was none of his business. Still, she was the reason he didn't seem to be able to focus on the topics under discussion. Finally he gave up. Back in his room, he changed into jeans and a T-shirt, then got out his laptop and looked up her name in a private and very expensive database.

He found Olivia Stapler quickly. What he read matched the facts she'd given him, but it was only part of the story. Until four months ago, she'd been dancing in the popular show at a top Vegas hotel. After that, he found medical records and a notation that she'd been forced out of her former apartment for nonpayment of rent.

Clearly she was in financial trouble and had been putting off paying some of her bills. Her phone was about to be cut off and the electricity bill was weeks overdue. They'd shut that off that, too. Then she'd get kicked out of her apartment if she couldn't come up with the rent.

He went a bit further back into her life. The family was from Paterson, New Jersey. The father had been an auto salesman who'd lost his wife and struggled to hold the family together. Olivia had been an excellent student, but her grades had slipped after her mother's death. She'd taken dance lessons since she was ten, the star of the local recitals. And she'd come to Las Vegas a couple of years ago. Was the brother already here, he wondered, or had he followed her?

With a sigh, Noah looked up men with the same last name and finally came up with Pearson Stapler—the brother, who had a record of arrests and convictions. He'd done several jail terms for assault and robbery. No surprise, from the way he'd come across in the brief encounter with his sister in the lobby.

Noah wasn't sure exactly what Pearson had in mind for his sister, but it was obvious Olivia didn't like it.

As he read the background information on Pearson Stapler, Noah felt a knot of dread forming in his stomach. Unable to shake off the sick feeling, he knew he had to go to her apartment. Leaving the hotel, he retraced his steps toward her apartment building.

The closer he got to the run-down complex, the faster he walked, so that he was almost running by the time he reached the front of Olivia's building.

As he stood near the entrance, debating what to do, a woman came down the stairs and looked at him from the landing above, before descending to the mailboxes and opening one with a key.

After taking out the mail, she gave him an inquiring look.

"Can I help you?"

"I'm waiting for someone."

"I hoped maybe you were here to help that poor girl."

"That, too."

The woman walked up the stairs, then turned to look at him as he headed down. When he gained the lower landing, he heard raised voices coming from apartment 1A.

Quietly, he moved closer, listening to the argument on the other side of the door.

"I'm tired of you telling me what to do." The speaker was Olivia.

"You don't have a choice." That was a man, probably Pearson Stapler.

"The nursing home called. Dad's pretty out of it. He couldn't speak to me and he won't be able to speak to you, either."

"You bitch. You're giving up a chance to make some real money."

"I don't want that kind of money."

"Well, I do. And whether you want it or not, you're going to help me out."

"No."

"Listen, I never had a chance. You got all the breaks."

"That's bull. I made my own breaks by working hard. Get out of here. Now."

"You're going to be sorry."

The voices stopped, and he heard scuffling sounds from inside the apartment.

Quickly, Noah reached for the doorknob. It turned in his hand.

When he stepped into a dimly lit room, the two people inside were so focused on each other that neither one of them noticed he'd come in.

Olivia had backed into the kitchen, her hips pressed against the cabinets.

Her voice came out hard and clear as she said, "I swear to God, if you don't get away from me, you're going to be sorry."

Her brother laughed. "Oh yeah, and what are you going to do about it, Miss Gimp?"

"This." Reaching into the drawer next to her, Olivia took out a knife and held it in her fist. "Get away from me. Now."

The smart thing would be for the brother to back off. Instead he snarled, "You wouldn't dare," and charged toward Olivia.

She was desperate enough to slash at him with the knife, but it looked like she didn't really want to hurt him, because the blade didn't come close.

He jumped back, just out of range.

"Get away from her," Noah shouted.

Pearson was focused on Olivia, but she raised her eyes in shock to stare at Noah.

The distraction gave Pearson the opening he needed, and he leaped forward. Twisting her wrist and taking the knife away from her, he held the top of the gleaming blade directly over Olivia.

Chapter Five

With a sick feeling, Noah realized he had tipped the balance in the wrong direction. While Olivia was distracted, Pearson brought his arm down in a savage strike.

Her dancer's reflexes had her dodging quickly aside, and the knife would have missed her entirely if she hadn't slammed into the side of the cabinet. Instead, the downward arc of the blade tore through the fabric at the side of her blouse, and she screamed.

It happened in seconds.

When the brother raised his hand for another blow, Noah sprang forward and grabbed for the knife. The blade caught him in the palm. Pain lanced through him, but he ignored it, twisting Pearson's wrist with the other hand. Stapler screamed and dropped the weapon.

Noah kicked it away. It clattered across the floor and slid half under the stove.

"Go after someone your own size," Noah ground out right before he punched Stapler in the chin. The man grunted and went down with a satisfying thunk.

Noah snatched up the knife and shoved it into his belt, then raced toward Olivia who lay on the floor, a red stain spreading across her dress.

Still ignoring his own injury, he looked wildly around and

saw nothing to stanch the bleeding from Olivia's wound. His only option was to pull off his T-shirt and use that. When his arms were out of the sleeves and his head was covered, he heard Olivia's frantic shout, "Watch out!"

Scrabbling feet told him that Stapler was up and moving. As Noah pulled his head through the shirt, smearing blood across the fabric, the brother came crashing into him, knocking him sideways. He fought to throw the man off him, but he felt fists pummeling his chest, his face. Then a punch to his kidney sent pain shooting through his back.

From the corner of his eye, he saw Olivia lift her leg and kick out with her foot, catching her brother squarely in the shoulder.

"You bitch."

Pearson's focus shifted as he lunged for Olivia. But Noah was already grabbing for him. Clawing his fingers into the back of the man's shirt, he heaved him across the room, where he landed with a whooshing sound. This time, he didn't get up.

Somewhere in Noah's consciousness, he heard a siren wailing. Ignoring it, he pulled the shirt off and hurried toward Olivia who lay wide-eyed on the floor.

"You're hurt," he said as he knelt beside her and pressed the fabric to her side.

"So are you."

"It looks worse than it is," he said, using an old fallback line. "You're the one who needs medical attention."

Before he could say anything else, two uniformed police officers pounded into the room.

The brother pushed himself up to a sitting position and turned toward the cops, spewing a bunch of bull that had Noah staring in amazement.

"Thank God you're here. My sister's hurt. This man broke in and attacked her. Watch out. He's got a knife. It's right there, sticking out of his belt."

"That's a lie," Olivia shouted. "Noah didn't attack me. It was my brother who did it. Noah got him off me."

Both cops drew their weapons. The one whose badge identified him as Clairmont looked from Noah to Stapler and back again. "Throw down the knife. Very carefully."

Noah pulled the bloody weapon from his belt and tossed it onto the floor, where it clattered across the tiles.

"Now both of you guys, raise your hands," Clairmont growled.

Shirtless, Noah turned and faced the cops, his hands in the air. His right palm was still bleeding, but the cut was already closing.

He'd been arrested many times over the years, and he knew that if you made the wrong move, you could get hurt. He wasn't worried about himself. But Olivia was injured, and he wasn't going to leave her twisting in the wind.

Speaking slowly and distinctly he said, "The woman on the floor is bleeding. I was trying to make a compress out of my shirt. She needs an ambulance."

The cop's gaze flicked from him to Olivia. "She doesn't look so bad."

Noah forced himself not to leap across the room and grab the guy. "How the hell do you know?"

Clairmont made a dismissive sound. "Women like her are resilient."

"Like what?"

The cop gave him a smirking look. "You know the kind."

Noah's hands clenched. He wanted nothing more than to punch the cop, but that would only get him arrested and then he wouldn't be able to help Olivia.

The cop spoke into the microphone attached to his collar, calling for backup and an ambulance.

"Arrest him," Stapler spat out, repeating his lie. "He came in here and started attacking my sister."

Noah kept his own voice calm. "It's just the opposite. If you talk to the woman upstairs, you'll find out that Stapler arrived before I did and started beating up on Olivia."

Clairmont looked like he might be persuaded to Noah's point of view. Then the other officer stepped forward.

"Not so fast. We've gotten reports on the two of them. They've been hanging around the Fountain Bar at the Calvanio. They're up to their eyeballs in some kind of dirty scam and we're going to find out what it is."

Noah heard Olivia gasp. He gave her a reassuring look, wondering exactly what he was going to say now, but he'd learned over the years that ideas came to him when he was in the midst of a crisis.

"It's not Olivia's fault," he said, then gestured toward the man on the floor. "Her brother, Pearson Stapler, is trying to blackmail her."

"Oh yeah? What's she done?" the second cop asked.

Noah was instantly sorry he'd put it in those terms. "Nothing," he spat out. "But her father is in a nursing home. Pearson's been threatening to tell him a pack of lies about her, just like he's lying now."

Olivia gaped at him. He was sure she wanted to ask how he knew that piece of information, but he gave his head a small shake, telling her to keep her mouth shut until the two of them could speak privately.

She was smart enough to take the silent suggestion.

On the other hand, the brother was dumb enough to keep digging himself deeper into a hole. "I saw you leave the bar with her," he shouted. "She went up to your room for some fun and games, and you just met her!"

Noah kept his own voice mild. "You may have seen us the other day, but I guess you didn't see us before. She and I are old friends." Addressing the cops, he said, "I'd appreciate it if you could cut her some slack. She's been hurt."

"That's bull! Tell me where you met her before," Stapler bellowed.

The cop turned to him and snapped. "Button it up, buddy. We've got to sort this out."

The brother looked like he wanted to strangle Noah for interfering with his plans, but Clairmont hoisted him off the floor, cuffed him, then patted him down.

After taking care of Pearson, he advanced on Noah. "Put your hands behind your back."

He hated going to the police station shirtless. But he figured that Olivia needed the shirt more than he did.

Teeth clenched, he let the cop cuff him.

Two more officers hurried into the room, and Clairmont explained the situation, then added, "The two guys are going down to the station. The woman's going to the hospital, under guard. We'll reassess her status after she sees a doctor."

One of the newcomers grabbed Stapler's arm.

Noah's gaze shot to Olivia. "It's going to be okay," he said, wondering if he was lying. Then he switched his attention back to the cops. "I'm registered at the Calvanio Hotel. I'm also registered at the Longevity Conference being held there. You can check me out with Dr. Sidney Hemmings. He personally invited me to the conference."

"You a doctor?"

He was tempted to say that he was a philanthropist who gave millions to medical research, but he knew it was better to maintain his low profile. "Just a private researcher," he answered.

Clairmont snorted. "A hanger-on."

"No!"

Before Noah could say anything else, they hustled him out of the room. His last glimpse of Olivia was of her white face as Clairmont crouched beside her.

AT LEAST they hadn't booked him, Noah thought as he looked at the palm of his hand. The cut had been a quarter-inch deep,

Now it was only a thin white line. In the next few hours it would be gone entirely.

Nobody had asked him about the injury. Probably they'd all assumed it was Olivia's blood on his shirt.

They'd left him to wait in an interrogation room at the downtown Las Vegas police station and they'd even given him a white T-shirt. He'd said again that he was registered at the hotel and the conference. He'd asked them to run his driver's license and he'd given the same address that he'd given to the cops on Grand Cayman. His San Francisco condo. It was a legitimate address. It just wasn't where anybody was likely to find him.

They'd taken the information and told him to wait.

Early in his checkered career, he'd gotten into some interesting scraps. Like the time he'd succumbed to temptation and let the nobles of a small European country set him up as their king. For a few glorious years, he'd enjoyed lording it over the locals, taking his pick of the kingdom's wealth and its women. He'd been enjoying himself too much to realize that one of the dukes was setting him up to lose a nasty little war so that the duke could take over the throne.

Noah had ended up sneaking out of the kingdom in the middle of the night, leaving his mistresses and most of the royal treasury behind.

That had been an important lesson. He'd decided that his best strategy was to live as a member of the upper-middle class. He'd shunned positions of power until the medicine man of a Native American tribe had designated Noah, alias Eagle Feather, as his successor. He'd counseled the tribe against going up against the soldiers in the area, only to see a troop of cavalry swoop into camp and kill everyone in a horrendous bloodbath. Of course, the outcome would have been the same for the tribe if they'd decided on an attack, but they would have taken a bunch of soldiers with them.

The troops had left Eagle Feather for dead, along with the

rest of the men, women and children who had just wanted to live their lives on their ancestral lands.

Noah had recovered, of course, and slipped into the soldiers' camp, where he'd quietly slit the throats of fifteen of them before he'd gotten the hell out of there.

After that, he'd cut his hair, stolen some clothing from a cowpuncher and built up his capital as a card shark in a bunch of two-bit western towns. A couple of times, he'd been shot by a sore loser, but he'd always survived the attack and gone on to kill the would-be assassin.

Those were the bad old days of the Wild West, when the law was on the side of the strong and the ruthless. Life was supposed to be more civilized in twenty-first-century America.

As the rule of law asserted itself, Noah had enjoyed a period of peace and prosperity. As much as possible, he'd lived his life out of the spotlight, but modern technology had made life more difficult for him again.

With the advent of surveillance cameras and computer databases, everything was on record and it was harder to keep the details of his life away from prying eyes, like the Las Vegas Police Department.

Although he knew a camera had to be noting his reactions, he couldn't sit still in the hard wooden chair pulled up at a scarred table.

As he paced back and forth, he thought about all the mistakes he'd made in his life. Olivia was likely one of them.

But he couldn't get her out of his mind.

Was she in the hospital or had they discharged her and brought her down here?

She'd been through some tough times in the past few months, and she'd survived better than most people could. Another woman would have sunk into depression and given up. She'd hung in and tried to figure out a new direction for herself. Too bad her brother was determined to screw with her life.

As he paced back and forth in the small room, he glanced at his watch again, wondering how long they were going to let him stew. Wasn't an hour long enough for them to look up Stapler's record and verify that he was a petty criminal?

He was about to bang on the door in frustration when it opened, and Clairmont stepped in. A man in a rumpled summer-weight sports jacket and dark slacks was with him.

"This is Detective Waterford," Clairmont said. "He'd like to ask you some questions."

Noah nodded. He wasn't about to say nice to meet you. Instead, he demanded, "What's happening?"

"I thought you could tell us," Waterford answered.

Noah's nerves had been stretched tight as he'd waited for someone to interview him. Or tell him he was free to go. Now a new surge of tension zinged through him as he and Waterford stared at each other. Two men, sizing up each other.

Only Waterford had been watching him on the monitor, and Noah was seeing the detective for the first time.

Still, he had an advantage the cop couldn't know about. In his long life, Noah had been in this situation many times. And he understood that at the beginning, you rarely knew which way to jump. You just had to feel your way carefully through the shark-infested waters and hope you didn't get bitten.

"I know the brother has a record," Noah said.

"Uh-huh."

Noah looked into the detective's narrowed, dark eyes. "Do you want to know something specific?"

"The brother says he cut you. Let's see your hand."

OLIVIA huddled on a padded table in the emergency room. The cubicle was chilly and she was shivering in the thin hospital gown they'd given her hours ago.

Apparently Mrs. Litton from upstairs had confirmed that Pearson had arrived first and threatened Olivia. She'd added that he'd been to the apartment before and made trouble. While Olivia had been in pain, a detective had asked if she wanted to press charges against Pearson. She hadn't—for a lot of reasons.

Finally the medical staff had gotten to her. Somebody was going to have to pay the bill, she knew, and she wondered where she was going to scrape up the money.

Or did they consider her a charity case? Did they have charity cases in Las Vegas? Probably, because it was a town where people could lose all their money on the turn of a card, then get into a fight over the loss and end up badly hurt.

She pressed her face into her hands. The painkillers they'd given her were making it hard to think. What should she do when she finally got out of here?

She still hadn't pawned the jewelry. Maybe she'd have to use the money to pay the hospital bill.

And what about Pearson? He'd been so mad at her because she wouldn't run the scam with him again.

A sick feeling welled up inside her when she thought about what she'd already done. They'd tried his scheme once, to her everlasting shame. Or half done it, because she hadn't been willing to actually go through with everything she was supposed to do.

She'd gone to a man's room. Not at the Calvanio. Another hotel on the Strip. But when the guy had reached for her, she'd ducked out of his embrace. Pearson hadn't known she'd gotten cold feet and had barged in anyway.

The guy had laughed at their stupid plan, and they'd gotten the hell out of his room. But what if he'd gone to the cops? What if she was already in more trouble than she could imagine? The police claimed they knew she and Pearson were up to something.

Again she thought about Noah Fielding. He'd showed up at her apartment to rescue her, and she couldn't help wishing that he'd walk through the door now.

Then she brought herself up short. He'd already gotten hurt trying to help her. She couldn't pull him any further into her problems.

NOAH shrugged, then held up his hands, palms outward. "He made a swipe at me. I guess my reflexes are better than his."

Waterford stared at Noah's palms and said, "Where did the blood on your shirt come from?"

"From Olivia. I was trying to stop the bleeding from the wound in her side when the brother attacked me. It was a pretty wild few minutes. I can believe Stapler doesn't have all the details right."

The comment was followed by stone silence.

Noah understood the technique. If the other guy stopped talking, you were likely to jump in with a comment to fill the empty space. So Noah ordered himself to relax while he waited out the detective.

Before either one of them could break the stalemate, another man appeared behind Waterford.

Noah couldn't hide his relief when he saw Sidney Hemmings.

"The police contacted the hotel to see if you were registered at the conference," the researcher explained. "I told them you were. When I found out that you'd gotten into some trouble, I figured you might like to see a friendly face."

"Yes. Thanks."

Waterford jumped into the conversation. "You're free to go." Finally!

"Where is Olivia Stapler?" Noah asked the question that had been stewing inside him since he'd first arrived at the station.

"She's still at the emergency room, as far as I know," the detective answered.

"And the brother?"

Waterford shrugged. "When I talked to her, she wouldn't press charges against him."

Noah stared at the detective. "Why not?"

"Maybe she's afraid of the consequences or maybe she wants to give the jerk another chance."

Noah bit back a curse, thinking that Pearson Stapler could be waiting in the parking lot to jump her as soon as she walked out of the emergency room door. And Noah had better get there before it happened.

"Where can I get a cab?" he asked.

"I can give you a ride," Hemmings offered.

"Thanks." Noah looked at Waterford again. "Which hospital?"

"Las Vegas General."

"I appreciate this," Noah said as they climbed into Hemmings's rental car.

"No problem."

When they pulled away from the police station, Noah breathed out a sigh. He was finally out of the clutches of the cops, yet he had a gut feeling that this wasn't over.

Hemmings spared him a look as he drove. "Were you hurt in the scuffle?" the researcher asked.

"I'm fine," Noah snapped, then apologized. "I'm sorry. I'm kind of on edge."

"What happened? I don't know anything other than that they were asking questions about you and that you were at the police station."

Noah apologized for dragging Dr. Hemmings into his mess. Then he explained, "I met Olivia Stapler at the hotel. I've been worried about her, so I went over to her apartment. I came in just as her brother was assaulting her."

Hemmings sucked in a sharp breath. "Good timing. What did he do to her?"

"He cut her with a knife. When the cops showed up, the brother started spewing a bunch of lies about who did what to whom. Which is how I ended up at the station. Now I want to find out how Olivia is."

The researcher looked like he wanted to ask more questions, but he pressed his lips together.

When they arrived at the hospital, Hemmings pulled up at the emergency room door.

Noah jumped out and looked around, trying to spot Stapler. When he didn't see the bastard, he turned back to Hemmings. "Thanks for the ride."

"I don't want to leave you alone."

"I can handle this," Noah said in a firm voice. Without waiting for an answer, he ran to the door.

Inside, he hurried to the reception desk. "I'm looking for Olivia Stapler," he said.

The receptionist consulted a clipboard in front of her. "She's in the back."

"What's her status?"

"I can't give out that information, sir."

"I'd like to see her."

"Family only, I'm afraid."

"I'm her fiancé," he clipped out, then wondered where that outrageous idea had come from.

The woman eyed him. Maybe he looked desperate and worried enough for her to take pity on him, because she picked up the phone on her desk and made a call. A few minutes later, a nurse led him into the treatment area.

He found Olivia sitting on a table inside a small room. She was wearing a hospital gown, and he could see from the bulge under the left side that they had bandaged her wound. He could also see her breasts through the thin fabric of the gown. Her nipples were puckered from the cold, clearly standing up against the fabric.

He dragged his gaze away from her chest as she looked up at him. Her eyes seemed clouded, but they cleared when they focused on him.

"Noah?"

"How are you?" he asked.

She waited a moment before answering. "Not too bad." She raised one shoulder. "They gave me something for the pain."

"Can you leave?"

"I think so." Her expression turned confused. "What are you doing here?"

"I wasn't going to just abandon you."

A FEW minutes ago, Jarred Bainbridge had been stopped dead. Now he was back on track. Noah Fielding had apparently gotten into some trouble in Las Vegas, and there was a police write-up on the case, which Jarred had accessed.

But the police report was less interesting to him than the private information he'd just acquired. Apparently Fielding's hand had been cut in a fight with a guy named Pearson Stapler. Then miraculously, the wound had disappeared.

So what did that mean? Did Fielding have some secret formula that healed him? Or was the story about the hand bunk?

Jarred wanted to see for himself. In fact, he was eager to repeat the experiment—perhaps with some kind of deeper cut that would be harder to miss.

Until a little while ago, Fielding had been cooling his heels at the downtown Las Vegas police station. According to a contact in the police department, when they'd let him leave, he'd gone straight to the hospital to see about Stapler's sister.

That sounded like a good place to scoop him up.

So how should he do it? He could use his contacts in the police department or he could use a private contractor.

After considering his options, Jarred reached for the phone and gave the orders.

Noah watched a wealth of emotions chase themselves across Olivia's face.

"I'm sorry I got you into trouble."

"Not your fault."

"Of course it was!"

"Let's not argue about it," he said gently.

She swallowed hard. "I thought when they took you away, I wouldn't see you again."

"They held me for a while. Then they let me go. I got here as quickly as I could."

He stepped toward her, wanted to pull her into his arms. She looked fragile, but he needed the reassurance of touching her.

Slowly he took another step and another. When she didn't draw back, he reached for her.

She moved easily into his embrace, her head coming to rest on his shoulder, a sigh escaping from her.

He felt her trembling. Maybe he was trembling, too. When she lifted her head, he lowered his, and their lips met.

A small sound escaped her. He hoped it was an invitation, because the need for more intimate contact suddenly filled him. The first touch of his mouth to hers sent sensation surging through him like a volcano of emotions.

He angled his head to taste her lips, sipping from her, drinking in the wonderful taste of her. He remembered the last kiss, remembered the out-of-control passion. He wasn't going to let that happen now, not when she was in the emergency room after being treated for a knife wound. He swore that to himself.

Yet he couldn't make himself lift his mouth, couldn't stop his hand from stroking her shoulders and arms.

As he touched her, erotic images assaulted him. He pictured her opening her legs for him where she sat on the side of the table. He pictured himself unzipping his pants and entering her as he stood in front of her.

The image almost undid him.

And what was she thinking?

He reached to cup one breast, and she swayed against him, her hardened nipple abrading his palm through the gown. He was already hard, more than ready to make love with her, and he thought he would go mad with wanting her—even when he knew he couldn't have her. Not now.

The way she quivered in his arms told him that she wanted this as much as he did.

Did she have on panties under that gown? He was reaching for the hem to find out when a stab of good sense stopped him. Maybe they both wanted to make love, but she was on pain medication, and he was the one who was thinking clearly.

Or almost clearly.

"We can't," he murmured against her lips.

"I know."

Still, she kept kissing him, her arms tightening around him until he heard her wince.

He eased back. "I'm sorry. I shouldn't have."

"You didn't do anything I didn't want."

"I hurt you."

"Of course not." She ducked her head and when she didn't raise her gaze again, he was pretty sure she was staring at his white T-shirt.

"You used your shirt to stop my bleeding," she murmured.

"The cops gave me a clean one."

"What about your hand?"

"I'm fine."

"But you were hurt."

When he held up his palm to show her, she shook her head. "I thought…" Her voice trailed off in confusion.

"It was your blood on the shirt," he said in a thick voice. He'd told that lie twice already and he hated repeating it now, especially when he'd been so intimate with her moments before, but for the time being it was his only option.

The time being? He struggled to clear his head. What was he thinking, that he was going to tell her the story of his life? The story he hadn't told anyone but Thomas in over a hundred years.

Before she could say anything else, he asked, "Your brother cut you. Why didn't you press charges against him?"

She gave him a pleading look. "I was in shock when they brought me here. I couldn't think straight, and that policeman was pressing me to have Pearson arrested." She looked at him helplessly. "I needed time to decide whether it was the right thing to do."

He stared at her. How many people would have given that bastard the benefit of the doubt? But Olivia's goodness had made her stop and think before she charged her brother with assault.

"He could be waiting outside for you," Noah pointed out, keeping his gaze steady on her.

She caught her breath. "I didn't think of that."

"Because you're too moral. You're going to let me protect you."

"Moral? I did something…" Her voice trailed off.

"We'll talk about it later."

"I don't feel good about it."

"Later," he repeated. "The quicker I get you out of here, the better." He gave her a long look. "You need some clothes to wear. Wait right here. Don't let them send you back out front."

"I might not be able to—"

"Stay here. Tell them I'm coming to pick you up. I'll be back as soon as I can." He turned and hurried back toward the waiting room. When he looked through the door, he saw Hemmings sitting on one of the chairs. And Detective Waterford was just walking in the door like he owned the place.

Chapter Six

Noah ducked back around the corner, hopefully before Waterford saw him. Was the cop looking for him or for Olivia? And why?

He'd like to know exactly what kind of mess he'd stepped into, and now he wondered if he should have let Olivia confess whatever was bothering her.

Still, in the absence of that information, he knew something for sure. His plans hadn't really changed. With Olivia in no shape to be interrogated, he was getting her out of the line of fire before the detective started in on her again. And before her brother could take another crack at her.

He hurried down the hall, opening doors, seeing nothing she could wear. He was out of the emergency room and into the hospital proper when he came to the gift shop. At this time of night, it was locked, but when he looked through the glass, he saw what he needed.

After glancing around to make sure nobody was watching him, he stepped to the door, gave the knob a hard twist, and rammed his shoulder against the door. He was stronger than he looked, and over the years he'd learned techniques for getting into places where he had no business being. The lock wasn't very effective. After twisting the knob open, he stepped inside and headed for a rack of Las Vegas General Hospital

T-shirts. To change his appearance a little, he took a navy one of those for himself.

He found a plain yellow blouse for Olivia that opened down the front so she could get into it easily. He also took a running suit that had the hospital logo.

He scribbled a note saying what he'd appropriated and left it with more than enough money under a ceramic crock on the counter. Mission accomplished, he sprinted back to the room where he'd left Olivia.

When he shot back through the door, she looked up in alarm.

"Sorry I scared you." He crossed to her. "How are you feeling?"

"I'm still spacey."

"Can you walk?"

"I think so."

She eased off the table and stood on shaky legs. Noah looked toward the door, thinking Waterford might come in at any minute. To make sure they didn't collide with the detective, he took Olivia's arm and helped her walk several doors down the hall, to an empty cubicle.

She looked exhausted from the short trip, so he told her to sit on the table while he changed his shirt and stuffed the white one in a trash can.

Then he turned back to her. "You've got to take off that gown."

Her brow wrinkled. "I don't have a bra on."

"I know."

"Oh right," she murmured, apparently remembering that he'd found that out for himself.

This time when he touched her, he tried to stay all business as he untied the fastenings and eased the gown off her shoulders. But his fingers burned when he touched her bare back. And when he carefully pulled the garment off her body, the sight of her high, firm breasts made him draw in a quick breath.

Glancing up at her face, he saw her staring at him intensely.

He managed to give her a crooked grin, then helped her put the arm on her bad side through one sleeve. She winced.

"Sorry."

"It's okay. I think I'm going to have a little trouble dressing for a few days."

They got the other arm through the sleeve, and he stepped back, relieved to have broken the contact.

His voice came out low and thick when he asked, "Can you button it?"

She raised her left arm and lowered it to her side again. "Sorry. I don't think I can maneuver very well."

Bending again, he clamped his lower lip between his teeth as he pulled the fabric over her breasts, then fastened the buttons, trying not to touch her as he worked. But her shallow breathing told him she was just as aware of him as he was of her.

The next task was getting the pants of the running suit on her, and he was thankful that she was still wearing panties.

She braced her hand on his shoulder as she pushed first one leg and then the other into the pants. When she was finally dressed, he realized he'd forgotten something.

"Damn!"

"What?"

"Your shoes," he muttered. "I don't want to go back for them. Can you walk barefoot?"

She nodded.

After checking the hallway, he led her out of the cubicle and toward the main part of the hospital.

When he heard someone coming up rapidly behind him, he turned, expecting to find that Waterford had figured out they weren't leaving the way they'd come in.

Instead it was another man, dressed in a business suit who had his arm down by his side, partially concealing the gun in his hand.

Noah looked from the man to Olivia. She was in no shape to run. And what good would it do them? They might as well be in a shooting gallery, if blasting them was what the guy had in mind.

"FBI. I want to talk to you."

Noah had seen enough federal agents to be sure the guy wasn't one of them. Not when he was coming at them with a weapon in his hand.

"What's your name?" he asked.

"Agent Barenson."

"You have ID?"

"You don't need to see it."

Olivia's eyes had gone wide.

Noah gave her a quick, reassuring look, then turned back to the man with the gun.

"What can I do for you?" he asked as he stepped forward, putting himself between the gun and Olivia.

"We should get out of the hallway."

"Okay."

"Walk ahead of me. Both of you."

Noah still didn't know whether the guy was after him or Olivia. Or both of them.

As they walked down the hall, his mind was coming up with plans and discarding them just as quickly. It didn't matter whether he got shot. But it mattered a great deal what happened to Olivia.

She shuffled along beside him.

"Hurry up," Barenson growled.

"I'm sick," she whispered.

Noah knew she must be frightened out of her mind, yet he was pretty sure she was deliberately slowing down the gunman, and when he gave her a sideways glance, he saw her lips were firmed.

She also looked to the side, and their gazes met. He knew

she was trying to tell him something and he wanted to shout at her to stay out of the way. Too bad he hadn't developed tele-pathic capacities over the past few hundred years.

"Turn right," the fake agent ordered.

They turned, taking a side corridor.

"Stop here," Barenson said.

They were standing in front of a door that said "Supply Closet."

Their captor tipped his head toward Olivia. "Open it. Then step inside."

She walked to the door and reached for the knob, but her hand wavered.

"I'm too sick," she whispered. "I think…I'm going to faint." Then she toppled to the side.

Barenson cursed and swung toward Olivia.

Taking advantage of the chance she'd given him, Noah spun around, grabbed the guy's head and slammed his face into the wall.

The gunman gasped as he went down.

Recovering instantly from the bogus swoon, Olivia pushed herself up.

"Can you open the door?" Noah asked.

"Yes." She turned the handle. Noah grabbed the guy by the shoulders and shoved him inside, where he lay unmoving on the floor next to a pile of cardboard boxes.

Noah turned on the lights, revealing shelves lining the walls. They were filled with various disposable hospital goods. "Get inside."

After stepping through the door, which Noah closed behind them, Olivia stared wide-eyed at the attacker. "Who is he?"

"Probably not an FBI agent named Barenson. You don't recognize him?"

"No."

"Thanks for helping fake him out."

"I didn't know if you figured out I was going to try something."

"I did. And I was thinking you could get hurt."

"Better than whatever he was going to do."

"Yeah." Taking a chance on staying another sixty seconds, Noah knelt and rifled through the man's pockets. He had no ID of any kind. But in the breast pocket of his suit, he did have a hypodermic needle full of something. Careful not to dislodge the cap, Noah pocketed the hypo along with the gun. Another gun, he thought, to go with the one from Pearson.

"We'd better get the hell out of here. He could have friends."

Opening the door a crack, he looked out. The hall was still empty. As he hurried Olivia toward the lobby, an uncertain look crossed her features, like she was coming out of a fog. "Shouldn't I check out? And…and…how am I going to pay?"

He laughed. "We'll worry about that later."

Once again, he was making and discarding plans. Hemmings might still be in the emergency room waiting area, but Noah didn't want to go back that way.

In the lobby, he was still trying to figure out what to do when a cab pulled up at the front door. As a white-haired man got out and shuffled toward the building, Noah walked around to the driver's side and asked if the cabby could take another fare.

"Where to?"

He hadn't gotten that far. After thinking for a minute, he named a small luxury hotel, the Royal Crescent. It was off the Strip, and he'd stayed there a few years earlier when he'd wanted a quiet location in the gambling town.

After he'd given the address, he went back for Olivia and helped her into the backseat.

When the cab pulled away, he let out the breath he'd been holding. He hadn't been sure they could really make their escape, but here they were. On the run from Lord knew who.

Olivia leaned her head on his shoulder as the cab headed across town.

When they arrived at the hotel, Noah helped her out of the cab and into a seat in the lobby while he registered. Because he always carried a couple of IDs with him, he checked in as Noel Feldman. Too bad he'd registered at the Calvanio as Noah Fielding, but he hadn't wanted to confuse people, like Hemmings, by using an alias.

After whisking Olivia into the elevator and into their room, he tucked her into bed. Then he went out to the well-stocked bar in the living room and poured himself a bourbon.

A New World liquor. He didn't usually drink, but he figured he deserved a couple of shots.

After taking a long swallow of the fiery liquid, he sat down on the sofa and sipped more slowly.

He had sprung Olivia from the hospital and gotten the two of them away from a gunman in the hallway, but he wasn't kidding himself. They weren't going to be safe until they got out of town.

And maybe not then.

He set down the glass on the coffee table and leaned his head back, thinking that his life had taken some very unsettling turns in the past few days. He'd been bombarded with one mess after another.

That sometimes happened. Events swirled together to surround him in good fortune or bad. But in the game of his life, the odds were better than at the Las Vegas casinos. His experience gave him an advantage. Seldom did he encounter a situation that was totally new.

So what was going on now?

And how did Olivia fit into the balance?

He was strongly attracted to her and he wanted to help her. But he couldn't deny that she was causing some of the problems. First, there was her brother. The two of them were up to something that he still didn't understand. Then the guy posing as an FBI agent named Barenson. He could have been after her, although Noah's gut told him that he'd been the target.

Which made him remember the hypodermic needle. He brought it out and looked at it, wondering what it contained. Too bad he didn't have access to a lab here. With a sigh, he went into the bathroom and emptied the syringe into the sink. Then he flushed the needle and kept the barrel, hoping he could analyze the residue later.

He wished dealing with Olivia was as easy. He wanted to make sure she was all right, but then what?

Meanwhile, he still had his own problems to deal with.

Unfortunately, he had to go back to the Calvanio. His belongings were expendable, except for his laptop. It had too much information stored on it. Of course, the hard drive was password protected, but someone with computer skills might be able to break into it. The gun in the drawer was another problem. He didn't want someone stumbling onto it and wondering why he had it.

It flashed into his mind that he might call Sidney Hemmings and ask him to take care of the computer. But that presented a number of complications. Hemmings would have to get permission to enter his room. Even if they could manage that, Noah wasn't perfectly sure that he trusted Hemmings. And certainly not with the gun.

Noah walked back to the bedroom and saw that Olivia was still sleeping. He didn't want to wake her, but he couldn't just leave her alone. Nor could he write a note because she might wake up and panic before she saw the message.

He eased onto the bed and lightly stroked her cheek. She made a small sound and stirred in her sleep. When he slid his finger to her mouth and traced the curve of her upper lip, her eyes opened.

As he'd anticipated, her eyes went wide with panic until

they focused on him. He saw her struggling for calm as she took in the darkened room.

"Where are we?"

"The Royal Crescent Hotel."

When she tried to sit up, she winced.

"You're hurting."

"I guess we left the hospital without any pain medication."

He cursed under his breath. "I was so busy getting you out of there that I didn't think about that."

"It's okay."

"No, it's not. But I can do something to help."

"What?"

"Have you ever tried hypnosis for pain?"

"Does it work?"

"Yes. But first I need to tell you something. I woke you up because I have to go back to the Calvanio and pick up my laptop."

She caught her breath. "Is that safe?"

"If I'm careful."

"But—"

"I'll be fine. I'll be back in a half hour. Meanwhile, let's take care of your pain. Look up at the line where the wall meets the ceiling."

When she'd done as he asked, he began to speak to her in a slow, even voice. "You're very relaxed. You're going to a place where you'll be very relaxed and comfortable. Where is that?"

She answered immediately. "The ocean. I love sitting and looking at the waves. We lived near the ocean when I was a little girl."

"Good. You're at the ocean," he continued in a mellow, reassuring tone, confident that she would follow his lead. "You have a nice comfortable chaise longue in the sun, but you're not going to get sunburned. You're feeling warm and nice and safe. You're not in any pain. Do you feel any pain?"

"No," she murmured.

"That's good."

"Stay with me," she whispered.

"I have to get some things but I'll be right back," he answered.

When she moved restlessly on the bed, he went back through the steps of relaxing her, and she settled again.

He had made her feel better and it was tempting to take one more step. While she was in this state, he could ask her about the scam with the brother, and she'd tell him what was going on. But he didn't want to use hypnosis to force information out of her. He wanted her to trust him enough to tell him on her own.

So he only said, "You're going to sleep on your chaise now. With the warm sun making you feel so good. You won't feel any pain. You'll be very comfortable. And when you wake up, I'll be right here with you."

"Okay," she answered in a lazy voice.

He stood up, thinking that he'd forgotten more than pain medication. She should be on antibiotics, too.

He knew a doctor was on call at the hotel and he was pretty sure that with some extra money for the man's trouble, he'd be able to get the medication from him.

Taking the hypo and the gun, he left the Royal Crescent and walked back to the Calvanio. Thankful for the eternal twilight of the casino, he was able to slip through it and into the elevator. In his room, he quickly packed the clothing he'd brought, along with the laptop.

OLIVIA smiled and tipped her head toward the sun. Noah had brought her to this beautiful, private beach, and…

Was he here with her?

Yes! That was the way she wanted it. The two of them were relaxing in the sun on a double chaise. A very comfortable double chaise. Almost like a bed, in fact.

She was wearing a very tiny two-piece bathing suit. Well, the bottom part, at least. She'd taken off the top to get a better tan. Noah was wearing a bathing suit, too. Not those big clunky trunks that American men wore. It was the skimpy European kind. She could see everything he had through the thin fabric. And she could see that he was hard.

As she stared at his erection, her insides turned liquid. They wanted each other and they were going to make love right out here in the sun.

He reached out to stroke her breasts, his fingers playing lightly over her nipples, sending shivers of sensation through her.

"You're going to make me explode," she gasped. "Just like that."

He gave her a knowing look. "That's the idea, sweetheart."

She grinned back and rolled toward him, then winced.

Something was wrong. Her ribs hurt.

When her eyes snapped open, she saw that she wasn't on a sunny beach at all. She was in a bed, in a darkened room.

Oh Lord, where was she?

Panic threatened to choke off her breath, but she struggled for calm.

Memories surfaced. Noah had brought her here after the hospital.

Gritting her teeth, she pushed herself up. She might be having sexual fantasies about him, but he had taken her to this hotel because he was being kind to her.

She sat for a moment, catching her breath, trying to be honest with herself. There was something about Noah Fielding that she couldn't define. He was different from any other man she'd ever met. He had a steadiness and a confidence about him that she envied. And he knew so much. Really, she was sure that she had only scratched the surface of what he was. There was a depth to him that she wanted to explore, and a firmness of resolve she hadn't encountered in a long, long time.

She'd been physically attracted to him right from the start, and she could fall hard for the guy, if she let herself. The problem was, she wasn't any good for him. Maybe if she were still dancing and felt good about herself, she could pretend she was his equal, even though she wasn't. He was obviously educated and doing well, and she needed to find some way to support herself while she finally went to college. Then there was that mess with her brother. No, it wasn't meant to be for her and Noah.

She gathered up a handful of the top sheet, trying to bring the past few hours into focus. He'd done something to her mind—hypnosis she guessed it was. Then he'd gone out, thinking she'd stay asleep while he was away.

He'd be coming back soon, and she had to get out of here before that happened. Otherwise, she'd let him talk her into what she wanted so desperately.

Gritting her teeth, she pushed herself off the bed and wavered on unsteady legs. When she looked down at herself, she grimaced as she saw that she was still wearing the mismatched blouse and pants Noah had given her in the hospital.

At the time, she hadn't questioned him about them. But where had he gotten clothing at that hour of the morning? Surely the gift shop wasn't open, so had he…stolen them?

Yes, probably that was it. Which just proved her point about being no good for him.

She staggered across the room and made it into a sitting area, then found that she was completely winded.

Gripping the arms of the chair, she thought about how she was going to get out of here. She needed shoes. This was a high-priced hotel. Maybe they provided guests with slippers.

The question was, did she have the energy to go back into the bedroom and look for them?

AFTER stuffing Pearson's gun in his bag and checking the room to make sure he hadn't left anything important, Noah hurried back to the Calvanio's registration desk where he checked out a day early. He also left a sealed envelope with a note and more than enough cash to pay Olivia's emergency room bill. The clerk added a stamp and put it into the outgoing mail.

Noah had just pocketed his copy of the hotel bill when his luck ran out. As he turned away from the desk, he saw Detective Waterford walking rapidly toward him.

"I'm glad I caught up with you," the cop said.

Noah could think of several rejoinders, none of which contained the same sentiment. Instead, he was imagining a hole opening up in the floor under the man. He could drop to the depths of hell and Noah could be on his way.

The cop zeroed in on his suitcase and computer bag. "Are you leaving?"

"Yes."

"Let's find a quiet place to talk."

Noah shrugged and followed the cop to a seating area at the side of the lobby, but both of them remained standing.

Neither of them spoke, and Noah waited, determined not to break the silence by asking what the man wanted.

"Ms. Stapler left without checking herself out of the hospital."

"Uh-huh."

"She was in no shape to get out of there on her own."

Again, Noah waited.

"Someone took some clothing from the gift shop. And someone bashed up a local thug."

A local thug. Interesting. Noah only shrugged.

"Were you involved in any of that?"

Noah shifted his weight from one foot to the other. "What makes you think so?"

"Deductive reasoning. And the T-shirt we gave you was found in the trash can several doors down from where Ms. Stapler was being treated."

"I'm in a hurry," Noah said.

"To get to the airport?"

Noah wished he'd kept his mouth shut. Instead of answering, he went back to the silent technique.

"Do you know where Ms. Stapler is?" Waterford asked. "She owes the hospital for her treatment."

Honesty forced him to say, "I mailed them some money."

"Where is she?"

"She's resting at another hotel."

"Which one?" the detective demanded.

"I'd rather not say."

Waterford kept his gaze on Noah. "We need to know her location."

This time it was impossible to keep silent. "Why? Are you charging her with something?" he asked.

"The brother has been mouthing off. He's threatening to kill her, if he can find her."

Chapter Seven

Noah felt the blood in his veins turn to ice as he struggled not to give away his reaction. He had met a lot of women in his life and he'd come to care about some of them. Nobody in a long time had affected him the way Olivia Stapler did.

He wanted to turn around and run back to the Royal Crescent, but if he did, Waterford was going to follow him, and he'd lead the cop straight to her.

As they stood facing each other, Noah ordered himself to think this through. Cops were allowed to tell you anything they wanted, whether it was true or not. Which meant that Waterford could have dropped that story about the brother because he wanted to question Olivia about the scam she and Stapler had been working.

Even if the brother had made the threat, it still might not be true. The jerk could have simply been letting off steam.

Noah could see the detective was watching him carefully. For a split second, he thought about trusting the guy. He could tell Olivia's location, and the cops would give her protection.

As soon as the notion surfaced, he dismissed it. Trusting this guy was not a smart move.

"Thanks for the information," he said, then glanced at his

watch. "I've got a little time left. I think I'll get in a couple of last licks at the tables."

"You can play the slots at the airport," Waterford said.

"I hate slots. I'd rather play a game where judgment counts for something." Quickly he turned and walked into the darkened casino. It was early in the morning now, but the lighted signs on the machines still flashed their come-hither call and the sound of coins dropping into the slots made a clanging background noise. A siren sounded and lights flashed as someone won a jackpot. A man and woman holding cups of change plowed toward the cashier, and Noah dodged around them, heading for the poker tables. After ducking around a pillar, he looked behind him.

Waterford had entered the casino but didn't look like he knew where his quarry had gone.

Noah plunged farther into the noise and confusion of the card-playing area, watched a few moments, then headed for an exit—this time into the garden where he and Olivia had encountered Gary Carlson.

That seemed like a decade ago, or maybe Noah's life was passing at lightning speed. Certainly it had felt that way since the diving accident off Grand Cayman.

Circling through the garden, he made it to the sidewalk again and took off along the side street. Only when he'd rounded the parking lot of the next casino did he head back in the direction of the Royal Crescent, constantly alert for Waterford or anyone else following him.

He got back to the hotel in record time and took one of the elevators to the fifth floor. As he let himself into the suite, he allowed relief to flood through him. But when he charged into the bedroom, it was empty.

His next stop was the bathroom, but Olivia wasn't there, either.

Although she had vanished, the sink felt warm, telling him she'd very recently run hot water.

She couldn't have been gone long.

He dashed out of the suite again and took an elevator to the lobby. Improvising, he said to the desk clerk, "I was expecting my fiancée to be here. We were supposed to go out together. Did you see which way she went?"

"I believe she turned left," the clerk said without missing a beat.

"Thanks."

Noah exited the building and turned left, praying that he would somehow find Olivia—before her brother did. Or the cops.

As he jogged down the street, he studied every woman he saw. None of them was Olivia, and he felt his throat constrict with worry. He was just about to acknowledge defeat when he finally spotted her. He uttered a little prayer of thanks. She hadn't gotten very far, only a couple of blocks from the hotel. Obviously winded, she was huddled on one of the benches provided by the city at bus stops.

He was about to call out to her when a battered silver Honda zipped by him, then screeched to a stop beside the bench.

Noah didn't know who it was, not for sure. Still, his heart was in his throat as he watched the driver's door open.

His worst suspicions were confirmed as the brother barreled out of the car, raced around the vehicle and started yelling at Olivia.

"Got ya, you bitch."

"Get away from me."

"In your dreams." As he shouted the last words, Stapler grabbed Olivia and tried to drag her toward the car.

Noah knew she was weak and in pain, but she grabbed on to the bench as Stapler struggled to pull her toward the car.

Get off her, you bastard, he silently screamed as he ran toward the pair, praying she could keep from getting dragged into the vehicle long enough for him to get there.

Fueled by determination, Noah put on a burst of speed.

Finally, between pants for breath, the words shrieking inside him burst from his lips. "Leave her alone."

He was less than half a block away, and both Stapler and Olivia jerked toward him. He could see the shock on Olivia's face and the determination on the brother's.

When Stapler redoubled his efforts, Noah knew that he had to get there in the next few seconds or it would be all over.

He had never run faster in his life as he flew toward the car. His lungs were burning and he could feel the pavement pounding the bottoms of his feet through the soles of his shoes.

The effort was wasted.

Stapler lifted Olivia off the ground. As Noah watched in sick horror, the brother managed to throw her into the car and slam the door, then run back to the driver's side.

Get out. You can get out, Noah screamed inside his mind.

But she must have used up all her strength in the fight, because she didn't open the door.

PEARSON slammed Olivia against the car door, stunning her and jarring her injured side. Her vision swam and she fought to catch her breath.

When she fumbled for the door handle, he slapped her, then stepped on the accelerator.

"You want to get killed? Go ahead and jump," he taunted.

Her body ached and her head throbbed as she stared at him through eyes that stung. "Why are you doing this?"

"Because you lied to me. You never had any intentions of helping me, did you? The one time you went upstairs with a guy, you screwed up."

Unable to play games with him any longer, she whispered, "That's right."

"You bitch. You were always a bitch, weren't you, even back home with Pop, when you were pretending to be oh-so-nice."

"I worked to make a home for the two of you. I cooked dinner. I kept the house clean. I did the laundry. You didn't help."

Ignoring her protest, he plowed ahead. "All you cared about was your damn dancing."

"That's not true. Let me go."

"And you got what you wanted, didn't you? Pop loved you. He never loved me."

"Is that what this is about?"

"Shut up."

He flicked her a look, probably thinking he had her under his control. He might be her brother, but he'd resented her all these years. Maybe he'd even forced her into his wild scheme because he wanted her to get in trouble with the law. Never mind what happened to him.

Now he had her in his clutches, and the look in his eyes made her blood run cold. But she had always been a fighter and she wasn't going to let him win.

She had to get away and even if she made him wreck the car, that would be better than whatever he had in mind for her.

She wanted to close her eyes, but she was afraid to take them off Pearson as she huddled against the door, gathering her strength.

NOAH kept running after the Honda, his eye never leaving the vehicle. He wanted to howl in anger and frustration, but he couldn't waste the breath on anything besides running.

The brother had said he'd kill Olivia. Well, he had her and he could take her anywhere and do whatever he wanted.

The thought kept Noah running.

As the car sped straight up the street, Noah almost gave up hope of catching them. Then, as he watched, it jerked to the right and then to the left.

Noah tried to imagine what was happening. Was Olivia grabbing the wheel?

He didn't know for sure, but he could tell she was doing something.

"Yes!" he shouted, redoubling his efforts as he watched the vehicle weave from one lane to the other. Another driver swerved to the side, honking loudly as the Honda barely avoided a collision.

The car lurched into oncoming traffic, straight into the path of a truck, and Noah's heart leaped into his throat. At the last second, it jerked out of the way of the two-ton truck, but overcompensated and jumped the curb. A pedestrian leaped out of the way as the Honda plowed across the cement. The car came to a stop, but not before it bashed into a trash can and dragged the container down the sidewalk.

Noah was ten yards from the car when the passenger door opened and Olivia rolled out. The brother came crashing out of the driver's side and barreled toward her, murder in his eyes.

Noah reached him first, spun him around and delivered a right hook to his jaw. As he had in their previous fight, the bastard went down.

Noah rounded the car and knelt beside Olivia. "Are you all right?"

Her lips moved but no words were spoken. She looked dazed.

"We've got to get out of here." Lifting her up, he carried her back to the car, set her gently on the front seat, then climbed behind the wheel. The engine was still running, and all he had to do was turn the wheel and back up to disengage the trash can.

The vehicle made a rattling sound but kept moving.

Noah took his eyes from the wheel long enough to look at Olivia. "What did you do to make the car swerve like that?" he asked.

"I started hitting him." She'd found her voice.

"Good."

"He was yelling and cursing at me."

"But you kept him from driving straight."

She heaved in a breath and let it out. "I guess I should have pressed charges."

"Yeah."

He turned down a side street and circled back toward the hotel.

"When I went back to the Calvanio for my stuff, I ran into Detective Waterford. He said your brother was telling people he wanted to kill you. When I rushed back to the Royal Crescent, you were gone."

"Sorry," she whispered.

"How did he find you?"

She made a snorting sound. "It was just blind luck! He was driving around and spotted me."

He swallowed around the lump in his throat. "Why did you leave?"

"I…" She spread her hands.

"Why?" he pressed.

She kept her gaze straight ahead. "You've done too much for me already, and I figured I was only going to get you into trouble. It looks like I was right."

He ignored the last part and said, "I haven't done nearly enough. I'm getting you out of town. I'm taking you where you'll be safe."

"He'll come after me. Then you'll get hurt, too."

"He won't be able to find us. And you'll be safe—if you're under my protection as my wife."

Her head jerked toward him and she stared at him, wide-eyed. "What did you say?"

"I said, you're going to marry me."

"I—I can't marry you."

"Of course you can."

She leaned back against the seat, her eyes closed. "You could be making the worst mistake of your life."

He laughed. "You'd be surprised at some of the mistakes I've made."

"Like what?"

"We'll talk about it later," he answered, wondering exactly what he was going to say. He could give her plenty of incidents, like the time he'd led a group of insurgents into battle against an overwhelming force. They'd had right on their side, but he was the only one who had survived. He thrust that memory away. He wasn't going to tell her about that, even if he changed some details and changed the century.

He tightened his hands on the wheel. More lies. That was the central tenet of his life. Lies.

Could he have something better with her? After keeping his own counsel for years, he longed for an honest relationship, even if he couldn't have it yet. But if he told her the truth, it would change the way she thought about him, and he wasn't ready for that.

He hadn't been paying attention to his driving and he hit the brake hard when the car in front of him stopped for a red light.

Beside him, Olivia made a sharp sound, and his gaze shot to her. Her skin had turned pale and her brow was covered with sweat.

"You're hurting."

"I'll be okay."

"As soon as we get back to the hotel, I'm getting you a doctor." And a minister, he silently added. Well, maybe not a minister, but someone who would marry them. In this town, that shouldn't be a problem.

She'd go along with it, because Noah Fielding usually got what he wanted.

He pulled up at the hotel entrance, where the doorman was obviously shocked to see a car with a caved-in bumper at the Royal Crescent.

"Have this put in valet parking," Noah said as he stepped

out and hurried to the passenger door. "And call the house doctor. My fiancée got a little bashed up."

As the doorman scurried to obey, Noah helped Olivia out of the car. She winced as she stood, then wavered on unsteady legs.

Noah glanced around, half expecting Detective Waterford to come popping out of the shadows like a jack-in-the-box. But the detective apparently hadn't found their hideout.

They made it to the suite without incident, and Noah eased Olivia onto the bed.

A few minutes later, the front desk called to say Doctor Turnbull was on his way up.

"I understand you wanted a physician right away," he said when Noah opened the door. The way he said it conveyed the definite impression that the speedy service was going to be expensive.

Sticking to the medical issues, Noah said, "My fiancée was cut. And then she was in a car accident. I'm afraid she hasn't done the original wound any good."

"Cut?"

"Her brother attacked her with a knife," Noah clipped out, making it clear that he didn't want to get into a long discussion about the incident. "She's resting in the bedroom."

Taking the hint, Turnbull crossed the sitting room.

When the door opened, Olivia turned her head toward them, and Noah could see that she was ready to slide off the bed and bolt, although he knew she couldn't get very far.

"This is Doctor Turnbull," he said in a soothing voice. "He's going to examine you and give you some medication for the pain."

The doctor asked him to leave while he did an examination. When he opened the door again, Noah tried to read his expression.

"How is she?"

"Pretty good, under the circumstances. But she needs to

mend. No more excitement. I've already given her a painkiller.
I can leave a prescription for more with the concierge, and also
for an antibiotic."

"Thanks so much."

"And my fee will be included in your hotel bill."

"That's fine. Thanks again," Noah said. He could tell the
doctor wanted to ask some questions about the knife incident,
but Noah had no intention of answering them. Instead, he
ushered the man out of the suite so he could hurry back to Olivia.

JARRED Bainbridge picked up the phone and spoke to one of
the men who did special jobs for him. "Did you get him?"

"Negative."

"What the hell happened this time?"

"After he assaulted Lex, he took the woman out of the
hospital and disappeared."

"Left town?"

"We don't know."

"Find him."

"If he's in town, we will."

"Check the airports. And the car rental companies." He
thought for a moment. "How did he get to the hospital? How
did he leave?"

"We're working on that."

"And canvass the other hotels."

"We're already on that."

He considered the female angle. "What about the woman?"

"She signed into the emergency room as Olivia Stapler."

"Did you check her address?"

"Yes. She hasn't been back."

"Call me as soon as you know anything, and see what you
can find out about her. And the brother. Maybe he'll turn out
to be useful."

Jarred set down the receiver very carefully so as to avoid

the temptation of throwing the instrument across the room. Once, he would have indulged in such behavior. Now he had to be careful about his bones.

Noah Fielding had disappeared again, which meant that he had something to hide. But he couldn't stay hidden forever, not from someone with the massive resources of Jarred Bainbridge.

And perhaps Fielding had made himself vulnerable. If he'd gotten Olivia Stapler out of the hospital and taken her with him, she must be important to him. That might be the way to get him to talk about himself when they finally scooped him up, which was simply a matter of time.

OLIVIA was only half-asleep, but she kept her eyes closed. She could sense Noah in the doorway looking at her. They should talk, but she didn't know what to say to him.

He stayed where he was for long seconds, then stepped back and closed the door.

She could hear him in the next room, talking on the phone. Later she heard a soft knock at the door, then the murmur of voices in the sitting room. Minutes later he came back into the bedroom.

Feeling like she couldn't hide from him any longer, she opened her eyes.

"How are you?" he asked softly.

"Better. Who were you talking to out there?"

"The clerk in one of the shops downstairs. She brought you some things to wear. I thought we'd have the wedding ceremony in here and you could wear this."

Wedding ceremony? So he'd been serious.

He stepped away from the doorway, then came back with a white nightgown. It had spaghetti straps and lace edging the bodice. The matching robe was also trimmed with lace.

She drew in a quick breath. "These are beautiful."

"They suit you." He shifted his weight from one foot to the

other. "Probably not the wedding dress you always dreamed of, but I think it'll do under the circumstances."

Olivia kept her gaze on the man who seemed determined to change her life. Her mind was muzzy from the medication the doctor had given her, but she needed to hear some things from Noah. "You're serious about getting married?"

"You don't want to?" he asked in a gritting voice. "If you think it's too crazy an idea, I'll back off."

Olivia kept her gaze steady as she replied. "At my apartment, before Pearson came over, I was having fantasies about you marrying me and whisking me away from here."

He seemed to visibly relax. "Good."

When he eased down on the bed beside her, her eyes searched his. She wanted to ask him a million questions, but she didn't know where to start. Not when she was half out of it on painkillers. He had secrets and he was more than he seemed on the surface. She knew that much.

But there were some things he couldn't hide from her. He had a basic integrity that showed in every action he took and he seemed determined to keep her from harm.

Still, she couldn't stop doubts from swirling in her mind, so she chose the question that might answer all the others.

"What am I to you?" she asked softly.

"You're a very sweet and appealing woman who's gotten into trouble you don't deserve."

"Sweet?"

"How would you describe yourself?"

"Tough."

"Yeah, you had to be tough to get away from your brother in the car. You did it, but now you've run out of resources," he added.

She nodded. "And you're the knight on the white horse."

He gave her a small smile. "You could say that."

"Why do you care about me so much?" she pressed.

"You remind me of someone I…lost."

"I remind you of her. But I'm not her. And you can't bring her back."

A look of resignation crossed his features. "I know." He reached out and took her hand. "But once we're married, we'll get to know each other as well as any man and woman, and we'll mean something important to each other."

Noah's words traveled through the haze that was her brain, sparking synapses until she finally understood. As her husband, he would be entitled to all marital rights and privileges—including sleeping with his wife.

Chapter Eight

"You want to marry me and have children?" Even her own ears couldn't discern what she heard in her voice. Was it shock or fear…or desire?

She was, however, able to read his expression. The regret was back in his eyes. "I can't have children."

"How do you know?"

He shrugged. "It's never happened."

"Did you have yourself tested?"

"No."

"So maybe it's not really true."

He switched the focus back to her. "Are children important to you?"

She took a moment to think. "I guess I always thought of them as something in my future. But I wasn't real serious about it. I was selfish. My career was more important."

"That's not selfish."

"What would you call it?"

"Honest." He cleared his throat and changed the subject, no doubt sensing her unease. "You know, you needn't worry about your brother anymore. I'm taking you where he can't find you."

"Which is where, exactly?"

"I have a ranch in California. Not a working ranch. But it's out in the country."

Touched by his concern, she decided right then to tell him everything. She made her voice firm. "Before we go any further, I have to tell you what happened. I mean about Pearson's and my scam."

"It wasn't your fault."

"I let him talk me into it."

"Because he was going to lie about you to your father."

Her brow wrinkled. "I remember. You said that to the cops, but how do you know?"

"I read your lips when you were talking in the lobby."

"You read lips?"

"It's not that hard." He shrugged it off and took her hand again. "Look, Olivia, you don't have to explain any—"

"No, I do." She squeezed his hand and took a breath. "Pearson said he got an idea from that presidential candidate who got into trouble for cheating on his wife." She raised her chin when she said it.

"You're not having an affair with a married man."

"But I worked for an escort service. That was enough for Pearson to call me a prostitute."

"Did you—" his voice hitched "—have sex with any of the men you escorted?"

"No." She shuddered. "I had to make it clear to some of them that that wasn't part of the package. But Pearson thought that if we could catch men in compromising situations, they'd pay us to keep quiet. He was going to burst into the room when I was with somebody. I…I said I wouldn't do it."

She didn't want to admit the rest, but she forced herself to tell him all of it. "He kept at me and at me. Finally I let a man pick me up, and I went up to his room. Then I hated what I was doing and I didn't…" She stopped and started again. "Pearson thought he'd find us in bed. He burst through the door, and the guy laughed at us." When she finished, her face was flaming.

He reached out and eased her into his arms, holding her gently. "It's all right."

"How can it be?" she asked in a small voice.

"You were brave to tell me all that when you thought I might change my mind about marrying you."

"You don't care that I let myself be talked into that scam?"

"I care. Because I know what it's like to be out of money and desperate. I know what it's like to be forced to do things that make your insides curdle."

She raised her face to him. "You do?"

"Yes."

"Are you going to tell me about it?"

A shuttered look crossed his features. "Now it's my turn to worry that you won't marry me if you know some of the things I've done."

"Tell me something you did that you're ashamed of. Maybe that will put us on a more even footing."

He sighed. "When I got kicked out of the community where I was living, I stole money and clothing to give myself a new start."

"You're not making that up?"

"No."

"What else?"

He sighed. "I took the identity of a dead man when the cops were after me."

"Noah Fielding?"

"No. I made up that name."

She gave him a considering appraisal. "How old are you?"

"Older than I look. I've had time to get into a lot of trouble."

"But you seem…so moral."

"Well, I changed myself. That woman I told you about helped change me. She taught me that anything can be forgiven, if you vow to go forward with a different set of values."

"Anything?"

"Yes. Stop beating yourself up. One little scam isn't so bad in the grand scheme of things."

She was about to keep arguing, but he shook his head. "Can we leave it at that for now? I'm not perfect. Nobody is. Everybody has done things that make them cringe when they think about it later."

She nodded, wondering if she was making a mistake. Her parents had had a happy marriage, until her mother had died. They'd given her a good model to follow, and she wondered if she could do as well.

When a knock at the door interrupted the conversation, her would-be husband looked relieved.

"I'd better get that," he said as he rose from the bed.

A few minutes later, he was back with three women.

"Let me introduce you to Sandy, Beth and Teresa," he said. "They're here to help you get ready. Sandy and Beth are practical nurses." He gestured toward a thin brunette and a chubby blonde, both of whom wore light green uniforms.

"And Teresa is a beautician," he continued, indicating the third woman, whose dark hair with silver highlights and a short black dress accented a beautiful face and a slim figure.

"Nice to meet you," Olivia murmured.

"I'll leave you girls—uh, women—alone," Noah said.

When he withdrew from the room, the three newcomers hurried over.

"He's a doll," Teresa said with a nod toward the door.

"Did he bring you here to get married?" Sandy asked.

"We met here."

"Lucky you!" Beth said. "That's the dream of every woman who works in this town."

Olivia nodded, knowing that was only a slight exaggeration.

"He says you were at the wrong place at the wrong time and got hurt."

She nodded, thinking that was a rather delicate way to put the facts. But then, Noah did have a way with words.

"Let me just have a look at your wound," Beth said. She and the other nurse guided her into the bathroom where they re-dressed the cut, then helped Olivia wash and put on the white gown. After that, Teresa helped her to the dressing table chair, where the beautician went to work on her hair and makeup.

Standing back, she gave her a studied inspection. "You look lovely."

Olivia eyed herself in amazement. She'd been injured only a few hours ago, but nobody would know it, unless they zeroed in on the bandage below her gown. Teresa had done a very subtle, very natural job with the makeup.

"I should take lessons from you."

"I'll leave you notes on what I used."

"Thank you. And thanks to you all," she said, looking around at the group. "I want to thank you so much."

An hour after they'd arrived, she was back in bed, propped against a mountain of pillows and wearing the matching robe over the gown. She was feeling like a queen, but her anxious gaze went to Noah when he came back in.

The look on his face confirmed that the women had done wonders with her.

"You look lovely," he said.

"Thank you."

While she'd been busy, he'd changed into dark slacks and a crisp white shirt that he must have gotten at the hotel shop.

Behind him was a short, balding man in a dark suit who introduced himself as Reverend Hartley.

The two nurses were the witnesses, and Teresa also stayed for the ceremony.

It was a very nontraditional wedding, with the groom sitting on the side of the bed holding the bride's hand.

Olivia tried to focus on the words Reverend Hartley was

speaking. This was her wedding, one of the most important days of her life. Even if it was under very strange circumstances.

When Noah produced a ring, she could hardly believe her eyes. He must have gotten that in the hotel, too. Or maybe he'd had time to run out to a jewelry store. When he slipped it on her finger, she felt her whole body tingle.

There was kind of a strange moment when the preacher got Noah's name wrong. Then she remembered he'd registered at this hotel under a different name. But they got it straightened out and they were married as Noah Fielding and Olivia Stapler.

Were they really married?

She guessed she'd find out soon enough. And she'd find out what she'd gotten herself into.

He'd even ordered champagne and a small three-tiered wedding cake. When she saw the words "Noah and Olivia" on the top, entwined in a heart, she had to fight back tears. He'd gone to a lot of trouble to make this a memorable occasion—and it had to be for her. Unless he was a blatant sentimentalist.

All the guests had a piece of cake and a glass of champagne. Still feeling like the main character in a Cinderella story, Olivia took a few bites of cake and a sip of the champagne. After a few minutes of small talk, Noah offered the rest of the cake and champagne to the wedding guests, who took the hint and left the bride and groom alone.

As soon as Noah had ushered everyone out, he came back to Olivia, who was looking dazed.

"I hope that wasn't too much for you," he murmured.

"It was…more than anyone has ever done for me."

He eased onto the side of the bed. "You sound like you're not sure that's good."

"It's kind of overwhelming."

He gave her a crooked grin. "I'm hoping you'll adjust to being pampered."

"That's not how I ever pictured myself." She ducked her head a moment, then looked back at him. "Do you have a cook at your ranch?"

"Yes."

"Will she teach me your favorite recipes and let me cook them?"

"Of course," he answered, wondering if Margarita was going to feel like her space was being invaded.

"What *are* your favorite foods?" Olivia asked.

"My favorites?" He thought for a moment, his mind ranging back over all the dishes he'd enjoyed. It was almost impossible to choose, but she looked so hopeful that he said, "Shashlik."

"What's that?"

"Like shish kebab but made the Greek way."

"You had it in Greece?"

"Um. And I like a good polenta with a fresh marinara sauce."

"And you first had that in Italy?"

"Yes. It's amazing how the Europeans have taken to corn."

"What do you mean?"

"Well, it's a New World plant."

"Oh, I never thought of that. You're so much more educated than I am," she whispered. "And well-traveled."

"Actually, I never graduated from college."

"Really?"

"I learned a lot from books. You can do that, too. And I can teach you a lot of what I know. Now that you don't have to worry about supporting yourself."

She sighed. "You're right. I never had the time to spend on myself. I mean when I wasn't practicing my dancing."

"We can study whatever you want and we'll travel together. I'll take you anywhere you want to go."

"To China?"

"Why China?"

"I got interested in it when the Olympics were in Beijing. The country seems so exotic."

Noah nodded. He still hadn't figured out how to talk about his background. But they'd deal with that. Reaching up, he brushed back her golden hair, thinking she looked so young and vulnerable. When she quivered, he prayed that he'd done the right thing.

He'd said he wanted to keep her safe, but he knew he was being selfish just the same. He had been alone for a long time and he knew this woman could end that loneliness for a time—unless he messed things up.

That thought made his stomach knot.

"This is our...wedding night." She glanced toward the window, then back at him. "Well, not night, yet. But we don't get to take full advantage of the moment."

"We will. I've had a lot of practice waiting for what I want." He leaned over and brushed his lips against hers. Then because he needed more, he pressed a bit harder.

When she made a small sound and opened for him, he tipped his head so that he could fit his mouth more tightly to hers, moving his lips in little nibbling motions.

Then he reminded himself that she was recovering from a very rough couple of days, and the doctor had said she needed to rest. Instead he had rushed her into a wedding ceremony. A wedding night was out of the question.

"I'm sorry," he murmured.

"About what?"

"Not letting you relax."

She lay back against the pillows, gazing up at him, and a smile flickered at the corners of her lips. "This is very relaxing."

He grinned back, then sobered as he dipped a finger under the edge of her bodice, stroking the tops of her breasts.

She was his wife. It had been a very long time since he had

taken that step, and now the need to make love with her surged inside him.

He couldn't do that, not when she needed to mend. But he couldn't stop himself from going a little farther. His gaze fixed on hers, he tugged at the elastic top of her gown. When she didn't flinch, he pulled the bodice below her breasts. The elastic cradled them and raised them temptingly toward him. He gazed down at her creamy breasts, crowned by her tightened nipples.

She stared up at him, her expression part shock and part invitation. He accepted the invitation, stroking his fingers over the peach-colored crests, then squeezing them gently, entranced by the sensual view. When he bent to swirl his tongue around one distended bud and suck it into his mouth, she sighed her approval. Before he realized her intention, she reached out to press her hand over the erection straining at the front of his slacks.

When she slid her hand up and down his length, he leaned back, enjoying her touch for a few moments before lifting her hand away.

"You can't," he whispered.

"I want to."

"I know. So do I. But we'll wait until you're better," he managed to say, even though he had pushed himself to the edge. Pushed both of them.

As he studied her flushed skin and accelerated breathing, he decided he didn't have to leave both of them in need.

Kicking off his shoes, he swung his legs onto the bed. Then, his focus on her pleasure, he dipped one hand under the covers, slipping under the hem of her gown and working his way up toward her most intimate flesh.

When he found her wet and swollen for him, he made a low sound of approval.

"Maybe we could…" she whispered.

"We're not going to do anything too strenuous. Just let me please you."

He bent to play with her breasts again, using his lips and tongue and teeth while he slid his hand into her folds in long strokes that dipped inside her, then moved upward to the point of greatest sensation.

He had a lot of experience pleasing women. And even though he hadn't been with anyone in years, he was gratified to find that he hadn't forgotten the moves. He listened to her breathing, judging her reactions, doing exactly what worked best for her, pushing her toward the point of no return.

When she came undone for him, he kept up the pressure, drawing out the pleasure of her climax—for both of them.

Her eyes blinked open and she stared at him, looking dizzy.

"That was…wonderful."

"I'm glad."

"What about you?"

"There will be plenty of time for me."

"I should…"

"You will. But not yet."

His heart was pounding and his body was on fire, but he eased down beside her, linking his fingers with hers.

"I've never met anyone like you," she whispered.

I'm sure you haven't, he thought, but he only squeezed her hand.

He felt her relax beside him and wished he could do the same, but his body was still humming.

Closing his eyes, he tried to unwind. This was the start of something good—for him and for Olivia. For the first time in years, he would have an intimate companion. Someone he could trust besides Thomas.

Or would it work out that way? For real intimacy, he'd have to let her past the barrier he'd erected between himself and the world.

"What's wrong?" Olivia murmured.

"Nothing."

"Don't start off evading me," she whispered.

He was searching for an answer when the phone on the bedside table rang.

He fumbled the receiver out of the cradle.

"Mr. Feldman?"

He almost said no, until he remembered that that was the name he'd registered under.

"Yes."

"This is Harold at the front desk. You asked me to contact you if anything unusual occurred."

He sat up, instantly alert. "What happened?"

Beside him Olivia pushed herself up, a look of alarm on her face. He kept his free hand on hers and squeezed it reassuringly.

The desk clerk was saying, "Someone was asking if you were registered. Well, not by the name Feldman."

"What name?"

"Fielding. I said you weren't here. Then he described you and your…wife."

"Who was asking?"

"A tough-looking man."

"The police?"

The desk clerk hesitated. "He might have been, except that he offered me money."

Noah fought a bolt of alarm. "But you said I wasn't here."

"That's right."

"Okay. Thanks. I believe we're going to check out, but I need to make some arrangements. I'd like you to contact a private ambulance service, so my wife will be comfortable on the way to the airport."

"When do you want the ambulance?"

"As soon as possible."

He climbed off the bed and ran a hand through his hair.

Olivia's look of alarm stabbed through him.

"Somebody was asking about us at the front desk."

"Us?"

"A couple looking like us. So we're getting out of here."

"Where are we going?"

"Home."

JARRED Bainbridge was leaving nothing to chance now. He was keeping in close touch with his men in Las Vegas.

When the phone rang, he picked it up before it finished ringing. "Well?" he demanded.

"We checked the luxury hotels," Wexler told him.

"And?"

"Nothing. Nobody admits to seeing anyone like Fielding and the Stapler woman."

He thought about Fielding's strategy. He could have left, except that Stapler was injured, and she probably couldn't be moved easily. Which brought up another point. Fielding could have checked them into a dive, but he probably wouldn't have wanted to subject the woman to any place where she wouldn't be entirely comfortable.

"Go back to the same hotels and try again. Offer more money." He paused for a moment, thinking. "If possible, speak to different people than the ones you talked to the first time. Just a minute before you hang up," he said.

Reaching for the glass of water and the bottle of pills on the table next to his padded chair, he took some pain medication. His damn body was failing and if he didn't find a cure soon, he was done. Pushing away a feeling of desperation, he looked through his notes. "And talk to that research doctor, Sidney Hemmings, again. He might know more than he's saying."

OLIVIA pushed herself up and winced, but Noah stopped her.

"You don't have to do anything. I'll take care of getting us out of here."

"I have to get dressed."

"We're taking a private plane. You can wear that."

"I want to have my clothes on."

He gave her an exasperated look, then seemed to check himself.

"I'm sorry. I'm upset about the call." He walked into the sitting room and came back with a couple of bags. Opening them, he dumped out a running suit. "This should be comfortable."

"Yes, thanks."

"I'll help you dress."

"I think I can do it."

"You're sure?"

"You've got things to do."

He nodded and picked up the phone again. As she gingerly pulled the gown over her head, she heard him talking, apparently to a company that flew executives around in private jets.

At first it sounded like he didn't like what he was hearing. Then he said, "How about for an extra fee?" After a few seconds, he answered, "Okay. Good."

Hanging up, he looked up, caught her naked and grinned. "Very nice." His expression turned regretful. "Except for the bandage."

She kept her eyes on him as she reached for the loose T-shirt that went under the jacket and pulled it over her head. He came over and helped her get her left arm through the sleeve.

"I get the feeling you have a lot of experience making quick getaways," she whispered.

"Yeah."

When he'd left the room, she sat for a minute staring at the door, fighting the feeling that she'd jumped from the frying pan into the fire. The worst part was that she was falling in love with Noah—even though she knew that he could hurt her badly.

Closing her eyes, she sat with her hands clenched, fighting

the feeling that she was being swept down a raging river by a strong current.

Then she straightened her shoulders.

Noah was doing everything he could to get them out of town. She wouldn't hold him up. So she finished dressing, then looked in the bag for shoes. He'd bought a pair of running shoes for her that were just about her size, and flip-flops.

"The running shoes are a better choice," she heard Noah say from the doorway. "Easier for balance."

She turned to him. "But I can't get them on."

"I'll help you."

He knelt by the side of the bed and helped her put on socks and shoes.

When she was dressed, he left the room and came back with a travel bag, into which he stuffed the rest of the clothing he'd bought her.

"They'll call us when the ambulance arrives."

"Okay." She cleared her throat. "You think this has something to do with my brother?"

"I don't know."

"Who else has a grudge against you?"

Chapter Nine

Noah swallowed. "You mean besides Eddie Carlson's brother?"

"Yes."

"I think I…defused Carlson. I mean, he knows that I hated to see those men die and I wanted to provide compensation for their widows and children."

Olivia nodded.

Noah continued the analysis of his situation, trying to be as honest as he could. "There's the Las Vegas PD. But I think that has more to do with you and your brother than with me."

Again she nodded.

"But we have to consider the incident in the hospital with the guy who claimed to be from the FBI. I think that either your brother did something we don't know about or someone is trying to get to me, and I don't know which."

"Pearson could have been involved in something."

"When I get home, I'm going to put the Light Street Detective Agency on it."

"You've worked with them?"

"No, but they impressed me—with the way they turned up my location. And I like the idea of hooking up with an organization I haven't used before."

"You made a snap decision about them—the way you did about me. You do that often?"

"I'm a good judge of character." He could have added that he wouldn't get involved with a detective agency without doing a background check, but that would lead to a discussion of whether or not he'd vetted Olivia.

"Could you—" She stopped.

"What?"

"I hate to create another problem."

"Just tell me."

She looked down as she spoke. "If we're leaving, could the Light Street Detective Agency get something from my apartment? My mom's jewelry. It's all I have left from her."

"Where is it?"

"In a dresser drawer. In a blue box."

"Of course I'll make sure it gets to you."

"Thank you."

His cell phone interrupted the conversation. It was the travel company, telling him the flight was ready, which led to a lot of activity. He had to check on the ambulance, pack the clothing that he'd bought for himself, hide the guns in his suitcase and make sure the oversized seat he'd requested was on board for Olivia.

Forty minutes later, they were at a private terminal at the airport.

"Don't we have to go through security?" Olivia asked.

"Not with this kind of flight."

"Okay."

He got her settled on the plane, then buckled up before takeoff. As soon as he could get up, he went forward to confer with the pilot about the arrangements for landing.

The convenience of air travel never ceased to amaze him. He'd spent so many years of his life traveling by foot, horse, cart, wagon train and canoe. Steamboats had been a tremendous improvement.

People today complained about waiting around airports and

delayed flights. Instead, they should thank God they weren't on a wagon train traveling a few miles an hour across the desert. Or crammed into a small sailing ship crossing the Atlantic.

He'd come to Las Vegas through L.A., but this time, to avoid the large airport, they were landing in Santa Barbara.

He went back to the passenger cabin to see how Olivia was doing and found that she'd fallen asleep.

As he stood looking at her, his heart squeezed. He really had acted in extreme haste getting involved with her. Whisking her away. Marrying her. Had he done the best thing for her, or had he let his own selfish reasons sweep away good judgment?

He didn't know. And he didn't know how he was going to handle letting her in on his secret. In the beginning, he'd have to be cautious about how much he told her. Either way, it was going to create trust issues between them.

He sighed. Honesty compelled him to admit that he'd plunged into this marriage too hastily. The urgency had come from his own needs and he had nobody to blame but himself.

Turning away from her, he picked up his laptop. Of course, the restrictions on using his computer were not the same as they would have been on a commercial flight. After informing the pilot of what he was doing, he took a seat several yards away from where Olivia slept and began doing some research on the Light Street Detective Agency. By the time they were on their final approach to Santa Barbara, he was pretty sure that he was going to hire them. But an in-depth phone call to the agency would have to wait until they got back to the ranch.

As he made that decision, another thought flitted through his mind and he cursed under his breath.

He'd been so wound up with events in Las Vegas that he'd forgotten to alert Thomas. Knowing he was going to set a whirlwind in motion, he made a call to the ranch.

"Is there something wrong?" Thomas asked when he recognized Noah's voice.

"I ran into some trouble in Las Vegas. We'll talk about it when I get there."

"Okay."

Noah cleared his throat. "I'm bringing someone back to the ranch with me."

"Dr. Hemmings?"

Noah laughed. Hemmings was another detail that had slipped his mind. "No, actually, my wife."

"Your wife?" Thomas asked, his voice incredulous.

"Yes. Her name is Olivia. It's a long story and I'll tell you about it when I get back."

"Yes, sir."

He thought about the sleeping arrangements at the ranch. "She was injured. It might be a good idea to put her in a guest room for now."

Thomas agreed.

"I know this is a bit of a shock to you. It's a bit of a shock to me, too."

"Yes, sir. When can we expect you?"

"We're landing in Santa Barbara in twenty minutes."

"Twenty minutes! That doesn't give us much time."

"Can you send a car down to the airport for us? I guess the SUV would be best."

"I'll have Pablo leave right now. You may have to wait for a few minutes."

"We'll stay on the plane until he tells me he's in the parking lot."

"Very good."

He ended the call and looked up to see Olivia watching him. "How are you?"

"Better. When I first woke up, I couldn't figure out where I was. There have been so many changes in the last few hours that I can't keep up."

"Likewise."

She kept her gaze on him. "Do you really want to put me in a separate bedroom?"

"Away from temptation—my temptation—until you're better."

"I *am* better."

"We'll see." He took the seat next to her and buckled his seat belt for the descent.

Pablo must have left the ranch immediately and not run into much traffic because he was at the airport fifteen minutes after they landed. Ten minutes after that, they were on their way north.

Olivia watched the scenery change from urban sprawl to dry brown hills.

"You do live out in the country."

"I like my privacy," he answered, wondering how it was going to work for Olivia. "As soon as you're better, I'll take you to some of the clothing stores in town."

"Okay."

"And you might want to do some redecorating at the ranch. I'm afraid I haven't made much attempt to be stylish."

"You're sure you trust me with redecorating?"

"Of course," he answered, wondering what her taste was like. "Unless it's something really weird, I won't much care. But I know that women do."

Thomas opened the gate by remote control and he watched Olivia taking in his landscaping. She caught her breath when she saw the house.

"You approve?" he asked.

"It's perfect for the location."

"Thank you."

"Did an architect design it?"

"I did."

She gave him a surprised look. "Another talent I didn't know about. What else should I know about you?"

"I guess we'll find out."

Thomas had lined up some of the staff, and Noah wished his majordomo had skipped the formality when he saw the overwhelmed look on Olivia's face as she was introduced first to Thomas then to Margarita, Caesar and Benita.

"Do you need to lie down?" Noah asked her when the staff had gone back to their work.

"No," she answered. "I just got here."

"Then let's go to the sunroom."

He led her through a dark and outdated living room to the glass-and-wood enclosed space that he'd filled with orchids and other plants.

She sat down on the chaise longue and looked around, wide-eyed. "You're rich," she whispered. "But I guess I knew that already."

He shrugged. When he saw Thomas hovering in the doorway, he hesitated for a moment. They'd have to talk about what they were going to say. But until then, he knew his old friend was smart enough not to give anything away, so he motioned him in.

"Why don't you sit down, Thomas?" he said.

His chief of staff perched on the edge of a wicker chair.

"Sit," Noah said again, and the other man slung his body into the seat.

"Thomas is a friend of mine as well as the man who keeps the household running," he said to Olivia. "If you need *anything*, just ask him."

Thomas smiled at her. "It's a pleasure to meet you."

"And you, too. I know you're going to be an enormous help to me." Olivia cleared her throat. "I take it there hasn't been a lady of the house recently."

"True."

"I'll try not to get in your way."

"This is your home," Thomas answered. "I hope we can

make you entirely comfortable here. Starting with something to eat. What can I get you?"

When her mind blanked out, Noah came to her rescue. "Some iced tea," he said. "And some sandwiches. Chicken or beef or ham?" He looked at her again.

"Fine," she answered, probably wondering how long it would take her to get used to this lifestyle.

JARRED Bainbridge struggled to control his fury. After the screwup by the local guy he'd used, he'd sent a crack team to Las Vegas to round up Noah Fielding, but apparently the man was no longer in the gambling paradise.

"You say you found out what hotel he'd moved to, but he checked out?" he asked in a dangerously quiet voice.

"Yes, sir."

"Where is he now, do you think?" he asked, the question sounding almost conversational, but anybody who knew Jarred Bainbridge would be wary of his tone.

"Because he has a contract with a company that flies private jets, we're going through their records now and we'll be able to tell you where he went."

"According to the information he gave the Las Vegas PD, he has an apartment in San Francisco. But he might not have gone there."

"You have the address?"

"Yes, sir."

"When you figure out where to find him, I want a plan to bring him here," Jarred said. "And if I don't get results very quickly, you will be looking for a new job."

Ignoring the threat, his man said, "The woman is with him."

"And?"

"She was driven to the plane in an ambulance. She must be important to him. I believe there's a way to use her to get to him."

Jarred had been thinking along those lines, too. But he wanted some input. "What do you suggest?"

"We located the brother. He's a petty criminal and a bitter man. He blames her for his current troubles. He may have already tried to kill her. I believe we can have his full cooperation in getting her back, if we promise to turn her over to him. And I believe he is absolutely ruthless."

"Good," Jarred answered. He was feeling cautiously optimistic again.

OLIVIA gave Noah and Thomas a considering look. "So do I get some information along with the food?"

Thomas kept his expression neutral, but he shifted in his seat, and Noah was sorry he'd put his old friend into a delicate situation. Another reason why he should have thought through this whole scenario.

Thomas answered with a catalog of the estate's amenities. "We have a full gym. An indoor-outdoor swimming pool. An excellent library, including a collection of DVDs. The latest computer equipment. Satellite TV. A well-stocked kitchen. Horses and riding trails. And Maria, one of the staff, does my wife's hair. You can also avail yourself of her services."

"This is a very self-contained place," Olivia murmured.

"Yes. And if we don't have it here, we can get it for you." Thomas stood up. "I'll go tell Margarita to get started on the food."

When the man had left, Olivia looked at Noah. "Am I free to wander around?"

"Of course. But you probably shouldn't go into the labs alone."

"What labs?"

"They're across the courtyard from the main house. I have a number of experiments going. Some of them on longevity."

"Okay."

"I'm also fiddling with some electronics equipment."

She nodded, then leaned back and closed her eyes.

"Maybe after you eat, you should get some rest," he suggested.

Her eyes snapped open again. "Maybe you're right. But I'd like to sleep in our room, if that's all right."

"Yes. Yes, of course," Noah answered.

The food came very quickly, and he could imagine Margarita in the kitchen, cracking the whip to make sure they impressed the woman who was now Mr. Noah's wife.

While Olivia was nibbling on a turkey sandwich, he wolfed down a roast beef and a ham sandwich.

"Not hungry?" he asked.

"Maybe after I get some rest." When she started to push herself up, he helped her, then showed her down the hall to his room, trying to see it through her eyes.

It was very spartan and very masculine.

She stared around. "It looks like a monk lives here."

He laughed. "I did spend some time at a monastery long ago. It taught me lessons in simplicity."

"Is there anything you haven't done?"

"Not much." He shifted his weight from one foot to the other. "I know this has to be overwhelming."

"You have a gift for understatement."

He laughed again, then pulled the spread and cover aside. "I guess so." Remembering that her suitcase was in the spare room, he said, "I'll get your bag."

"I'd rather just sleep in one of your shirts."

"Okay."

Because it was chilly in the bedroom, he chose a soft wool shirt and brought it back to her.

She'd already pulled off her slacks and blouse, and he caught his breath as he took in her body again. This time the bandage over her knife wound seemed to only accentuate her tiny waist. His fingers itched to touch her smooth skin there, to trail downward to her…

He stopped his imagination cold.

Before he could start anything he shouldn't finish, he merely helped her into the shirt and into bed.

"We'll talk at dinner. What do you want?"

"I can have anything I want?"

"Pretty much."

"Barbecued chicken, potato salad, baked beans."

"Done. You sleep. I'll come and wake you in a couple of hours."

Glad to escape, he stepped out of the room and closed the door. He was out of practice living with anyone and he'd have to brush up his husband skills.

First he stopped at the kitchen to order dinner, which took longer than he expected because everyone wanted to congratulate him. They also wanted him to tell them about Olivia, so he told them she had been a dancer, then made his escape as quickly as possible.

Then he went to his office. After closing the door, he booted his computer, checked his mail and got the number of the Light Street Detective Agency in Baltimore.

A man named Hunter Kelley answered.

"This is Noah Fielding."

Kelley's tone immediately turned wary. "How can I help you?"

"Actually, I was impressed with the work you did for Eddie Carlson's brother. I'd like to hire you. Unless it's against the rules."

The man whistled through his teeth. "It's not against the rules. Just unusual for someone we've located for another client to turn around like that. What can we do for you?"

"I'd like to know who's trying to either kill me or capture me."

"Gary Carlson's back in Baltimore," Kelley informed him. "He says he doesn't have any further need for our services."

"I don't think it's him. This must not be my month, because somebody else has it in for me."

"You lead a busy life."

"I try not to. But things have gotten kind of…crazy lately."

When he started to elaborate, Kelley stopped him. "This is our public line. We have a secure computer hookup where we can set up a videoconference call. You can talk to several of our agents."

"That sounds fine."

"Can you wait until tomorrow morning? Or are you in immediate danger?"

"I'm back home, which is a pretty secure environment."

They made an appointment, and Noah got off the phone. Thinking he would check on Olivia, he went back to his room.

When she wasn't in her bed, panic seized him.

A noise from his closet sent him rushing through the door where he found Olivia pawing through his things.

As she looked up wide-eyed, a million thoughts rushed through his head—none of them good. He'd impulsively married this woman and brought her home—and now she was spying on him.

Chapter Ten

Olivia saw the instant mistrust in Noah's eyes and her stomach balled into a tight knot. Suddenly, she was seeing another side to this man whom she'd married in such haste.

"What exactly are you doing?" he asked in a voice that could have etched glass.

As she took in his tone and his rigid stance, she went cold all over, wondering if he was going to believe what she said. "I…" Her throat clogged and she had to start again. "The shirt you gave me must be wool. It's making me itch and I need something else to wear." She gestured over her shoulder. "You have all these expensive shirts. I'm looking for something I won't ruin…if I used it as a nightgown."

The tight expression on his face eased, along with some of the tension coursing through her.

She wanted to tell him that a husband and wife had to trust each other, but she wondered if it could be true in this case. Could he ever trust her? Or was he just not used to sharing his life with someone?

Feeling like she was rushing headlong into the unknown, she watched him stride into the closet, rifle through the contents and grab what looked like a perfectly good dress shirt.

"How about this one?"

She came from a family where clothing purchases were

carefully considered, and your possessions carefully cared for.
Well, that was how she'd looked at it. Pearson hadn't been
quite so frugal.

"I'll muss it up."

"That's not a problem. We have very good laundry
service here."

She accepted the shirt and started to unbutton the one she
was wearing, but her fingers were too clumsy to accomplish
the simple task.

When he reached to help her, their hands collided.

"Let me do it," he said, his voice suddenly thick.

"Okay."

She tried not to tremble as he unbuttoned the shirt,
slipped it off her shoulders and put on a new one. Apparently he wasn't looking directly at her, and she felt his hand
stiffen when he realized she'd taken off her bra after he'd
left the bedroom.

His gaze dropped to her breasts, taking in the tight points
of her nipples, then quickly closed the shirt, covering her.

"You thought I was spying on you," she said in a voice that
wasn't quite steady.

She saw him swallow.

"I wasn't. I'm not a spy. I'm just what I seem to be. No
more, no less." She forced herself to add, "But now you're
thinking you rushed into marrying me."

"It's hard for me to trust people."

"But you took a chance on me. That's a good start." She
kept her gaze on him. "What can I do to make things right
between us?"

"You're a very wise woman, with excellent instincts. Just
be yourself. Don't do things or not do them because you're
calculating how I'll react."

"Okay." She caught his hands and cupped them over her
breasts. "I think I know how you'll react to this."

"I thought we agreed not to do anything now," he said in a gritty voice.

"You told me to trust my instincts. I want you. And I want to give back the pleasure you gave me."

And I want this to be a real marriage, she silently added. She wasn't sure what that meant in this case; she only knew that things hadn't started off very well between them.

They'd both rushed along on a course of action that would seem insane when examined closely. Now she wanted to make things normal. If they could be normal.

Reaching between them, she curled her fingers around his erection through the fabric of his slacks.

An exclamation hissed out of him.

"I like *that* reaction," she whispered as she brought her lips to his.

"You're sure?"

"Very," she answered, then followed the assurance with the passion of her kiss.

When their lips finally broke apart, they were both trembling, and she had to hook her hands over his shoulders to keep from swaying dangerously.

"You need to get off your feet."

"That's a good plan."

He scooped her up and carried her back into the bedroom, then laid her on the bed.

Looking behind him, he stared at the open door and made a low exclamation.

"Be right back."

He crossed the room quickly and locked the door. While he was gone, she slipped out of the shirt, then pulled the covers to the tops of her breasts.

Turning, he gave her a warm look. "I think we can put this on a more equal footing."

Quickly he pulled off his shirt. When he reached for his belt buckle, she said, "Not so fast."

"Why not?"

"I want to look at you," she answered. That was true, but she was also a little nervous. "I like your chest. It's broad and muscular."

"I thought chest hair was out, judging from the guys I see in the movies."

"I like it. It looks masculine. And I like the way it feels."

"Against your breasts?" he asked, his voice sultry.

"Against my breasts. And my fingers," she answered, feeling her temperature rise as she spoke.

She hadn't thought she could get playful with this scene, but she found she liked it. And she could see he was enjoying himself. Slowly, he worked the buckle on his belt, then lowered the zipper of his slacks.

"Should I try to find some music to strip by?" he asked.

"The visuals are enough to push me to boiling point."

With a grin, he slicked his pants down his legs and kicked them out of the way, leaving him wearing black briefs. There was a confidence in his stance that she admired. He knew his body was in good shape and he didn't pretend otherwise.

"Nice." She swallowed. "Now I'd like to see the rest."

He grinned again. Then his expression turned serious as he pulled down the briefs and stepped out of them.

Her breath caught as her gaze fastened on his erection. It was large and firm and stood straight up against his body. In response, moisture gathered between her legs.

They hadn't touched each other, yet she was aroused. Very aroused.

"Your turn," he said. "Pull down the covers so I can see you."

"That's fair," she said, her voice going breathy.

She kept her gaze fixed on him as she grabbed the edge of

the sheet and dragged it slowly downward, the fabric seeming to abrade her skin as it traveled down her overheated flesh.

The smoldering look in his eyes sent her temperature shooting up several more degrees.

Still, she held her breath until she heard him say, "Beautiful. You're so beautiful."

Their eyes locked as he walked toward her, then sat on the edge of the bed. Her whole body tingled as she waited for him to gather her in his arms.

Instead, he reached out to stroke her collarbone. The light touch sent a firestorm through her.

It grew more intense as he stroked her arms, the ribs on her good side, the indentation of her waist, the outsides of her thighs. Everywhere that shouldn't jolt up her need but did.

She moved restlessly on the bed. "Please," she gasped out.

"What do you want?"

"You know."

"Tell me."

"Touch my breasts. Between my legs."

The look in his eyes was enough to scald her as he lightly brushed the backs of his fingers against her nipples.

"Harder…" she begged.

"Like this?" he asked, turning his hands over and taking her between his thumbs and forefingers, squeezing gently, and then harder as he watched her reaction.

She surged toward him, then grabbed one of his hands, dragging it downward toward the throbbing place between her legs.

He obliged her, dipping into her folds, feeling the swollen wetness there.

"I need you inside me," she begged, reaching to close her hand around his erection, knowing that he wouldn't be able to hold back.

He made a sound low in his throat.

"Your injury isn't healed. I don't want to hurt you. Let's try this way." He helped her up, turning her to the side of the bed where he still sat with his feet on the floor.

She understood what he intended and straddled his lap. As she stood with her legs on either side of his knees, their eyes locked. Slowly, building the anticipation, she lowered herself, bringing his erection inside her.

They both gasped at the joining, and she surged upward, then came down on him again. Instead of allowing her to continue, he pressed his hands against her thighs, holding her in place.

His gaze stayed locked with hers. "I want both of us to remember this."

"Not much chance of my forgetting," she managed to say.

He let go of her thighs, and she moved again, frantic to bring them both to completion.

He reached down with one hand, stroking her sensitive core, while he used the other to play with her breasts.

The twin pleasures kindled an explosion that flashed through her, and she gasped as climax took her.

He cried out as he followed her, his face a study of intense awareness.

They clung together for long moments. Finally he helped her off his lap, then settled her in the bed again. Pulling up the covers, he lay beside her cradling her in his arms.

She snuggled against him, feeling safe and secure for the first time in…she couldn't exactly remember when.

"Well, we know we suit," he said.

"Suit?"

"I mean suit each other in bed." He turned his head toward her. "I guess that's a kind of old-fashioned phrase."

"Where did you pick it up?"

"I used to read a lot of eighteenth-century novels."

"Why?"

"One of my strange hobbies."

She nodded against his shoulder. He was quiet again, and she wanted to simply drift on the euphoria of the moment.

But he cleared his throat. "I know I'm not going to be the easiest guy to live with."

"We both want it to work."

"Yes." Now that he'd brought up the subject, she felt a question burning behind her lips. After dragging in a breath and letting it out, she asked, "Are you going to tell me your secrets?"

His voice stayed relaxed, but she felt his muscles stiffen. "What makes you think I have secrets?"

"Well, you wall yourself off from everyone on this estate."

"I have my reasons."

"Are you going to tell them to me?"

He shifted so that he was facing her. "Yes. But you're going to have to let me do it in my own way."

"Are you afraid that I won't want to stay with you…when I find out."

He swallowed hard. "Yes."

"That will never happen, Noah."

"What if I told you I was dying and I selfishly wanted to spend my last days with you?"

Alarm shot through her. "Are you dying?"

He sighed. "No. That was just an example of the kind of thing I'm dealing with."

"How could…" She stopped herself before she finished the question. What could be worse than his dying? He was going to have to tell her, but if he couldn't talk about it yet, she understood because she knew how hard it had been to tell him about Pearson's scam. "Okay."

"Okay, what?"

"I'm not going to argue with you. And I'm not going to pressure you. I just hope you decide to trust me sooner rather than later."

He breathed out a small sigh. "Thank you."

She settled down beside him and tried to relax. But her mind was churning now. All sorts of possibilities assaulted her. Had he murdered someone? She couldn't see him doing that on purpose. Maybe it had been a terrible accident, and now he needed to stay out of circulation so that the law wouldn't catch up with him. But if he had to stay out of circulation, why had he come to Las Vegas? And what about their recent run-in with the cops? They hadn't arrested him.

She struggled to make the disturbing speculations go away. Maybe he knew what kind of anxiety he'd created in her, because he began to stroke her again and kiss her and before long, they were back where they'd been a little while ago, hot and bothered and craving sexual release.

Only after making love a second time was she able to sleep. Wrapped in Noah's arms.

Noah woke her some time later. "I told the cook we'd be wanting dinner around now."

"Yes. Right."

"I can have it brought to the bedroom because you're obviously recuperating."

"I'd feel less awkward if we did what we're normally going to do. What's that?"

He laughed. "Sometimes I have a tray sent to the lab. Or to the library, if I'm working. But we can pick a place to eat."

"You have a dining room?"

"Yes, but it's not all that friendly."

"Well, what about a table in the library or the sunroom?"

He got out of bed. "Let's try the library." He reached for the phone on the bedside table and pressed one of several buttons, which apparently gave him the kitchen. It seemed like a kind of old-fashioned arrangement, but Noah modernized it.

"You'll have to show me the system," she said when he finished giving directions.

"Yes."

She watched him walking around, picking up clothing.

"I'm going to take a quick shower."

She looked down at her bandage. "I guess I can't do that yet. Or maybe you can help me take this off and put on another bandage after I wash."

"Yes."

The bathroom was large, but it felt awkward using it with a man she hardly knew.

Her husband, she reminded herself as he carefully removed the bandage.

"The cut's looking a lot better," she said, as she inspected herself in the mirror.

"Yes. I'll bring your suitcase. And I'll clear out one side of my closet."

"I hate to inconvenience you."

"I have things I should give away anyway. In a few days, we can drive into Santa Barbara and go clothes shopping."

"Thanks."

They walked hand-in-hand to the library, and she felt awkward again as a maid gave them a speculative look. Was that woman going to straighten the bed while they were at dinner and note the evidence of lovemaking? And so what? she asked herself. They were newlyweds. Of course they'd be making love.

Still, when she'd imagined being married, she'd pictured herself and her husband living in a little house alone, not surrounded by people who were noting their every move and talking about them in the kitchen. Because she had no illusions about that.

Noah Fielding was the center of attention on this estate, and that made her the center of attention with him.

The meal she'd ordered was delicious and she ate more than she'd expected. Just like that, she'd asked and been taken care of.

It was sinking in that she'd married a man who lived in a way that few people could match. And also that she was now living in a self-contained world.

"That was wonderful. I'm going to have to watch out or I'll gain weight on Margarita's cooking."

"She'd probably like to hear that."

"Of course." It felt strange at first to stop in the kitchen. But Margarita put her at ease. Could they turn out to be friends? Would she have any friends here? That was something else to worry about.

THE next morning, before breakfast with Olivia, Noah kept his videoconference appointment with the Light Street Detective Agency.

"I appreciate your talking to me," he told the three men who sat around a long table.

One of them was Hunter Kelley, the guy he'd initially talked to. Also at the meeting were Sam Lassiter and Max Dakota.

"So you think you have a stalker?" Dakota asked.

"It's complicated," Noah answered, and he gave an account of the past week.

"You have been busy," Lassiter said when Noah finished.

"You agree that I've got a problem that I can't handle on my own?"

"Yes. We'd better start by finding out where the brother is. We'll also see if we can get a line on the guy who said he was an FBI agent."

"And Sidney Hemmings should be on the list," Lassiter added.

"Hemmings? He's been…" He'd started to say "a friend for years." But he couldn't actually be sure. Instead, he uttered his agreement.

"I think there's a factor we haven't figured out yet," Dakota said.

Noah concurred. "That's what I'm worried about."

"Do you want one of us to come out there?"

"No. Our security is excellent."

They talked for a few more minutes, during which Noah asked if someone could pick up the jewelry box.

"What should we do with it?" Hunter asked.

Noah gave them the address of his post office box in San Francisco.

"We'll have more information for you tomorrow," Hunter said.

"I'll call you in the afternoon." Noah was unwilling to give them his number. He liked these guys, but he wasn't able to trust them fully. Not yet.

"WE found out his home base. It's not that apartment in San Francisco. That's just an address he uses occasionally."

"Finally!" Jarred snapped. "Where is he?"

"On a ranch above Santa Barbara."

"Then go in and get him."

"It's heavily fortified. We can't touch him there."

"You mean you don't want to take the chance."

"You want somebody to get killed? You want the press all over this?" his informant asked.

Jarred didn't particularly care about the collateral damage, but he recognized that press coverage could be inconvenient.

"What do you suggest?" he asked, working hard to keep his voice calm.

"He can't stay there forever. He has to leave some time and then he'll be vulnerable."

"I don't have forever," Jarred snapped. "I'll give you five days. Then we go in."

NOAH called Light Street the next day from the office in his lab.

"It would be more convenient if we could call you," Hunter Kelley said.

"For now, let's keep it this way."

His new security contractors didn't argue about it.

"What have you found out?" Noah asked.

"The jewelry box is on its way. But that's the only good news. The brother has disappeared. The man posing as an FBI agent has disappeared. And Hemmings has disappeared."

Noah sucked in a sharp breath, trying to figure out what kind of scenario would produce those results. "You think they're all in the same place?"

"We don't know, but we're working on it."

Feeling unsettled, Noah went to find Olivia and discovered her talking to Thomas.

He paused outside the door to his chief of staff's office, listening to the exchange.

"I can see you're devoted to Noah's welfare," Olivia was saying.

"He... I mean an ancestor of his saved the life of an ancestor of mine. There's been a bond between our two families ever since."

"Do you have a son who will take over when you retire?"

Noah heard the sorrow in Thomas's voice. "My older son is ill. I'm hoping that my younger one can take the position."

Noah stepped into the room, noting Thomas's look of relief. "Your wife came to speak to me because she needs some things from town," the man blurted.

"What kind of things?" Noah asked Olivia.

A flush rose in her cheeks. "Well...underwear. I've been washing out the panties I have."

Noah thought for a moment, weighing his options. He didn't want Olivia to feel like a prisoner on his estate, but at the same time, he knew he had to be concerned about safety—until the Light Street people came up with some hard information.

Noah turned to Olivia. "We could go shopping. If you're up to it."

She hesitated, undoubtedly taking in his guarded expression. "Could you send someone into town to buy me...underwear. And we'll put off the shopping trip for a few days?"

"I'll send Benita. She'll love the excuse to do some shopping."

"Thanks. It's probably good for me to get comfortable here and rest for a few days."

He nodded, thinking that she was being sensible, which relieved some of his anxiety. "Let's shoot for the beginning of next week."

"That sounds good."

Two days later, he was able to hand her the jewelry box and felt his heart squeeze when he saw how much pleasure it gave her to get back her mother's modest pieces.

He'd like to give her a six-carat engagement ring, but he knew that would be too overwhelming right now. That could wait, but every time he saw her watching him, wondering when he was going to trust her completely, he felt a pang of guilt.

By the end of the week, he knew she was feeling restless hanging around the house. Because he saw that she was getting her strength back, he told her that Pablo would drive them into town.

"Can't we just go by ourselves?" Olivia asked.

The suggestion was tempting, but he was still being cautious. "For now, it's better to have someone with us."

OLIVIA couldn't help feeling a pang of alarm. He'd said they could leave, but she knew he was still worried. "Are you saying we need a guard?"

"Just a precaution," he answered, and she wondered if they should be leaving the compound at all.

"I'm not going to be locked in here," he snapped, then immediately softened his voice, "Sorry. We'll go to La Cumbre

Plaza, the closest shopping center. Then let's have lunch out—somewhere on the ocean."

"That sounds like fun."

He gave it some consideration. "The Biltmore, I think. You'll love the view and the gardens."

Noah's Mercedes wasn't a stretch limo, but it was a large car with a window between the front and back seats. After giving Pablo instructions, Noah closed the window to give them privacy. It was another symbol of the life Olivia had stepped into.

"So why do we need a bodyguard?" she asked.

"I'm being cautious until…"

"What?"

"I asked the Light Street Detective Agency to check into the situation in Las Vegas. Your brother has disappeared."

She stared at Noah, trying to take all that in.

"They'll find out where he's gone."

"I hope he can't get to us here."

"I don't think so, but I'm not taking any chances. Let's talk about our outing."

An outing. Another old-fashioned term.

She stopped focusing on Noah's language. She was sure her brother was up to something unsavory and she wanted to hear Noah's thoughts. But she couldn't see how endless speculation would help. Instead, she tried to focus on the shopping trip.

"I'm not sure of the rules," she said as the big car reached the suburbs of Santa Barbara. "Like, uh, do I have a spending limit?"

"You can get whatever you want."

She smiled at him. "That could be dangerous."

"I'm betting that I married a levelheaded woman."

"I hope so." She reached across the seat and laid her hand over her husband's and said something she'd been wanting to say for days. "I love you."

She saw the mixture of emotions that crossed his features. He looked stunned, happy, then a little sad.

"You didn't want to hear that?" she asked, thinking she'd like to hear those words from him.

"I'm hoping I'm worthy of you."

"How could you not be?"

"Maybe you'll think I rushed you into marriage."

A little twinge of dread shot through her, but she brushed it away. "You did, but that was lucky for me."

Again his face wasn't exactly sanguine. "I hope so," he murmured.

She'd given him the opportunity to tell her what was bothering him, but he didn't take it. Maybe the car wasn't a good setting. Maybe they'd get to it when they were sitting in front of the fire in the evening. Or in their bed. Yes, that was where they'd have the most privacy.

Instead of talking about Noah, they discussed details of the household, how she was settling in and what DVD they wanted to watch that evening.

When they arrived at an upscale shopping mall in one of the wealthiest communities in the United States, Pablo found a space close to one of the entrances, then followed discreetly behind them as they walked into one of the anchor department stores.

"Where are we going first?"

"Wherever you want. I want to see what you choose for yourself when you don't have to worry about the cost."

"Old habits die hard. I'll probably be looking for sales."

He shrugged. "That's not a requirement."

She led him to the lingerie department where she bought ten pairs of panties and a couple of bras. She could have been absolutely practical. Instead, she chose some skimpy little numbers that she knew would please him. When he saw her selections, he gave her a wicked grin and added four sexy nightgowns.

Then they went on to the sportswear department, where she picked out shorts, slacks and casual shirts.

"I'll have to try these on," she told him.

He looked around and found a chair. "I'll be right here. Come out and show me how the outfits look."

"Okay."

Pablo was still hovering in the background when she stepped into the fitting room area and found a cubicle. Just as she was hanging up the clothing she'd selected, the door opened, and she looked up in surprise as a man stepped into the room.

A couple of the hangers fell to the floor as she stared at her brother.

"What are you doing here, Pearson?" she managed to ask through a tight throat.

"You and I need to talk."

When she took in the hard look on his face, panic rose inside her.

NOAH kept looking expectantly toward the dressing room area. When Olivia didn't appear, he checked his watch, then looked toward the entrance again.

Olivia had been badly cut a little over a week ago. What if this trip was too much for her and she was in trouble?

He was just about to walk over to the young brunette at the sales desk when his cell phone rang, and he pulled it out of his pocket, thinking that it must be Thomas.

Checking the number, he saw it was out of the area and unfamiliar.

As soon as he made the connection, a man started talking. "This is Max Dakota."

"How did you get this number?"

"Your man, Thomas, gave it to us."

"You have my home phone, too?"

"Yeah, but that's not the important point. We know that Pearson Stapler landed at the Santa Barbara airport on a private plane a couple of days ago. I suggest that you get back to the house as soon as possible."

OLIVIA tried to duck around her brother, but she still didn't have her full strength.

Pearson grabbed her by the shoulder, his fingers digging into her skin.

"Get off me." She tried to call out to Noah, but Pearson swore and pressed a cloth to her face. That was the last thing she knew.

Chapter Eleven

Noah charged into the dressing area.

"Sir! Sir!" the clerk called after him. "You can't go back there."

"My wife has been sick," he shouted over his shoulder. "She may be in trouble."

Noah turned right, looking into open cubicles. Pablo turned left, doing the same thing.

In one dressing room a pile of clothing lay on the floor. And beside it was the purse that Olivia had taken shopping. He knew it didn't contain much, but he also knew something basic about the female sex. No woman left her purse lying around in a public place.

"Crap!"

Someone was calling his name, and he realized he'd never closed the phone.

As Pablo charged down the hallway toward him, Noah put the cell back to his ear.

"What happened?" Dakota asked.

"Olivia has disappeared from a department store dressing room." He cursed again. Cursed himself for being so stupid. He'd taken Pablo along as a precaution, but he hadn't really thought anything was going to happen in Santa Barbara.

"We'll be there as soon as possible."

"Anything could happen in five hours."

A clicking noise told him that someone was trying to contact the cell.

"Someone's calling me," he told Dakota.

"Do you recognize the number?"

"No."

"Answer it. Make it a conference call."

Noah pushed the button. "Noah Fielding?" someone said. He couldn't tell if it was a man or a woman, because the voice was electronically distorted.

"Yes."

"We have your wife."

Noah's heart stopped, then started up again in double time.

"If you want to see her alive again, you will do exactly what we tell you."

"Is this about money?"

"No questions!"

"All right."

"You will not contact anyone. You will go to the Santa Barbara airport, where someone will meet you. Go now."

"All right," he said again, then hung up on the second line.

Max Dakota was still there.

"What the hell do I do?" Noah asked.

"What they said, only we'll meet you on the way to the airport and make sure we can track your location."

"Meet me? How? You're in Baltimore and I'm in Santa Barbara."

"We were anticipating problems, so we sent Hunter Kelley out a couple of days ago. Go back to your car. Drive to the La Cumbre Road exit of the parking lot and stop. Hunter will get in the car."

Noah swore again, this time in admiration. He'd hired these guys because he knew they were good. He hadn't known just how good.

"We'd better get off. Hunter will give you further instructions."

Noah hung up, unable to suppress the sick feeling in his gut as he and Pablo returned to the car and followed Max Dakota's directions.

This could be about Olivia, but he didn't think so. Someone wanted him, and they knew how to get him. Was it a revenge thing—like with Eddie Carlson's brother? Or what?

Too many unpleasant possibilities swirled in his head.

The car slowed, and the lean, dark-haired man he'd seen on the teleconference call ran out from between two cars, climbed into the backseat and folded himself onto the floor.

"Keep driving toward the airport," Hunter said.

Pablo followed directions.

"I'm sorry to be meeting you under these circumstances," Hunter said.

"Yeah, but I'm glad you decided to come out here."

The other man nodded. "We're going to put a tracking device on you."

"If they're as thorough as I think they are, they'll find it."

Hunter laughed. "I don't think so. You're going to swallow it."

The idea had very little appeal, but he didn't see any alternative. Apparently the Light Street Detective Agency had made a lot of contingency plans.

Hunter reached into the knapsack on the floor beside him and brought out something that looked like a large capsule. He also produced a bottle of water, which he handed to Noah.

Noah held the pill in his hand. A lot of strange things had happened to him in his long life, but he had never imagined anything like this.

"Swallow it," Hunter said.

Noah did, feeling it travel down his throat.

"They may have put a tracker on your car," he said, "so

you'd better not detour. I'll get out at the next traffic light. We won't try to communicate with you until we have a better idea of the situation, but we'll zero in on your location. And we'll be as close as we can get, ready to bust in and scoop up you and your wife."

"I hope," Noah muttered.

"We have a very good closure rate."

"All right." It was more than he should have been able to hope for, actually, given his own stupidity. He should have kept Olivia safe at the compound, but he'd been too arrogant for that.

"If we can send you a signal or a message, we will," Hunter said.

"How?"

"That will depend on the circumstances." Hunter looked up as the car slowed for a red light. "Got to go. Good luck."

He opened the door, ducked low and rolled out of the car, landing in the gutter. Then he scuttled away, and Noah hoped to hell that the escape hadn't been noted by whoever was calling the shots.

Pablo drove to the airport. "What should I do?" he asked.

"Go home and wait for me," he said, hoping that he'd be back—with Olivia.

He got out and watched Pablo drive away, then he shoved his hands into his pockets and stood on the sidewalk waiting. Moments later, a man approached him. It wasn't anybody he'd ever met before.

"Noah Fielding?"

"Yes."

"Your plane is waiting."

"Where's my wife?"

"No questions!" the man clipped out. "Come this way."

They walked to a van, and Noah felt his chest tighten. He'd thought they were flying out of the Santa Barbara airport. Instead, when he stepped inside the van, something slammed into the back of his head.

He woke up groggy, on the floor of an airplane, with the taste of dried blood in his mouth. When he explored his lips with his tongue, he found out he'd been cut, probably from his own teeth. That would heal soon enough, but it didn't solve any of his other problems.

He didn't know how long he'd been out, but it wasn't just from getting whacked on the back of the head. He was pretty sure he'd been given something to keep him unconscious. And he'd bet they'd searched him. Luckily the transmitter was where they couldn't find it.

He tried to move his hands and found they were cuffed. His feet, too, were tied. Because he wasn't Houdini, he probably wasn't going to free himself. Instead, he tried to evaluate his surroundings.

The aircraft was small and of limited range, and if he craned his neck, he could see blue sky out the window. Which didn't prove much of anything, he decided.

He didn't bother speaking to the pilot or copilot because he was sure they weren't going to give him a progress report on Olivia's health.

His chest tightened. He never should have taken her into town. Not until the Light Street operatives told him it was safe, but he'd seen the questioning look in her eyes and he'd wanted to wipe it away—at least for a while. Too bad he hadn't tried the honest approach and simply told her the truth.

But their relationship was still so new, and he'd been afraid that she'd walk away from him.

He felt the shift in the plane as it angled down for a landing.

The runway was short but the pilots were skilled. They were on the ground shortly.

Noah tensed as he waited to find out what would happen

next. The door opened, and he heard the pilot conferring with someone outside.

The man came back with a pistol in his hand. His companion untied Noah's legs.

"Get up."

When Noah pushed himself to a sitting position, one of the men grabbed his arms and hauled him to his feet.

"Where are we?" he asked.

"You'll find out what you need to know when you need to know it," the man growled. "Come on."

Outside, two more men were waiting, both of them armed with automatic weapons. Behind them was a desolate landscape. It looked like they were in the southwest, on a high mountain plateau.

Ahead of them, in a cleared area, was a small structure that might have been a modest vacation home.

What were they going to do, leave him out here and fly away? Panic rose in his chest. "Is Olivia here?"

"Stop asking questions." To emphasize the order, one of the men backhanded him across the mouth, and he stopped trying to get information. He could rush them, but that wasn't going to help Olivia. He had to find out where she was.

His guards led him to the house, which turned out to be a sort of elevator lobby.

Great, he thought. One elevator going down into the mountain. It would be very easy to keep an attack team from getting in.

When the three of them stepped into the car, it carried them down several levels, into a structure that must have been carved out of the native rock.

They led him along a rockbound corridor lined with doors, then stopped in front of one. The taller of the two guards unlocked his handcuffs, then punched in numbers on a keypad. When the door opened, the man shoved Noah into a small cell.

There was a narrow bed along the wall, and as he stumbled into the room, he saw someone scramble to her feet.

Olivia!

The door slammed behind him as she rushed toward him. "Noah! Thank God, Noah," she cried out, then stopped when she saw the blood on his mouth. "You're hurt," she breathed.

"It's not bad."

He reached for her and she went into his arms, clinging to him with all the strength she possessed. He held her just as tightly.

"How are you?" he murmured, praying they hadn't been as rough with her as they had been with him.

"Scared."

"Did they hurt you?"

"No. What's going on?"

He stroked her back, her hair, taking comfort from the contact. "I don't know. How did they get you?"

Her hands tightened on his shoulders. "I was in the dressing room and my brother came in."

"Your brother? *Your brother* pulled this off?"

She shook her head. "I don't think so. I heard him talking to someone else."

"Okay. We'll figure it out."

"How?"

He laughed. "I don't think someone brought both of us here just to lock us in a cell. Eventually, they have to tell us what they want."

When he said the word *cell,* she started to tremble, and he tightened his hold on her.

He made a harsh sound. "Forgive me for getting you into this." As he spoke, his lips skimmed her cheek.

"This isn't your fault," she answered.

He wanted to tell her it was, but he saw no point in insisting when there was something much more important he had to say. Emotions surged inside him as he said, "I should have told you before. I love you."

He felt her sharp breath. "You're not just saying that because you think we're going to die?"

"We're not going to die," he said in a gritty voice. Confessions flashed through his mind, but this wasn't the time for them. Instead, he said, "I married you because I love you. Only I hadn't figured it out yet."

"That means a lot. I guess each of us saw something we needed in the other."

"Yes."

She nestled against him for a long moment, then leaned away from him and managed a small laugh. "We're an odd pair. You were lonely, and I came along at the right time."

He shook his head. "Don't sell yourself short. It's a lot more than that. I was very lucky to find you. You have some very rare qualities. You're warm and generous. And you know what's right and what's wrong."

"But I…"

"No. That's why you gave your brother so much grief over the scam he wanted to pull."

She dragged in a breath and let it out. "You said this is about you. But it's about me, too. Somebody's given Pearson the chance to get even with me."

As she finished speaking, the door opened again.

Noah whirled to see the men who had brought him from the plane.

He eyed their guns as he put himself between the guards and Olivia, estimating his chances of taking them. It wouldn't do any good to rush them. He couldn't get out of this with brute force. They'd shoot him, and he'd be out of commission for hours. He needed his wits. And he probably needed the Light Street Detective Agency.

They knew where he was. Maybe they were already working on plans to get him and Olivia out of here.

Yeah, sure. Out of a fortress built into a mountain.

"Mr. Bainbridge wants to see you now," one of the men said.

Noah had never heard the name. "Who is Mr. Bainbridge?"

"You'll be talking to him directly. Come on."

Noah reached for Olivia's hand.

"Not her," the guard said. "She stays here."

Noah folded his arms across his chest. "Then I stay here."

"If you give us any trouble, we have orders to shoot her," the man said.

Noah's throat clogged. When he turned toward Olivia, her face had drained of color. "I'll come back as soon as I can," he said, even when he was pretty sure he had no say in the matter.

She answered with a tight nod, and he stepped out of the room with the men. When the door closed behind him, he felt his heart squeeze painfully.

Yes, he'd gotten her into this. And he was deathly afraid for her.

He thought again about going after the guards. It didn't matter if they shot him. Olivia was out of the line of fire now, but he still wouldn't recover quickly enough to do anything for her, so he retraced the route to the elevator.

This time, they rode to a higher floor.

When they stepped out, it was like stepping into another world—into the opulence of a five-star New York hotel.

The floor was polished marble, cut so that each huge block of stone mirrored another one along the corridor. The ceiling looked like it had come from a French palace. And fabulous antique chests and tables were arranged along the walls. Apparently Mr. Bainbridge was very rich and he liked to remind himself of his wealth.

"That way," one of the guards said, pointing to a doorway on the left. As he stepped inside, Noah took quick stock of his surroundings. The room was furnished with comfortable couches and more antique cabinet pieces. Heavy drapes were drawn along one wall, but Noah suspected there might not be real windows behind them.

Two men were sitting in the room facing a large flat screen TV which showed a view of Olivia huddled in the cell he'd just vacated.

The picture made his blood boil, and he turned to the men in the room. One of them looked frail and wasted, and Noah was sure he had never seen him before. The other was Sidney Hemmings.

Noah focused on Hemmings. "What the hell is going on? What are you doing to Olivia?"

The doctor ignored the second question and said, "After you left Las Vegas so precipitously, Jarred contacted me and asked if I could help find you. Actually, I couldn't. You've covered your tracks very well, but Jarred's operatives are persistent. You used a different name at the Royal Crescent in Las Vegas, but we confirmed through fingerprint evidence that Noel Feldman was you."

Hemmings smiled. "We've had some very enlightening discussions about you. You're quite an interesting man."

"And so you kidnapped me and my wife?" Noah asked, making an effort to keep his voice calm, when he felt like his life was unraveling before his eyes.

"I apologize for the dramatics," the other man said. "I'm Jarred Bainbridge."

"I can't say that I'm glad to meet you."

Bainbridge gestured toward an easy chair. "Why don't you sit down."

"I'd rather stand."

"As you wish."

"What the hell is this all about?" Noah repeated.

"Yes, in your position, I'd want some information, too. All

right, I'll get to the point. I'm dying of a very nasty disease. Multiple myeloma. I've been searching for a way to extend my life. You first came to my attention as the result of a newspaper article from the Cayman Islands."

Noah felt a chill ripple over his skin as he thought over everything that had happened over the past few weeks. How much of it had to do with Bainbridge?

Hemmings said, "When we met in Las Vegas, I was shocked at your apparent age. I used my ring to take a cell sample from you. Your cells have an amazing ability to regenerate themselves."

"A cell sample! That's an invasion of privacy."

The doctor shrugged.

"So you got involved in some kind of diabolical scheme with your new best friend?" Noah asked.

Hemmings lifted one shoulder. "As you know, I'm always interested in scientific research. Jarred has the funds to carry out research that would be beyond my scope. There's considerable benefit to me in joining him in this venture."

Bainbridge jumped back into the conversation. "Dr. Hemmings has come up with some very interesting theories about you."

"How helpful of him," Noah said through gritted teeth, then ordered himself not to let anger sweep him away. He had to understand these men. Bainbridge was no problem. He was a very rich man used to getting his way, and his illness was an unexpected blow, something he couldn't control. Yet he was trying desperately to change the equation. Unfortunately, it appeared he didn't care who got hurt, as long as his own purposes were served.

Hemmings was another matter. Noah knew he'd always been a tireless researcher. It seemed that Bainbridge had given him an opportunity to study a fascinating anomaly. Or was Bainbridge giving him a great deal of money for his assistance?

"Of course, I wanted to test the theories for myself," Bainbridge continued. "If Sidney's hypothesis is true, then I'll want to see how your remarkable recuperative powers can be transferred to me."

"They can't," Noah snapped.

"Pearson was very helpful in getting you here," the frail man said, ignoring the interjection.

"Where is he?"

"Dead. He served his purpose and he was too dangerous to keep around."

The offhand way Bainbridge spoke deepened the chill in Noah's flesh. And when the man continued, the chill sank all the way into Noah's bones.

The billionaire gestured toward the television set. "We watched that tender reunion between you and your wife. It was very enlightening. Now I'd like to find out what lengths you'd go to to save her if her life was in danger."

Chapter Twelve

"Leave Olivia out of this," Noah shouted, then wished he'd kept his mouth shut when he saw the twisted look of satisfaction on Bainbridge's gaunt face. He had something in mind, something that made Noah's heart start to pound.

"I've been thinking of various dangers," he said. "We already know you survived without oxygen for hours in that drowned submarine. And I've found out that you were shot in the chest on your ranch last week with no lasting damage. But that leaves many interesting possibilities. What about fire? Can you survive that?"

Noah clenched his fists.

"We'll set up a little experiment—with Olivia—to find out."

"No!" Noah screamed, but he might as well have kept his mouth shut.

Bainbridge picked up a phone on the table beside him and spoke, but there must have been some kind of damping device on the instrument, because Noah couldn't hear what he was saying. And because he cupped his hand over his mouth, his lips were hidden.

Still, it took only a few moments for him to find out what order had been given. On the screen, the door to Olivia's cell opened, and two men came in. One of them held a gun on her while the other cuffed her hands in front of her. Then they led her through the door and out of the picture.

"Leave her alone," Noah shouted again. His gaze flicked to Hemmings, who was sitting rigidly in his chair, his face a stark mask. Did that mean he hadn't given his approval for this experiment, whatever it was? Could Noah use that?

He turned to Hemmings, but the doctor avoided his eyes.

"Come on," one of the men behind Noah said. He wanted to sit down on the floor and make them carry him, but he was afraid that he would only be putting Olivia in serious danger, so he went along.

Behind him, Bainbridge got slowly to his feet. Noah hoped the man was in pain. At least that thought gave him some small satisfaction.

Hemmings also stood, and they walked back to the elevator. Noah tried to focus on the layout of the underground building. There couldn't be only one entrance, could there?

That would be too dangerous.

But his heart was pounding so hard that it was difficult to focus on the details of his surroundings. They exited into a kind of reception area, with several doors and a large viewing window. Through it, he saw Olivia standing on a platform at the far end of the room. She was tied to a wooden post, and straw and wood were piled around her on the platform.

Straw and other flammable materials covered the floor between her and the door.

"The fire will start at this end of the room and move toward your lovely wife," Bainbridge was saying. "You'll have to run through it to get to her. Once you get there, you'll find a fire hose you can use to put out the flames."

"You bastard."

"I'm sure you'll disregard your own safety and do your best

to save her," Bainbridge said. "Because you love her so much. Or were you telling her the truth?"

He pressed a switch beside the door, and a line of flames sprang up across the middle of the room. They leaped high, shooting ten feet into the air. And they were at least three feet thick.

Beyond them, Olivia gasped. When the fire started moving toward her, she began to struggle, trying to free herself from the post. But she was tied securely in place.

Noah threw the door open and bolted into the room. The fire continued to advance, getting wider as it crept toward Olivia.

"Noah!"

"I'll save you," he shouted, staring at the ten-foot wall of flames that now separated them. His only option was to run straight for the fire.

His clothing caught immediately, and the flames seared his skin, sending agonizing signals from his nerve endings to his brain, but he kept running, his goal was to reach the fire hose.

Olivia's screams echoed in his ears as he made his desperate dash. He could feel his flesh burning deeply now. The pain was incredible, but he gritted his teeth as he reached the fire hose, turned the cock and felt a rush of relief as water gushed from the nozzle.

He was enveloped by mind-numbing pain as he sprayed Olivia, sprayed the straw and wood around her, then turned to spray the flames licking at his feet.

Olivia's screams were still echoing in his ears as he fell over, into the fire.

WHEN his eyes blinked open again, he was lying in a bed with Hemmings and Olivia standing over him. He saw tears trickling down her face.

"You killed him," she whispered. "How could you stand there and let it happen?"

"No, he's already healing," the researcher said.

Noah dragged in a rattling breath, and both of their gazes shot to him.

"I'm sorry," he whispered, his eyes fixed on Olivia.

"Noah. Oh, Lord, Noah."

He raised his hand toward her, but it fell back on the bed. He still didn't have much strength.

"It's the secret I couldn't bring myself to tell you," he whispered. "I don't die. No matter what happens to me, I just come back to life. That's the damn secret."

She stared at him, and he knew she was having trouble taking that in. Who wouldn't?

Well, Bainbridge for starters. And Hemmings.

He turned toward the researcher. "What do I have to do to make sure you don't put her through anything like that again?"

The researcher's expression turned eager. "Cooperate with me."

Noah felt his stomach clench, but he kept his voice even as he asked, "How?"

"I want to do some tests on you. And I want to know everything you've learned about longevity."

"It won't help Bainbridge. As far as I can tell, I'm unique, so you'll be wasting your time. I can't even reproduce. I've never had any children."

"Maybe. But I'd like to find that out for myself. How long will it take you to recover?"

"Several days," he said, lying. He'd be functioning sooner than that, but he was hoping he could buy himself some time while he figured out how to get the hell out of here.

Hemmings nodded.

He gave the researcher a direct look. "If you want any kind of honest cooperation from me, do not lock Olivia in a cell again. I want her with me in comfortable quarters."

"Maybe that can be arranged," Hemmings said.

"It better be." He stopped talking and closed his eyes, partly because he needed to rest and partly because he couldn't cope with the wounded look on Olivia's face. He had lied to her, and she'd found out in the worst possible way. But maybe that was part of the fun of the experiment for Bainbridge.

After a few minutes rest, he said, "Where's our host?"

"Resting."

"I hope he's in pain."

"He is."

"Glad to hear it. Do you know what burns over ninety percent of your body feel like?"

Hemmings winced.

"Unendurable pain is often the consequence of not dying," Noah said.

"Maybe that can be controlled."

"I doubt it." He kept his focus on the researcher. "I want to be alone with my wife."

"All right."

To Noah's vast relief, Hemmings turned and walked out of the room. Noah took a deep breath before shifting his gaze to Olivia.

"I asked to be alone with you, but that's a relative term. We'd better assume that anything we say and do is being monitored."

"Yes," she whispered.

"Like I said, I'm sorry I got you into this. Bainbridge apparently thinks I can save his life." He paused for a moment and thought about what he wanted to say, then stared at her with an intensity he hoped conveyed his urgency. "But Hemmings is a brilliant researcher. And I've had years of experience in the field of longevity. Maybe working together we can figure it out. So for now, I'll cooperate."

Olivia nodded.

Although afraid of her answer, he asked her, "How do you feel about me?"

"I don't know."

"Yeah, it's hard to wrap your head around my abnormality. It was hard for me."

"That woman you loved a long time ago. Did she know?"

"Yes. I told her."

"You trusted her enough," she said, her voice sad.

"I trusted you enough, but I was terrified that I'd lose you. I was just trying to figure out how to work my way up to a confession."

"And she accepted it?"

"Yes."

Olivia nodded, and he knew she still hadn't made any decisions about what this meant for her. He wanted to swear to her that he'd rescue her from this outpost of hell on earth where anything could happen. But because he didn't want Bainbridge to know that was his goal, he couldn't say anything.

"Do you know why you've lived so long?" she asked.

"No. My family died of the plague in a little village in Britain. Monks found me as a boy wandering around, starving. They took me in, and I grew to adulthood and lived with them for a while—until some of the brothers started wondering why I didn't get sick. They tried to kill me. I survived. I've had a lot of lives. I'll tell you anything you want to know about them."

It was a relief to come clean with her, although he still didn't know what the future held for them. If—when—he got them out of here, he'd give her a divorce if that's what she wanted. And enough money so she'd never have to worry again. Then he would go back to his lonely existence.

They were still huddled together when Hemmings came back. "You're being moved to a guest suite," he said. "Near the lab. Then you and I can start talking about your research."

"We've been corresponding about it for years."

"Yes, but I want all the facts you didn't share," he said and there was something in his tone that made Noah wonder about his motivation. Could he be having second thoughts about Bainbridge's methods? Could he actually be stalling for time?

Too bad they couldn't be clear on that point.

"Can you walk?" Hemmings asked.

"I'd like a wheelchair," Noah answered, because he was still pretending that he was in worse shape than he really was.

"I'll show you the suite. Then I'd like to do a physical exam."

The suite was comfortable, although not as opulent as the sitting room where Noah had spoken to Bainbridge and Hemmings.

"I'll be back as soon as I can," he told Olivia. The look she gave him when Hemmings wheeled him away for the physical made his stomach knot.

WHEN Noah and Dr. Hemmings had left, Olivia breathed out a sigh. Her insides were churning. She wanted to be with Noah—her husband—and at the same time, she wanted to be alone.

Seeing him fighting to save her life, even as flames enveloped him, had been the most wrenching experience of her life. She'd known he must be in agony. When she'd thought he was dead, she'd felt like her own life had ended.

Men had carried his charred hulk into another room and laid him on a table. When they'd let her go in, she'd been sobbing, thinking she was saying goodbye to him. Then his chest had moved as he'd sucked in a breath of air, and Hemmings had told her that Noah had remarkable recuperative powers.

His secret.

She understood why he'd kept it to himself, although she was pretty sure he'd been working up to telling her.

She knew exactly what it meant for the two of them. She would grow old and die and he wouldn't.

Or maybe not. Not if Bainbridge had his way and finished her off. Maybe the only way to prevent that was to help Noah figure out how to get out of here, because she was pretty sure that's what he was doing.

No doubt she was being watched, she thought, as she walked around the suite. The drapes were drawn, and behind them she found only a wall. There were two doors to the rooms, both of which were locked. There were also two bathrooms. One was fairly small, with a pedestal sink, a toilet and a shower stall. The other was larger, with a long vanity. When she looked under it, she could see an access panel to the plumbing.

Would they have cameras in here, too?

Stepping inside the bathroom, she closed the door and began looking through the drawers of the vanity, where she found some beauty supplies and a manicure kit.

Could she open the panel with it? And would armed guards come rushing in if she did?

She stopped and squeezed her eyes closed, fighting tears as the irony of the situation reached out and grabbed her. Yesterday she'd dared to embrace the happiness Noah had brought her. Today her dream of a normal life with him was shattered. She might end up going back to some kind of life on her own, where she'd try once again to dig herself out of debt and stay out of her brother's clutches.

She shuddered, hating to imagine that alternative.

She still loved Noah, and she had to give him her support—at least until this was over.

Deciding she had nothing to lose, she firmed her lips, crawled under the sink and used the nail file to work on the screws that held the panel closed. When she got it open, she found a space large enough to squeeze behind the pipes. In fact, she could see a kind of tunnel leading away from the bathroom.

Was she looking at an escape route? Even if she was, exploring it on her own was a bad idea. After loosely screwing the panel back again, she used the facilities, then went back to the bedroom to wait for Noah.

THE medical complex turned out to be on the same floor of Bainbridge's little kingdom. Noah looked around, hoping for something he could use to help him escape.

Hemmings wasn't in a very chatty mood as he did the examination. Other than issuing orders, he didn't speak until he was finished.

"You're in excellent shape," he said then. "I don't think you need that wheelchair."

"You could be right."

"Put your clothes back on and meet me in the lab," he said. "It's just down the hall. And don't try to get out of here. The cameras will pick it up and the guards will go after your wife."

Noah gritted his teeth, knowing Hemmings was right.

When he was dressed, he found Hemmings in a state-of-the-art bio lab. He saw an autoclave, a fluorescent-activated cell sorting machine, tissue culture hoods, an electron microscope, biological safety cabinets, an incubator for growing and protecting tissue samples and a lot more specialized equipment. It was clear that Bainbridge had spared no expense in outfitting the facility.

Hemmings was sitting at a computer station at the end of the room.

"So was this lab here last week?" Noah asked.

The doctor looked up. "Partly. I had carte blanche to get what I needed."

"How did they get it in here?"

"You don't need to know that," Hemmings snapped. "Let's get back to you. How old are you?"

Noah shrugged. "I was born in the early fourteenth century."

Hemmings reacted with an exclamation of surprise. "I guess you've seen a lot."

"Too much."

"I can't tell you exactly when I was born. We didn't do much record keeping in my village."

He talked a little more about his background, hoping to establish some kind of rapport with the researcher.

"You should write all that down. And also your lab notes on your experiments," he said.

"I'd do better if I had my records."

"Maybe if I gave you access to this facility, you could reconstruct some of your observations," the researcher said. "Unfortunately, the door between your quarters and the lab is locked."

Noah stared at Hemmings. He'd like to know what the man had in mind. Was this his way of telling him about the door? He couldn't ask, so he said that he had reached his energy limit and needed to rest.

To his relief, Hemmings agreed.

An armed guard escorted him through the hallway and back to the suite, where he found Olivia pacing the carpet.

A wealth of emotions gathered on her face when she saw him. "I was starting to worry about you."

"I'm fine."

Before they could say anything personal, the door opened and two men came in, one of them holding a tray and the other a gun.

"Dinner," the one with the tray said and set it down on a table at the side of the room.

When they were gone, Olivia declined the food. "I'm not hungry."

Long years of practicality made him say, "But you'd better eat because we don't know when we get more food."

She answered with a little nod.

They sat at the table, both of them quiet as they picked at the steak, baked potato and green beans that had been delivered. Yesterday he and Olivia had been so warm and close. Now they might have been strangers, and he fought the fear that this was the emotional end of their marriage.

When Olivia finally spoke, her words confused him. "Come in the bathroom."

"What?"

"Maybe we can take a shower together," she said.

He stared at her, astonished that she wanted to get that close to him. Or maybe she knew that might be the only place where they could have some privacy.

He didn't object as she led him into the bathroom, closed the door and turned on the water in the shower.

Instead of taking off her clothes, she got down on her hands and knees and pointed to a panel under the sink. Then she opened a drawer and got out a nail file.

"That's very creative of you," he murmured, his admiration for her surging.

She met his gaze. "I want to…I mean, do you think they're watching us in here. I'd be embarrassed if they were."

"Let's assume we've got some privacy in here. At least that there's no camera."

He didn't know where they stood, but he couldn't stop himself from reaching for her and pulling her into his arms, holding tight.

"I love you," he said again.

She nodded against his shoulder, but she didn't wrap her arms around him and she didn't return the words.

He held her for a few moments longer because he needed the contact to steady himself. Finally he stepped away and started working on the screws, which she had obviously already loosened. When he removed the panel, he could see a tunnel.

He pointed inside, then pointed to himself.

When she gestured to herself, too, he shook his head.

She made a face but just handed him the small flashlight that was in another drawer. Nice of Bainbridge to provide it, but he supposed it was a necessity in a home that was completely inside a mountain.

He squeezed into the area behind the sink, then started crawling. It was a good thing he had the flashlight because he might have fallen down a shaft about twenty yards farther along the tunnel. There were metal rungs on the side. When he shined the light down, he couldn't see the bottom.

Another man might have worried about falling. He just started climbing upward, with the flashlight gripped in his teeth.

There were branch tunnels on what he figured was every floor. He might have done some exploring, if he'd had more time. But he and Olivia were supposed to be in the shower.

He was looking up, wondering how far he had to climb, when a voice spoke in the darkness.

"Noah, stay cool."

Chapter Thirteen

When he heard the disembodied voice, Noah almost dropped the flashlight in his mouth.

What the hell?

Struggling to retain the light, he clenched his teeth.

"This is Max Dakota from Light Street," the voice said. "You can't answer me, but I can speak to you. And I'm assuming you're picking this up. It's coming from the magic capsule you swallowed. In addition to the transponder, the capsule has a small transmission device inside."

The voice stopped, and Noah waited with his heart pounding.

After several seconds, the voice started again. "Sorry. We have to do this in bursts, so they won't figure out what's going on."

Yeah, right. Was this some kind of trick? The voice sounded like Max Dakota, but he couldn't be sure. And he was having trouble believing what the guy said.

Then he reminded himself that nobody could know about the capsule except the Light Street guys.

"We had to wait until you were alone to send a message. We have a schematic of the facility and we know where you are. We're in a helicopter within range of the facility."

The voice stopped again, and once more he waited in the darkness, his heart pounding.

Was he really in contact with the Light Street men? Or was

Noah Fielding so desperate for help that he was making up voices in his head?

He clenched his fingers around the rung of the ladder. He'd lived a long time and had been in some tight spots, but he'd never made up imaginary friends.

In this case, the logical conclusion was that the Light Street operatives had figured out some very sophisticated technology. He'd like to talk to them about that, if he ever got the chance.

Max Dakota began speaking again. "We know you're in an access shaft that leads to the top of the mountain. The exit above you is on the roof of the facility. If you can get outside, we can scoop up you and your wife. But we need you to create some kind of diversion in there. Something that will have them running around so they're not aware of us swooping in for the pickup. We're hoping you can do that. We'll stand by."

Okay!

He couldn't say it aloud, but he felt a surge of hope. Light Street was in position to get them off the mountain. Noah's job was to get back to Olivia and figure out how to screw up Bainbridge's security force.

Reversing his direction, he started back down the ladder, moving faster than when he'd climbed up, yet it seemed like a long way down. He kept scanning the darkness and finally he saw the light shining through the access panel where he'd entered the shaft.

When he scrambled back into the bathroom, Olivia was staring at him with a question on her face—a question she couldn't ask because she understood that Bainbridge's men might be listening.

He gave her a thumbs up sign.

"Wow. I feel good. That was a great idea about the shower," he said, hoping that anyone listening would assume they'd been fooling around. He ached to tell her what had happened with the access shaft and the communication from Max Dakota, but he couldn't take a chance on Bainbridge's men hearing the news.

He thought about the door to the lab. Hemmings had said it was locked, but Noah had had a lot of practice getting out of confinement.

"Wait here," he mouthed, then took the nail file through the bedroom to the living room of the suite.

When he looked around, Olivia was right behind him. He wanted her out of danger, but he suspected she wasn't going to cooperate.

Without too much trouble, he opened the door, and they both stepped into the lab.

Hemmings had told him the area was under surveillance. But would the guards be focusing on the lab when it was empty?

He didn't know, but he had to take the chance.

Putting his mouth to Olivia's ear, he whispered, "We don't have much time. Look for fire accelerants."

She nodded and began opening cabinets.

He ran back to a storage room he'd seen and started his own search.

OLIVIA rummaged through the cabinets, glad to have something to occupy her mind. Since she'd found out Noah's secret, her thoughts had been in turmoil. Could she live with him, knowing that she would grow old and he would stay the same? Could she be happy with him under those circumstances?

She'd known he had a secret. Of all the things he could have told her, she never would have expected this. Not in a million years. And she still couldn't come to grips with it.

She clenched her teeth, angry with herself. She was all wound up with herself. But what about Noah? What was it like to live for centuries and lose the people you loved? You'd wall yourself off to avoid pain. Noah must have done that, yet he'd picked *her* out of all the women he could have married.

Absorbed with her thoughts, she missed the sound of a lock opening. But when a door swung open to her right—not the door she and Noah had come through—she pivoted to face it.

Dr. Hemmings stepped into the room, a gun in his hand.

When she saw him, she went stock-still. So did the doctor.

"What are you doing here?" he asked in an icy voice.

She scrambled for an answer, knowing she had to keep the man's attention so that he wouldn't discover what Noah was doing.

Raising her voice so it would carry to the back of the lab, she said, "Mr. Bainbridge is setting up another experiment and he asked me to get some things."

Hemmings snorted. "If he were, he wouldn't involve you in the planning." He regarded her with narrowed eyes. "How did you get in here?"

"Through the door." Compounding her previous lie with another, she added, "Maybe I've switched sides, and you didn't get word. Call your boss and ask."

"He's not my boss!"

Her heart was pounding as she waited for Noah to realize they weren't alone. Finally, behind Hemmings, she saw a flicker of movement. It was Noah, creeping quietly toward the doctor's back.

Noah looked like he was about to leap at Hemmings, when the man must have sensed there was someone behind him. He whirled and fired.

She screamed as she saw the bullet strike Noah's shoulder, but his reaction wasn't that of a normal man. He kept charging forward.

And she knew Hemmings couldn't deal with Noah and her at the same time. Weaponless, she leaped on his back, bringing him crashing to the floor. The gun discharged again, but this time the bullet only struck the bottom of a cabinet.

Hemmings rolled one way and then the other, trying to dislodge her, but she wasn't about to let go.

Noah surged forward, grabbed the gun and kicked out a foot, slamming it into the doctor's ribs with bone-jarring force.

Hemmings gasped as Noah trained the gun on him.

"How do you like a little pain?" he growled. "Want another kick?"

"No. Please."

"Sit up. Hands behind your head," he ordered through clenched teeth.

Hemmings grimaced as he sat up.

Olivia's gaze swung between them. When she saw the blood spreading on Noah's shirt, she couldn't hold back a little sob.

"You're hurt."

He made a rough sound. "As we all know, I'll live."

"You're a priceless resource," Hemmings said to Noah. "Don't do anything to endanger this project."

"You think setting me on fire isn't endangering the project?"

"You recovered. Just like you'll recover from the bullet wound."

"Yeah, but you didn't know that for sure before you tried that human torch experiment."

Hemmings's voice turned desperate. "It was Bainbridge's idea! I couldn't change his mind."

"That's a convenient excuse."

"Listen to me. We can both be rich if you cooperate with him."

"I have all the money I need."

"Work with me!"

"Is that why you were being accommodating—to soften me up?"

Hemmings didn't answer.

"We're wasting time," Noah snapped. "Olivia and I have to get out of here."

Noah made a wide circle around the man, then handed the gun to her. "Keep him covered."

She took the weapon and held it in a two-handed grip, her focus on Hemmings. From the corner of her eye, she saw Noah run to the back of the storeroom again. He returned with two bottles and a pile of towels.

"Alcohol and benzene," he said, as he began to pour the liquid onto the towels.

Olivia could see Noah move around the lab, his teeth clenched. He was turning on the five Bunsen burners on the tables.

"What are you doing?" Hemmings gasped.

"Starting a fire. Turnabout is fair play, don't you think?"

Hemmings eyed the gas jets. "This place is going to go up like a torch."

"Uh-huh."

As Noah lit one of the towels, Hemmings leaped up and lunged for Olivia. She was too stunned to shoot, but Noah must have been ready for the move. Once again, he used his foot, this time against Hemmings's back, slamming him to the floor again.

But the man was obviously desperate. He hurled himself at Noah, who battered him down again. This time Hemmings stayed on the floor.

Noah worked methodically, emptying the bottles onto the towels. When the terry cloth was soaked with benzene and alcohol, he used the burners to light them, then flung them around the room. Finally, he extinguished the flames on all but one of the burners but left the jets on.

As Hemmings watched what he was doing, the researcher gasped. "Are you crazy? The gas will explode."

"That's the idea."

"You can't leave me here."

"You were perfectly willing to kill Olivia if I hadn't gotten to her in time. You just watched."

"I didn't have a choice."

"You'll have a chance to get out—after we do."

The smoke from the burning towels was already making Olivia cough.

Noah whirled toward her. "Go into the bedroom. I'll be right there."

But she wasn't going to leave him alone with Hemmings.

As the flames leaped higher, the doctor made a desperate grab for Noah, and she shot him in the shoulder.

He screamed as he fell backward into the flames, then screamed again as his clothing caught fire.

Hemmings begged for help.

Shocked at her own actions and her unfeeling reaction, Olivia ignored him.

"We'd better split," Noah ordered, "before the gas blows."

They both turned and ran. Just as they stepped through the doorway, an alarm rang.

"Hurry," Noah shouted. "The guards are going to be here any minute."

THE alarm woke Jarred Bainbridge. For a moment, he couldn't figure out why a bell was ringing. Then the speaker beside his bed crackled.

"Sir, there's a fire in the laboratory."

His immediate reaction was anger. "How the hell did that happen?"

"The lab was vacant. We put it on an eight-minute surveillance cycle."

"You idiot," Jarred screamed. "Noah Fielding is next door. Get him out of there."

"Yes, sir."

"And keep me informed."

"Yes, sir."

The voice clicked off, and Jarred was left alone in his bedroom.

Struggling up, he started for the door, but the smell of smoke stopped him. Apparently it had gotten into the air ducts.

He pressed the communications panel again, but nothing happened, and fear clawed at his chest.

For years he'd always been in command, but somehow since he'd started stalking Noah Fielding, the situation had gotten out of his control. He'd thought he'd been so clever bringing Fielding here. Now he knew he'd made a bad mistake.

Smoke was filling the room, and in his weakened condition, he couldn't breathe.

Panic seized him and he struggled for calm.

The floor. You were supposed to get down on the floor to get away from the smoke.

He tried to crawl toward the door, but he wavered on unsteady arms and knees.

"Help. Someone help me," he called out, his voice barely carrying across the room.

No one came.

The last conscious thought he had was a curse.

NOAH ran for the access panel. Just as they reached the bathroom, the door burst open, and two armed guards pounded in.

"Go," he shouted to Olivia. "There's a shaft about twenty feet down the tunnel. Start climbing up."

She gave him a desperate look.

"Go," he shouted again as he fired at the guards. Neither one of them had expected him to be armed, and he was able to take both of them out. Leaping forward, he grabbed an automatic weapon from one of the bodies and headed for the panel.

Earlier it had been dark inside. Now he saw emergency lighting along the interior of the shaft. Maybe the alarm had triggered the lights.

Olivia had already disappeared inside, and he heard her gasp.

"How far down is it if I fall?" she asked.

"Don't look down. Keep going up. I'll be under you."

He climbed in, just as another guard charged into the room. He dropped the guy the way he'd taken out the others, then slung the gun's strap over his shoulder so he could climb.

His right shoulder still hurt, but it was getting better. He could feel the slug working its way out, the foreign object being rejected from his body the way he knew it would.

Below him, another guard had crawled into the tunnel and started firing upward.

Noah cursed under his breath as he paused on the ladder, turned and fired back.

Bullets whizzed past him, and he prayed that one of them wasn't going to hit Olivia.

Then from below, a massive explosion shook the ladder. In the dim light, he saw Olivia waver on the rungs.

"Hold on. Just hold on tight," he called out, following his own advice.

His heart leaped into his throat as he watched her feet scramble for purchase, but finally she stabilized herself. When she was steady again, he ordered her to climb, praying they could get to the top before the whole structure collapsed around them.

She kept going, but he could hear her breathing hard, and the smoke was following them up the shaft.

They had another problem, too. Since the initial contact, he hadn't heard anything from the Light Street men. Were they really out there, or had something happened?

When Olivia reached the top, Noah breathed out a small sigh. There was a narrow platform and an access hatch. Olivia climbed off the ladder and onto the platform. Leaning back against the wall, she sagged to the side.

His heart stopped as she wavered toward the guardrail. Swiftly he reached for her, propping her against his side with one hand while he aimed the machine gun at the hatch with the other and fired a stream of bullets at the panel. The door flew off, letting blessed air into the shaft.

"Come on."

Olivia didn't move.

"Come on," he said again, lifting her up and heaving her through the opening.

She flopped limply onto the surface above, and Noah scrambled out after her.

In the distance, he could see the small house with the entrance to the elevator shaft, and he knew they were on the same plateau where he'd landed yesterday. Or maybe it was the day before.

He looked back at the escape hatch, thinking that if someone came through, he and Olivia were too exposed.

"Olivia?"

She made a small sound, but she didn't move.

"We have to get away from here."

Gritting his teeth, he lifted her in his arms. His shoulder still hurt after the long climb up the ladder. Carrying Olivia several yards away, he rounded an outcropping of rock and set her down gently on the ground.

Desperation clawed at him as he scanned the sky. They were out of the underground facility, but where were the Light Street guys?

While that question circled in his mind, he felt the ground quake below him, and knew that another explosion had shaken the complex.

Was the whole top of the mountain going to blow? With them on it? That might solve the Noah Fielding problem once and for all.

"Please, Lord. Not now," he whispered. "Not when I've found Olivia."

But even if, by some miracle, he got her out of this, would she stay with him?

Chapter Fourteen

Behind them, Noah heard a whooshing sound. Whirling, he was in time to see the building with the elevator burst into flames. So much for anybody inside using that escape route.

Unless someone came up the access shaft, it looked like everybody down there was done for. Including Bainbridge.

That realization gave Noah a moment's satisfaction as he crouched over Olivia. The unprincipled bastard had been looking for a way to prolong his life—and he'd only succeeded in shortening it.

Nobody from inside the complex was coming after them. Unfortunately, he had the feeling they were sitting on a man-made volcano that was going to blow the top off the mountain.

Desperately, he shook Olivia's shoulder. "Wake up. You have to wake up."

She didn't respond, and he felt everything inside him twist and cramp. They had to get away from the mountaintop, but after climbing the shaft with a bullet in his shoulder, he knew that he couldn't carry her to safety.

Gently he tried to rouse her. When that didn't work, he grasped her arm and shook her.

"Olivia, we're still in danger. We have to get out of here. Sweetheart, I love you. If something happens to you because of me, I'll never forgive myself. Never. Please, wake up."

Centuries passed in those moments. When her eyes opened, he breathed out a grateful sigh.

She looked around, dazed.

"Sweetheart. Thank God."

She focused on him. "Where are we?"

"Outside."

A grin flickered on her lips. "We made it."

"Sort of. We can't stay here," he said, even when he didn't know where they were going.

When she pushed herself up and fell back, he grabbed her under the arms and steadied her.

"Are you okay?"

"Yes," she said, but her voice was weak.

He helped her to her feet, even when he knew that she was in no shape to walk.

From her standing position, she scanned the barren landscape, that ended in a drop-off in every direction. "Where are we going?"

"The Light Street Detective Agency is coming for us." *I hope,* he silently added.

Before the lab fire, he'd been in communication with Max Dakota. At this moment, there was no indication that anyone from the agency was still in the area. If they ever had been.

But he knew he and Olivia couldn't stay where they were. The dry brush around the elevator building had started burning, sending a cloud of smoke into the air. Before they had a repeat of the scene with Olivia tied to the stake, he urged her away.

"NOAH Fielding? Can you hear me, Noah Fielding?"

There was no answer, and Jed Prentiss cursed under his breath.

"I still can't reestablish contact with him," Jed Prentiss said into his com unit. He was piloting a helicopter circling in the air near the mountain where Noah and his wife were being held.

"They're still jamming?" Hunter asked.

"Yeah."

Moments ago, an underground explosion had sent shock waves through the air around them. Now smoke from a brushfire on the mountaintop was pouring into the air, blocking their view.

"Noah Fielding," Jed tried again.

Once more he was met with silence.

"You think they're dead?" Max asked, voicing Jed's worst fear.

"Maybe they made it to that access shaft and got out," Hunter Kelley said.

"Even if they're out there, we could miss them in all that smoke if they can't tell us where they are."

While Jed circled into the haze, he and the other men in the chopper scanned the mountaintop, looking for the two escapees, but they spotted no one.

As he watched the fire and smoke, Jed knew the whole mountain could blow and blast the chopper out of the sky. But if they didn't get closer, they weren't going to spot the Fieldings—if they'd managed to get to the surface.

WHEN Noah and Olivia reached the edge of the plateau, he stopped. They were hundreds of feet in the air—like in one of those TV commercials with a vehicle on top of a giant rock, and you had to wonder how it got there. Only in this case, the rock was big enough for a short landing strip. And the strip was on fire.

Noah stared at the ground so far below, wondering whether they really could climb down. But it seemed to be the only escape route. Damn, he wished he had a rope. He had some experience rock climbing, but Olivia probably didn't.

She swayed on the edge of the cliff. "That access shaft was bad enough. This is too wide open. I can't go down there."

"You have to."

When he walked to the very edge, she winced. Leaning over, he could see a ledge about six feet below them. He could get to it and help her down.

But then what? Would the wall of the cliff shield them from an explosion?

He had just swung his leg over the edge when a voice near his ear stopped him cold.

"Noah Fielding. Can you hear me, Noah Fielding?"

"Yes!" he shouted, although he knew the communication was only one way.

"If you can hear me, give me a sign. We're having trouble seeing you through the smoke."

Noah yanked off his shirt and swung it back and forth in the air. When he heard a noise in the distance, he pivoted in that direction and saw a helicopter.

Answering his unspoken question, the pilot said, "They jammed us when they went into emergency mode. They must have had an automatic interference system that kicked in."

Noah exhaled a breath and pointed to the rapidly approaching chopper. "That's the Light Street Detective Agency."

"But how?" Olivia breathed.

"After you were kidnapped, they set up a transmission link to me."

The helicopter swooped low, and Noah moved Olivia back from the cliff edge to make sure she wouldn't be blown off in the wash from the rotors.

The chopper didn't attempt to land. Instead, while it hovered in the air, Dakota came down on a ladder that swung back and forth in the wind.

Olivia bit her lip as he reached for her.

"Go!" Noah ordered.

When she was safely in the copter, he pulled on his shirt, then scrambled up the ladder and slid in beside her.

As soon as he was in his seat, they took off.

Just in time.

As they zoomed away, a tremendous explosion rocked the mountain behind them. When Noah twisted around in his seat, he saw the whole top of the plateau fly apart, spewing chunks of rock into the air.

The helicopter shook as shards of rock hurtled past the windows. Noah held his breath, praying that they wouldn't be knocked out of the sky, but the pilot kept the chopper on a steady course.

"So much for Bainbridge," Noah muttered, then glanced at Olivia. She was staring white-faced at the place where they'd been only a few minutes earlier, probably thinking that getting onto the ledge below the plateau wouldn't have done them a damn bit of good.

It was noisy in the machine, and they didn't have headsets like the rescue team, which meant he couldn't say anything to her. When he reached out and squeezed her hand, she looked at him, then away, and he felt his stomach knot. Since he'd woken up after Bainbridge's twisted experiment, he'd ached to talk to her in private. He wanted to know where he stood with her. Would she stay with him? Or would she flee this hasty marriage as soon as she could get away?

That discussion would have to wait, but there was something else he wouldn't be able to put off. He needed to think about what he was going to tell the Light Street men who had come through for him and Olivia under heroic circumstances.

He'd made his decision by the time they landed in a clearing next to a lodge that he judged to be about fifty miles away. He thought they were somewhere in Arizona.

Olivia was still unsteady on her feet, and he helped her into the house.

"Thank you for getting us out of there," Noah told the men as soon as they were inside and away from the noise of the chopper blades.

"A pleasure," Max Dakota answered. "We researched Bainbridge. He was into some nasty stuff. He was born rich and made sure he got richer. His whole life seemed to have been lived for his own aggrandizement. He didn't care who he hurt or stepped on, so long as he got what he thought he wanted or needed."

"Nice guy."

A group of Light Street agents was waiting for them in the lodge. Besides the men Noah had met in the teleconference, there were two more on the team. Jed Prentiss, who had piloted the helicopter, and a guy named Thorn Devereaux. After the introductions, everybody settled down in the rustic but comfortable living room.

Noah sat next to Olivia, aching to be alone with her, yet dreading it, too. When she clasped her hands in her lap, he kept himself from reaching for her.

"So what, specifically, did Bainbridge want with you?" Sam Lassiter asked.

Noah had been steeling himself for this moment. For years, he'd kept himself safe by protecting his secret, but these men had pulled out all the stops for him and Olivia.

When he glanced at her, she was staring at him intently. Her expectant expression tipped him over the edge. When he spoke, it was as much for her sake as to enlighten the Light Street team.

"Bainbridge was dying of multiple myeloma and he was looking for a way to extend his life, so he was researching people who made miraculous escapes from death. I guess you know he found out that I'd survived a submarine accident off Grand Cayman," he said, knowing that the long explanation was really a stall.

"Yeah," Jed said. "That's why Carlson came to us."

Noah dragged in a breath and let it out. "Okay, here's the crux of it. I was born in the early fourteenth century. I have no idea why I've lived this long. Bainbridge wanted to find out and use my secret to save his life."

There were exclamations around the room.

Thorn Devereaux cut through the babble. "We knew there was something unusual about you. We didn't figure out what it was."

The matter-of-fact way he said it helped Noah relax a little. "I've made a habit of keeping it hidden."

"I can imagine," Jed answered.

"But I decided I owed your group the truth after what you did for me and Olivia."

"You don't have any clues to your longevity?" Sam Lassiter asked.

Noah shook his head. "And I have a state-of-the-art longevity research laboratory. I haven't been able to find any reason for my long life. I just know that I recover from injuries that would kill an ordinary man."

He lowered his gaze and spoke in a flat voice. "Once when I was chained in a prison, I cut off my left hand to get free."

Olivia gasped.

He held up his hand. "It grew back. I wasn't sure it would, but I took a chance and cut it off."

There was a buzz of excited talk around the room, until Thorn Devereaux began to speak again.

"The Light Street Foundation does some basic medical research. It's headed by Travis Stone. When he recovered from leukemia, he set up some endowments."

"I'd like to talk to him," Noah said.

"That can be arranged," Jed answered.

Thorn cleared his throat. "We have a lot of unusual men in our organization." He grinned at Noah. "I was part of an outer space exploration team that came to your world fifteen hundred years ago."

Noah's jaw dropped as he struggled to take that in. "You what?"

"You heard me right. But I haven't exactly lived as long as you. I was in suspended animation for most of the intervening years, until my wife rescued me. And I know what it's like to be hunted by a megalomaniac because he wants to use you."

While Noah was grappling with that, Jed said, "I was turned into a zombie by a voodoo priest." He laughed. "I don't know how it's affected my life span, though." He continued. "We also have Nick Vickers working for us. He's been around for over two hundred years. But then, he's, uh, a vampire. And then there's one of our technical guys, Luke McMillan, who's sharing his body with the spirit of an ancient warrior."

Noah tried to process all that. Apparently he'd gotten a lot more than he bargained for when he'd called up the Light Street group.

"I'd like to meet Vickers."

"Yeah." Max laughed. "You can talk about old times."

Noah glanced at Olivia, who was looking stunned. As for himself, he'd lucked out. He'd thought he was the only guy in the world with his unusual problem.

When Olivia began to speak, everyone turned toward her. "My husband's probably not going to tell you about it, but Bainbridge had an interesting way of testing Noah. He had me tied to a stake and set the room on fire. The only way to save me was for Noah to run through the flames and put out the fire." She swallowed hard. "He was horribly burned, and I thought he was dead."

"Nice guy," Max muttered.

To fill out the picture, Noah added, "I'd been corresponding for years with Sidney Hemmings. He invited me to a conference in Las Vegas, where we finally met. He scraped my hand with his ring and apparently took a cell sample. I think Bainbridge contacted him, and they got excited about testing me." He gave Olivia a pointed look. "He was at Bainbridge's headquarters and he died in the fire."

There was something else Noah needed to say. He kept his gaze on Olivia. "I didn't want to put anything else on you while we were in captivity. So I didn't tell you that Bainbridge killed your brother."

She nodded numbly.

Jed cleared his throat and looked at Olivia. "In case you don't know it, Ms. Stapler, your brother arranged to have you run over in Las Vegas so he could rope you into his…extortion scheme."

Her jaw dropped. "My brother is responsible for my accident? How do you know?"

"As soon as your husband hired us, we started researching all aspects of the case."

Olivia started to shake, and Noah put his arm around her and held her close. "I'm so sorry," he murmured.

She gave him a shattered look. "He was always jealous of me, always looking for ways to get even. I guess he thought he'd found the perfect scheme," she whispered. "He ruined my career. Then he thought he could control me."

"Only you proved he couldn't."

She huffed out a breath. "I tried. It took you to get me out of there."

Once again Noah wished they could be alone. He was wondering how to gracefully excuse themselves when a cell phone rang.

Max Dakota got up to answer it. He returned a few moments later, his expression serious.

"It's for you," he said, handing the phone to Noah.

"Hello?" he said.

"Noah, you're all right!" It was Thomas.

"Yes."

"The Light Street Detective Agency contacted me when you were kidnapped. But I hadn't gotten a report in hours."

"I guess they were a little busy getting us away from a fiend named Jarred Bainbridge."

Thomas cleared his throat. "There's a situation here. I need you to come home."

"What's wrong?"

"I'd rather not say over the phone." He paused for a moment, then added, "You have to come here."

Noah knew Thomas well, and the tone of his friend's voice told him that something was badly wrong at his estate.

"I'll be there as soon as I can."

After signing off, Noah stood up. "There's a crisis at home. Thomas needs me." He looked at Max Dakota. "I'm hoping I can leave right away."

"We have a plane standing by."

"Thanks. And I'd like to have Olivia stay with you until I know it's safe."

When he started for the door, Olivia closed the space between them and put a hand on his arm. "You're not leaving me behind."

"I don't know what's going on at the ranch. I don't want anything to happen to you," he said, his tone rougher than he intended.

Her eyes narrowed. "Maybe you'd better get used to what being married means."

He felt his stomach drop. She had a point, but she'd picked a bad time to insist. Was she saying she was planning to stay with him—or did her decision depend on *his* decision?

She had put him in an agonizing position.

Would she walk away if he gave her the wrong answer? Hoping he could negotiate, he said, "If you're coming, we'd better do this smart."

"I'm listening."

He managed to laugh. "Unfortunately, in this situation, I don't know what smart is." He ran a shaky hand through his hair, wishing he'd had more sleep. And wishing he knew what they'd be facing back home.

Jed Prentiss jumped into the conversation. "Perhaps we can discuss it on the way. It's an hour and a half flight to Santa Barbara."

"You're coming with us?"

"Why go it alone when you can have help?"

They all headed out of the house and got into an SUV which took them to an airstrip where a Gulfstream G500 waited.

"Nice plane," Noah said.

"We share it with Randolph Security. Our two companies are linked together," Sam said. "Actually, Jed and Thorn work for Randolph."

Jed headed for the copilot's seat, and after quick introductions to their pilot, Steve Claiborne, they took off.

The seats in the plane were grouped around a low table. Hunter broke out some sandwiches and soft drinks, and both Noah and Olivia ate and drank hungrily. He longed to get some sleep, but he couldn't afford that luxury.

Still, he leaned back and closed his eyes for a few moments. When he opened them again, Olivia was staring at him. "You look worn out," she said.

"You don't look so good yourself."

She touched her hair. "Thanks."

"We've got a fully equipped bathroom in the back," Jed said. "It's small, but it's got a shower. And we have a change of clothes for both of you, in the back cabin. Why don't both of you freshen up?"

"Good idea," Noah answered. He looked at Olivia, "You want to go first?"

"It will be the fastest shower on record." She got up and walked toward the back of the plane, then reappeared less than ten minutes later looking refreshed and wearing a very nicely cut pair of jeans and a knit shirt.

"How do you feel?" he asked.

"Energized." She sat beside him. "I can't stop thinking about it. What do you think is wrong at your house?"

Noah was facing another mess he didn't want to talk about. This was family business, but in this case, he had to clue them in.

"Thomas, my chief of staff, has a son, Simon, a paranoid schizophrenic who's been fixated on me for years. He shot me in the chest a few days before I came to Las Vegas."

"You've had a pretty eventful couple of weeks," Jed muttered.

"I could do without the excitement." He sighed. "We sent Simon to a private mental hospital. If I had to guess, I'd say he's escaped and is threatening the household."

Olivia's eyes were wide. "He knows he can't kill you."

"Maybe he thinks he's found a way to do it. Which makes me wonder what he's cooking up. And I wonder who else is going to get hurt."

"An explosion?" Jed suggested.

"That's one possibility."

Noah stood up. "I might as well think about it while I'm in the shower."

Like Olivia, he made it fast. When he came back, they were discussing the problem.

"I've got to get in there and find out what's going on," Noah said as he sat back down. He looked around the group. "There's a secret tunnel that leads into the compound."

"Odds are, he forced Thomas to tell him about it," Hunter said.

"I won't know until I get there."

"Until *we* get there," Olivia corrected.

Noah looked at her. "I want you safe."

"He'll know that, which will make me the wild card he's not expecting."

Noah wanted to argue. Unfortunately he knew she was right. The question was, why did she want to put herself in danger when she could stay out of this?

He ached to ask her, but her reasons would have to wait.

Although they made some tentative plans, Noah knew that it was impossible to get on top of the situation before they arrived. There were just too many variables. He needed to know how many people Simon was holding captive and where.

Or was it even Simon? He was the most obvious choice, but there was no way to know for sure.

In Santa Barbara a car was waiting at the airport for them, and they started north.

When they were within a couple of miles of the estate, Noah asked Jed to slow the car.

"Because Simon's probably using my long-range scanning system, we'd better stop here."

Jed nodded. "Where should I leave the car?"

"There's a grove of live oaks up ahead. Pull in there."

When they were out of the vehicle, they tested the communication equipment the Light Street men had brought. It was a lot more conventional than the capsule he'd swallowed the day before, and it allowed for two-way transmissions.

As they looked toward the house, Jed turned back to Noah. "Do you also have the monitors set to capture foot traffic?"

"It can be calibrated that way, but that takes some special adjustments."

"Can we get under it?"

He laughed. "Crawl for a mile? I don't think we're up to that kind of stress at the moment. We can walk until the last three hundred yards."

To minimize their exposure, they came in single file, with Noah in the lead. He took them to the front entrance and opened the locked gate, thankful he'd gotten Olivia to agree to go with the others. Hopefully, he'd be the only one in real danger when he went in through the tunnel.

Olivia made his throat constrict by asking, "What if we're in a tight spot, and you need to distract Simon?"

He had thought they were all set. Now she tried to upset the plan. "I don't want you calling attention to yourself."

She kept her gaze focused on him. "What signal would you give me if you need me to do something to get his attention?"

"Nothing."

"Don't say nothing. I want to agree on a signal—just in case you need my help. The way we worked it when we were escaping from that guy in the hospital. Only I don't want either one of us having to guess about what we're doing."

He sighed. "Okay. If I say…" He thought for a moment. "If I say 'Kiss my ass' to him, you can jump into action."

The men around him laughed, and he knew they assumed it was never going to happen.

It wasn't. But if having a signal made Olivia happy, fine.

"We'd better get going," Max said.

"Right."

Unable to keep his feelings to himself, he reached for Olivia, pulled her close and gave her a hard kiss.

"Take care of yourself," he whispered.

"You, too."

"We'll talk when this is over," he promised, then slipped along the wall toward the tunnel.

No one challenged him as he pushed aside the brush that hid the entrance to the tunnel and stepped inside.

His weapon at the ready, he hurried toward the main compound until a noise over the com unit stopped him cold. It sounded like Jed urgently calling his name.

He pressed the button. "Sorry, I can't understand you. Try again."

When the only answer he got was static, he knew something was wrong—either with the communications equipment, or they'd badly misjudged the situation inside the house.

He was trying to decide what to do, when a voice behind him gave a sharp order.

"Hold it right there, or your wife and your friends die."

Chapter Fifteen

Noah whirled around and stared at the man with the gun, trying to figure out if he was hallucinating.

"How did you get off the mountain?" he asked.

Pearson Stapler answered with a satisfied smile. "I guess I lead a charmed life. Your friend Dr. Hemmings wanted to find out more about you. He'd learned where you live, so he sprang me from Bainbridge's prison and sent me here."

"Bainbridge said he killed you."

Pearson shrugged. "He gave the order, but Hemmings made sure it wasn't carried out."

Too bad, Noah was thinking as he kept his gaze trained on the man. He'd helped himself to some clothing from Noah's closet—a pair of black slacks, a white dress shirt and a beige cashmere sweater.

"If you're thinking about jumping me, don't. Simon's got your friends, your wife and Thomas under his control. I made sure of that before I let you know I was behind you. And he can hear what we're saying. Understood?"

"Yes," he answered, trying to keep his voice unemotional when he wanted to scream in rage.

Stapler smiled in satisfaction. "When I got here, I found Simon had taken over the house. He was surprised to see me, but he realized I could be an asset because there are two ways into this place and each of us could cover one. He's a fount of information about you. And thanks for the change of clothing, by the way. I was a little the worse for wear after that cell on the mountain."

"If you trust Simon, you're making a big mistake," Noah answered, punching out the words.

"The way I see it, he's a very logical guy. You're going to pay us a lot to get us out of your life."

Oh sure, Noah thought. *I just bet you're going to volunteer to get out of my life.* What he said was, "All right."

"Thomas spilled the beans about the Light Street Detective Agency. Simon figured you'd take the more dangerous route in here and send in the main party through the front door. He was waiting for them there."

Noah bit back a string of curses. Instead, he kept his voice even when he said, "Let the rest of them go."

"We can't do that. You'd jump us. Because Simon's sure you can't be killed, the others are our hold on you." As he spoke, Stapler clicked the microphone clipped to his collar. "I'm bringing Fielding around. If you don't continue to hear from me, eliminate the others."

"Is Thomas all right?" Noah asked.

"I guess you'll find out."

Noah fought the sick feeling rising in his throat. He wanted to shout that Simon was crazy and trusting him was like playing Russian roulette. But if he said any of that, Simon would hear. Which was also dangerous.

His mind scrambled for a way out as he walked ahead of Olivia's brother. He expected to go to the main house. Instead, they headed for one of the old buildings that he used for storage.

As they walked, he kept scanning the grounds. Nobody else was around. So was his staff dead?

He struggled to keep his fear for them under control. A lot of people could have gotten hurt, and it was his own damn fault.

When he stepped into the storage building, he found Olivia and Thomas sitting on wooden packing crates against the wall. They were handcuffed, and Thomas appeared to have been beaten.

Olivia's gaze shot to him. "Are you all right?"

"Are you?"

"Shut up," Simon growled.

Dread leaped inside Noah. "Where are the men who came with me?"

Simon shrugged.

Unable to control himself, Noah bellowed, "Dammit! Tell me where they are."

Thomas's son gave him a satisfied look. "They're in a separate storeroom. We don't need them for this meeting. This is an executive session."

Were they still alive? There was no way to know. If they were, maybe they could free themselves. Still, he couldn't count on that.

While he considered all the angles, Noah struggled for calm. He had to get control of this situation somehow. The logical place to start was an evaluation of Simon. His hair was neatly combed, his clothing clean and well-fitting, his face smoothly shaven. If Noah had met him on the street, he'd have thought he was normal, except for the bulky jacket he was wearing and the gun in his hand. What was with that jacket?

Noah's attention darted back to Olivia as he heard her gasp. Apparently her brother had stayed beyond the doorway to make a dramatic entrance.

"Pearson?" She stared in disbelief at him. "I thought you were dead."

He smiled at her. "I keep coming back like a bad penny, don't I?"

"How…how did you get away?"

"Like I told your husband, Dr. Hemmings knew I could be of use to him. He freed me and sent me here."

"That's enough chatting," Simon said. "Good work. You can put down your gun now."

"I'd rather keep it."

"I'm the only one who can have a gun in this hostage situation," Simon said, with an edge in his voice.

"Okay." Looking reluctant, Pearson set down his weapon, then said, "We should get the money and get going."

As he picked up the weapon and pocketed it, Simon shook his head. "That's not the plan."

"You said—"

"Shut up!"

Pearson clamped his lips together, his face going from smug to panicked. Maybe he was just now realizing that he was dealing with a man who was as predictable as a hurricane.

Simon pulled out another set of handcuffs. "Put these on and join your sister."

"But—"

"Do it!"

When Olivia's brother still hesitated, Simon shot at the floor in front of his feet, barely missing his running shoes.

With a shriek, Pearson jumped back. "Stop. Okay, stop."

"Put on the cuffs and sit down."

He clicked the handcuffs onto his wrists, then sat on one of the boxes.

"Just so we get everything straight," Simon said in a conversational voice, "I want you to know that I'm wearing one of those vests like the suicide bombers use. So if anyone in here tries anything funny, I'll blow myself up." He giggled, and the sound scraped against Noah's nerve endings.

The blood drained from Olivia's face.

"I'm sorry," Thomas said.

"Shut up, Father dear. I brought you here as a hostage, not

to give your opinion. Well, maybe later we can have a family confab, but right now I have to deal with Fielding."

Thomas closed his mouth again.

Simon pulled out another pair of handcuffs, which he kicked toward Noah. "Put them on, then join the peanut gallery." He pointed to another packing crate about ten feet away from the other prisoners.

Silently raging against the helpless feeling in his gut, Noah clicked on the cuffs and sat.

Simon's attention was still on him. "So now you're finally going to tell us all the truth," Simon said, "or I start shooting my father and your wife. And I don't mean shoot to kill. I'll start with stuff like knee caps. And I don't think they're going to regenerate the way you do."

Noah ground his teeth together.

"My father's been keeping your secret all his life," Simon said. "But I figured it out. When I was a kid, I used to poke around here and in your other storerooms. I found stuff. You weren't just an antique collector. You saved a lot of personal things from your past lives, didn't you?"

"Yes."

"How old are you?" Simon asked suddenly.

Noah sighed. He'd given away that secret a couple of times already in the past few days. "I was born in the fourteenth century," he said.

"I thought so!"

Noah doubted that Simon had been that precise, but he wasn't going to argue about it.

"And when did you kill your first man?"

Noah glanced at Olivia, then away. "In Italy. When I was exporting antiquities to England in the fourteenth century. I was suspicious of one of my employees and followed him to my warehouse. He was robbing the place. When I confronted him, he went after me with a knife, and I turned it on him."

"So you say."

"Why would I lie?"

"To make yourself look better to your wife," Simon spat out, and Noah heard the hatred in his voice.

"She knows exactly what I am," he said.

"How many women have you raped over the years?" Simon suddenly asked.

"None."

"I don't believe you. You're completely immoral."

"Suit yourself."

"You've kept my father in bondage his whole life."

"No!" Thomas protested. "He was always fair with me!"

Simon swung the gun toward him. "One more outburst like that and you're dead."

The way Simon said it and the tone of his voice sent a chill skittering up Noah's spine. Simon was teetering on the edge of control and he might not last much longer. If he went berserk, he could kill Olivia and Thomas, no matter what Noah did. And Pearson would be collateral damage. Too bad for him that he hadn't had the sense to get out while he could. The prospect of acquiring some of Noah Fielding's wealth had been too tempting.

"How many men have you killed?" Simon asked Noah.

"As few as possible." He stared at Simon, who was also sitting on one of the packing crates. For the first time, Noah looked at the words written on the side and realized with a jolt that it contained stone blocks from a garden wall he'd built in France. He'd loved that garden and he'd wanted to take part of it with him when he had to leave.

Perhaps those blocks gave him an option. If Simon was on the floor on the other side of the box, the stone might be thick enough to shield the other people in the room if Simon set off the explosives he was wearing. Or was the thick jacket just a bluff? That was a possibility, of course. But Noah couldn't risk Thomas's and Olivia's lives on that assumption.

Noah calculated the distance between himself and Simon. How fast could he spring across those eight feet?

His gaze flicked to the captives. Thomas looked angry, Pearson looked like he was about to wet himself and Olivia clenched her hands in her lap, her shoulders rigid. When he looked at her, she looked back, her gaze boring into him, and he knew that she was trying to remind him of their earlier agreement.

He'd wanted to keep her out of this, but she was smack in the middle of the action. But just maybe she was the key to neutralizing Simon.

"I want to know how many men you've killed. You must have kept count," Simon prodded, relentless. "Answer me, you bastard, or you'll be sorry. And don't you dare lie, or your wife is going to get it in the knee!"

Knowing it could all go wrong in the next instant, Noah glared at Simon and growled, "Kiss my ass."

Olivia made a strangled sound as she stood up. "Leave us alone," she shouted. "You're the bastard. We haven't done anything to you so leave us alone."

She started to scream at the top of her lungs, and Simon turned his gun on her.

Noah made his move, leaping across the eight feet that separated him from Simon. The gun swung back toward him, but Noah was already there, grabbing for Simon's hands as he shoved the man over the box and onto the cement floor, where he landed with a thud.

For a moment Noah thought he was home free—that the suicide bomber's vest was just a bluff.

Beneath him, Simon struggled to move his arm. The explosion came seconds later, and Noah was engulfed by searing pain. Maybe this was it.

Finally.

The end of Noah Fielding.

Chapter Sixteen

Noah woke up the way he always did—probably because the bulletproof vest under his clothing had saved him from the worst of the blast. He'd objected to wearing it when the Light Street men had given it to him. Now he was glad he'd listened to them.

Still, his chest hurt like a son of a bitch. And he knew from the pain in the lower part of his body that he'd suffered some damage to his legs.

When his eyes blinked open, he saw that he was lying on his own bed and that Olivia was in a chair beside him.

"You're awake," she said softly.

"We have to stop meeting this way," he managed to say.

When she burst into tears, he groped for her hand and held it tightly. "I'm sorry," he got out.

"For saving my life?"

He could see her struggling for control. "No. Not that. Never that."

"For what?"

He might have said, *for being alive.* But he was glad to be here, more glad than he had been in a long time.

"For putting you in danger again."

She swiped her hand across her eyes and gave him a direct look. "You didn't *put* me in danger. I volunteered."

"And you were very brave to pull Simon's attention toward you."

"I think it was the only way."

"Are you all right?"

"I got hit by some debris. No big deal." Still needing to know the exact situation, he asked, "What happened to Thomas and the Light Street guys?"

"The Light Street men are all right. Like Simon told you, they were in another building. We freed them." She laughed. "They were embarrassed at being caught at the front gate."

"Better embarrassed than dead. I can identify with that."

"Nobody expected my brother to have both entrances covered."

"How is Thomas?" Noah asked, anxious for word of his old friend.

"He took a few hits the way I did, but I pulled him behind the crate with me when you made your move." She heaved in a breath and let it out. "Simon's dead. And so is Pearson. Instead of ducking for shelter, he ran for the door, and some serious pieces of debris caught him in the back."

"I…"

"Don't say you're sorry again. He was rotten. I never knew how rotten until Jed told me about his arranging that accident in the parking lot."

"Yeah. It's hard to believe he could do that to you."

"I still have trouble wrapping my mind around it." She kept her hand in his, which seemed like a good sign for the two of them.

"Thomas is waiting to speak to you. Will it upset you to see him?"

"No. Send him in."

She jumped up and went to the door. Moments later, Thomas was standing by the bed.

"Sir, I'm so sorry."

"Yeah, everybody's sorry," Noah said, trying not to sound weary. "But it worked out."

"I caused you a lot of trouble."

Noah shook his head. "Not you. Simon. He had a real talent for breaking out of that hospital."

Thomas nodded. "This time he used bribes. He'd told some of the staff that he could make them very rich."

"I assume they've been fired?"

"Yes, sir."

The mention of staff made Noah think about his own people. "What about everyone else here? Are they all right?"

"Some, like Pablo, were bound and gagged. Simon forced me to tell the others that there was a threat here, and they had to clear out."

Noah sighed. "I hope we can get them back."

"Margarita is already in the kitchen fixing you chicken soup. And some of the others are on the compound, too."

"Good. We'll have to give everybody who comes back a nice fat bonus."

"An excellent idea."

He could see Thomas needed more time with him.

"Do you want me to leave?" Olivia asked.

"No. Please stay," they both said.

She hovered near the door while Noah and Thomas talked.

"Are you planning to stay here—at this estate?" the chief of staff asked.

Noah glanced at Olivia, then back at his old friend. "I believe everyone who knew my secret is dead. Well, except the Light Street men, and I trust them implicitly. I believe it's safe to stay here while we evaluate our options."

"Your options," Thomas said.

"Both of us. I'd never discount your counsel."

Thomas nodded gravely. Then Noah asked to see the Light Street men.

Jed and Thorn came in, looking sheepish. "Sorry we got scooped up," Jed said.

"We're not used to getting caught with our pants down," Thorn added.

"We were all in a hurry," Noah answered. "If I hadn't rushed you into danger, we would have had time to figure out the situation."

They spoke for a few more minutes, with Noah doing his best to assure the men that nobody could have done any better.

Finally, he told them he was worn out and needed to rest.

"Come here," Noah said to Olivia when they were alone together.

She took her seat again. "You made them feel okay about what happened."

"It *was* okay."

"But you always know the right thing to say to people."

"Everyone but you," he said in a gritty voice. "Now that we're finally able to talk, tell me why you insisted on putting yourself in danger."

"I guess I was testing myself—to see if I have what it takes."

"For what?"

"To be the woman you deserve." She looked down at her hands. "Well, that's impossible, of course."

He felt like a great weight had settled on his chest. "I have a lot of experience with women. I knew right away that you were the right one for me."

"Except for the fundamental problem that I'm going to grow old and die and you'll still be young. There's nothing we can do about that."

"We can try," he said softly. "Medical science is making new discoveries every day. Remember what the Light Street men told us about the foundation that's run by Travis Stone? I want to talk to him about putting a major amount of money into longevity research. I'll submit to any test they can think of, if they want to study me. Except running through fire."

"Oh Lord." Her voice hitched. "That was horrible."

Pushing himself up, he reached for her. When she came into his arms and nestled against him, he let out the breath he'd been holding. "I love you. I'll do everything I can to make you happy."

"I love you." Raising her head, she looked him in the eye. "I had a lot of time to think about what your life must have been like. I know how lonely you've been and I hope I can make you happy."

His heart swelled, but he knew they still needed to work some things out. "I wasn't thinking about what you needed when I brought you here. Well, beyond keeping you safe. Really, I was being selfish about wanting you in my life."

When she started to speak, he held up his hand. "Let me finish. I know that puttering around in the kitchen and decorating the house aren't going to keep you busy and happy. Do you have any better suggestions?"

"I'd want to visit my father."

"Of course." He stroked his hand up and down her arm. "If you want to bring him out here, we could have round-the-clock nurses for him."

Her eyes shone. "That would be wonderful! If he's up to it."

"Anything I can do for you or your father, I will."

"It's just sinking in—how much my life has changed," she whispered. Raising up, she met his eyes. "Money's really no object."

"Well, unless you want something like a flight to the moon. And maybe even that could be arranged."

"Nothing so out of the ordinary. I used to dream of having a dance studio. Would you mind if I had a studio in Santa Barbara? I can't dance professionally but I can still teach kids the skills I love."

"Of course."

She sighed. "I was afraid you wouldn't want me going into town every day."

"Maybe we can compromise on four times a week," he answered.

"That gives me an excuse for limiting my hours. I can say my husband wants me home." She tightened her hold on him. "Yes, I definitely think my husband and I need a lot of quality time together."

"You could start by locking the door."

She raised her head and grinned at him, then looked uncertain. "We still have guests in the house. The Light Street men."

"I'm sure Thomas is making them comfortable. We'll come out and join them in a few hours. But they know we're just married. They probably figure we want to be alone for a while."

"Just married," she murmured, her eyes warm. "You made me an offer I couldn't refuse. I just didn't understand what the two of us would mean to each other."

She hugged him, then climbed off the bed, walked to the door and clicked the lock. She was magnificent looking, so tall and straight with a dancer's grace. He watched her possessively. His wife. He marveled again that they had met and that he'd had the sense to make her part of his life.

"You could have left me after that stunt Bainbridge pulled," he said in a thick voice. "I'm so thankful you gave me a chance."

"You proved how much you loved me when you saved me. I just had to figure out how I was going to cope."

"I—"

She put her fingers against his lips to silence him.

Then she leaned over and replaced her fingers with her mouth, giving him a long, passionate kiss.

Noah wrapped her in his embrace and brought her down beside him on the bed.

For long moments he simply held her. When he needed more

assurance, his hands began to move urgently over her. As he cupped her breasts and began to play with the tight buds of her nipples, she arched into the caress—then suddenly pulled away.

"What?"

She raised her head and met his questioning gaze. "I want you to know how much I love you. Do you have any objections to a woman in charge?"

"Of course not," he answered, wondering what she had in mind, but sure he was going to like it.

"Then lie back and relax."

He plumped one pillow behind his head, then stretched out, his gaze never leaving her.

When he'd gotten comfortable, she knelt beside him on the bed and stroked his shoulders, pushing the covers down so that her fingers could comb through the hair on his chest before finding his nipples and playing with them.

When he exhaled sharply, she grinned in satisfaction, then slowly rolled down the covers farther, exposing him from the knees up.

As she reached to cup her hand over the erection straining at the front of his briefs, he couldn't hold back a heartfelt exclamation. But why hold back? He wanted her to know how much he was enjoying this.

"I see you love getting a rise out of me," he murmured, unable to keep the grin out of his voice.

"Oh yeah. Help me out a little. Raise your hips."

He did as she asked, and she slid his briefs down his legs, exposing him to her hungry gaze and touch. Slowly, she stroked his ribs, then his abdomen. His muscles jumped under her fingers. When she bypassed his erection and ran her nails down one of his thighs to his knees, he made a pleading sound.

"Maybe I'd better get comfortable," she murmured.

Smiling at him, she stood and unbuttoned her shirt, tossing it to the floor. Then she slowly unhooked her bra and flung it after the shirt, standing proud to give him a view of her magnificent breasts.

It was all he could do to keep from surging off the bed and grabbing her. But he ordered himself to stay where he was and let her torture him.

He'd obviously married a very talented woman and he wanted to find out how she would finish this, if he didn't go crazy first.

As he watched in appreciation, she unzipped her pants and slicked them down her legs, along with her panties.

Unable to stop himself, he reached toward her. "Come here," he begged.

She shook her head and tortured him some more by playing with the blond hair at the juncture of her legs.

"Have mercy," he whispered.

Arching her back, she lifted her hair off her shoulders, then let it fall again, smiling as his gaze followed every move she made.

Finally, to his vast relief, she slid back onto the bed. Reaching out, she delicately glided one finger along his swollen length. To keep from grabbing for her, he caught two handfuls of the sheets.

"Look at what you're doing to me," he breathed.

"To me, too," she said, continuing to stroke him with one finger, before closing her fist around him.

He gasped, then moaned as she lowered her head, replacing the hand with her mouth as she swirled her beautiful hair against his chest.

The feel of her lips and tongue on him was exquisite, pushing him toward what he knew was going to be a rocketing climax.

"Not like this," he pleaded. "I want you with me. All the way."

"Oh, yes."

In one quick motion, she straddled him, bringing him inside her.

He struggled to wait for her, but he found he didn't need to. As she leaned forward and moved frantically above him, he felt her contract around him, heard her cry out in satisfaction.

Seconds later, he followed her over the edge.

When she collapsed on top of him, he gathered her close, kissing her and stroking her back and hips.

"I love you," he said.

"I love you—for as long as I can have you."

"I think we've found a love that defies the ages," he answered, clasping her to him.

She slid to the surface of the bed and nestled beside him. For a few moments, she seemed relaxed, until he felt tension gather in her.

"What is it?"

When she raised her head, her eyes were uncertain, but she kept them focused on his face. "You said you couldn't have children, right?"

"Yes. I'm sorry."

She pressed her fingers over his lips. "I should have gotten my period. I'm always right on time. And now…now I feel different. I was saying something to Margarita—not anything, you know, revealing. But she's pretty smart. And she had one of those early pregnancy tests…."

He raised his head, staring at her. "Are you trying to tell me you…you're pregnant?" he asked in a strangled voice.

"Yes."

"Oh Lord!"

Her eyes clouded. "You hate the idea? Or you don't think it's yours?"

"Of course I think it's mine!" He sat up and raked his hand through his hair. "I mean, I know you…" He stopped and started again more softly, "This is a miracle."

"Maybe it means something important," she murmured.

"Yes." He gathered her to him. "Children. I've had so

many in my life, but never one of my own. Finally. After all these years."

She stroked his cheek with her lips. "I'm so happy that I could give you something nobody else ever has."

"Something precious."

They held each other for long moments.

"I want to savor this, but we should see to our guests," she murmured.

"Right. The sooner we go thank them again, the sooner we can be alone for some quality snuggling."

She laughed. "You're being devious."

"Only in a good cause," he answered, his heart overflowing with love for this woman and all the gifts she had given him.

* * * * *

5 MINUTES TO MARRIAGE

BY
CARLA CASSIDY

Carla Cassidy is an award-winning author who has written more than fifty books. Carla believes the only thing better than curling up with a good book to read is sitting down at the computer with a good story to write. She's looking forward to writing many more books and bringing hours of pleasure to readers.

Prologue

He stood on the curb across the street from the casino with its glittering lights and flashy marquee, and the ball of hatred inside him expanded to make him half-breathless.

Harold Rothchild owned this casino, the same Harold Rothchild who had built his fortune on the destruction and blood of others, the same Harold who had destroyed his life.

A small smile curved his lips. Poor Harold's life had taken a turn for the worse. "And it's all because of me," he whispered to himself.

He'd killed Harold's daughter and he now had in his possession the invaluable Tears of the Quetzal diamond ring. He'd done everything he'd set out to do, but as he started at the grand entrance of the casino, he realized it wasn't enough.

That was the funny thing about revenge—just when you thought you'd achieved it, that gnawing hunger for more rose inside you.

He felt it now, burgeoning in his chest, and he clenched his hands into fists at his sides. Rage. It roared through him like a hot wind, stirring his need to inflict more pain, more heartache.

He wasn't through with the Rothchilds, not yet, not by a long shot. He wouldn't be through until Harold Rothchild and his family fell to their knees and wept for all they had lost.

Chapter 1

The evening began with such promise. The house was in order, the kids had been bathed and dressed in matching outfits and Jack Cortland was looking forward to his date.

He'd met Heidi Gray in the grocery store on one of his rare trips into town. The sophisticated, attractive blonde had smiled at him, and before they'd left the produce section, they'd made a date. Since that time they'd been out three times, and tonight was the first time she would meet his children.

Ten minutes before she was set to arrive, he sat down with his two sons on the sofa. Four-year-old

Mick sat on one side of him and three-year-old David was on the other.

"Now, boys, this is a really important night. I want you both to be on your best behavior and be nice to Miss Heidi when she gets here," he said.

"Heidi tighty whitey," Mick exclaimed.

"Heidi tighty whitey," David echoed, and the two broke into gales of laughter.

"Now, now, boys," Jack said in an effort to gain control, but it was too late. Their giggles increased in volume, and Jack sat and waited until finally they'd worn their giggles out.

"I do not want to hear you say that again," Jack said as firmly as possible.

David frowned at him. "Bad Jack," he said. "No yelling."

"I wasn't yelling," Jack protested, and then sighed. "Why don't the two of you go play in your room until our guest arrives."

He watched as they raced out of the living room and down the hallway toward the bedroom. When they disappeared out of sight, he released a sigh of exhaustion.

The boys had been in his custody for a little over four months, ever since their mother, his ex-wife, Candace, had been murdered. And in those months he'd realized they were undisciplined, wild and had absolutely zero respect for him.

Jack knew how to beat a rhythm on the drums to

stir the blood. He could sing the rock and roll that was in his soul. He knew how to entertain a stadium of fans with his music. There had been a time not so long ago when he'd also known how to drink and drug himself into oblivion, but he didn't know anything about parenting.

He pulled himself up from the sofa and went into the kitchen, where the delicious scents of pot roast wafted in the air. Betty, his cook, stood before the sink, washing the last of the dishes before she left for the day.

"Everything is done and in the oven waiting to go on the table," she said as she turned away from the sink and dried her hands on a towel.

"Sure you don't want to stick around?" Jack asked hopefully.

She gave him one of her dour gazes. "I told you when you hired me that I cook and that's it. I don't serve, I don't clean house and I definitely don't babysit." She grabbed her purse from the top of the counter. "I'll see you tomorrow morning, Mr. Cortland."

As she headed for the back door, Jack squashed the panic that threatened to rise in his chest. He told himself that the night was going to be a rousing success.

He wandered into the dining room, where Betty had set the table with the good dishes and linen napkins. It was probably a mistake to share the meal with both his date and his sons, but it was important to him that whatever woman he invited into his life knew that his sons were part of the package deal.

For a year following his divorce from Candace, Jack had rarely seen his sons. Candace has spent much of that year globe-trotting, and Jack had been in no condition, either financially or emotionally, to chase after her.

When Candace had been murdered the boys had come to live with him, but Jack knew Harold Rothchild, Candace's father, was just waiting for him to make a mistake so he could swoop in and take the boys away.

Jack's stomach tightened at the thought of Harold. There was no question the wealthy, powerful Las Vegas mogul wanted his grandsons, but the only way he could take custody away from Jack was to prove that he was an unfit father. Jack was doing everything in his power to make sure that didn't happen. He was determined to be the best father he could be.

The doorbell rang, signaling the arrival of Heidi, and Jack hurried to the door to welcome her. From the direction of the bedroom came the sounds of the boys laughing, and once again he mentally muttered a prayer that the evening went well.

The first thirty minutes were relatively successful. On their previous dates Jack had found Heidi to be a good conversationalist, and it didn't hurt that she was jaw-droppingly gorgeous. He was male enough to enjoy the scent of her perfume in the air and the hint of cleavage that her V-neck blouse offered him.

After a brief introduction to the boys, they returned to playing in their room, giving Jack and Heidi time alone.

When it was time to move into the dining room for the meal, there were several minutes of chaos as Jack got the boys settled in their booster seats at the table, then hurried into the kitchen to bring out the meal that Betty had prepared.

Pot roast and potatoes, broccoli florets with cheese, homemade dinner rolls and a Jell-O salad all went to the table, and after filling the boys' plates, Jack returned to his seat.

"This looks yummy," Heidi said. "Did you do all this?"

"I wish I could take credit for it, but no. I have a local woman who comes in to cook for us." He smiled at her, then blinked as a piece of cheesy broccoli smacked her chest and slowly slid downward before falling into the vee of her blouse.

Mick giggled.

Jack stared at his son in horror. "Mick!" He turned back to Heidi. "I'm so sorry."

Another cheese-covered floret struck her in the head, and this time it was David who laughed uproariously. Suddenly the broccoli was flying and

Jack was yelling. Heidi jumped up from the table in an effort to escape the onslaught of food, her features tight with aggravation.

"Mick, David! Stop it right now," Jack exclaimed.

"Bad Jack," Mick yelled.

"I'm out of here," Heidi exclaimed. "I wasn't sure that I was at a place in my life to be an instant mother, and now I know the answer. I'm definitely not ready for this. Your children are undisciplined little boys, and you all need more than I can offer." She grabbed her purse and marched out of the dining room. Jack ran after her, muttering apologies that she obviously didn't want to hear.

As she slammed out of the front door, Jack leaned against the wall and closed his eyes. She was right. His boys were unruly animals, and he didn't know what to do about it, but something had to be done.

He could just see the tabloid headlines now: "Rock Star Children Belong in a Zoo." He hoped Heidi wasn't the type to cash in by selling the tale of the evening to the tabloids.

By ten that evening the boys had finally fallen asleep, David on the living-room floor and Mick on the sofa. Jack carried them into their room and put them into their beds, then returned to the living room and called his lifelong buddy, Kent Goodall.

Within fifteen minutes Kent was at the house and the two men were seated at the kitchen table sipping coffee as Jack told Kent about the disastrous date.

"I need help," Jack said. "Heidi was right. The boys are out of control, and I don't know how to fix things."

Kent swept a strand of his long blond hair behind one pierced ear. "I know a woman, a professional nanny. Her name is Marisa Perez, and she lives right here in Las Vegas."

"How do you know her?" Jack asked. Kent had no children. He wasn't even married.

"Remember the woman I dated? Ramona with the big hair and bigger chest? She's a friend of Marisa's. Last I heard Marisa was saving money to open up her own nanny agency."

Jack frowned. He didn't want to just invite anyone into his home and into the lives of his sons. As he recalled, Ramona with the big hair also had a pea brain. She'd been working as a showgirl in one of the casinos. He wasn't sure being a friend to Ramona was necessarily a good qualification for interacting with his children.

"I'm not sure Ramona vouching for somebody makes me comfortable," he finally said.

Kent grinned. "Trust me, I hear you, but it wouldn't hurt for you to interview Marisa and see if she's everything Ramona said she was. I'll call Ramona and get her number for you."

Jack wrapped his hands around his coffee mug and nodded. "I have to do something. If Harold gets wind of how badly I'm mangling the parenting stuff, he'll have me back in court fighting for custody." A painful knot formed in Jack's chest as he thought of the possibility of losing his boys.

For the next few minutes the men talked music and bands. When Kent and Jack had been teenagers, they'd formed a band that had played local clubs and at weddings. The band had been successful on a regional level, but Jack had hungered for more.

At the age of twenty-two he'd left Las Vegas for Los Angeles and eventually had hooked up with a group of musicians who had become the rock band Creation.

While Jack had ridden the rise of fame and fortune, then eventually crashed and burned, Kent had remained in Las Vegas with his band members, playing local gigs whenever they could get them.

It was after midnight when Kent finally left, and Jack had finished clearing the dishes from the dining-room table.

When he was finished he went down the hallway toward the bedrooms. The first one he stopped in was the boys' bedroom, and he stood in the doorway and stared at his sons.

Mick slept on his side, his legs and arms curled into a fetal position. David lay sprawled on his back, arms and legs thrown to his sides as if he'd fallen asleep in the middle of a leap off a building.

A surge of tenderness flowed through him as he watched them sleep. The love he felt for his sons was like nothing he'd ever experienced before.

Although he didn't want to think ill of the dead, Candace had possessed the maternal instincts of a rock. Jack had hoped that the birth of the boys would somehow domesticate the wild, beautiful woman he'd married—and for a while it had worked. But it didn't take long for the novelty of motherhood to wear off and for their marriage to self-destruct.

The boys had so many strikes against them. A mother who had been murdered and a father who was a recovering addict and knew nothing about being a dad.

They needed somebody else in their life, a nanny who could teach them how to be good boys—and the sooner the better.

"You are stupid to even consider this," Marisa Perez said aloud to herself as she drove down the dusty Nevada road in the direction of Jack Cortland's ranch.

He'd called her earlier that morning and asked her about her services as a nanny. Against her better judgment she'd agreed to meet with him at his house.

It had been big news when Jack had moved back to his family home two years ago following a very public divorce from Candace Rothchild.

For years Jack and Candace had been a favorite topic of gossip in the tabloids. Their lifestyle of excess and drugs and alcohol had been legendary.

The public had loved stories of the hard-rock star and his beautiful heiress wife.

From everything Marisa knew about Jack Cortland, she was not impressed. She glanced out her side window, passing land that her parents probably owned.

Like Candace, Marisa had come from wealth, but unlike Candace, Marisa had decided early on that she wanted to make her own way. She didn't want to work for the family in their real estate ventures. What she loved was working with children.

She tightened her grip on the steering wheel as she turned into the long, dusty driveway that led to the Cortland ranch.

This visit was more to satisfy her curiosity than for any other reason. Since moving back here Jack had kept a low profile, rarely being seen out of his home.

She'd read the stories about Candace's tragic murder and knew there were two little boys in Jack's custody. More than anything she'd been driven to come out here to check on those boys.

She might not think much of Jack Cortland as a person, but he had a low, deep voice that could weaken the knees of a soldier. After talking to him on the phone that morning, it had taken her several minutes to get that sexy voice out of her head.

The farmhouse came into view, and as she pulled up front and parked, she saw a towheaded tot wearing only a diaper racing across the grass and heading toward a large barn in the distance.

Marisa turned off her engine and expected at any moment some adult to come running out of the house to collect the child. When that didn't immediately happen, she jumped out of her car and hurried toward the little tot.

"Hi," she said when she caught up with him.

He stopped and smiled at her, and her heart crunched in her chest. He looked like a little angel with his pale hair and bright blue eyes. "Hi," he replied.

"What's your name?" she asked.

"David." He glanced toward the barn, as if eager to be on his way.

"I'm Marisa. You want to play a game?" His eyes lit up and he nodded. "Do you know how to jump on one foot?" He nodded again and began to jump up and down. "Let's see who can jump on one foot all the way to the house."

He took off, alternately hopping and running. Marisa followed after him, silently seething over the fact that a baby was outside alone with no adult supervision in sight.

David's laughter rang in the air as he hurried toward the house with Marisa at his heels. They had just reached the porch when the front door exploded open and Jack Cortland flew outside.

His gray eyes were wide with alarm as he took

the stairs of the porch two at a time. "David! Thank God." He grabbed the boy up in his arms, then stared at Marisa, panic still gleaming in his eyes.

She said nothing, merely stood drinking in the sight of the infamous Jack. She'd expected a man who looked dissipated, a man with sallow skin and the lines of debauchery slashed deep in his face. Instead his dark hair gleamed richly in the overhead sunshine. He sported a healthy tan and arm muscles that looked as if he wasn't a stranger to hard work.

He was hot...and for just a few seconds, Marisa forgot what she was doing here. It was only when David squealed in protest and struggled to get out of his father's arms that her brain reengaged.

"I'd say you have a problem with basic safety issues," she said.

"He's Houdini reincarnated," Jack said with obvious frustration. "I assume you're Marisa?" She gave him a brief nod, and he gestured her toward the front door. "Welcome to the zoo."

"I need to get some things from my car," she said. "I jumped out when I saw David racing across the grass and no adult in sight." She couldn't keep the thick disapproval from her voice.

"I didn't know he'd escaped," he replied with a grimace. "Get whatever you need and come on in." He didn't wait for her reply, but instead disappeared into the house.

Marisa headed back to her car and tried to still the

crazy butterflies that had gone dancing in her stomach at the sight of him. She couldn't remember when just looking at a man had caused such a visceral reaction. Certainly when she'd first met Patrick she hadn't felt the burst of heat that the sight of Jack had evoked.

The man was a mess, she reminded herself as she grabbed her purse and briefcase from the passenger seat.

Still, as she headed toward the front door she steeled herself against his obvious attractiveness. She was here to contemplate a job and nothing more. She had a boyfriend, her life was on track and the last thing she needed was for some thirty-year-old drummer with a disastrous history rocking her world.

She swept through the front door and into a small entry and then into a large living room that was obviously the heart of the house.

Jack stood in the center of the room, which was littered with toys and kids' clothes and had the faint scent of a dirty diaper. The boys were wrestling on the floor, and as Jack looked at her, once again his soft gray eyes held an appeal. "I need help."

She felt her resolve not to get involved fading away. He looked so utterly helpless in the midst of the chaos. "Is there someplace we can sit and chat?" she asked.

"Boys, why don't you go to your room and play," Jack said.

David jumped up and smiled at Marisa. "Watch," he said, then hopped on one foot down the hallway. The other boy followed his brother, and the two of them disappeared from view.

Jack swept a handful of blocks and toy trucks off the sofa and gestured her to have a seat. Then he sat in the chair opposite the sofa.

"I've had the boys in my custody for almost four months," he said. "They came to me undisciplined and wild, and as you can see, I haven't managed to change things much in the time that I've had them."

"Exactly what are you looking for from me, Mr. Cortland?" she asked.

"Jack, please make it Jack." He smiled, but the gesture didn't quite erase the worry from his eyes. "Isn't it obvious that I need somebody to train the boys and to teach them how to behave?"

Marisa didn't think Jack was ready to hear that. In her experience it was usually the parents who needed training, not the children.

At the moment she saw nothing of the hard-rock star. What she saw was a concerned father worried about his sons. She held on to her heart. There was something about Jack Cortland that made her think that if she allowed it, it would take about five minutes for her to fall crazy in love with him.

But of course she wouldn't allow it. She wasn't even sure she was going to take this job. Just because Jack had beautiful gray eyes fringed with sinfully long lashes, just because he had lips that looked as if they could drive a woman wild didn't mean she was eager to work as a nanny for him.

She opened her briefcase and pulled out a sheath of papers. "Here are my credentials and references," she said as she held them out toward him.

He waved his hand in the air. "Trust me, I've already checked you out, Ms. Perez. I wasn't about to allow just anyone into my home with my boys." He shot her a level gaze. "You graduated from college with a degree in early childhood education. You're twenty-seven years old, live alone and you're particularly close to your aunt Rita, who has worked as an FBI agent for the last twenty years."

Marisa raised an eyebrow. "Please, call me Marisa," she said, impressed by the fact that he'd done his homework where she was concerned. "How many other people do you have working for you here in the home?" she asked. "I need to know who the children interact with on a daily basis."

"I have a cook who comes in the morning and leaves right after she fixes the evening meal. Other than that, it's pretty much just me. The nanny Candace had used for the boys got another job."

"No housekeeper?" she asked.

One corner of his mouth turned up in a rueful grin as he looked pointedly around the room. "If I had a housekeeper, I would have definitely fired her by now."

"You understand this would be a live-in position," she said.

"There's a spare bedroom across from the boys' room. You'd have your own private bath and of course free access to the rest of the house." He leaned forward in his chair. "Tell me you'll take the job, Marisa. You have no idea how important this is to me."

But she did see how important it was to him. A frantic desperation shone from his eyes, something that looked remarkably like fear.

There was more going on here than just his need for her to teach the boys to be well-behaved. She was definitely intrigued.

The fee she collected from this job would put the final dollars in her bank account that she needed to start her business, but she had no idea how far Jack had come from the bad-boy rocker he had once been. Was this really a man she wanted to work for?

"Okay," she heard herself saying before she even knew she'd made a conscious decision. "But I have a condition."

"Just name it," he exclaimed.

"We agree to a weeklong probationary period. If at the end of that week you wish to terminate me, or I decide to leave, then you pay me for the week and I'm on my way. At the end of that week if we're both agreeable, then I have a contract to sign that will assure me two months here."

"Just two months?" he asked.

"I'm a troubleshooter. I only work temporary positions. If you're looking for somebody for long-term, then when I finish my two months I'll help you hire somebody for a permanent position."

"Sounds reasonable to me. When can you start?"

"Tomorrow morning around nine?"

"Perfect," he said with a sigh of relief. She stood and so did he.

She was far too aware of him just behind her as she walked back to the front door. She turned back to him, finding him standing ridiculously close to her. The scent of him washed over her, a clean scent coupled with the faint remnants of a spicy cologne.

She stepped back, her breath catching in her chest as that crazy surge of heat swept through her. He held out his hand, and she stared at it for a long moment, almost afraid to touch him, afraid of how that touch might make her feel.

"I'll see you in the morning," she said as he awkwardly dropped his hand to his side. She flew out the door and hurried toward her car.

Dear God, what was wrong with her? She was acting like some silly, empty-headed fan—and she hadn't even liked his music or his band.

She was doing this strictly for the kids. It was obvious they needed some loving attention and a firm hand. Still, as she thought about moving into

Jack Cortland's home the next morning, she couldn't
help feeling that it might just be the biggest mistake
she'd ever made in her life.

Chapter 2

"What's he like?" Marisa's aunt Rita asked. Rita had invited Marisa and Marisa's current boyfriend, Patrick Moore, for dinner that evening. They were all seated around the dining table in Rita's apartment.

Marisa picked up her glass of ice water, as if needing the cold against her skin as she talked about Jack Cortland. "Desperate," she replied. "The little boys are a mess and from all appearances are the ones running things."

"I still don't like it," Patrick exclaimed. "That man has a terrible reputation. I don't like the idea of you living in that house with him."

Marisa smiled at the handsome man across from her at the table. "Initially it's just for a week. If I see behavior that makes me uncomfortable, then after that week I'll be done."

There were times she thought Patrick was too good to be true. Not only was he incredibly handsome and charming but he also had a good job as an accountant and seemed to have fallen head over heels in love with her.

They'd been dating only a couple of weeks, but Patrick had already made it clear that he believed she was the woman he wanted to spend the rest of his life with.

Although Marisa liked him a great deal, she wasn't about to fall into a hot, passionate affair with a man she'd been dating only a brief time. She'd done that once before in her life, and the results had been devastating.

She took a sip of her water and wondered why thoughts of a hot affair automatically brought a vision of Jack to her mind.

"I was a fan of Jack's band for a while," Patrick said. "Creation did some awesome songs, but once he married Candace Rothchild the band seemed to go straight downhill."

"Such a shame about her," Marisa said. She looked at her aunt. "You were working that murder case for a while, weren't you?"

"Still am," Rita replied. "Unfortunately, there

aren't many leads to follow." Rita shook her head. "I can't imagine having to bury a child, even a child who was thirty years old at the time of her murder."

"It doesn't seem to have slowed down her father. What's he on now—his third or fourth wife?" Patrick asked.

"Third wife," Rita replied. "This current one is a former showgirl considerably younger than him. Rumor has it that the thrill is gone and the marriage is in trouble."

"I'm sorry that Harold lost a daughter, but I'm even sorrier that David and Mick lost their mother," Marisa said.

Patrick smiled ruefully. "From all accounts, she wasn't much of a mother."

"I know, but I still feel bad for those little boys," Marisa replied.

"Just don't get too emotionally involved," Rita said with a gentle smile.

Marisa laughed. "Aunt Rita, I've been a nanny for quite some time now. I know how to separate myself from my little charges. I never lose track of the fact that I'm only in their lives temporarily."

Rita was the only person on the face of the earth who knew what had happened to Marisa in college. Eventually if she and Patrick decided to marry, she'd have to tell him before any vows were exchanged. But it was far too early in their relationship for deep, dark secrets to be exposed.

The rest of the dinner was pleasant, and when they were finished Patrick excused himself from the table and disappeared down the hallway toward the bathroom while Marisa and Rita began to clear the table.

"I like him," Rita said as she rinsed off one of the dinner plates. This was only the second time Patrick and Rita had shared any real quality time together. Rita had entertained them over dinner a week earlier.

"He is great, isn't he?" Marisa handed her another plate. "He couldn't wait to get to know you better. He knows how important you are to me."

Although Marisa's parents were lovely people, they'd never really understood their daughter's desire to make her own way in the world rather than follow them into the very lucrative family real estate business.

Marisa had always been particularly close to her father's sister, Rita. It had been Rita who Marisa had confided in when her world had fallen apart in college.

"How are you doing?" Marisa asked and gestured to the bandage on the side of Rita's head. She and Jenna Rothchild had been kidnapped, and Rita had suffered a gunshot wound to the head. It had rendered her unconscious, and although she and Jenna had managed to get away neither of them had been able to identify the man responsible or why they had been kidnapped in the first place.

"I'm okay—a little headache now and then, but that's all," Rita replied. "You're taking things slow with Patrick?"

"Absolutely. I want to marry once in my life. I'm not about to jump into anything too intense too fast."

Rita smiled. "I think Patrick has other ideas. He seems quite smitten with you."

At that moment he walked back into the kitchen and any further conversation with him as the topic halted.

After cleaning up the kitchen, the three of them moved into the living room where the conversation revolved around Las Vegas life, Patrick's work and a new casino that had opened in town. Rita never discussed her work, but she was a charming hostess who kept the conversation flowing until Patrick and Marisa decided to call it a night.

It was just after nine when Patrick pulled up in front of the small house Marisa rented. "I like your aunt," he said.

"She liked you, too," Marisa replied.

"What's not to like?" He flashed her a bright smile.

"I'd invite you in, but I really want to get a good night's sleep before the morning," she said as he parked the car.

"Am I going to see you at all over the next week?" he asked.

"Probably not," Marisa admitted. "The first week

in a new position is always pretty intense. But it's just for a week, Patrick." She opened the passenger door and got out.

Patrick got out of the car as well and fell into step next to her. He grabbed her hand in his as they walked to her front porch. "And what happens after the first week? What if you take the position for the next couple months? Does that mean I won't be able to see you the whole time?"

She disentangled her hand from his to reach into her purse for her keys. "Not at all. If Jack Cortland and I agree that he needs my services for that long, then I always make sure I have most weekends off."

She unlocked her door then turned back to face him. "Good night, Patrick." She reached up and kissed him on his smooth cheek, but he quickly pulled her into his arms for a real kiss.

It was pleasant, but it didn't curl her toes or weaken her knees. When the kiss ended he reluctantly released her. "Then I guess I'll see you in a week or so?"

"I'll call you and let you know how things are going," she replied.

"You know I'll be waiting for your calls," he replied.

She watched as he walked back to his car. He was a man who could easily turn female heads. Tall and slim, with the dark features of his Hispanic heritage, he always dressed with an understated elegance and looked both handsome and successful.

Minutes later as she undressed in her bedroom she thought of that kiss and Patrick. Maybe one of the reasons she was attracted to Patrick was because there weren't wild fireworks when they kissed, there wasn't that sizzle that came from a simple touch and the breathlessness of a mere glance.

She'd experienced that crazy hot passion once in her life and never wanted it again. It had destroyed her life, and the thought of feeling that way again frightened her.

She pulled her red silk nightgown over her head, turned out the light and crawled into bed. Maybe real love was just that faint warmth that filled her when Patrick smiled at her or the quiet friendship they were building together.

She frowned as she thought of Jack Cortland. So what was it about him that had caused that sizzle inside her? Why did a man she had little respect for, given his past, fill her with a wild sense of anticipation at the very thought of seeing him again?

Jack worked until almost three in the morning cleaning the house. The boys had finally fallen asleep around eleven. He'd moved them into their bedroom, then had tackled the living room with a vengeance.

Toys went back into the boys' room, dirty plates and cups carried back to the kitchen. He polished and washed and vacuumed until the room looked presentable. Then he went into the guest room that Marisa would call home and cleaned it as well.

It had needed to be done for the past couple months, but the days were so full with keeping the boys occupied and trying to oversee the work being done on the ranch. By the time the boys fell asleep at night Jack was comatose, and cleaning was the last thing on his mind.

He'd considered hiring more help but had put it off, hoping to get the boys better acclimated to him before bringing other people into their lives.

When he finally fell into bed he thought sleep would come quickly, but instead he found himself thinking of Marisa Perez.

He hadn't expected her to be so sexy. Even though he'd known before he'd met her that she was twenty-seven years old, he'd expected a maternal type, someone who was overweight and not particularly attractive.

Marisa had been more than attractive. Her long, dark brown hair had sparkled with honey highlights and dark, sexy lashes fringed her large chocolate brown eyes. She had the bone structure of a model, but her body wasn't model thin; rather, it was lush with curves in all the right places.

He'd eventually fallen asleep and dreamed of her…and in those dreams she'd been soft and yielding in his arms. Her kisses had stirred him like none had ever done.

He awoke at dawn and hurried into the shower, eager to get dressed and maybe choke down a cup of coffee before the boys awoke.

Betty wouldn't arrive for another hour so he made the coffee, poured himself a cup and sat at the table, trying not to remember the dreams that had bordered on downright erotic.

He breathed in the peace and quiet of the morning and stared out the window where his herd of cattle grazed on whatever vegetation they could find in the hard, dry earth.

His father had raised cattle here, as had his father before him. Jack's dad had wanted Jack to follow in his footsteps, to take over the ranch and continue producing quality cattle. He'd wanted Jack to live by the values they'd tried to teach him instead of the ones Jack had learned on his way to fame and fortune.

It would always grieve Jack that both his parents had died before he had returned here. Worse than that, he suspected that they had died brokenhearted by the bad choices their son had made in his life as a rock star.

He wouldn't make the same mistakes now. He wanted his boys to grow up and be proud of him. He wanted to give them a solid foundation of love and good values. More than anything he wanted to be the man his parents had known that he could be.

By eight-thirty Jack looked forward to the arrival

of Marisa. The boys had been fed their breakfast and were dressed in clean clothes.

The living room was still relatively clean, and the boys were playing quietly with their trucks in the middle of the floor.

Jack was grateful that he was going to get some parenting tips from Marisa, but he also recognized that his interest in her wasn't solely that of a father needing help with his kids.

It had been a man's interest that had kept him awake the night before, and it had been a shocking desire for her that had filled his dreams, reminding him that he'd been alone for a very long time.

At exactly nine o'clock his doorbell rang and he hurried to greet her, surprised that his heart was pumping harder than it had in months.

He opened the door, and she offered him a bright smile that made him believe that this was going to be a very fine day. "Good morning, come on in."

As she walked past him into the living room he caught her scent, a floral spice that seemed to shoot right to his brain. "What a pleasant surprise," she said. "You've cleaned."

He gave her a sheepish grin. "I didn't realize how bad things had gotten until I saw them through your eyes. Here, let me take that." He gestured to the suitcase she held in her hand. "I'll just take it to your room."

"Thanks," she replied.

He took the case and hurried down the hall. When he returned she was in the middle of the floor with David and Mick. The boys were showing her the trucks that were their favorite toys.

"So how does this work?" he asked. "You just teach them what they need to do?"

She smiled and rose from the floor with a sinuous grace. "It's not quite that easy, Jack. What I'd like to do this morning is just kind of sit back and observe what would be a normal morning for you and the boys. Then at lunch we'll sit down with a game plan."

"Oh, okay." He shoved his hands in his jeans pockets and stared down at his sons, then back at her. "All of a sudden I'm feeling very self-conscious," he admitted.

At that moment Mick hit David with one of the trucks, and within seconds both boys were crying and Jack was yelling. He grabbed Mick up into his arms. "You don't hit, Mick. That's not nice."

"Bad Jack," Mick cried and wiggled to get out of his arms.

"Bad Jack," David yelled, obviously forgetting that it was his brother, not his father, who had hit him in the head.

"Both of you go to your room," Jack exclaimed as he set Mick back on his feet. "Go on. You're both in trouble."

As the boys went running down the hallway, Jack

slicked a hand through his hair in frustration then looked at Marisa. "I handled that badly, right?"

"We'll talk at lunch," she said, her beautiful features giving nothing away of her emotions.

The morning passed excruciatingly slow for Jack. The boys seemed to be on their worst behavior, and he was overly conscious of Marisa watching his every move.

Then, right before lunchtime, while he was in the bathroom with Mick, David climbed through the window in his bedroom and snuck out of the house. As soon as he realized what had happened, Jack raced down the front porch to grab David. Marisa and Mick stood in the doorway and watched him.

Jack was exhausted and his patience was wearing thin. He hadn't hired the lovely nanny to stand around and observe. She was supposed to be fixing things, not watching from the sidelines.

When Betty announced that lunch was ready, Jack had never been so happy for a meal. He set the boys in their booster seats at the dining-room table then gestured Marisa into the chair opposite his as he introduced her to the cook.

"About time you did something," she said to Jack, then glared at Marisa. "I don't babysit, and I don't clean. I don't leave this kitchen except to serve the breakfast and lunch meals. I don't serve dinner. I just cook. That's all I do."

"That's good to know," Marisa replied with a friendly smile. Betty harrumphed and disappeared back into the kitchen.

"I pay her for her cooking skills, not her sparkling personality," Jack said with a dry chuckle.

Marisa laughed, and the sound of her laughter filled a space in him that had been silent for a very long time.

He couldn't remember the last time he'd shared any laughter with anyone. For the past couple months everything had been so tense; the stakes had been so incredibly high.

"One of the first things we need to address is David's ability to escape out any door and window," she said. David smiled at her, his mouth smeared with mustard from his ham sandwich. "You need to purchase childproof locks for every door," she continued.

"I agree. It's only been in the past week or so that he's developed this new skill," Jack replied.

The afternoon sun drifting through the window played on those golden highlights in her hair, making it look incredibly soft and touchable. Her lipstick had worn off by midmorning, but she had naturally plump, rosy lips that he found incredibly sexy.

"What's bedtime like?" she asked.

"Bedtime?" Memories of the visions he'd had of her the night before in his sleep exploded in his head, and he felt a warm wave seep through his veins.

"Do the boys have a regular bedtime?"

He shoved the visions away. "It's regular in that their bedtime is whenever they fall asleep."

"And they fall asleep in their beds?"

"They sleep wherever they happen to fall," he replied.

"They're bright, beautiful boys," she said.

Her words swelled a ball of pride in his chest. "Thanks. I just want them to be good boys as well."

"Good boys," David quipped and nodded his head with an angelic smile, then threw a potato chip in Jack's direction.

After lunch the boys played for a little while, then both of them fell asleep on the floor. Jack carried each of them into their room, put them in bed for their afternoon nap and then returned to where Marisa sat on the sofa.

He sat on the opposite end from her, close enough that he could smell the enticing scent of her perfume. "They should sleep for about an hour," he said.

"What's in the barn?"

He blinked at the question that seemed to come out of nowhere. "What?"

"Both times David got out of the house he was heading for the barn. What's inside?"

"A small recording studio, memorabilia from my old band, my drum set." He shrugged. "My past."

"You miss it?" she asked.

He considered the question before immediately replying. "Some of it," he admitted. "I miss making music, but I don't miss everything that came with it. Why do you ask?"

Her dark eyes considered him thoughtfully. "I need to know that you're in this for the long haul, that the number one priority in your life is your boys. I don't want to spend a month or two of my time helping you here only to have you decide fatherhood is too boring and you'd rather be out on the road making music."

There was a touch of censure in her voice that stirred a hint of irritation inside him. "Nothing in my life means more to me than David and Mick. When Candace and I divorced I rarely got to see the boys. Usually the only time I saw them or heard about them was if they were mentioned in an article in a tabloid." He exhaled sharply. "I'm sorry Candace is dead, but I'm glad the boys are with me now—and I intend to do right by them not just for a month or two but for the rest of their lives."

Warmth leaped into her eyes, and that warmth shot straight into the pit of his stomach. He couldn't remember the last time a woman had affected him so intensely. He wanted to reach out and tangle his hands in her long hair. He wanted to press his lips against hers and taste her.

"It's not going to be easy to turn things around here," she warned.

He smiled. "Over the past couple of years I've fought some pretty strong personal demons. Two little boys aren't going to get the best of me."

"'Bad Jack.' Where did they learn that?"

Jack's smile fell and he frowned instead. "I suppose from Candace. They refuse to call me anything but that."

She leaned back against the cushion. "I hate to tell you this, Jack, but what we need to work on most is your behavior. Those boys are crying out for positive attention and boundaries."

"I'm game," he replied.

"Good." She stood. "I'm going to go unload some things from my car."

He jumped up. "Need help?"

"No, I can handle it." Her eyes twinkled with humor. "Besides, you'd better save your strength. You're going to need it."

He followed her to the front door and watched as she went down the stairs, her hips swaying invitingly beneath the navy slacks she wore.

The background check he'd done on her had told him a lot of things about her, but it hadn't told him what he wanted to know at this moment.

Did she have a boyfriend? Was she in some kind of a committed relationship? Would he be a total fool to get involved with the woman he'd hired as a nanny?

He scoffed at his own thoughts. He'd be a real fool to think that a woman like Marisa would have any interest in a man like him. He was nothing but a washed-up rocker who she'd already seen as useless and ineffectual.

She was bright and beautiful and he could want her, but it was a desire he didn't intend to follow through on. She was here for his boys and that was enough for him…it had to be enough.

Chapter 3

As the day wore on Marisa told herself again and
again that she was here for David and Mick and
nothing more.

She could not allow herself to get caught up in
her overwhelming attraction to Jack. She refused to
allow herself to admit that she liked him. Still, she
could admire the man he was now despite the fact
that she had a feeling she would have disrespected
the man he had once been.

During the afternoon she met Kent Goodall, who
was one of Jack's closest friends. He was a tall,
blond man who told her he used to play bass in a

band with Jack when they'd been teenagers. He was affable but didn't stay long.

She also met the two ranch hands who worked for Jack. Sam and Max Burrow were brothers who had the dark leathery skin of men who had spent their entire lives out in the elements. They appeared quiet and uncomfortable as they stepped into the kitchen through the back door.

Sam had been sent to town to pick up childproof locks for the windows and doors in the house. Once he gave them to Jack the two disappeared back outside.

As Jack put them on, Marisa sat with the boys on the sofa and read them a story. David snuggled next to her on one side and Mick on the other. She had already lost her heart to the boys, who were definitely rambunctious but also responding to her gentle guidance.

It was at bedtime that things got wild as Marisa instructed Jack to put the boys to bed in their room. Every few minutes the boys came out of the bedroom and Jack carried them back in and tucked them in once again.

The boys screamed and cried, and Jack shot Marisa frustrated looks as he carried them back to their beds. It was after one in the morning when he returned from their bedroom and flopped on the sofa. Silence reigned.

"It will be easier tomorrow night," she said.

He scowled at her. "I hope that's a promise."

She smiled. "I forgot to mention that there are

going to be moments in this process when you'll probably hate me."

His scowl lifted, and he offered her a sexy half grin that ripped at her heart. "I'm not mad at you. I'm mad at myself for not doing this when I first got them here." His smile fell, and he gazed at her curiously. "Why aren't you married with a dozen kids of your own? It's obvious you love children."

The question pierced through her, bringing forth a longing that she knew would never really be satisfied. "I'm young. I have plenty of time for all that in the future," she replied airily.

"Are you seeing somebody?"

She nodded. "Yes, I have somebody I'm seeing." She needed to let him know that, but she also needed to remind herself. Patrick. Patrick was the man in her life at the moment and she definitely needed to remember that.

She stood, suddenly needing to escape from Jack. "Time to call it a night," she said. "Tomorrow is a brand-new day."

He got up as well, and together they walked down the hallway toward the bedrooms. "You'll let me know if you need anything?" he asked as they stopped in front of the room where she'd be staying.

"I'm sure I'll be fine," she replied. She released a soft gasp as he reached out and grabbed one of her hands.

"I just want to tell you how glad I am that you're

here," he murmured huskily. "You have no idea how grateful I am."

Those crazy butterflies winged through her stomach, and she pulled her hand from his, uncomfortable by the way his touch made her feel.

"Good night, Jack." She escaped into the bedroom and closed the door behind her.

What on earth was wrong with her? She had to get hold of herself and stop thinking about Jack as a man rather than a client.

She moved into the bathroom to get ready for bed. Her attraction to him wasn't just a physical one. There had been moments in the day when she'd sensed a deep loneliness inside him—one that had called to something deep inside her.

She was intrigued as well. There was a desperation about him that went far beyond a father concerned with his sons' behavior.

The light of dawn awoke her the next morning, but she remained in bed for several long minutes, going over the things she intended to accomplish that day.

She wondered why Jack hadn't already hired a nanny or a babysitter for the kids. Surely he needed to be outside doing things to keep the ranch running smoothly.

For the past four months, since the boys first came here, his life had been on hold, and it showed in the stress lines on his face when he dealt with the boys. He was muddling through parenthood, but he wasn't having any fun.

It was forty-five minutes later when she left her bedroom, freshly showered and dressed in a pair of jeans and a coral-colored tank top.

The house was quiet, but the scent of fresh brewed coffee led her through the house and to the kitchen. Jack was there, seated at the kitchen table as he stared out the window.

He didn't see her, and for a moment she simply stood in the doorway and looked at him. Once again she was struck by the sense of loneliness that clung to him. This man had once had thousands of adoring fans, but at the moment he simply looked like a man in over his head and so achingly alone.

"Good morning," she said as she walked into the room. She waved him down as he started to stand. "Just point me to the coffee cups and I can help myself."

He pointed to a nearby cabinet. "Did you sleep well?"

"Like a baby," she said as she poured herself a cup of coffee. She joined him at the table and tried to ignore the kick of pleasure she felt at the sight of him.

He was dressed in a pair of jeans and a gray T-shirt that enhanced the gunmetal hue of his eyes. His jaw was smooth-shaven, and his hair was still damp from a shower.

"What time does Betty usually get here?" she asked.

"She doesn't work on the weekends, so we're on our own for today and tomorrow. Meals are usually as easy as possible on Saturdays and Sundays."

"This morning I'd like to have breakfast alone with the boys," she said. "You can take an hour or two and go outside to chase a cow or ride the range or whatever you need to do."

"Really?" He sat back in his chair and looked at her in surprise.

She smiled. "Really." She took a sip of coffee and then continued. "Jack, you need to relax a bit. You're so tense when you're around the boys, and I think they're picking up on that. What you need to do is enjoy the process of raising them. You need to have fun with them."

He looked at her as if she were speaking a foreign language. "Fun?"

She laughed. "Remember fun, Jack?"

He smiled ruefully. "Actually, I don't remember it."

"That's what I'm going to bring back to your life, but I have to warn you things are going to get a little tough around here for the next couple days. You'd better enjoy your morning because there are going to be times you won't know who you want to strangle more—me or the kids."

He laughed. "I can't imagine that."

It was the first time she'd heard him really laugh, and the sound of his deep, rich laughter reached inside her and touched her heart. She mentally steeled herself against it, against him.

"You'd better go on before I change my mind about giving you some time off," she said with a businesslike briskness.

"You sure you don't want me to hang around and help you with breakfast for the boys?"

"I'm quite capable of taking care of it." She suddenly wanted him gone. She wanted him to take his deep, sexy voice, his clean male scent and his gorgeous robbing eyes and leave her be.

"Okay, if you insist." He got up from the table, carried his cup to the sink, then grabbed a cowboy hat from a hook near the back door. "I'll be back in a couple hours."

She nodded, and it was only when he left the house that she felt as if she could draw a deep, full breath.

There was no question that something about Jack Cortland touched her. She had never considered herself a rescuer, except when it came to the lives of children.

She had to maintain some emotional distance. She needed to focus only on her reason for being here, and that reason had nothing do with making Jack smile, bringing laughter to his lips and chasing away that cloak of loneliness that clung to him.

* * *

Jack lifted his face to the sun as he sat on the back of his horse, Domino. This was the third morning Marisa had chased him out of the house for a couple hours.

He'd been more than eager to get away this morning. He was irritated. The beautiful nanny who stirred him on a number of levels in the past two days had transformed into a mini drill sergeant barking orders.

Over the past two days she'd introduced so many new techniques his head was spinning. There was a little red chair that was a time-out place where the boys each had spent an abundance of time, and there had been times when he suspected Marisa would have liked to put *him* in that time-out chair.

She'd promised him fun, and she'd given him a rigid structure that had both he and the boys feeling downright cranky.

As he headed across the pasture, he focused his attention on the fencing, noticing several places where repair was needed.

The ranch hadn't been in great shape when Jack had returned here after his parents' deaths. He'd been back for two years, but the first year he'd done nothing but anesthetize himself with alcohol and drugs, and the ranch had fallen into more disrepair.

He waved to Sam, who was on a tractor cutting back weeds from around the barn. Then with a glance at his watch Jack realized it was time to get back to the house.

Even though he was irritated with Marisa, he couldn't help being eager to get back to the house with her and the boys. No doubt, the cute little nanny was definitely making him more than a little crazy.

He quickly brushed down Domino then put him back in his stall. Eventually he wanted to teach the boys to ride. Maybe it was time to buy a couple ponies.

He entered the house through the kitchen where Betty was working on lunch preparations. "Best thing you ever did was hire that woman," she said.

"I agree," he replied, although he'd liked Marisa better when she hadn't been riding him so hard.

"You can love them, but you also need to demand decent behavior from them. That's real love," she said.

He had just walked into the living room when the phone rang. He answered on the second ring, vaguely aware of the sound of laughter coming from the boys' bedroom.

"Jack, it's Harold."

A knot twisted in Jack's gut as he heard the sound of his ex-father-in-law's voice. "Hello, Harold."

"How are the boys?"

"Fine. They're getting along just fine," Jack replied.

"Really, that's not what I've heard."

Jack's stomach dropped to the floor. "What exactly have you heard?"

"That they have the table manners of hyenas."

Heidi. Damn, how had Harold found out about that dreadful meal? Had Heidi gone to the wealthy casino mogul man and told her tale for a price? Jack gripped the receiver more tightly against his ear.

"You don't have to worry about it, Harold," he said, pleased that his voice sounded cool and calm. "I've got a professional nanny working with them on their manners, along with some other things."

"Is she one of your bimbos from your past?"

A tide of anger swelled up inside Jack, but he stuffed it down, refusing to be baited into a screaming match with the man. Harold had never believed that Jack was faithful to Candace during their marriage. It didn't matter to Harold that his daughter probably hadn't been faithful to Jack.

"Her name is Marisa Perez. Check her out, Harold. I'm sure you'll find her credentials impeccable." At that moment Marisa and the boys came into the living room. They were all laughing and looked so happy he wanted to be a part of it. "Look, Harold, I've got to go. I'll talk to you later." He disconnected the call.

"Problems?" Marisa asked with a frown.

"I hope not," he replied, then forced a bright smile on his face. "And what has my two favorite boys laughing so hard?"

As Mick went into a long story about a bug on the floor in the bedroom, love swelled Jack's heart. He would do anything within his power to keep these boys with him.

That night he found himself alone in the living room with Marisa. The boys had gone to sleep in their beds at eight-thirty without a fuss.

"This is amazing," he said to her as he listened to the silence of the house.

She smiled. "And you were probably getting ready to fire me."

He grinned. "There have been moments in the past couple days that I thought you'd ridden me hard," he admitted. "It's taken me a while to realize that giving kids consequences for bad behavior isn't abusive."

"On the contrary, it's the most loving thing you can do for them," she replied.

All day long Jack had felt a simmering tension where she was concerned. He felt it now as he smelled the scent of her perfume, noticed how her T-shirt tugged across her full breasts.

She has a boyfriend, he reminded himself. *She's unavailable.* Still, thinking those words didn't ease the desire for her that seemed to grow stronger every day.

His irritation with her that morning seemed like an alien emotion as this afternoon he'd begun to see the results of her firm hand both with the boys and with him. By no means were things perfect yet, but they were definitely better than they had been before she'd arrived.

"I guess I should go to bed," she said.

"Don't go yet," he protested. "It's still early, and I enjoy your company."

Her cheeks turned a charming pink as she settled back into the sofa cushion. "It is early. I guess I could stay up for a little while longer." She looked at him curiously. "I might be overstepping my boundaries, but I couldn't help but hear you mention my name on the phone earlier."

A new tension twisted in Jack's stomach. "That was Harold Rothchild on the phone. Apparently he heard about a dinner that went bad just before I hired you." He quickly told her about the dinner with Heidi and the flying broccoli. When he was finished a small smile curved her lips.

"I'm sorry. I know it isn't funny," she exclaimed with her laughter barely suppressed. "But I'm just imagining that cheesy broccoli sliding down the front of her chest."

Suddenly they were both laughing with an abandon that felt wonderful. The stress of the past four months seemed to melt out of Jack.

"That felt good," he said when the laughter finally stopped.

"You need to do more of that," she replied, her brown eyes brimming with warmth.

"I haven't had anything to laugh about for a very long time," he confessed. "First there was the divorce from Candace, then my band fell apart and all the other members were ticked off at me. But the worst part was after the divorce when I wasn't getting to see the boys and I knew if I fought for custody I'd lose." He sighed heavily. "Then Candace was murdered. Now I'm struggling to pick up the pieces of my boys' lives. I still worry about losing custody."

She looked at him in surprise. "Why?"

"There's nothing Harold Rothchild would like more than to take the boys away from me—and the only way he can do that is to prove I'm an unfit father."

"Surely he couldn't do that," she replied.

Jack grimaced. "I'm not so sure. I have two strikes against me already. I'm a single man, and I don't exactly have a sterling past—and it will only take one screwup and he'll come swooping in."

"Then we can't have a screwup, right?" she replied.

She smiled, and at that moment Jack wanted nothing more than to move from his chair to the sofa and pull her into his arms. He wanted to explore exactly where that sexy scent emanated from on her body, what those lush lips tasted like in the heat of a kiss.

"Tell me about Harold Rothchild," she said, and

the question tamped down any wild desire that might have possessed Jack. "I heard he's some big casino tycoon and his family made their fortune in the diamond business."

"They owned some diamond mines in Mexico. There was a Mayan legend that one of the big diamonds that was found there held some sort of special powers. Its magic caused people to fall in love. It was made into a ring that Candace was wearing on the night of her murder."

"I read something about the ring. It was stolen that night, right? Isn't the diamond called The Tears of the Quetzal?"

Jack nodded and frowned as he thought of the man who at the moment was the bane of his existence. "Harold is working on his third wife. His first wife, June, died giving birth to Candace's youngest sister, Jenna. He and his second wife divorced, and from what I've heard the third wife is on her way out as well. Harold is powerful, and I think he hates me."

"Why would he hate you?"

"Because of my divorce from Candace. I think he believes that we split because I was sleeping around on his daughter. It doesn't seem to bother him that in all probability she was cheating on me. Maybe he thinks that if Candace and I had stayed together she wouldn't have been murdered."

"Were you in love with her?" Marisa asked.

Jack considered the question a long time before

answering. "Initially I was in lust with her. She was wild and beautiful, and we partied together for months in L.A. before we impulsively hopped a plane to Vegas and got married. Almost immediately she got pregnant with Mick. and I was ready for the partying to stop."

"But she wasn't ready to stop," Marisa said.

He nodded. "And then David came along. At the same time a couple of record producers contacted me. They told me they wanted to make me a star in my own right, turn me into a solo performer. I thought I had it all—two little boys, a gorgeous wife and a shot at becoming an artist of real standing."

His laughter held a touch of bitterness. "It wasn't until Candace and I split that I realized the record producers were more interested in her than in me. The deal fell apart, and the members of Creation were angry with me for even thinking about going out on my own. The band broke up and my marriage did the same. But I haven't answered your question, have I?"

He turned his head and stared out the window as he thought of the woman he'd married. He finally looked back at Marisa. "Did I love Candace? I loved the woman I hoped she'd become as the mother of my children, but that woman didn't exist."

"I'm sorry," Marisa said softly. "I'm sorry for you, but I'm also sorry for your boys. And now, I really should call it a night," she said and rose from the sofa.

Jack got up from his chair. "Me, too. Mornings come early with two little ones in the house."

Together they walked down the hallway, and when she got to the door of her room she turned to look at him, her gaze soft and warm. "Everything is going to be all right, Jack. You're a great father, and nobody is going to take those boys away from you."

He wasn't sure if it was her words or the fact that she looked so achingly feminine, so soft and touchable, but the desire that had simmered inside him for the past couple days returned with full force.

Almost without his volition he reached up and touched a strand of her long hair. He half expected her to jump back from him, but other than a slight flare of her eyes, she remained in place as if anticipating his next move.

He placed his hand on the back of her head and pulled her toward him until they stood breast-to-chest, hip-to-hip.

"I'm going to kiss you now," he said, unsure if it was a threat or a promise.

"I know," she replied breathlessly just before he lowered his mouth to hers.

Chapter 4

As Jack's lips claimed hers Marisa welcomed the kiss. She'd wanted this since the moment she'd met him. She'd needed to know just what his mouth would taste like pressed against hers.

Hot. It tasted hot, and as his tongue touched the tip of hers, she opened her mouth to him, allowing him to take the kiss deeper and more intimate.

In the back of her mind she knew this was wrong—that they were crossing a line that shouldn't be crossed, but she found herself helpless to stop it.

Instead she leaned into him as he wrapped his arms around her and pulled her more tightly against him. Here were the fireworks she'd missed on the

Fourth of July a week earlier, she realized as he kissed her with a mastery that weakened her knees.

It was only when he pulled her close enough and she could tell that he was aroused that her senses returned. She pushed against his chest and stepped back from him.

"That probably wasn't a good idea," she said as her heart banged rapidly in her chest.

He dropped his arms to his side. "You're right, but it was something I've wanted to do since the first moment I met you."

"Bad Jack," she said teasingly, even though she wanted nothing more than to back in his arms. "And now it's really time for me to say good night."

She escaped into her room, her heart still beating an unsteady rhythm.

Patrick's kisses had never stirred her like this. He'd never made her feel the breathless excitement that now coursed through her veins.

For the next three days that kiss haunted her. Neither she nor Jack mentioned it again, but the memory of it was there in the air between them, snapping with energy and making things just a little bit uncomfortable.

It was mid-afternoon, and the boys were down for their naps when Jack and Marisa sat at the table in the dining room to discuss her further employment. The week of probation was over, and she had to decide if she was going to stay in his employ for the next two months.

From the kitchen the sound of a portable television played a soap opera, entertaining Betty as she began the preparations for the evening meal.

Even though Marisa's attraction to Jack made her more than a little bit nervous about continuing on here, her real concern was that she was losing all her objectivity where the boys were concerned.

She had fallen in love with Mick, who had a wonderful sense of humor and was surprisingly protective of his younger brother. And David had stolen her heart as well despite his attraction to getting through locked doors and windows.

Although they still hadn't bonded with Jack in the way she'd like to see them do, they had bonded to her, desperate for her attention and love.

She now faced Jack across the width of the dining-room table. "Our probationary week is over," she began.

"And I want you to stay until the boys are teenagers," he replied half-seriously.

She laughed and shook her head. "I can give you two months, Jack. By the end of that time the boys should be socialized enough to enter a preschool program. They need that. They need to learn to play with other children before they start school, and we need to get David out of diapers as soon as possible."

"I'll start working on that with him," Jack replied.

"You also need to understand that if I make the commitment for the two months, then I'll need my weekends off. I'd also like to take tomorrow evening off. Patrick has invited me to dinner." She needed to see the man she was supposed to be dating and was hoping that being with Patrick could banish the power of Jack's kiss from her brain.

"Why don't you invite him here for dinner?" Jack asked.

Marisa's first impulse was to say no, that she preferred to keep her work and her private life separate. But she knew that Patrick had mentioned he'd been a big fan of Jack's band, and maybe it would clear her head to see the two men together.

"That's very nice. I think he would enjoy meeting you. He told me he was once a big fan of yours," she replied.

"Good, then I'll tell Betty to make sure and set an extra plate at the table for tomorrow evening," Jack replied.

At that moment noise from the bedroom let them know the boys were awake from their naps, and with the next two months of employment arranged, Marisa got up from the table to tend to the boys.

Throughout the afternoon she reminded herself that whatever Jack felt for her was tied up in who she was professionally. She was the woman who had brought order to his chaotic existence. It was no wonder he'd kissed her. She was positive what had

prompted him to do so was a healthy dose of gratitude and nothing more.

She had to remember that. She had to remember
that Jack Cortland might make her heart race, but
she'd be a fool to fall into thinking Jack had any real
feelings for her. And Marisa had been a fool only
once in her life for a man. She wasn't about to repeat
the same mistake.

Rita Perez was frantic. She'd been frantic ever
since she'd realized the ring, Harold Rothchild's
million-dollar diamond ring, was missing.

It wasn't just a piece of expensive jewelry. It was
the ring Candace Rothchild had been wearing the
night she'd been murdered. The ring they called The
Tears of the Quetzal.

The ring not only had a Mayan legend attached
to it but it had also had a crazy past since it had come
into evidence, having been stolen from police
custody and then recovered.

And now it was gone once again.

For the hundredth time in the past week, she knelt
on the floor under her desk and searched the carpet,
even though she knew it wasn't there. The ring
hadn't accidentally fallen on the floor; it hadn't
dropped into a desk drawer. It had disappeared from
a small box that she kept locked in her gun safe.

She should never have checked it out from the
evidence room and brought it home, but she'd been

fascinated with it and had wanted to research more thoroughly how it had come to belong to the Rothchilds.

A wave of despair washed over her and made the wound on the side of her head bang with nauseating intensity. She'd probably be fired. Worse than that, if Harold found out the precious ring was missing again, he'd sue not only her but also the entire department for her negligence.

How had that ring disappeared from her gun safe? Whoever had stolen it had been a professional. They'd known just where to look and how to get in and out without her even knowing they were there.

What was she going to do? Sooner or later she was going to have to tell her superiors what had happened, and then all hell was going to break loose.

With a new burst of energy she began to pull out the desk drawers, hoping, praying that it would be found.

Once again Jack and Marisa were in the living room. It was just after nine, and David and Mick had been in bed asleep for half an hour.

"I still can't believe how easy bedtime has become," he said. "It's like a miracle."

Marisa smiled at him. "All it takes is a firm hand and consistency. That's the secret of good parenting."

"What about your mom and dad? Were they good parents?" he asked curiously.

"Absolutely." She leaned back against the corner of the sofa and drew her legs up beneath her. "Like Candace and the Rothchilds, money was never a problem in my family. My parents are quite wealthy, but they taught me values that had nothing to do with money. I started babysitting when I was about fourteen and even through college worked a variety of jobs. What about your parents?"

"They were terrific people, hardworking and possessed good old-fashioned values." A flash of pain darkened his eyes. "They taught me right, but when I got to Los Angeles and had more money than sense, all their lessons went right out the window. I think I broke their hearts."

There was nothing more appealing than a man who recognized his own frailties and regretted them, Marisa thought. "I'm sure they'd be proud of the man you've become," she said softly.

"Yeah, I'm just sorry they passed before they saw me pulling my life back together again."

"I'm sure they were confident that eventually you'd come back to the values they'd taught you as a young man," she replied.

He nodded. "You think the boys will ever call me Daddy?"

She heard the wistfulness in his voice and knew how important that was to him. "Maybe when they feel safe with you. I don't know much about their lives when they were with Candace, but from what little you've told me I would guess that most of the people who entered their lives were there only on a temporary basis. When they know you're not going anywhere and they can trust you, then maybe you won't be Jack anymore. You'll be Daddy."

He smiled at her. "What made you so smart?"

"Trust me, I'm not always smart. We all have things in our pasts that we'd prefer to forget about."

Jack raised a dark eyebrow. "Now you have me intrigued."

For just a moment she thought about sharing with him the heartache that would always be a part of her, one that had forever changed what she would expect from life.

She knew Jack would understand how foolish she'd been, that he of all people wouldn't judge her. But it felt far too intimate to share that piece of herself with him.

Once again she realized the lines were getting blurred between them. She had to remember that he was her employer and nothing more. She had to remember that she was one of those temporary people not only in the boys' lives but in Jack's as well.

She got up from the sofa. As always when it was just the two of them, she felt the need to get away, to escape from him. It was too appealing, too intimate to sit in his living room with him while night fell outside.

This whole assignment would have been easier if Jack had a wife, but of course if he had a wife Marisa probably wouldn't be here.

"Good night, Jack," she said, hoping he didn't follow her down the hallway to her room, yet in a small little place in her mind wishing he would. She wouldn't mind sharing another kiss with him, and that realization worried her.

Thankfully, he seemed to be caught up in thoughts of his own, for he murmured a good-night and remained in his chair.

Over the past couple nights they had fallen into the habit of staying up talking until around midnight or so. During those hours she'd heard a lot about the Rothchild family, and she'd told him how close she was to her aunt Rita.

Even though the conversations during those hours of the night were light and not overly personal, the end result had been a growing friendship between them. Still, it wasn't that friendship that made the most simple touch from him sizzle inside her.

She now paused in the doorway of the boys' room before going to her own. How could she not fall in love with these boys? They were children who desperately needed a mother, and she was a woman who was meant to be a mom.

With a soft smile, she went first to Mick's bedside and pulled the sheet up closer around his neck. She smoothed a strand of his blond hair off his face and pressed a kiss on his forehead. He said something incomprehensible but didn't awaken.

She moved to David's bed and tucked in one of his legs and an arm. He mumbled and smiled, as if enjoying the pleasant dreams of innocence. She kissed him, too, then moved back to the doorway.

Two months. That's all she was giving herself with them. By that time she'd have taught Jack what he needed to learn to be a good father, and the boys would have a new respect and love for him.

This was her job, to make things right for parent and child, then to walk away. But somehow she thought it was going to be more difficult than it had ever been to walk away from the boys.

And from Jack.

With a tired sigh she left the boys' bedroom and went across the hall to her own. She stepped inside, flipped on the overhead light and froze as she saw a masked man sliding open her window.

She has a boyfriend. Jack had to keep reminding himself that Marisa wasn't available to him, that she was a temporary fix in his life.

The worst mistake he had made since she'd arrived was kissing her. The memory of that single kiss had haunted him each night since. *She* haunted him, stirring inside him a want that he hadn't felt for a very long time—perhaps never before.

He was a fool. She was intelligent and had big plans for her future. She was eager to start her own agency, and the last thing she needed was to be involved with a man with his kind of past.

A scream shot him out of his chair.

Marisa! His heart leaped into his throat as he raced down the hall toward her room. She stood just inside, a hand over her mouth. When he entered she pointed to the window where the screen had been removed and the window was partially opened.

"A man. He was trying to get in," she exclaimed.

"Go check on the boys," Jack said.

"Should I call the police?" she asked.

"No." Jack barked the single word as he raced down the hallway to his bedroom. Once inside the room he pulled a lockbox from his bedroom drawer, unlocked it and withdrew his gun.

As he ran back down the hallway he glanced into the boys' room, grateful to see them both still sleeping and Marisa standing between the beds.

The hot July air wrapped around him oppressively as he left the house. He moved with stealth, keeping to the shadows of the house and trees. He was grateful for the moonlight that made his search that much easier.

When he reached the window of Marisa's bedroom he tightened his grip on the gun. The window screen was propped up against the house, but there was no sign of the intruder.

As he extended the perimeter of his search outward, a thousand questions flew through his head. Was this about Marisa? Had somebody been trying to get inside to harm her? Or was it about him?

Whoever it had been, he was apparently gone now. Jack put the screen back up in the window, then went inside.

Marisa met him in the hallway, her eyes large and still holding an edge of fear. "Nothing?" she asked.

"Nothing." He motioned her to follow him into the living room. "Whoever was out there isn't there anymore."

She curled up on the sofa, as if her fear had made her unusually cold. He set the gun on the coffee table then began to pace in front of her.

"Did you get a good look at him?" he asked.

"He had on a ski mask. Are you sure you don't want to call the police?"

"Right, I can see the headlines now. Intruder looking for drugs at Cortland Ranch. Harold Rothchild steps in to save Candace's kids." A ball of tension expanded in his chest, and for a moment he had trouble drawing a full breath.

"You think that's what it was? Somebody looking for drugs?"

He stopped pacing and looked at her. "I don't know what to think. Unless you know somebody

who might want to break into your bedroom to
harm you."

"I can't imagine anyone wanting to hurt me," she
replied. "Surely Harold can't use it against you that
there was an attempted break-in."

"You'd be surprised what he could use against
me," Jack replied with an old touch of bitterness.

"Okay, if you don't want to call the police, why
don't you let me call my aunt Rita? She's FBI. She
can take a look around, maybe check the window for
fingerprints and we can trust her not to say anything
to anyone about this."

We. We can trust her. The use of the plural wasn't
lost on him, and there was a certain sense of relief
knowing that he wasn't in this alone.

"Would she mind coming over?" he asked.

In reply she uncurled herself and reached for the
phone. Minutes later as they waited for Rita to arrive,
they sat together on the sofa, and it was then that Jack
decided to tell her what scared him more than anything.

"When Candace died and I was granted custody
of Mick and David, Harold made a lot of threats. But
the one he told me that upset me most was that it was
possible that one or both of the boys might not be
mine." A new surge of emotion filled his chest.

"I don't care about biology," he continued. "As
far as I'm concerned both of them are mine, and I
don't give a damn what a blood test would show. But

one little mistake and I'm afraid Harold will order DNA tests. Then I risk losing the only thing that has given me any real meaning in my life."

She placed a hand on his arm. "Then we won't let that happen."

At that moment Rita arrived.

Jack immediately liked the no-nonsense woman who held an important role in Marisa's life. She briskly went about her work of checking for fingerprints in and around the window frame, but unfortunately there were none.

After looking around the area, she returned inside, where she sat with Jack and Marisa at the kitchen table. "If he was smart enough to wear a ski mask, then he was surely smart enough to wear gloves, hence no fingerprints," she said. She reached up and touched the bandage on the side of her head, then dropped her hand to her side.

"Maybe it was just somebody trying to get in to rob Jack," Marisa said.

"Maybe," Rita agreed. "Or I suppose it's possible it was an old fan wanting a piece of the famous Jack Cortland." She smiled at Jack, but the smile didn't last but a moment.

"What would concern me if I were you is that those two little boys of yours would be hot targets for kidnapping," she said.

Marisa gasped, and Jack sat up straighter in his chair, his blood chilling. "Everyone around these parts knows I spent most of my fortune years ago," he said.

"But not the Rothchild fortune," Rita replied. "Those boys are Harold's heirs, and everyone knows that he's probably worth more than the national debt. My recommendation would be that you beef up security around here."

An overwhelming sense of discouragement settled on Jack's shoulders as Rita stood to leave. He started to rise as well, but she waved him down. "Marisa will see me out," she said.

Jack nodded wearily as the two women left the kitchen. In the four months since he'd had the boys here with him at the ranch he'd never thought about the fact that they could be potential kidnap victims.

The idea of somebody taking his boys and using them for ransom was absolutely chilling. How did you keep children safe against an unknown threat? When there was no way to identify the face of a kidnapper? Somehow, some way he'd have to figure it out.

He forced a smile as Marisa came back into the kitchen. "Thanks for calling her."

She nodded, a worried frown creasing her forehead as she sat in the chair next to his. "She wasn't herself tonight. Something is wrong. I could feel it."

"Did you ask her about it?"

"Yes, but she assured me it was nothing, just something work related. I just hope it doesn't have anything to do with the wound on her head." She quickly told Jack about how Rita had gotten shot during the kidnapping of Jenna Rothchild.

"Yeah, I read about that in the paper," he said.

Marisa's gaze held his intently. "So what happens now?"

"I wish I knew. I guess the first order of business is to get a security system installed here. Maybe it was just somebody trying to get in to rob me," he said thoughtfully, "But it's definitely put me on notice, and I'm going to take whatever precautions I can to see that we're all safe here."

She reached across the table and gave his hand a quick squeeze, then got up. As she moved a strand of her shiny hair behind her ear, he noticed that her hand shook slightly.

Even though he knew it wasn't a good idea to try to comfort her, he got up and wrapped her in his arms.

She stood rigid for only a moment and then melted against him. He held her tight and felt the slight tremor of her body against his.

"I'm sorry you were frightened," he whispered against her ear, where he could smell that dizzying scent of her.

"It's not your fault," she replied as she buried her face into his shoulder.

"I should have had an alarm system put in here when I first moved the boys in, but nobody had ever bothered me out here and it just never entered my mind." He was rambling, wanting to keep talking, needing to continue holding her.

He'd felt alone for a very long time, but with her in his arms the loneliness no longer existed inside him.

When she finally raised her head to look at him there was no question that he was going to kiss her again. As he took her mouth with his, desire slammed through him. What he'd intended as a gentle kiss instead was hot and demanding.

She responded with a hunger that stunned him. She raised her arms and tangled her fingers in his hair as they stumbled backward and her back hit the refrigerator.

Their lips remained locked in a kiss that drove all other thoughts from his head. He slid his hands up the back of her T-shirt, wanting to feel the warmth of her bare skin against his palms.

She didn't protest but instead broke the kiss and leaned her head back, allowing him to trail his lips down the length of her neck and across her delicate collarbone.

"Marisa." He breathed her name on a sigh against her ear. "I want you. I've wanted you every day since you arrived here."

When she looked up at him he saw the flame of desire in her eyes, and that nearly shoved him over the edge. She didn't say anything but instead pulled his head back down so their lips could meet once again.

As he kissed her once again he leaned into her and slowly moved his hands from her bare back to her breasts. Her nipples pushed against the thin material of her bra, and he wanted her naked in his arms. He wanted her panting beneath him as he took her over and over again.

She moaned, a soft throaty sound that shot through him like a bolt of electricity.

He stepped back from her and took her by the hand. Neither of them said a word as he led her out of the kitchen, through the living room and down the hallway to his bedroom door.

They were just about to go into the room when Mick cried out from his bedroom. Both Jack and Marisa froze.

"Marisa," Mick cried. "I had a bad dream."

Jack dropped her hand. Whatever fire he had seen in her eyes moments ago was gone. "He needs me," she said.

Jack nodded. "Go on. I'll see you in the morning."

As she hurried back down the hallway to the boys' room two thoughts flittered through Jack's mind. Would he and Marisa ever be able to reclaim the moment that had just been lost? And would there ever come a time when his boys would cry out for him?

Chapter 5

By ten-thirty the next morning the new alarm system had been installed and Marisa prayed that these extra precautions would prevent another terrifying break-in from ever happening again.

After lunch and naps Marisa was on the floor in the living room playing with building blocks with the boys when Kent Goodall stopped by. She was grateful when the two men went outside on the front porch to visit.

Facing Jack this morning had been more difficult than she'd expected after the near intimacy of the night before.

She was grateful they hadn't followed through on

the desire that had momentarily flared out of control between them. She couldn't let herself get caught up in the heat of a moment that wouldn't last. That's what she'd done before, and she'd sworn she'd never allow it to happen again.

She was equally glad that Patrick was coming to dinner tonight. Patrick was safe. He didn't stir a craziness inside her.

She needed to see him. For the past week she and Jack had been living in a tiny bubble where it was just the two of them and the boys. She needed Patrick to bring the world in, to set her feet more firmly on the ground of reality.

"Marisa, watch!" Mick said as he built a tower of blocks higher and higher. He shoved his blond hair off his forehead with the back of his hand, a gesture Marisa had seen Jack do before.

"M'ssa, watch," David echoed and began slamming blocks one on top of the other. David's tower only got four high when the blocks tumbled to the floor. He laughed as if it were the funniest thing he'd ever seen.

As always, playing with the boys brought a wave of love into her heart. She knew from those late-evening talks with Jack that most of their early life had been spent in hotel rooms with hotel staff acting as babysitters. Then, after the divorce, Candace had shoved the boys off on nannies so they wouldn't hamper her wild lifestyle. There had been no sense of permanence and security for them from the moment they'd been born until they had come here to Jack's ranch.

They wouldn't even remember her. Within months of her leaving, the boys would forget the positive influence she'd had on their lives. It was the way it was supposed to be with professional nannies.

Still, she was surprised to realize this knowledge pained her more than a little bit. These boys had laughed and misbehaved their way right into the core of her heart like no other children had done before.

Maybe it was because on every other job she'd had in the past there had been a mother present. This was the first time Marisa had worked with a single parent.

The front door opened, and Jack stuck his head inside. "Kent and I are going to the barn. You and the boys want to come?"

Both of the boys headed for the door as Marisa pulled herself up off the floor. "Guess so," she said with a smile as the two boys barreled out the door and onto the porch.

Jack took Mick's hand and Marisa took David's. Together with Kent they all began to walk across the expanse of lawn toward the barn in the distance.

The July sun bore down on them with an oppressive heat that was searing. Marisa made a mental note to check with Jack about sunscreen for his fair little boys.

"I can already see a big change in the kids," Kent said to her. "They seem a little more calm than they were a week ago."

"That's because Jack is a little more calm," she replied with a teasing smile to Jack. "We still have a ways to go," she added.

"Still, it's nice to see them behaving better," Kent replied.

They hadn't gone far when she felt a prickly sensation in the center of her back. It was a whisper of intuition, the feeling that somebody was watching her.

She turned her head from side to side, seeking the source of the discomfort. She spied Max Burrow standing near the stables. The tall burly man leaned on a shovel, and it appeared that he was watching them…watching her.

The uneasiness increased as he met her gaze and didn't look away but rather stayed focused on them as they walked. She looked at Jack, then back toward Max, surprised to see that he had disappeared.

She mentally shook herself. Apparently the episode of the attempted break-in the night before had her more on edge than she'd thought. Surely Max hadn't been staring at her but was just resting for a moment before getting back to work.

Jack pushed open the barn door, and they all entered. Marisa caught her breath as she saw the wealth of memorabilia housed inside.

Life-size posters of the Creation band lined the walls and Jack's sparkling drum set was on a small raised platform in one corner. David released Marisa's hand and beelined to the drums.

"Welcome to Jack's past," Kent said to her. "And what a glorious past it was."

There were T-shirts and caps and CDs in glass frames. There was also a glassed-in room that Marisa assumed was the recording studio. "This stuff must be worth a fortune," she exclaimed.

"Yeah, Jack had it all after he left us poor folks behind for the big-time," Kent replied. He clapped a hand on Jack's back. "But we're glad to have him back here where he belongs."

David hit the cymbals and laughed with glee.

"David, I don't think you're supposed to touch that," Marisa exclaimed.

"He's all right," Jack replied with an easy smile. "He can't hurt anything."

"Maybe he's the next generation of drumming talent," Kent said.

"God, I hope not," Jack replied fervently. "I'd much rather see the boys go to college than join a band."

Mick had found a set of dolls fashioned after the band members and sat on the floor with them. "No wonder the boys like to come out here," Marisa said. "It's like a big wonderland." She winced as David banged on the snare drum.

Jack smiled and then touched Kent on the arm. "Come on, I'll get you that music you wanted."

As Jack and Kent went into the recording studio area, Marisa looked more closely at the posters on the walls.

Although his hair had been much longer and there had been a wildness in his eyes that was no longer present, Jack had still been one hot hunk when he'd been in his band.

She stopped in front of one particular photo and stared at him. He was standing at his drums, his sweaty T-shirt plastered against his broad chest and oh my…what a chest it was.

The memory of the kiss, the caresses they'd shared jumped unbidden into her head, and her body temperature rose at least ten degrees.

She whirled around as the two men came back out of the recording studio, Kent clutching several sheets of music in his hand.

"Thanks," he said to Jack. "I really appreciate it."

Jack shrugged. "I'm never going to do anything with it. Your band might as well use it." He smiled at Marisa. "We're done in here. Mick, David, come on. We're going back to the house."

David banged the cymbal once again as Mick put the dolls back on the stands where they belonged. David eyed his father with more than a hint of mutiny.

Marisa moved closer to Jack. "Give him a reason to do as you asked," she said softly.

"The time-out chair?" he asked below his breath.

Marisa smiled. "Why don't you try something positive?"

Jack frowned, and she tried not to notice that wonderfully clean male scent of him, desperately tried to forget how his hands had felt so hot and needy on her bare skin.

"Hey, buddy, let's go back to the house and we'll get out the trucks and make a road through the living room," Jack said.

David looked at him thoughtfully, then with a happy grin left the drums and approached Jack. Jack picked him up in his arms, and Marisa's heart expanded. Jack was learning and proving to be quite an amazing daddy.

"And we can make bumps in the road with pillows," Mick said eagerly as they all headed back to the house.

"Yeah, bumps!" David echoed.

Kent headed for his car and waved goodbye.

"You gave him music?" she asked Jack.

"A couple of songs I wrote a long time ago. I wasn't going to do anything with them, and Kent had some interest in using them with his band," he replied.

"That was a nice thing for you to do," she said.

He shrugged. "Kent's been a good friend over the years. It's really no big deal."

They entered the house, and for the next hour Jack sat on the living-room floor playing with his sons.

He's good with them, Marisa thought as she watched their play. He was patient and had a sense of make-believe that they responded to with glee.

As far as Marisa was concerned there was nothing more appealing than a man who could get in touch with the boy inside of him for the sake of his small sons. It didn't take long for the truck game to evolve into a wrestling match.

Marisa laughed as the two boys piled on top of Jack, screaming and giggling with abandon. It was the first time she'd seen the three of them just having fun together.

"Get M'ssa," David yelled, his bright blue eyes sparkling with excitement.

Suddenly it wasn't just the three of them on the floor in a pile but it was her as well. Jack had her on her back and tickled her ribs as the boys squealed with delight and danced around them.

"Stop, please," she cried amid bursts of laughter. He stopped, and for just a minute he remained on top of her, staring down at her.

There was no laughter in his eyes; rather there was a hot flash of fire that left her breathless in a way the tickling had not.

Instantly he stood and held out a hand to help her up off the floor. "Thanks," she murmured as she got to her feet. She didn't look at him as a blush warmed her cheeks. "Okay, boys, it's time to pick up the toys," she said.

"I'll see to the cleanup," Jack said, his voice deeper than usual. "I'm sure you'd like some time to shower and get ready for dinner."

Dinner with Patrick. She looked at her watch and realized dinner was less than an hour away. "Thanks, I appreciate it."

As she walked down the hallway to her bedroom, she tried to ignore the ball of heat that still burned in her stomach, a flame that had been ignited by the desire in Jack's eyes.

He'd confessed to her one night when the boys had been in bed that he hadn't been with any woman since his divorce from Candace. That was a long time for a man to go without a woman.

Surely it was nothing more than close proximity that had him looking at her as if she were his favorite dessert.

The worst thing she could do was allow herself to get caught up in the family atmosphere, in the intimacy of this particular assignment.

Jack was dangerous to her. She felt it in her heart, in her soul. The look in his eyes, the heat of his touch reminded her of that time in her life when she'd risked everything—and lost.

Jack didn't like him. It took him about fifteen minutes for him to make the judgment call that Patrick Moore was arrogant, abrasive and far too smooth.

He especially didn't like the way the man looked at Marisa—with a possessiveness that rankled Jack.

"It's a shame your band broke up," Patrick said as he helped himself to more of Betty's mashed potatoes. "But I guess that wild lifestyle really took a toll on you."

It was as if he wanted to remind Marisa that Jack was an old has-been with a questionable past. "It was time for me to move on to a new phase in my life," Jack replied easily. "I had more important things to do than make music." He looked pointedly at his sons, who so far had behaved admirably through the meal.

"Yeah, but I heard the transition from rock star to family man has been pretty tough for you. Didn't you have a stint in rehab?"

"Patrick!" Marisa let out a short uncomfortable laugh, and then gave him a look of disapproval.

"I'm just asking," he said with a look of innocence.

"It's all right," Jack said to Marisa, then turned his attention back to Patrick. "Actually, no. I never spent any time in rehab, and I'm too busy raising kids now to even think about drugs or alcohol."

"I didn't mean to offend you in any way," Patrick said hurriedly.

"No offense taken," Jack replied smoothly, although he found everything about Patrick offensive. His hair was too dark, too neat. His dress shirt didn't have a single wrinkle and he possessed a cool facade that annoyed Jack.

Marisa deserved a man with more passion, one who had a lust for life burning inside him. She deserved somebody like Jack. He mentally shook himself at this silly thought.

He conceded that his feelings for Patrick were colored by his growing desire for Marisa. He told himself he had no right to judge the kind of man Marisa dated.

Marisa was his employee, and in two months' time she'd be gone from his life. He needed to gain some distance from his lovely nanny.

Perhaps someday there would be a woman who would fit neatly into his life, but it wasn't going to be Marisa and it wasn't going to happen for a long time. David and Mick were all that were important to him, and what he wanted more than anything else on this earth was for them to trust him enough to call him Daddy.

The rest of the meal passed with pleasant, easy conversation, and when they were finished eating Jack took the boys into their bedroom to give Marisa and her boyfriend some time alone.

At seven-thirty he gave the boys their baths and got them into their pajamas. Once they had fallen asleep he remained in the room, seated between their two beds.

His mind raced back to the night before and what Rita Perez had told him. He'd never thought about his sons being likely candidates for kidnapping.

He'd been so busy just trying to get through each day with them he hadn't thought of the bigger ramifications of them living here with him.

There was no question that as Harold's grandkids, the boys would be worth a fortune to a potential kidnapper.

Was the man who had tried to break in simply a robber looking for a quick score of cash or drugs? Why break into a house where people were not only home but were still awake?

He frowned thoughtfully. If the intruder had watched the house for any length of time he might have known that it was habit for Marisa and Jack to stay up late talking in the living room. Perhaps he meant to use that time to get in, maybe steal whatever he could find in Jack's room, then get out before he and Marisa headed off to bed.

Or had he attempted to get in to somehow grab the boys? Had there been an accomplice standing outside the boys' bedroom window, waiting for sleeping kids to be handed to him? A rush of cold air blew through Jack at the very thought.

It was all assumption, but it was the kind of speculation that could keep a man awake at night.

He didn't know how long he'd been sitting there when the phone rang. He left the boys' room and went down the hallway to his bedroom, where he grabbed the receiver next to the bed.

"Jack, it's Harold."

Jack barely stifled his groan. "Hello, Harold. What's up?"

"Why didn't you tell me? I heard somebody tried to break into your house last night."

Jack stiffened. "How did you hear about that?"

"That isn't important. What's important is the safety of those boys. If you can't keep your home safe, then maybe it's time I step in."

"That isn't necessary," Jack exclaimed, his blood rushing to his brain in a burst of anger. "I've got it covered. In fact, I had a state-of-the-art security system installed this morning. I have it all under control, Harold. There's nothing for you to worry about."

"You're on notice, Jack. Keep in mind that it's very possible you have no real legal claim to the boys. If I hear any more news about potential threats to them, then I'll have them yanked out of your custody so fast your head will spin. And you know I have the power to do that."

"I'm well aware of what you're capable of," Jack replied dryly. "Like I said, everything is under control here. There's no reason for you to worry."

Jack slammed down the receiver, his stomach burning with frustrated rage. He hated the fact that Harold had managed to remind him that one or both of the boys might not be his.

"It's very possible you have no real legal claim to those boys." Harold's words whirled in Jack's head, making him feel ill. He'd like to think that

Harold wouldn't go there to get the boys, that he would be reluctant to paint Candace as a woman who didn't know who the father of her children had been.

But he knew that Harold was ruthless enough to do such a thing to get what he wanted. Candace's reputation wasn't exactly stellar to begin with, and if Harold decided he wanted custody of the boys then he'd do whatever necessary to get it.

He leaned his head back and listened to the sound of the boys' breathing. He felt like he'd already missed so many moments of their lives. He couldn't imagine them being ripped away from him now.

Who was feeding Harold this information? Did he have somebody watching the house? Or was somebody in his house sharing private info with the man?

He left the bedroom, and as he walked back into the living room Marisa came in the front door, apparently having walked Patrick out to his car to tell him goodbye.

"Thank you for this evening," she said and then frowned. "What's wrong?"

"Harold just called. He'd heard about the attempted break-in last night."

She sucked in a breath. "How?"

"I don't know, but I intend to find out." He motioned her to follow him into the kitchen, where he noticed she'd cleaned up all remnants of the evening meal.

They sat at the table, and he stared at her, his mind whirling at a frantic pace. "Somebody is feeding Harold information. When he heard about the dinner date gone bad I just assumed Heidi had somehow made contact with him. But this puts a whole new spin on things."

"Rita didn't know about your dinner date, and in any case she would never betray my trust," Marisa said quickly.

Jack nodded. "Then that leaves Kent, Sam, Max or Betty. And of course you," he added.

A stain of color crept into her cheeks, letting him know he'd made her angry. "If you really think I'm capable of such duplicity then you need to fire me right now," she exclaimed.

"I'm not saying you're responsible," he protested. "Marisa, think about it, I'd be a fool not to consider everyone right now." He sighed in frustration. "It appears that somebody I trust, somebody who is in my confidence, is betraying me."

Some of the color in her cheeks faded. "I know you have no reason to trust me, but it isn't me, Jack. I don't know Harold Rothchild. I've never spoken to the man in my life. I certainly want what's in the best interest of Mick and David, and I've told you that as far as I'm concerned that's having them here with you."

"I trust you, Marisa," he said, and as the words left his mouth he recognized the truth in them. Even though he'd only known her a little over a week, he trusted her without a doubt. "What I have to figure out is who is betraying me." He rubbed a hand wearily across his forehead. "Somebody is playing with my life, Marisa."

It had been a long time since Jack's anger had been directed outward instead of inward. But now a wave of anger bigger than any he'd ever known filled him. "More important, somebody is playing with my boys' lives, and when I find out who it is, I'll make them damned sorry they ever did."

Chapter 6

"I've invited Kent to have breakfast with us," Jack said first thing the next morning.

Marisa took a sip of her coffee and eyed him over the rim of her cup. He didn't look particularly friendly. A knot of tension throbbed in his jaw, and his eyes were stormy.

"You don't look too happy at the prospect of a guest for breakfast," she observed.

"I lay awake half the night thinking about who might be selling me out to Harold," he replied. He shoved his empty coffee cup aside and stared out the dining-room window, where despite the early hour the Nevada sun already looked blazing hot.

"What about Betty?" she asked softly, hoping the woman working in the kitchen wouldn't hear her. "Or maybe Sam or Max?"

Jack turned back to look at her. "I just can't imagine it. She's more interested in soap operas and talk shows than in what's going on in this house. As far as Sam and Max are concerned, I'm not even sure they knew what happened during my dinner with Heidi. That leaves Kent."

It was obvious by the expression on his face that the idea that his friend was capable of such a thing hurt him. "Maybe there's another answer. Maybe Harold has somebody watching the house," she offered.

She thought of those moments outside the day before when she'd thought somebody was watching her. Maybe it hadn't been Max's gaze that she'd felt on her. Maybe somebody else had been hiding nearby, watching her, watching them all.

"Maybe," Jack replied, but he didn't sound convinced. "I'll know by the time breakfast is over if Kent is really my friend or not." He shoved back from the table and stood. "He's always been a terrible liar. I'm going to head outside for a little while. I'll be back soon."

She watched him go and once again had the impression of a lonely man who wasn't sure who he could trust in his life.

What must it be like to have two precious

children and be afraid all the time that some powerful entity might steal them away?

She frowned thoughtfully and stared at his coffee mug. Did she dare? She knew what she was contemplating would far exceed the boundaries of her position, but nevertheless she grabbed Jack's coffee cup and carried it to her bedroom. A few moments later she then returned to the kitchen and asked Betty for a small paper bag.

Betty gave her the bag, then looked pointedly at the door, as if inviting Marisa to leave. But instead Marisa sat at the table and eyed the woman who had been working for Jack since the boys had come to stay.

"You enjoy cooking?" she asked, even though she knew it was a foolish question.

"It's what I know how to do," Betty replied.

"What made you decide to come and work for Jack?"

Betty stirred a simmering skillet full of hash browns then wiped her hands on a towel and turned back to face Marisa. "I was a good friend of Jack's mother. A fine woman, she was. When Jack put out the word that he needed some household help there weren't many people lining up for the jobs." She shrugged. "You know his reputation wasn't the best. But I knew Jack's mother would want those boys to eat well so I decided to come to work for him."

"And you like working for him?"

"The pay is good, between meals I get to watch my television shows and I'm in my own house by six every night. What's not to like?"

"Your husband doesn't mind you being here every day?" Marisa asked.

"My Joe left me a year ago. Dropped dead of a heart attack at a slot machine in downtown Vegas. We never had any kids." She sighed. "I knew early on that I wasn't one of those maternal types. This job fills in the long hours of the days."

"I know Jack appreciates you being here for him," Marisa said as she got up from the table. She wasn't sure what she'd hoped to accomplish, but like Jack she couldn't imagine this woman being the pipeline of information to Harold Rothchild.

She was about to walk out of the kitchen when Betty called her name. She turned back to face the old woman.

"That woman Jack married broke his heart. I hope you don't plan on doing the same thing."

Marisa stared at the older woman in stunned surprise. "I'm an employee, just like you," she replied.

Betty snorted and turned back to the stove.

Marisa hurried to her bedroom, where she tucked Jack's coffee cup into the paper bag. Then noise from the boys' bedroom let her know they were awake, and she hurried into their room to help them dress for the day.

It was eight o'clock when Kent arrived and they all sat down for breakfast. The conversation remained pleasant throughout the meal although Marisa could feel tension wafting off Jack. Kent seemed oblivious to the stress that tightened Jack's jaw and filled the air as the meal came to an end.

"I'll just take the boys to their room to play," Marisa said as she rose from the table.

"Why don't you let them play on their own? I'd like you to stay here," Jack replied.

She really didn't want to be a part of the confrontation she knew was coming, but she also didn't want to leave if Jack needed her to stay. She got the boys out of their booster seats, told them to play in their room and then returned to her chair at the table.

"What's up?" Kent asked as if for the first time feeling the tension that rode thick in the air. He looked at Marisa and then back at Jack.

"We've been good friends for a long time, haven't we, Kent?" Jack asked, his voice deceptively calm.

"Except for your Los Angeles years, sure. Best friends," Kent replied. Once again he shot a quick glance at Marisa, then looked back at Jack and shifted uncomfortably in his chair. "What's going on?"

"You've been a great friend to me, but I know you and your band have been struggling. I imagine money is tight," Jack said.

"Money's always tight," Kent said with a small humorless laugh. "There's nothing new about that, but I always get by."

"I've got a problem, Kent."

"What's that?" Kent gazed at him warily.

"Somebody close to me is feeding Harold Rothchild information about the boys." It was obvious from Jack's tone that this was difficult for him.

Kent sat back in his chair and stared at Jack. "Are you accusing me? You really think I'd do something like that?" His face reddened. "You invite me here for breakfast and then accuse me of something like that? You're crazy, man."

"Kent, I'm not accusing," Jack protested. "I'm just asking."

Kent scooted his chair back from the table and stood. "I can't believe you'd think I'd do something like that to you. You're my closest friend."

He slammed his hands down on the table and glared at Jack. "If I were you, I'd look a little closer to home." He looked pointedly at Marisa and then at Jack. "Remember Ramona? The showgirl who is friends with Marisa? Guess where she works, Jack. At Rothchild's casino. You want to find a snake? Beat the grass in your house, Jack."

Marisa gasped as Kent stalked out of the kitchen and a moment later the front door slammed shut with a resounding bang.

Jack reached for his glass of water and Marisa

couldn't help but notice that his hand trembled slightly. "That went well," he said dryly.

"Did you believe him?" she asked softly.

"I don't know what to believe." His eyes looked hollow and dark. "I just know I feel like I'm on borrowed time with the boys, and I don't know how to change that."

Mick came into the dining room. "David went out the window," he said. "He wanted to play the drums again."

Both Marisa and Jack jumped up from the table and raced for the front door.

"I thought these locks on the windows were child-proof," Marisa exclaimed.

"Apparently they aren't David-proof," Jack replied.

As Jack raced after the little boy who was halfway to the barn, Marisa stood on the porch and wondered how on earth this father was going to fight somebody as wealthy and as powerful as Harold Rothchild?

Jack wandered the living room long after the boys had gone to bed. Marisa had helped him get them settled in for the night then she had left to go visit her aunt Rita.

He was surprised by how much he felt her absence. It was as if she'd taken some of the energy in the house with her when she'd gone.

The fight with Kent that morning had left a bad taste in his mouth that had lingered throughout the day. Jack had never been the kind of man who looked for a confrontation. Nothing had ever been important enough for him to fight over until now. For Mick and David he'd confront a five-headed monster.

He went into the kitchen and decided to put on a short pot of coffee. He was reluctant to call it a night and go to bed until Marisa got home safe and sound.

It was funny how quickly she'd become a part of his routine. He liked the time they spent visiting after the boys had gone to bed. He enjoyed the sound of her laughter, a rich, joyous sound that never failed to make him smile.

It wasn't just the loving way she interacted with the boys that drew him to her. She seemed to know instinctively when to give him space and when to ride him hard.

He liked the way her hair sparkled in the light, how the scent of her flooded his senses.

In fact, there was nothing about Marisa Perez he didn't like.

After the coffee had brewed he poured himself a cup and sat at the table. He rarely sat in the kitchen, had come to consider the room strictly Betty's territory.

It was a nice, warm room, and he had many memories of meals at this very table with his mother and father. Many nights Kent had joined them, and Jack's mom had often joked that she must have been asleep when they'd adopted Kent.

He wrapped his hands around the warm coffee mug as he thought of Kent. Betrayal was always tough to take but particularly so when it came at the hands of a friend.

He was still sitting at the table at ten-thirty when he heard the front door open and the beep of the security alarm preparing to ring. The beeping lasted only a minute then stopped as the code was entered.

He smelled her before she entered the room, that slightly spicy floral that heated his blood and left him wanting more.

"Hi," she said. "I wasn't sure you'd still be up."

"I decided to make some coffee. There's a cup still there if you want it."

"No, thanks. Too late for caffeine for me." She sat in the chair across from him at the table. "Everything all right here?"

"Fine. I managed to fix the lock on the window where David escaped earlier today. If I ever have trouble opening a bottle of aspirin I'm giving the bottle to him."

Marisa laughed. "We're just going to have to be vigilant about keeping the alarm on not just at night but also during the day. That way we'll know when he manages to get a window or a door open."

"I don't understand why he keeps trying to get

out. Today he wasn't even running toward the barn. He was just running."

"Curiosity," she replied. "David is curious about everything. When he starts school he's probably going to challenge his teachers."

"I have a feeling he's going to challenge me. How was your visit with your aunt? Everything okay?"

She frowned. "I still get the feeling that something's wrong, that she's worried about something, but I can't get her to confide in me. She says it's work related and that's all she would tell me. You know she's been working on Candace's murder case."

"Maybe they finally have some leads to the killer," he replied. "It would be nice to see justice done and the guilty behind bars. I think maybe that would give Harold some peace."

"Have you heard any more from him? Any more phone calls tonight?"

Jack shook his head. "No, but I realize it's just a matter of time." A new wave of discouragement filled him. His heart felt as if it weighed about a hundred pounds.

"What made you decide to get clean and sober, Jack?" she asked.

He leaned back in his chair, surprised by the question. But he realized that in all the conversations they'd shared, they'd never talk about this particular part of his past.

"Candace and I were big on the party scene." He frowned thoughtfully. "It was what brought us together, and for a long time I think it was what kept us together. The only time we stopped was when she was pregnant with the boys."

He stared out the nearby window, thinking about those days with Candace. Many of the early days of their marriage were nothing more than a blur. They had rarely been sober back then.

He turned his attention back to Marisa. "It was after David was born that I tried to change our life. I wanted to be the kind of father the boys needed, and that meant no more booze and no more drugs." He sighed. "Ultimately I think that's why Candace divorced me—because I wasn't fun anymore."

"She wasn't ready to give up the fun?"

A dry laugh escaped him. "I'm not sure what it would have taken for Candace to turn her life around, but it wasn't me or the boys. So we divorced and she took the boys. She made it almost impossible for me to have any interaction with them. She took them to Europe for several months, then back to Los Angeles. She was rarely in one place for long."

"And so you came back here," Marisa said.

He nodded. "And proceeded to drink myself into a stupor. For the next six months I pretty much stayed drunk. It was Kent who came over to see that I ate, to check on me to make sure I was still alive." He grimaced. "It's a time in my life I'm not proud of."

"So what turned things around for you?"

"One morning I stumbled into the bathroom and stared at myself in the mirror. I looked dead. I looked like all I was waiting for was somebody to shovel dirt over me." He met her gaze. "On the sink in my master bath is a small photo of my parents. I stared at that picture and was ashamed of who I was, of what I'd become."

He thought of that single defining moment. It was as if his parents had reached out to him from their graves.

"I also realized at that moment that it was possible at some point in the future the boys might need me. I knew eventually I'd have to justify the choices I'd made in my life to them." His voice deepened. "I didn't know if it would be five years or fifteen, but some day those boys would want to get to know me and that got me clean and sober. Being a drunk wasn't something I wanted to have to explain."

Marisa stared at him for a long moment, then turned her head to look out the window, her brow furrowed in thought.

Jack tried not to notice the soft curve of her jaw line, how the yellow tank top she wore clung to her full breasts. His head filled with the memory of how those breasts had felt in his hands, how her mouth had clung to his as if they were both drowning.

He felt himself getting aroused at the very thought and chastised himself for letting his mind wander.

Needing to do something—anything—to cleanse the erotic images from his head, he got up from the table, poured himself another cup of coffee and stood with his hips against the counter. At least with this distance between them he couldn't smell her fragrance.

She finally looked at him, her gaze as somber as he'd ever seen it. "You told me that you have two strikes against you if push comes to shove over custody of the boys. The first was your past."

He nodded slowly, unsure where she was going with this.

"But you've never been arrested, and most of the stories of your legendary partying were in the tabloids, right?"

"Right," he agreed.

"Which are not always true."

"Definitely," he said dryly. "The tabloid reports were always full of untruths and exaggerations."

"You've kept a very low profile since moving back here to the ranch, and nobody can make a case that you aren't an upstanding citizen now."

He moved back to the table and sat, still unable to guess where she was going with all this. "I suppose that's right."

"So really the only issue is the fact that you're a

single man trying to raise two children alone. We could fix that. We could make sure that Harold couldn't use that fact against you."

"And how would we do that?" he asked.

She held his gaze intently. "You could marry me."

Chapter 7

Marisa saw shock take possession of his features. His eyes widened and his mouth fell open, and she took advantage of his momentary speechlessness.

"Think about it, Jack. It would be a strictly business relationship," she continued. "Everything would stay just as it is now, including our sleeping arrangements." She hoped the blush she felt inside didn't show on her cheeks. "The only difference would be the picture we present outside this house—as a happily married couple raising the boys in a two-parent home."

"That's a crazy idea," he said, but she couldn't help but see the hope that leaped into his eyes. "Isn't it?" he added.

"There's absolutely nothing questionable in my past, and raising children has been my job. No judge could look at me and the way I have lived my life so far and deem me unacceptable as a stepmother to the boys."

"But why would you want to do that?" He narrowed his eyes slightly. "What's in it for you, Marisa?"

"I'll get to raise Mick and David. Jack, I've fallen in love with your boys. I care about them. After all they've been through, they need a stable life, and I can help provide that for them. I wouldn't just be doing this for you but I'd be doing it for myself as well."

"But what about Patrick?"

"I told you that we were just casually dating. It's nothing serious," she replied.

"He didn't look like it was just casual for him." Jack took a sip of his coffee, his gaze not leaving hers over the rim of his mug.

"That doesn't matter. This is my choice, Jack." She'd thought about it all night and throughout the day. There was a part of her that knew it was an insane idea, but there was a bigger part of her that somehow felt it was right.

He lowered his cup to the table. "Marisa, you're bright and you're beautiful. Why would you want to get yourself involved in this kind of a relationship? Why not marry some man and raise kids of your own?"

Her heart squeezed painfully at the question. She looked down at the top of the table, unable to look at him as she revisited the most painful time in her past.

"I was a junior in college when I met a guy named Tom, and we started a wild, passionate relationship." Her throat grew dry as she thought of those nights with Tom—not because of any residual desire but rather because she'd been such a fool.

"I was crazy about him, and I thought he was crazy about me. I didn't realize I was nothing more than a booty call for him." This time she felt the heat that filled her cheeks. "I found out just how little I meant to him when I discovered I was pregnant and he told me I was on my own."

Jack's only response was a tightening of his jaw. "It was okay," she hurriedly added. "Even though the pregnancy was unplanned and Tom had disappeared, I was thrilled to be pregnant, and I wanted the baby desperately."

The knot of pain in her chest expanded, squeezing out the breath in her lungs. "I didn't tell my parents. I didn't tell anyone about my condition except Aunt Rita. I was going to tell my parents once I had it figured out how to continue college and be a single parent." A lump rose to her throat. "To be honest, I was afraid they'd try to talk me into getting an abortion, and that was something I'd never consider."

She halted, unable to go on for a moment as her

heart shattered all over again. Tears burned in her eyes, but she refused to allow them to fall. She'd cried enough tears to fill the ocean when she'd been going through the trauma.

Jack reached across the table and took one of her hands in his. He said nothing but waited for her to gain her composure.

The warmth of his hand, big and strong around hers, helped and she drew a deep, tremulous breath. "I was just beginning my sixth month when I started to bleed and then miscarried. I was devastated, but even more devastating than that was when the doctor told me in order to save my life they had to do a complete hysterectomy."

"God, Marisa, I'm sorry. I'm so sorry for you," he said. His features were filled with compassion.

She pulled her hand from his and instead wrapped her arms around herself. "Thanks, but now surely you understand why I'm willing to do this. I'm never going to have my own babies, Jack. I'm never going to have a family of my own." She swallowed hard. "So if you agree to this business arrangement we erase one of the strikes against you and I get to be a mommy to Mick and David."

She knew what she was proposing sounded impulsive, especially given the short time she'd known Jack and the boys. But she couldn't help but follow her heart, and her heart was telling her that this was where she belonged…at least for now.

He shoved a strand of his dark hair off his forehead with the back of his hand. "I need to think about this," he finally said. "I mean, this is all happening so fast."

"Of course," she agreed. She immediately got up from the table. "I'm going to bed. I'll see you in the morning."

She left him seated at the table, staring out the window into the dark of night. She had no idea if he'd agree to her plan or not. It was out of her hands.

As she got ready for bed she thought of the offer she'd just made to Jack. She wasn't sure when it had first blossomed in her head, but the moment it had she'd embraced it.

It made a crazy kind of sense. She could live in a loveless, passionless marriage if the payoff was being able to raise Mick and David. What she didn't know was if Jack was willing to make the same kind of sacrifice.

There was no question that there was a smoldering desire between her and Jack, but she wouldn't complicate matters by diving headfirst into something wild and hot and dangerous.

She fell asleep almost immediately and dreamed of Jack. In her dreams they were making love, and she awakened the next morning feeling restless and edgy.

After showering and dressing for the day, she remained in her room until it was late enough for her to call Patrick. Whether Jack agreed to her plan or not, she'd decided to call it quits with the handsome accountant.

She'd been comfortable dating Patrick because he didn't inspire great passion in her. Jack inspired passion, but she didn't intend to follow through on it. She was putting her heart far more at risk by offering to be Jack's wife, but as she thought of the two precious boys, she thought the risk was worth it.

Besides, it wasn't really fair to continue seeing Patrick knowing that they had no future together. Eventually Patrick would want to get married and have children, and that was something she would never be able to give him. It was time to cut him loose so he could find the woman who would be his future.

He answered his phone on the second ring, obviously identifying her cell phone number from caller ID.

"What a pleasant surprise," he exclaimed. "I was just getting ready for work and thinking about you."

"I've been thinking about you, too," she replied. She hated the fact that she was going to hurt him. But better to hurt him now in the early stages of their relationship than later.

"Patrick, you're a wonderful man and someday you're going to make some woman very happy," she began.

"Why do I get the feeling this call is a kiss-off?"

Marisa sighed. "Because I guess it is. Patrick, I've enjoyed the time I've spent with you, but I'm not in a place in my life right now to want a relationship. I'm focused on my work here and two little boys who need me."

"Have I done something to offend you?" he asked quietly.

"No, not at all," she hurriedly replied. "This is about me, Patrick, not about you. I just think it would be better if we stopped seeing one another."

"You know that's not what I want," he replied in a husky voice. "But I can't do anything but respect your decision. You know where to find me if you ever need anything."

"I do—and thanks." She was grateful it hadn't gotten messy and was rather surprised that it had been so easy. She hung up and went into the dining room, where Jack was already seated at the table.

"Good morning," she said and tried not to notice how handsome he looked in a short-sleeved blue shirt and his worn jeans.

The aroma of frying bacon came from the kitchen along with the faint noise of the small television.

Marisa sat next to him and a wave of heat shot through her as she caught the scent of shaving cream and minty soap that wafted from him. Yes, she felt desire for Jack, but she reminded herself that it was an emotion that caused more grief than pleasure.

"Did you sleep well?" he asked.

"Like a baby."

"Change your mind about what you proposed to me?"

She studied his features, trying to discern what he was thinking, but his face was schooled into an enigmatic mask that made it impossible to see into his mind. "No, I still think it's a viable plan."

At that moment she heard the sound of childish laughter and knew the boys were awake. "I'll be right back," she said.

It took her only minutes to wash and dress Mick and David and then get them buckled into their booster seats at the table.

By that time Betty had served breakfast and they all began to eat. Jack ate for a few minutes in silence, then put his fork down and looked at her once again.

"What happens if we go through with it and Harold manages to get custody of the boys anyway?" he asked.

"Then we divorce," she replied. "Quick and easy—no harm, no foul." She'd once held the idea that when she married it would be forever, that she would be with the man she chose to exchange vows with for the rest of her natural life. But fate had changed her expectations.

"You know we're both more than a little bit crazy to even be contemplating this." His gray eyes studied her thoughtfully. "I'm still not sure why you'd be willing to do this for me."

"I'm not doing it for you. I'm doing it for Mick and David, and I'm doing it for me," she replied. The last thing she wanted was for Jack to know that there was a small piece of her heart that belonged just a little bit to him. She didn't even want to access that place herself.

Strictly business, she told herself even as the thought of Jack's lips against hers created a small ball of warmth in the pit of her stomach.

"You have anything special planned for this afternoon?" he asked.

Her heart seemed to skip a beat. "Nothing out of the ordinary."

"Then why don't we get dressed up and head down to the license office, then visit one of the tacky wedding chapels Las Vegas has to offer?"

Now was the time for her to change her mind, she thought. Maybe it was crazy; perhaps she hadn't considered all the ramifications.

"M'ssa, look!" David said. He grinned at her as he balanced a piece of round oat cereal on the end of his nose.

"Marisa, look, I can do it, too," Mick said and dug into his cereal bowl.

As always, her heart filled her chest at their antics. Yes, this whole scheme was probably crazy, and she was positive she hadn't completely thought it all through. But she turned to Jack and smiled.

"Just tell me what time to be ready," she said,

knowing that she had just made a decision that would forever change her life. It could be a wonderfully positive change or it could leave her utterly desolate for the second time in her life.

Harold Rothchild had many things that he regretted about his life. At the moment there was only one regret on his mind as he gazed at the gorgeous blond trophy wife seated opposite him at the long mahogany dining room table.

He'd found her incredibly sexy when he'd initially met her and truth be told she'd stroked his ego by appearing to be crazy about him. They hadn't been seeing each other for long when she'd told him she thought she was pregnant. Impulsively he'd married her and regretted it ever since.

The pregnancy had yielded a son who was now five years old. Unfortunately the bloom had definitely worn off the marriage.

It hadn't taken Harold long to be bored—bored to tears with his young wife who could only have meaningful discussions about who had worn what to which charity function and what designer was having a tremendous sale.

It was enough to make a man think fondly of the wife he'd divorced. Anna had been a good wife and had tried to be a good mother to the three girls he'd brought into the marriage. And he'd come to love Anna's daughter, Silver, as if she were his own.

Lately he'd been thinking more and more about his second wife.

He focused his attention back on the financial section of the morning newspaper.

No matter how bad the economy got, people still loved to gamble. Business had never been better at the casino as people blew their money on the chance of hitting it big.

Still, he found his concentration wandering from finances to family matters. He wondered if things would have been different for Candace if his first wife, June, hadn't died.

Candace had been a handful from the moment of her birth. Wild and impetuous, beautiful and troubled, but Harold would always believe that the reason for her murder had been that damned diamond ring.

The Tears of the Quetzal, so named for the resplendent Quetzal bird of Mexico. Like the bird, the diamond had possessed magnificent colors of golds and greens and deeper hues of blue and violet. His stomach muscles clenched with tension as he thought of the diamond.

It had been found in one of his father's diamond mines, and Harold would never forget that day—it was burned into his head and occasionally gave him nightmares that awakened him in the middle of the night.

He knew the legend attached to the ring, that it

had special powers and would bring love to anyone who came into contact with it.

It was a charming little legend, but Harold knew the truth. He knew that until the ring was back in his possession, it had the potential to wreak havoc on his family. Candace's murder had only been the first of a string of tragedies waiting to happen.

Only Harold knew the true story, that from the moment the diamond had been found it had been bathed in blood. And he got up every morning and went to bed every night terrified by what might happen next.

Chapter 8

The chapel was gaudy, like so much of what Las Vegas had to offer. Jack suddenly wished he had picked another place to exchange vows with Marisa. She deserved better than this.

Marisa looked positively stunning in a pale-pink sundress that was cinched at her slender waist and emphasized the lush fullness of her breasts and hips.

She stood just inside the door with the boys on either side of her while Jack made the necessary arrangements for the ceremony.

There were a dozen wedding packages to pick from when it came to the actual ceremony. Aware that this was nothing but a business deal, he picked one that would let her carry a nosegay of roses but had fewer of the romantic accoutrements.

The minister had the scent of booze clinging to him, and the witness would be a paid stranger. It all felt slightly seedy.

Jack would have walked out but it was already after five and the boys had forgone their nap and were now getting cranky.

He also didn't want to give himself too much time to think, too much opportunity to let reason take over. He had no idea if this was a mistake or not, but he told himself that if it gave him an edge in a custody battle, then it couldn't be a mistake.

Still, he realized that Marisa should be wearing a white gown of ribbons and lace, and she should be exchanging vows with a man she loved beyond reason.

He wore a suit and tie for the occasion, but he had a feeling he also wore the expression of a deer caught in the headlights.

With the arrangements made and the ceremony paid for, he walked back to where she stood. "Last chance to bail," he said.

She smiled, but the gesture looked slightly forced. "I'm not going anywhere until this is done." She picked up David in her arms, and the toddler wrapped his arms around her neck and laid his head on her shoulder. "Let's just get it finished. The boys are getting hungry and tired."

It took fifteen minutes for Marisa to become Mrs. Jack Cortland. She held David during the brief ceremony, and Jack held Mick.

She only seemed to get emotional once and that was when Jack slipped his mother's wedding ring onto her finger. He'd never given it to Candace, who he'd known would have laughed at the small size of the diamond.

At the end of the ceremony the minister clapped Jack on the back as he walked them out of the chapel and told him he'd always been a big fan of Creation.

Thankfully there were no paparazzi hanging around outside so he didn't have to worry about their wedding becoming a tabloid story.

"I told Betty before we left that we'd be dining out tonight," Jack said as the four of them stepped outside the small chapel. "I thought we could grab a bite at one of the casino buffets or restaurants." He would have never attempted a meal out with the kids before Marisa had arrived and worked her magic with them.

"That's fine, although a restaurant would probably be easier than a buffet with the boys," she replied. David was no longer in her arms but at her side. She held his hand in hers, and in her other hand she clutched the bouquet of pink roses that had come with the wedding ceremony.

It was over a quiet dinner that Jack explained to the boys that Marisa was going to be their new mommy. David seemed to take it all in stride, but Mick looked at her worriedly.

"If you're our new mommy, does that mean you're going to go away?" he asked. His big blue eyes held far too much worry for a little boy.

"No, honey. I don't plan on going away," she replied. "Hopefully we're all going to be together for a very long time."

That seemed to satisfy Mick, who turned his concentration on dipping his French fries into the ocean of ketchup that pooled on his plate.

Marisa was unusually quiet during the meal. Jack watched her easy, loving interaction with David and Mick, and that eased the faint uncertainty that somehow they had made a mistake.

He wasn't worried about the mistake affecting him in a negative way. He'd made enough mistakes in his life to fill a book and had managed to survive them all.

But, he worried about Marisa. She might believe she was in this scheme wholeheartedly now, but how long could a woman exist happily in a loveless situation with just the comfort of two little boys?

There would come a day when she might regret not having a man in her life that she loved, when the love of two little boys just wasn't enough.

He tried to tamp down the simmer of desire that he always felt when he was around her. He had to put the memory of the kisses they had shared out of his mind.

She'd made it clear that this was strictly a platonic union and that the sleeping arrangements would remain the same.

She'd also emphasized that she was agreeing to this because of her own needs and the needs of his sons. She hadn't mentioned his needs at all when she'd made the offer.

Dinner was pleasant, and when they were finished eating they walked back to where they had parked his car. David was once again in Marisa's arms, and Mick rode on Jack's back.

Within the first five minutes of being buckled into their car seats, the boys were both sound asleep. As Jack headed back to the ranch, he cast a quick glance at Marisa, wondering what she was thinking, if perhaps she was already regretting the decision she had made.

"You okay?" he asked.

She turned and smiled at him. She looked re-laxed, not stressed. "I'm fine. What about you?"

"I'm good. I think I'm just having a hard time processing what we just did."

He felt her gaze lingering on him. "This is going to be far more difficult on you than it is on me, Jack."

"And why is that?"

"Sex." The word hung in the air.

He shot her a quick glance, fast enough to catch the charming blush that colored her cheeks. "What about it?"

"I know how important it is to most men, but it can't be an issue between us. Getting involved in a physical relationship will only complicate things if this all falls apart." She frowned thoughtfully. "If this condition really bothers you, I suppose it would be okay for you to have an affair if you could do it as discreetly as possible."

He was stunned by her words and by the fact that she would think so little of herself as to agree to such a thing. "I was married to Candace for a long time and never cheated on her. During all my years of partying, I might have done a lot of morally questionable things but I never knowingly slept with a married woman.

"I won't have an affair, Marisa, and I'll respect your wishes about not having a physical relationship with you." He offered her a smile. "Contrary to popular myth, going without sex does not kill a man."

Turning onto the road that would lead them home, he offered her another smile. "However, if you ever change your mind about the no-sex part of this relationship, I hope I'll be the first to know."

"Trust me, you'll be the very first person I tell." Once again deep color filled her cheeks, and he wanted nothing more than to take her in his arms and show her what she'd be missing.

He was definitely going to have to take up splitting wood or something equally physical to ease the burn of the desire she stirred inside him.

He could do it. He would do whatever it took to

keep Marisa in his life. He would do whatever it took to make sure that his boys stayed in his custody, and if that meant living in a sexless marriage, he would do that.

Once they were home Marisa went into her bedroom to change her clothes, and Jack took the boys into the bathroom for a bath and to get them into their pajamas.

The tub was filled with bubbles, and the two boys splashed like fish. They wore the bubbles on their head and on their chins like little white beards.

"Look, Jack." Mick giggled as he built a tower of bubbles on his head. "It's a hat."

"Watch me, Jack," David exclaimed, vying for attention with his brother. He put his face into the water and blew, then raised his head and grinned with obvious pride.

"That's great, David, and Mick, I love your hat," he replied.

Love buoyed up inside him. He couldn't lose them. He needed them in his life and he liked to believe that they needed him.

By the time he got them out of the tub and dried and dressed, he was as wet as they had been. He handed them off to Marisa at the doorway so she could tuck them in and he could change his drenched shirt.

In his bedroom he pulled on a clean white T-shirt, then stood in the boys' bedroom door as Marisa got them into their beds.

"If you're our new mommy, then can we call you Mommy?" Mick asked her as she leaned over to give him a kiss on the forehead.

Marisa stood in obvious surprise and glanced at Jack. He shrugged to indicate that it was her call. She bent down next to Mick and smoothed a strand of his hair away from his face. "I think you should call me whatever you feel comfortable with," she said.

"And you'll be here in the morning when I wake up?" he asked.

Jack's heart squeezed. They had never asked about Candace in the months that he'd had them, and Mick's question indicated to Jack that there had been many mornings when the boys had awakened and not had their mother there.

"I'll be here," Marisa answered simply.

"You promise?" he asked.

"I promise," she replied.

"Okay, then good night, Mommy," he said with a sleepy sigh.

"Now me!" David exclaimed. "Kiss me good-night."

Marisa laughed and quickly kissed Mick on the forehead then moved to David's bedside. "'Night, Mommy," he said and Jack's heart squeezed even tighter.

"Now my turn," he said as Marisa moved toward the door. "Good night, son," he said to Mick as he bent down to kiss him.

"Good night, Daddy," Mick replied.

For a moment Jack remained frozen as a joy he'd never known coursed through him. Daddy. Finally, he'd heard that word from his son's mouth. Never had a single word sounded so sweet.

When David said the same thing, he left the room with a sense of wonderment. As he and Marisa walked out in the hallway he caught her by the shoulders and stared at her for a long moment.

"You did this," he whispered. "I don't know how you did it, but you accomplished a miracle."

She smiled, her eyes shining brightly. "It's no miracle, Jack. They love you, and finally they're willing to trust you. I didn't do this, you did."

He couldn't control himself. His joy was so great he had to kiss her. He grabbed her into his arms and commandeered her lips with his.

For a moment he could think of nothing but the happiness in his soul and the pleasure of her warm lips beneath his.

It was only when he felt her stiffen against him that he dropped his hands and stepped back from her. Jeez, they hadn't even been married five hours and already he had stepped over the line.

"I'm sorry," he said awkwardly. "I just got carried away with the moment. I won't let it happen again." He didn't wait for her reply but instead walked down the hallway to his bedroom.

Chapter 9

Marisa stood on the porch and watched the car pulling away from the house. She sighed in exhaustion. She'd arranged for a playdate for the boys and had spent the morning entertaining not two but four rambunctious, energetic little boys.

She was about to turn and go back into the house when she saw Sam and Max Burrow standing near the barn, their gazes directed at her. A small chill worked its way up her back.

During the course of the past week since the marriage, she'd felt them staring at her far too often. It gave her a creepy, unsettled feeling, and she couldn't help but wonder if Jack had vented his rage about who was feeding Harold information on the wrong person.

She closed the front door and set the alarm, then collapsed on the sofa in the living room, where Mick and David were playing with their truck collection.

The visitors had been previous charges of Marisa, the two sons of Margaret and John Covewell, who worked at one of the casinos. She'd worked for them for four months, until they had gotten themselves into a financial position where Margaret could be a stay-at-home mom.

Although the first hour had been a little rough as David and Mick weren't used to sharing either toys or attention with any other children, the last hour had gone remarkably smoothly.

Jack was outside somewhere. In the past week they had fallen into a routine that allowed him to work on the ranch during the day, then spend his late afternoon and evenings with the boys.

There had been no more interaction between Jack and Kent, and Marisa knew the rift weighed heavy on Jack's mind. They still had no idea what the man had wanted who had tried to break into the house, but thankfully nothing alarming had happened since then.

That wasn't exactly true, she thought. The most alarming thing happening in her life at the moment was the growing intensity of her desire for Jack.

It was hotter than anything she'd ever felt for her

boyfriend in college. They were all living like a happy family, but at night when she climbed into her lonely bed she ached for something more. And when she finally fell asleep it was to erotic dreams of making love with Jack.

In those dreams it wasn't just the sex that overwhelmed her. It was the fact that Jack whispered his love for her—a love that had nothing to do with his sons but rather that indefinable emotion between a man and a woman.

What she had to remember was that she was just a means to an end to better his chances if a custody battle should ensue. Their relationship was only about the boys, not about love.

Seeing that the boys were playing well together, she went into the kitchen, where Betty was finishing up the preparation of the evening meal.

"Is there anything I can do to help?" she asked.

Betty looked at her as if she'd just suggested murder. The old woman had been particularly cantankerous over the past week. "Do I look like I need help?" she asked. "Have you noticed the food not tasting right lately? Am I getting the meals ready on time?"

"No, I mean yes." Marisa frowned. "Betty, I didn't ask because I think you needed my help. I just wondered if you'd like any help."

Betty set down the knife she'd been using to cut up vegetables. "Just tell me now. Am I going to lose my job?"

Marisa looked at her in surprise. "Why would you ask?"

Betty shrugged her skinny shoulders. "With you and Jack married now, I've been wondering when you'd decide to take over everything in the house."

"I have no intention of taking over your job," Marisa assured her. "To be perfectly honest with you, there are some things I do very well, but I never really got the hang of cooking."

The taut line of Betty's mouth relaxed, and she picked up the paring knife once again. "It's not that hard if you put your mind to it."

Marisa leaned a hip against the counter. "How well do you know Sam and Max?" she asked suddenly.

"I've known those two since they were teenagers. Why?"

"I was just curious about what kind of men they were." Marisa didn't want to say that she had questions about their loyalty to Jack, and she definitely didn't want to mention that the two occasionally gave her the creeps.

"They're good men, not too bright but hard workers. Jack could do a lot worse."

At that moment there was a cry from the living room, and Marisa rushed from the kitchen to tend to a fight between the two brothers.

That night after the boys had been tucked into bed, Marisa and Jack sat in the living room as was their custom.

"Are you okay?" she asked. He'd been unusually quiet the entire evening.

"I'm fine. Why?"

"You just seem like you have a lot on your mind." She wondered if he was regretting the marriage. He'd reached a place with the boys where they would have been fine without her. Jack had learned to be consistent with discipline, and the boys had begun to trust him to be there for them.

He leaned back in his chair and released an audible sigh. "Things have been quiet for the past week. I haven't received even one phone call from Harold. I somehow feel like it's the calm before the storm."

"Have you heard from Kent?" she asked.

He shook his head, his eyes deepening in hue. There was no question that the topic of Kent hurt him. "But I didn't expect to."

"Maybe you should talk to him again, Jack. It would be a shame to throw away all those years of friendship that the two of you shared, especially given the fact that we don't even know for sure if he is the one who is feeding Harold information."

He rubbed two fingers across his forehead, as if fighting a headache. "I've lost all objectivity about all of this. Maybe you're right. Maybe I need to sit down with Kent and talk. I'll go over to his place tomorrow." He dropped his hand from his forehead and smiled at her.

That smile of his warmed a place inside her that no other smile had done. "You know, just because we got married doesn't mean you can't still pursue your dream of owning your own nanny agency," he said.

"To be honest, I haven't even thought about it for the past couple of weeks," she admitted. "But it is something I'd like to do. I'd need to create a Web site and do some advertising, and I'd also need to interview prospective employees but it's all something I could do from the house. I'd never have to leave the boys."

"I want you to do what makes you happy, Marisa." His deep voice was as soft as a caress. "You've already sacrificed so much for me. I'll support whatever it is you want to do as far as an agency is concerned."

It was far more difficult than she'd expected to maintain an emotional distance from him. She'd tried desperately since the moment she'd met him to keep herself detached, to ignore the simmering burn he evoked in her. But it was getting more arduous with each day that passed.

"I think I'll go to bed," she said, releasing a tired sigh. "The playdate today exhausted me." At that moment Mick cried out, obviously suffering from one of his nightmares.

"I'll take care of him," Jack said and got up from his chair. As Marisa went into her bedroom Jack disappeared into the boys' room.

She went into her bathroom and got undressed and into her silky nightgown, then pulled her robe around her and crept out into the hallway just outside the boys' bedroom.

Her breath caught in her chest as she heard Jack singing, his deep, melodious voice whispering of circus clowns and treasures found, of big balloons and smiling moons.

Marisa leaned with her back against the hallway wall and closed her eyes as warmth rushed through her. It was a warmth coupled with a horrible sense of dread as she realized she'd fallen hopelessly in love with her husband.

Jack sang until Mick fell back asleep. He remained in the chair next to the bed for a long moment, breathing in the scent of his boys, then quietly got up and left the room.

He nearly collided with Marisa, who was standing in the hallway just outside. She looked up at him with her liquid brown eyes, and the smile that curved her lips made his heart pound just a bit.

"That was beautiful," she said, her voice a husky whisper.

"I might not be good at a lot of things, but I always could sing," he replied. Every muscle in his body tensed as she didn't move away. He feared he might lose his mind if she didn't stop looking at him like that.

He shifted from one foot to the other. "Well, I guess I'll just say good-night," he finally said. He started to walk by her to return to the living room, but she stopped him by placing her delicate hand on his forearm.

"Jack?" Her eyes were luminous as she gazed up at him.

"Yeah?" The air between them seemed to shimmer with an energy that made it difficult for him to breathe.

She moistened her lips with the tip of her tongue, and Jack felt his blood pressure shoot through the ceiling. "I told you that you'd be the first to know if I changed my mind," she said.

Jack shoved his hands in his jean pockets, afraid of where they might roam, afraid that he might misunderstand what she was talking about. "Changed your mind about what?" He fought the urge to cough to clear away the huskiness of his throat.

A wild desire had crashed through him the moment she'd touched her lips with her tongue. The thin cotton robe she wore did nothing to hide her curves, and the tiny peek of red silk he saw only further heated the blood rushing through his veins.

"About not having anything physical between us." Her cheeks flamed, but she held his gaze with an uplifted chin. "I mean, if you were interested in having something physical between us, I wouldn't be upset."

"If I'm interested?" He pulled his hands from his pockets. "Marisa, I've been interested in a physical relationship with you since the moment you walked through my front door."

He felt frozen in place, afraid to move too fast, afraid to move too slow, scared somehow that he'd do something to shatter the moment and that gorgeous light in her eyes.

She took a step closer to him, engulfing him in that delicious scent of hers. "So do you intend to do something about it or are you just going to stand there and stare at me?"

Her upper lip trembled slightly, letting him know that she was nervous, that she was putting herself on the line and wasn't sure what reaction she might get from him.

He pulled her into his arms and placed his lips against hers. Softly, tenderly he kissed her as he cradled her against him. But the kiss didn't remain soft or tender. As she wrapped her arms around his neck and opened her mouth against his, his need roared through him like a loosened beast.

He wanted to devour her. He felt as if he'd been on a slow burn since the moment they'd met, and her sudden acquiescence was the fuel that exploded that simmer into a raging inferno.

He broke the kiss, wanting to get her into his bedroom, into his bed before she changed her mind.

As he stepped back from her he reached for her

hand and led her down the hallway toward his bedroom. She followed him without hesitation, but her hand trembled slightly in his.

The bedside lamp was on in his room, casting a faint golden light on the king-size bed he hadn't made that morning.

He dropped her hand and looked at her. As much as he needed to take what he wanted from her, he gave her one last chance to halt what they were about to do.

"Marisa, this wasn't what you offered to me when you agreed to marry me. I don't want to take advantage of you," he rasped out. "I want you, but I don't want you to feel pressured in any way to do this."

She didn't reply. She untied the belt at her waist and allowed the robe to fall to the floor behind her. The red silk nightgown hit her mid-thigh, and the deep V-neck exposed the swell of her upper breasts.

Jack bit back the moan that tried to escape him as he saw that her nipples were already hard and pressed tauntingly against the silk material.

"Trust me, Jack. I never do anything I don't want to do." She took a step closer to him, her eyes a pool of darkness that he could easily submerge himself in.

He felt as if he were in a fog as he grabbed her to him once again, his hands sliding down the silky gown to grab her buttocks and pull her as close to him as possible.

Once again their lips met in a hot, wild kiss that

had him hungering for more. He slid his mouth from hers and instead rained kisses across her jaw and down the length of her neck. She gasped in pleasure as he found a sensitive place just behind her ear.

The sound of her gasp ignited the flames inside him even more, and he stumbled back from her and yanked his T-shirt over his head.

At one time he might have been smooth, but it had been so long and he felt like a teenager preparing for his very first time. His fingers fumbled with his button fly as she pulled the nightgown over her head and slid in under the sheets.

He kicked off his shoes and finally got out of his pants, and then he tore off his socks and joined her in the bed. She was clad only in a little pair of red panties and he in a pair of briefs, but as they came together their naked skin warmed with the intimate contact.

He tangled his hands in her luxurious hair as he kissed her hungrily. She returned his kiss with a fever of her own, her tongue swirling with his as she pressed her naked breasts against his chest.

It didn't take long for Jack to want more than kissing. He rolled her over on her back and captured the tip of one of her breasts in his mouth. Gasping with pleasure, she writhed beneath him.

He laved first one nipple, then the other, fired up by the sounds she made as he cupped her breasts and made love to them.

She didn't remain a passive partner. Her hands roamed his body. She clutched his shoulders, then smoothed her palms down the length of his back.

Jack had forgotten the wonder of human touch, of body heat shared. But that wonder all came rushing back as their foreplay grew more intimate.

Smoothing his hand down the flat of her stomach, his heart pumped fast and furious. As he reached the waist of her panties, he felt her catch her breath.

He glanced at her, and her eyes glowed almost feral in the splash of illumination from the lamp. He held her gaze as he pressed his hand against her panties, her heat radiating out from the wispy material.

Even though he knew she was turned on, he sensed that she was holding back. He wanted her mindless. He wanted that control to shatter, wanted her to go to the place where there was nothing in the world but him and what they were sharing.

He caressed her through the panties, and a low moan escaped her lips as she thrust her hips upward to meet his touch.

Jack was quickly reaching the end of his own control. He grabbed hold of the sides of her panties and pulled them down. She aided him by rising up, her eyes filled with urgency.

He pulled off his own briefs and tossed them to the floor, then gathered her back in his arms for another soul-searing kiss.

As he kissed her, she reached down and closed her fingers around his arousal. The intimate touch nearly undid him. He grabbed her wrist. "Don't," he said in a raw whisper. "If you touch me for another second it will all be over."

Her eyes flared slightly, and she pulled her hand away from him as he once again began to caress her intimately. He moved his fingers against her moist heat, wanting her to tumble off the edge of reason, fall into the place where thought wasn't possible.

"Let go," he said softly. "Marisa, just let go."

She gasped and closed her eyes, and he felt her relaxing, welcoming his touch without reservation.

It didn't take long before her body began to tense and her breathing grew ragged. She arched her hips, and he felt the wave of release that shuddered through her.

Before she had a chance to recover he moved between her thighs. Her eyes opened and she looked up at him, but by the wild glaze there he knew she wasn't seeing him. She was lost in the sensual pleasure, and as he entered her, he let go of the last of his own control.

Chapter 10

Marisa awoke first. The faint glow of dawn crept into the window as she lay spooned against Jack. One of his arms was flung across her waist, and for just one sleepy moment she felt at peace and she felt loved.

Illusion, she told herself. Still, she didn't move, unwilling to break this magical spell until it was absolutely necessary.

Making love with Jack had been beyond anything she'd imagined. She'd expected passion. She'd anticipated fast and hot and wild. What she hadn't expected was his tenderness.

And there had been a wealth of tenderness. She

closed her eyes, her head still filled with thoughts of Jack.

She recognized that the hard-rocking, headbanging drummer that he'd once been had been a facade. The real Jack Cortland was a sensitive man who cared deeply about family and friends and perhaps maybe a little bit about her.

But she had no illusions about what had occurred between them the night before. It had been sex. Nothing more, nothing less. It had been an explosion of the sexual tension that had existed between them from the moment they'd met.

Jack wasn't in love with her. He might love her for what she was doing for him—and for the boys. But there was a difference between loving somebody and being in love with somebody.

She was in love with Jack, in a way she'd never been with Tom in college, but she had a terrible feeling that ultimately this all would eventually end in her heartbreak.

One day at a time, she told herself. Her days would be filled with taking care of Mick and David and building the business she'd dreamed of owning. And her nights—she wasn't sure where she'd be spending them, although she knew where she wanted to be…right here beside Jack.

His hands smoothed down the outside of her thigh, letting her know he was awake. "Good morning," he whispered against the back of her neck, his warm breath sending a shiver of pleasure through her.

She told herself she should get up and get out of his arms, but she remained where she was as she murmured a good-morning back to him.

She'd never had a morning with Tom. She'd never awakened in his arms after a night of lovemaking. She'd been nothing more to him than a quick convenience, and she had a feeling that's what she had become with Jack.

This thought drove her out of his arms and out of the bed. She grabbed her robe from the floor and pulled it around her nakedness.

"Gee, I was kind of looking forward to an encore," he said as he sat up.

He looked roguishly appealing with his hair tousled from sleep and a lazy, sexy smile curving his lips. His smile fell as he studied her features in the semidarkness of the room. "Please don't tell me you have morning-after regrets."

"No, no regrets," she replied. It was true; there was no way she could regret making love with him. "I just have a lot of things I want to get done today, and I thought I'd get a head start before the boys got up."

"You going to work on your business venture?" he asked curiously. She nodded and belted her robe more firmly around her waist. His smile fell. "We haven't talked about what you intend to do with your house. Are you planning on selling it?"

She thought of the little bungalow her parents had bought her as a college graduation present. She loved the little house, but if this had been a real marriage she would have sold it in a minute and completely melded her life with that of her husband's.

But this *wasn't* a real marriage, and she wasn't comfortable giving up everything without a crystal ball to see into the future.

"I don't plan on doing anything with it for a while," she replied. "I'm going to go shower. I'll see you in the kitchen in a few minutes." She left the room and went down the hallway to her own bedroom.

Eventually if she remained here with Jack and the boys she'd want some of the things from her house. But even though she'd made a commitment to remain here, in the back of her mind she couldn't help but feel that this whole arrangement was temporary. Keeping her house was a safety net in case everything fell apart.

The morning passed as always with Jack out on the ranch with his men and Marisa entertaining the boys and taking care of some of the housework. It was Saturday so they were on their own for meals. Breakfast was cereal, lunch was sandwiches and Marisa had ambitious plans to make spaghetti sauce for dinner.

It was when the boys went down for a nap that Jack told her he was going over to Kent's to have a talk.

"Good, I'm glad," she replied as she sank down onto the sofa.

He frowned thoughtfully. "I keep thinking about how it was when I moved back here after the divorce. I was in bad shape, and if it wasn't for Kent I'm not sure I would have survived." He leaned against the chair, and his gray eyes gazed at her thoughtfully. "What about your friends, Marisa? I don't ever hear you talking on the phone with anyone except your aunt and occasionally your parents."

"After I lost the baby, I pretty much withdrew from everyone." Emotion swelled in her chest as she remembered those dark days after the miscarriage. "I went through a period of mourning followed by a depression."

She pulled her legs up beneath her and leaned her head back against the cushion. "My friends didn't seem to understand that this wasn't something I could just put behind me, and they weren't comfortable with my grief. By the time I graduated from college I'd pretty well isolated myself, then I immediately began to work as a nanny. That kept me too busy to miss any of my friends."

She smiled at him, wanting to take away the frown that tugged his eyebrows low. "Don't look so worried, Jack. I'm relatively well-adjusted, and I'm open to the possibility of making new friends. Go on, get out of here and make peace with your friend."

"I shouldn't be too long," he said as he headed for the front door.

"Take whatever time you need. I'm going to do a little work on the computer, then see about making a pot of the best spaghetti you've ever eaten."

He grinned at her. "Sounds great. I'll see you later. Don't forget to set the alarm after I leave."

The minute he went out the door she pulled herself off the sofa and reset the alarm, then returned to her bedroom, where her laptop was plugged in.

She'd just started working on a Web site for her nanny agency when Jack had first hired her, and she eagerly dove back into it now. She tinkered with it for a half hour before the boys awakened from their naps.

As they played in the living room she made a call to the newspaper to place an ad for young women interested in becoming nannies, then joined the boys in the middle of the floor for playtime.

They were in the process of building a fort from several empty cardboard boxes when there was a knock on the door.

She looked out to see Patrick standing on the porch. What was he doing here? As she reached for the doorknob the ring that Jack had placed on her finger sparkled in the sunlight.

"Patrick." She greeted him with a cautious smile. "What a surprise."

"Hi, Marisa. I just thought I'd stop by and see

how you were getting along." He hesitated a moment, then offered her a smile. "Can I come in?"

She opened the door wider to allow him inside. "Come on into the living room. We were just in the process of building a fort."

Mick and David barely paid attention to Patrick as they colored the boxes in shades of brown and black.

"I miss you, Marisa," Patrick said. "I've given you a little time, and I was hoping that maybe you changed your mind about me…about us."

Marisa drew a deep breath. She had to tell him about marrying Jack, but she had to make a fast decision about what, exactly, she intended to tell him.

For some reason her pride wouldn't allow her to tell him the truth, that she and Jack had made a business arrangement for the sake of the two little boys who were now coloring their fort with purple and red crayons.

"Patrick, I'm sorry. I haven't changed my mind. In fact, as crazy as it sounds, I've fallen in love with Jack, and he's fallen in love with me. Last week we got married."

For a moment he looked stunned. "Wow, that was really fast. Are you sure you haven't made a mistake?"

"Positive," she replied without hesitation. "I've never been happier." The minute the words left her mouth she knew they were true. She had no idea how long this happiness would last, but she intended to embrace it for as long as it existed.

"Then I guess I'm happy for you," he said with a tight smile.

She relaxed. "Thanks."

"Well, then I guess I should get out of here." He headed for the door then paused and turned back to her. "I've heard Jack has a whole bunch of Creation memorabilia in the barn. Do you think I could take a peek at it?"

Marisa remembered him telling her that he'd once been a fan. "I guess it would be all right. I don't think Jack would mind. Boys, you want to go to the barn for a few minutes?" Just as she expected, the two raced to her side.

"Mick and David, you remember Patrick," Marisa said.

The boys murmured hellos, and Patrick raised a dark eyebrow. "Mick and David, as in Jagger and Bowie?"

She smiled. "That's right. Apparently Candace was a big fan of the legendary rock idols. Come on, let's take a walk."

The four of them left the house, the boys jumping and skipping with boyish energy. "I don't know how you keep up with them," Patrick exclaimed. There was a suppressed impatience to his tone that made her think perhaps Patrick wasn't so fond of children.

They would have never had a chance for a future together, she thought. One way or another children would have always been a big part of her life.

Neither Sam nor Max were in sight as they reached the barn. She figured the two were out someplace on the acreage. Jack had told her they were mending a section of fence almost two miles from the house.

The barn door creaked open, and the four of them entered. Patrick gasped in amazement. "My God, I'd heard rumors that he had a bunch of stuff in here, but this is amazing."

Marisa smiled as she watched him move around the room. David headed directly to the drums, and Mick found the dolls that he'd played with the last time they had been inside the building.

As he began to bang on the cymbal, Patrick winced. "Can you make him stop that?" he said, a touch of irritation in his voice.

Marisa looked at Patrick in surprise. She was definitely seeing a side of him she didn't find attractive. "David, come here, honey," she said, but he ignored her.

"Hey, I've got an idea," Patrick said. He pulled a chair in front of him and smiled at Marisa. "Why don't we play a game of cops and robbers?" He reached into his pocket and pulled out a small revolver. "Sit down, Marisa," he said, all attempt at levity gone.

She stared at him in incomprehension. "What are you doing? Patrick, what's going on?" Her heart thumped painfully hard in her chest.

"I said sit down," he replied. "You don't want me to get angry and upset the kids."

She sank down on the chair, almost hypnotized by the weapon in his hand. "Is this about me breaking up with you?" she asked.

"Don't be stupid," he exclaimed as he pulled a length of rope from his pocket. "Hey, boys, let's play a game and tie up Marisa." He leaned closer to her ear. "If you don't cooperate I'll kill them both."

The low menace in his voice coupled with the hard glaze of his eyes made her believe him and her blood ran cold. "Patrick, please. Jack is going to be home at any moment. I don't understand. Why are you doing this?"

As he began to bind her hands behind her, the boys came to stand nearby, watching as Patrick tied her to the chair.

"Jack won't be home anytime soon," he said. "My partner will make sure he doesn't arrive here until it's too late."

He didn't speak again until both her hands and feet were bound to the chair. As he stepped back from her she tried to pull her hands free, but there was no give in the rope.

"Patrick, why are you doing this?" She tried to keep her voice as calm as possible, not wanting to frighten Mick and David, who were watching the two of them with widened eyes.

He drew himself up straight and proud. "My name isn't Patrick. Over the years I've had lots of names and lots of identities, but my real name is Paz Marquez. It was my father who found the diamond, The Tears of the Quetzal. It should have belonged to him, but Joseph Rothchild, Harold's father, found out about it."

Paz's handsome face twisted into a mask of hatred so intense it nearly stole Marisa's breath away. "Joseph killed my father. He buried him alive in a cave and walked away with the diamond. I got it back from Candace the night I murdered her, but it slipped through my fingers once again…and I've been targeting the Rothchilds ever since."

Marisa gasped. He'd killed before. He'd killed Candace. And clearly he was responsible for those other mysterious acts against the family that had been splashed all over the tabloids. Her sense of danger rose dramatically as fear lodged in her throat.

"I finally got it back." He smiled, and it was a cruel, hard gesture. "It's back where it belongs in my possession."

"Patrick, I had nothing to do with any of this. The boys had nothing to do with it. Let us go." Her voice trembled with terror.

"The boys have *everything* to do with this," he replied, seething anger still rife in his voice. "Right,

Mick? Right, David?" He cast the boys a friendly smile. "I figure they're worth at least a million a piece. Their grandfather is easily capable of paying that, and it's the least of what he owes me."

The blood that had been cold inside her turned even icier. "Patrick, you have the Rothchild ring. Isn't that enough? You have the diamond you said belonged to your father."

"No, it's not enough." His hands tightened into fists at his sides. "I want the Rothchilds' blood. I want their tears. I want them to know the kind of pain I've known because of them."

She struggled against the ropes as a deep sob wrenched from her. She had to do something. She had to save the boys.

The only thing she could do was scream and hope that either Sam or Max might hear her cry. The shriek that ripped out of her came from her soul. She never saw it coming, but she felt the crashing blow that landed on the side of her head…then nothing.

Pain brought her back to consciousness, an excruciating pain in her skull that made her feel nauseous.

As she opened her eyes she realized two things had changed. There was now duct tape plastered across her mouth, and the boys were nowhere in sight.

Dear God, where was Mick and David? What had he done with them? With a new fervor she pulled against the ropes that held her tight in the chair.

"Ah, I see you're back." Patrick stood in front of her, a large red can held in his hand.

Frantically she struggled to get free, screaming into the tape with a growing sense of horror. She cried out as the chair toppled to its side with her still bound to it. She lay with the side of her face pressed against the ground, and tears began to burn in her eyes.

"It's been nice knowing you, Marisa," Patrick said from someplace behind her. "Those two little boys are my ticket to wealth. Unfortunately you're worth nothing. Still, I'm hoping your death will make both Jack and Harold shed a tear or two."

She realized at that moment that it wasn't money that drove Paz, it was a rage-driven need for revenge. She heard the splash of liquid and instantly smelled the odor of gasoline. Fire! He intended to set her on fire.

The scent of the gasoline grew stronger as he continued to splash the liquid around the perimeter of the barn.

Marisa tried desperately to get herself untied, but it was a futile effort. Her wrists and ankles burned, and the fumes from the fuel were almost overwhelming.

Mick! David! Her heart cried out. She felt little fear for herself as her concentration was on the two little boys she'd grown to love with all her heart.

Jack, where are you? Come save your babies! Come save me!

"I guess this is goodbye, Marisa," Patrick said from behind her. She heard the strike of a match, then the loud whoosh of flames. The barn door slammed shut, leaving her alone with the fire that within seconds burned with a crackling heat.

Smoke billowed around her, making it difficult for her to see, almost impossible for her to breathe. She coughed and choked against the gag, and her lungs felt as if they were about to explode.

Dark shadows closed in, obscuring her vision altogether as unconsciousness reached out to her. Her last conscious thought was the bitter regret that somehow she'd brought a monster to Jack's door.

Chapter 11

It had taken a week for Rita to learn that Patrick Moore, the man Marisa had been dating, didn't exist.

She'd begun to get suspicious about him when she'd realized the last time she'd seen the ring had been just before he and Marisa had come over for dinner.

Rita knew her niece would never enter her office, and certainly would never take something that didn't belong to her. But she couldn't help but recall that Patrick had left the two women while they'd been clearing the dishes, supposedly to go to the bathroom, and gut instinct warned her that Patrick might have stolen the ring. However, she was still trying to wrap her brain around how he could have discovered where the ring was stashed and how he'd managed to seize it from a locked gun safe. This was clearly the work of a professional…

Yesterday she'd called the accounting agency where she knew Patrick worked, only to discover that he had quit his job there two weeks before. She'd gotten an address from them and had gone to the location late last night, only to discover that it was an empty lot on the outskirts of town.

While she stood on that vacant lot, a new fear had gripped her. Who was Patrick Moore, and why would he have a false address? It was something a criminal would do.

Rita had tried to call Marisa a few minutes ago to see if she could give her any information that might lead Rita to the young man's real identity or home address, but there had been no answer at Cortland's house.

Rita needed to recover that ring. Her career depended on it. But, more than that, she needed to alert Marisa that Patrick Moore wasn't the wonderful man they'd thought he was.

She had a sick feeling in her heart, one that usually portended something bad about to happen. She picked up the phone and dialed the Cortland ranch again. This time she just needed to check to make sure that Marisa was all right.

She sighed in frustration when there was still no

answer. She grabbed her keys and headed for her apartment door, unable to just sit still and do nothing.

She'd start with the accounting agency and see what Patrick's associates could tell her about the man that might lead to his whereabouts and the truth of his real identity.

"I really need to get back home," Jack said for the third time in the past fifteen minutes. He'd already been at Kent's for over an hour and a half. What had begun as a healing of the rift between the two men had transformed into a walk down memory lane.

"Hey, remember that time we played that gig in Riverside and the owner of the place paid us in beer?" Kent asked, obviously not ready to call a halt to the conversation.

Jack stood from the chair where he'd been sitting in Kent's tiny living room. "Yeah, I remember. We were all underage, and we ended up drunk for the next two days. Kent, I really gotta go. I need to get home to the kids."

Kent glanced at his watch and then stood as well. "Okay, I guess if you have to take off…"

"I really do," Jack replied.

"Hey, man, thanks for coming by," Kent said as the two of them stepped out on the front porch. "I really felt bad about our argument. I wish I knew who was feeding Harold information, but you should know I'd never do anything to hurt you." He held out a hand, and Jack gripped it in a firm handshake.

Minutes later as Jack headed back home, he still wasn't sure that he trusted Kent. Certainly Kent had mouthed all the right words, proclaiming his innocence with a resounding fervor, but Jack wasn't sure if it was just an act.

He realized that until he knew the truth of who Harold was talking to, the only thing he and Marisa could do was make certain nothing bad happened. If a mole had nothing to talk about, then he'd have to remain silent.

His thoughts turned to Marisa and what they had shared the night before. It had been amazing. They had fit together as naturally as if they'd been made for one another. Even now, just thinking about it, he felt himself getting aroused.

She had transformed his life and he would forever be grateful to her for all that she had done.

But the feeling that filled his heart when he thought about her had little to do with gratitude. He cared about her. He loved to see the light of a smile dance on her lips and shine from her eyes. The sound of her laughter filled him with a warmth he hadn't felt for a very long time.

Still, he wasn't convinced she was in his life for the long-term. If he needed any evidence of that it was the fact that she wasn't willing to give up her house. She was hedging her bets, making certain she had a fast and easy escape route if things went bad.

Funny how the thought of her not being in his home, in his life, filled him with regret.

He loved what she had done with his boys, but more than that he loved what she had done for him. She'd made him believe he could be the kind of man he wanted to be. She'd given him the confidence to not only embrace parenthood but also to hold close to who he was at his very core.

He saw the smoke as he turned onto the long gravel road that led to his ranch. It billowed upward, a dark gray snake slithering up in the sky.

His heart seemed to stop in his chest as he realized it was his barn that was on fire. He tromped on the accelerator and squealed to a halt in front of the burning building.

Sam and Max were already there with garden hoses spewing ineffectual sprays of water.

"Call the fire department," Jack yelled as he leaped out of his car.

"Already did," Sam replied above the roar of the flames.

Jack didn't give a damn about anything that was in the barn. It was just stuff from his past, things that no longer really mattered to him. But as he thought about how much Mick loved those stupid dolls and David adored the cymbals, he decided to try to get inside and at least retrieve those items.

He grabbed the garden hose from Sam's hand and sprayed himself down. Once he was soaking wet, he burst through the barn doors.

Visibility was next to nothing, and smoke seared his lungs as he raced toward the box where the dolls were kept. It was then that he saw her. Marisa—tied to an overturned chair and still as death.

He cried out in horror and raced to her. A million thoughts raced through his head. What was she doing out here? Who had tied her to the chair?

Overhead the fire raged, and the ominous sound of cracking wood made him realize the roof was about to collapse at any minute.

Instead of taking the time to try to untie her, he made the split-second decision to grab the chair with both hands and dragged it and her toward the door.

Don't be dead. Please don't be dead. The mantra went around and around in his brain as he struggled to get her out of the barn.

He nearly sobbed in relief as he pulled her out into the fresh air and her eyes opened. She began to cough, choking against the duct tape that rode across her lips.

He yanked off the tape, then straightened and looked back at the barn. *The boys. Oh, God, were the boys inside?* Once again his heart felt as if it stopped beating altogether.

"Marisa, are the boys in the barn?" he asked, his heart pounding so loudly he was afraid he might not hear her reply.

A breath whooshed out of him as she shook her head violently. But the relief was short-lived as she clutched him by the arm. "They're gone, Jack. He took them." Once again she was overcome by a spasm of coughing.

In the distance came the sound of sirens drawing closer. Jack leaned down to Marisa, the knot in his chest so tight he could scarcely draw a breath. "Who? Who has the boys, Marisa?"

Tears washed down her smoke-blackened face. "Patrick. Oh, God, Jack. I'm sorry. I'm so sorry." She began to sob as the fire engines pulled up in front of the barn and Jack's cell phone vibrated from his shirt pocket.

He straightened and walked back to his car as he pulled the phone out. The caller ID displayed the caller as anonymous.

"Cortland," he said as he got into his car and shut the door, grateful that the fire trucks had cut their sirens.

"I have your boys. If you go to the police I will kill them. If you talk to anyone in law enforcement, I will kill them. Do you understand?" Patrick's voice was deep and chilling.

Jack wanted to reach through the phone and kill him. He tamped down the rage, knowing that his sons' lives hung in the balance. "I understand. What do you want?"

"Two million dollars."

Jack barked a humorless laugh. "I don't have that kind of money. Don't you remember, I'm an old has-been who blew his cash on drugs and alcohol."

"You might not have it, but you can get it," Patrick replied.

"And how am I supposed to do that?"

"Harold Rothchild will be happy to pay that for the return of his grandchildren. I'll give you until nine o'clock this evening to get it together. I'll be in touch."

The line went dead.

Jack dropped the phone back into his pocket and gripped the steering wheel with both hands. Outside his car, chaos reigned. The firemen were losing the battle with the blazing barn, and Marisa was seated with an oxygen mask over her mouth and nose.

But the scene happening before his eyes had nothing on the drama that unfolded in his head. Mick and David were in danger, and tears stung his eyes as he thought of his precious sons.

His first impulse was to call the police, but as he replayed Patrick's menacing voice in his head he feared the consequences of that particular action. There had been an edge in Patrick's tone that had let Jack know he was capable of harming the boys.

Jack got out of the car and hurried over to Marisa, who pulled the mask off her face and burst into tears as he approached.

He pulled her up off the ground and into his arms,

knowing the particular kind of torture she must be going through.

"I'm sorry. I'm so sorry," she sobbed against his chest. "I couldn't stop him. He said he wanted to see some of your things from your band days. I never thought... I never imagined. He pulled a gun, and there was nothing I could do."

"Shh, it's all right," Jack said as he rubbed her back. "You need to pull yourself together, Marisa, and tell me everything that happened. You need to tell me everything he said."

Maybe he'd said something to her that would provide a clue as to where he had the boys.

She raised her head and looked at him, her brown eyes filled with torment. "He killed Candace, Jack. He told me that he killed her."

Ice rolled through Jack's veins. "Go get in my car," he said to her. "I'll be right there." As she headed for the vehicle he walked over to the fire chief. The fire was still burning, but it was obvious the barn was a complete loss.

Jack told the man in charge that he had to leave but would be in touch in the next day or two. Then he hurried back to his car where Marisa awaited him.

As he started the car Marisa began to tell him everything that had happened from the moment Patrick had appeared on the doorstep.

Jack's blood was cold as ice by the time she

finished telling him everything that lunatic had said. "Where does Patrick live?" he asked her.

"I don't know. He always came to my place." She wrapped her arms around her stomach, as if she were physically ill. "Are you going to call the police?"

"Patrick called me a few minutes ago. He told me he has the boys and if I contact the police he'll kill them." He gripped the steering wheel so tightly he feared he might snap it in half. "I believe him. I'm going to have to take my chances without any police reinforcement."

"He said he had a partner, Jack, and that partner would make sure you didn't get home too quickly. It has to be Kent," she said.

The flames that lit inside Jack's stomach were hotter than the ones that had consumed his barn as he thought of how Kent had stalled him again and again from leaving his place.

If he was going to find his boys, then it was possible the answer was with Kent. He tore down the highway toward Kent's place, the rage inside him building to mammoth proportions.

If anything happened to his boys and Kent had anything to do with it, then Jack would kill him. It was as simple as that.

He pulled up in front of Kent's small farmhouse, and as he got out of the car he was aware of Marisa shadowing just behind him.

The burn in his gut flamed hotter and when Kent opened the door, Jack swung his fist and punched him in the nose. Kent fell backward as blood blossomed and trickled from his nostrils.

"What the hell?" He scrambled to his feet and backed away as Jack came at him again.

"Where are my sons?" Jack roared. He would have hit the man again if Marisa hadn't grabbed on to his arm and held tight.

"I don't know what you're talking about," Kent yelled as he fumbled in his back pocket for a handkerchief. He pressed it against his nose and tried to look belligerent but Jack smelled fear.

"Patrick told me you were his partner just before he tried to burn me alive," Marisa said as her fingers bit into Jack's arm. "He killed Candace, Kent. Your partner is a murderer."

Kent's eyes widened and a gasp exploded out of him. "Nobody was supposed to get hurt," he said. "He promised me that nobody would get hurt."

"What have you done, Kent?" The words came from Jack in a tortured whisper.

"It was supposed to be easy. Just grab the kids, get the ransom then finally live on easy street for the rest of my life," Kent said.

"Why would you do something like this to me?" Jack asked as he stared at the man who was supposed to be his best friend.

Kent took a step backward from him, and his

eyes darkened with a hint of anger. "Because you left me behind. The whole time we were kids we talked about going to L.A. and building a band. Then you took off by yourself and never thought about me again. You had it all, and you left me here with nothing." His voice rose on the last few words. "Damn you, Jack. You just left me behind."

Jack stared at him in stunned surprise. This was about jealousy? "I don't have time for this. Where did he take my boys?"

"I don't know. He was supposed to call me when he had them, but I haven't heard from him." Kent pulled the bloodied handkerchief from his nose.

Jack wanted to smash him in the face again, but instead he whirled on his heels, grabbed Marisa's hand and raced back to his car.

"What do we do now?" Marisa asked as he pulled his cell phone out of his pocket.

"I've got to call Harold. I need two million dollars from him."

"When this is all over, he'll try to take the boys from you." Marisa's voice was a tortured whisper.

"Probably," he agreed and fought a wave of fear so intense it brought a mist of tears to his eyes. "But it's a risk I have to take."

He punched in the number for his ex-father-in-law, and when Harold answered his phone Jack explained to him what had happened and what he needed from him.

When he hung up he turned to Marisa and stared at her with a hollowness he'd never felt before. It was as if he were already grieving a loss too enormous to comprehend.

Marisa must have seen something in his eyes that spoke of the depth of his despair. She placed a hand on his forearm. "Don't give up, Jack. Mick and David need you to stay strong. Patrick wants money. Once he has what he wants he'll let them go."

"I hope you're right," he said. He started the car and pulled away from Kent's. Once he had his boys back safe and sound he would see to it that Kent spent the rest of his life behind bars. Right now all he cared about were his babies.

If anything happened to his boys, then there was no place on earth that Kent or Patrick could hide. Jack would make it his mission in life to find them and destroy them.

Harold Rothchild was a handsome man. His snow-white hair was in stark contrast to the black suit he wore with a casual elegance.

He'd arrived at Jack's moments ago with two large suitcases. He'd shown no emotion when Jack had introduced Marisa as his wife.

During the time that they'd waited for him to arrive Marisa had taken a quick shower, washing off the soot and ash that had covered her. As she'd stood beneath the spray of water she'd wept with fear for Mick and David. She'd cried uncontrollably for Jack.

Jack spent the first few minutes after Harold's arrival telling the tall, lean man what had happened in the past couple hours. Harold said nothing but his piercing blue gaze never left Jack's face.

They were all seated at the dining-room table, Jack's cell phone in front of him as he waited for another call from Patrick.

"Patrick Moore." Harold frowned as he said the name. "He's a dead man and doesn't even know it yet."

With everything that had happened since Jack had pulled her from the fire, Marisa suddenly remembered what Patrick had told her about his real identity.

"His name isn't really Patrick Moore," she said. Both men turned to look at her. "I just remembered, he told me his name was Paz…Paz Martin or Martinez."

"Paz Marquez." Harold's voice was flat as he stared at Marisa.

"Yes, that's it," she replied. "He said something about a diamond and his father being murdered."

Harold leaned back in the chair, his face turning the shade of ash. "This isn't about money. It's about revenge. It's about that damned diamond." He reached a hand up and rubbed his forehead, as if a headache had suddenly made itself known.

"What are you talking about? Who is Paz Marquez?" Jack asked.

"Antonio Marquez, Paz's father, found the diamond that we now know as The Tears of the Quetzal." Some of the natural color began to return to Harold's face. "He didn't turn it over to my father like he was supposed to but rather pocketed it and quit his job. My father found out about it, and one night he met Antonio in the mine, retrieved the diamond from him, then buried him alive." He bowed his head, looking as if he carried the weight of the world on his shoulders. "I was just a kid, but I was there and saw it happen. I never told anyone, and now it appears I'm paying for my silence."

He reached up and straightened his black and silver tie, as if finding comfort in the small gesture. Marisa noticed that his hands shook slightly.

"I tried to make it right," he continued. "As soon as I was old enough I began sending money to Paz's mother, Juanita. Because of my father she was left a widow with three small children. I arranged for her to move to Arizona and start a new life. I thought it would be enough."

"Apparently it wasn't," Jack replied.

Harold offered him a tight smile. "I always thought it would be you who did something stupid and put those boys at risk. I never dreamed it would be me who brought danger to them."

"It doesn't matter now," Jack replied. "It's just

important that you and I work together to bring the boys home."

Marisa turned her head to stare out the window. The emergency equipment had been carted away, and the barn was nothing but a pile of rubble. Dusk was falling and the coming of night terrified her.

Where was David? Where was Mick? Were they afraid? Were they crying out for her?

Her heart ached with the need to have David and Mick back in her arms. In the short span of time that she'd been in their lives they had crawled so deeply into her heart that she felt as if she'd given birth to both of them.

It wasn't just thoughts of the boys that shattered her heart. As she looked across the table at Jack she wanted to weep with his pain.

He looked as if he'd been shot in the gut and couldn't staunch the bleeding. His face was an unhealthy shade of pale, and his eyes were feverish shards of pain.

The evening passed in a torturous tick of the clock. Each minute felt like an eternity as they waited for Patrick to make contact.

Marisa made sandwiches that nobody ate and coffee that they all consumed with alacrity as they waited for the call that would hopefully bring the boys home.

Home. That's what Marisa had begun to think of this place with Jack and the boys. Since their whirlwind marriage she'd been happier than she'd ever been in her life.

Even though she'd known better she'd begun to have dreams about their future. She'd fantasized about school carnivals and baseball games, about family outings and laughter. Always in those fantasies she and Jack were proud parents who not only loved the boys but also each other.

But they were just fantasies, and she knew without question that no matter what happened tonight the fantasy was coming to an end.

Even if the boys were returned safe and sound, she had a feeling that Harold would fight Jack for them, and in Jack's current frame of mind, she wasn't sure he would fight back.

The knot that filled her chest at telling them all goodbye was as painful as her gasps for breath when she'd been inside the burning barn.

It wasn't just the boys that she would miss. It was Jack. She'd known in the first five minutes of meeting him that he was the kind of man who could own her heart. She'd tried to keep herself distant from him but to no avail. He'd ingrained himself so deeply into her heart then when she finally would have to leave, she would leave a piece of herself behind with him forever.

She'd just gotten up for the coffeepot to refill their cups when Jack's cell phone rang. For a moment it was as if everyone in the room froze.

Marisa's heart beat so loudly in her head she wondered if she'd only imagined the ring of the phone. It was only when Jack leaped forward and grabbed the cell phone that she realized it really had rung.

"Cortland," he snapped.

The tension in the room was so intense it made Marisa's stomach churn. She'd grieved long and hard for a baby she'd never held, a baby who had never drawn a breath of air. She couldn't imagine grieving for Mick and David. The pain was simply too unbearable.

"I've got the money," Jack said. "I want to talk to my boys." He rose from the table with such force his chair crashed to the floor behind him. "Damn it, you put Mick on so I can talk to him."

His angry features instantly transformed to something softer. "Hey, Mick. Are you okay, buddy? Don't worry—Daddy is going to come for you, okay?"

Marisa could tell the moment Patrick got back on the phone as a hard mask of rage replaced the tenderness on Jack's face.

"Just tell me where to meet you and I'll be there with the money," Jack said. "Yeah…yeah, all right. I got it." His eyes narrowed to dangerous slits. "And, Patrick, if either of those boys has so much as a scratch then I'll kill you." He hung up the phone.

"Where?" Harold asked, his features as ferocious as Jack's.

"Eleven o'clock tonight behind the old King's Inn casino downtown," Jack replied.

"Shouldn't we go to the police?" Marisa asked, afraid that something was going to go terribly wrong. She knew the location of King's Inn. It had been a dive where some of the locals had gone to gamble, but three months ago it had been closed down.

"No, no cops," Harold said, and Jack quickly echoed the sentiment.

"But what about Kent? Shouldn't he be arrested as an accomplice?" she asked. "For all we know he's already left town."

"We'll get him," Harold replied. "He's a stupid man who would sell out a friend for the price of a six-pack of beer." He looked at Jack. "I imagine you know that it was Kent who was keeping me apprised of what was going on here with you and the boys."

"Yeah, it's amazing when you realize who you can't trust in your life," Jack said. His gaze sought Marisa's and he smiled. "And it's equally amazing when you realize who you can trust."

Rather than make her feel better, the smile shot an icy chill through Marisa. If anything happened to Mick and David she would be devastated, but she knew in her heart, in her very soul, that the man she loved would be completely destroyed.

Chapter 12

Jack drove slowly down the street toward the old King's Inn casino. The downtown area that most people visited was the Fremont Street Experience, five blocks of casinos and restaurants beneath a large barrel canopy with light shows to enthrall the crowd.

There was a seedier Las Vegas downtown, where small casinos served a desperate crowd and drug addicts lingered in the shadows. Pimps and prostitutes yelled to passing cars, and pickpockets and muggers lay in wait for an unwary out-of-towner.

It was to that area that Jack drove.

He was alone in his car with two million dollars

in cash and was hoping—praying—that Patrick had enough morality left not to harm his boys.

More than a touch of fear rode with him in the car. The terror burned in his heart that beat with enough adrenaline to fuel a football team in a championship game.

Harold had insisted that he was coming along, but Jack had refused to allow him to ride with him. Patrick had demanded that Jack come alone, and he wasn't about to break the rules of a game where Mick and David were the trophies.

It was agreed that Harold and Marisa would follow him and park a block away from the rendezvous and wait for Jack to get the kids.

Jack knew the boys would want Marisa. They would need her loving arms wrapped around them and assuring them that everything was all right. Truth be told there had been moments in the long night of waiting where Jack had needed her arms around him.

As he pulled into the deserted parking lot behind the abandoned building that had once been a casino he glanced at his watch. He was fifteen minutes early.

He parked the car and turned out his headlights, then took a quick survey of his surroundings. An old trash Dumpster sat against the back of the building, barely discernible in the darkness. Other than that there was nothing in the area.

The streetlights from in front of the building barely pierced the darkness back here. Tension screamed inside him as he glanced at his watch once again.

He rolled down his window to allow in the stifling July night air, but the heat couldn't begin to melt the icy center inside him.

He touched the butt of the revolver on the seat next to him. There was no way he'd put himself in this kind of position without bringing a weapon. He had no intention of using it unless it was to save his own life. The last thing he wanted was to try to be a hero and wind up turning a volatile situation into something worse.

As far as he was concerned Patrick could have Harold's money as long as he returned Mick and David unharmed.

Money could be replaced.

Little boys could not.

He looked at his watch once again, apprehension roiling inside him. He had no idea from which direction Patrick would come so he swiveled his head in all directions as he waited.

"Don't take them away from me," he whispered. "I've only just learned to do it all right. Don't let it all be for nothing." Jack had never been an overly religious man, but he prayed now, hoping that God heard his prayers.

He was well aware of the fact that Harold would

probably push for custody when this was all over. Jack would fight him with every breath in his body. In his heart, Jack truly believed that those boys belonged with him.

And for the first time he recognized that he'd become the man he'd finally wanted to be—the man his parents would be proud of, the man Marisa had known was inside him.

He straightened in his seat as a car without its headlights on slid around the building and parked facing his. For several agonizing moments nothing happened.

A throb of tension beat at the base of Jack's skull, and his hands grew slick with sweat on the steering wheel.

Suddenly the car's high beams came on, half blinding Jack.

The driver door opened and Patrick stepped out. The headlights gleamed on the metal of the gun in his hand. Jack grabbed the revolver from the passenger seat and opened his door as well.

As he got out of his car he smoothly shoved the revolver into his waistband in the small of his back. "Where are my boys?" Jack asked harshly.

"First things first," Patrick replied. "Throw your weapon on the ground," he demanded. Jack hesitated. "Come on, Cortland, I know you wouldn't be stupid enough to show up here unarmed. Now toss it and we can get this over with. Slow and easy. Don't make me get nervous. Trust me, you don't want me nervous."

There was no way Jack intended to take a chance. He didn't want to piss off Patrick. He just wanted to get his sons and walk away.

With a slow movement he reached behind him and grabbed the revolver, then bent down and placed it on the oily pavement and scooted it away with his foot. It clattered and came to rest several feet from where Jack stood.

"Where are my boys?" he asked again.

"I told you, first things first. Where's the money?"

"Two suitcases in the backseat of my car," Jack replied.

"Get them out."

Jack did as he was instructed and pulled the two heavy cases from the backseat of his car. The fact that he didn't see the boys in Patrick's car worried him. He hoped they were there, perhaps asleep in the back.

"Now, bring them halfway to me."

"First tell me where Mick and David are," Jack countered.

"They're in a safe place, and I'll tell you exactly where they are once I have the money."

"How do I know I can trust you?" Jack asked.

Patrick's teeth gleamed white as he smiled. "Well, now, I guess you really don't know."

The red wash of rage threatened to take over Jack, but he tamped it down. He'd never wanted to hurt a man so much, but he realized in this drama he was powerless to do anything but what Patrick asked of him. The stakes were too high for him to gamble in any way.

As he carried the cases forward, his heart beat so frantically he thought he might be on the verge of a heart attack. A thousand thoughts raced through his head. His heart didn't just beat frantically for himself but also for Marisa.

She'd already suffered an enormous loss in her life, and she'd loved the boys enough to give up her personal freedom, to bind her life to his in the best interest of the children. If this all went horribly wrong he recognized that he wouldn't be the only one devastated.

He dropped the suitcases where Patrick indicated. "Now step back," Patrick said. The gun remained pointed directly at Jack's chest.

As Jack backed away Patrick moved forward, his dark brown eyes gleaming with triumph, with greed. He knelt to open the first case but kept the gun focused on Jack.

"It's all there," Jack said. "Two million dollars in unmarked bills. Now give me my kids. We had nothing to do with your father's murder."

Patrick's smile fell, and raw emotion shone from his eyes. "So you know who I am."

"Marisa told me. I managed to get her out of the barn. She told me that you're Paz Marquez. Harold's father murdered yours in a mine when you were a boy. This isn't my fight, Paz, and it certainly isn't Mick and David's battle."

Paz's features twisted with rage. "He ruined my life."

"And you killed his daughter. I'd say the score is even."

"It will never be even," Paz exclaimed, the cords of his neck standing out. "Yeah, I killed Candace because I wanted the ring, the ring with the diamond that should have been mine. But Candace's murder was just the beginning. I took it upon myself to make the Rothchilds' life hell ever since I rid the world of Harold's precious little girl."

"How did you manage to evade the cops for so long?" Jack demanded.

"I was a master of disguise…and highly motivated. He smirked. "It wasn't hard to camouflage my identity when I kidnapped Jenna Rothchild and Marisa's aunt. I would have gladly killed them both if that's what it would have taken to get back the ring—but it wasn't necessary." He shrugged. "I knew Rita Perez had the ring, and I knew the easiest way to get close to her was to get close to Marisa. They made it easy for me to take the ring from Rita's apartment."

He was wired, babbling with pride but the gun never wavered in his grip.

"Harold tried to make it right," Jack said, trying to appeal to any reason Paz might possess. "He sent your mother money. He moved you to Arizona so you could have a good life."

"A good life?" Paz spat on the ground. "My mother went through money almost as quickly as she went through men. Harold even had a brief affair with her, which is how I knew that he was the one behind our sudden good fortune." He sneered. "He'd throw us a few dollars and then go back to his multimillion-dollar lifestyle. The score isn't even. It will *never* be even."

"Just give me my kids," Jack said, his voice cracking with his emotion. "You have the diamond ring, and you have the money. What else do you want from me? You want me to beg? I'll beg. For God's sake, just give my kids back to me."

Paz drew a deep breath, as if to calm the rage inside him. "I've been thinking that maybe this is just the down payment," he said.

Down payment? The implication of those words created a red fog inside Jack's brain. "Where are my boys?" he raged as he took a step toward Patrick.

"Get back or I'll shoot you," Patrick yelled as Jack took another step toward him.

Jack heard the sound of the gun, a sharp crack that echoed in his head.

There was a split second when his heart cried out. Not because he believed he was about to die, but rather because he would die without seeing Mick and David's first day of school, he'd miss seeing them become teenagers—become men.

His heart cried not just for his children but for Marisa, whom he now recognized he loved not just as the mother figure to his boys but as the woman he wanted in his life forever.

He tensed, waiting for the killing bullet, but instead he watched in stunned surprise as Patrick crumpled to the ground.

Harold stepped out from around the side of the building, a gun in his hand. "I couldn't let him kill you," he said.

Jack stared at the unmoving Paz with a growing sense of alarm. "Oh, God, what have you done?" Jack raced to the fallen man, vaguely aware that Marisa had joined Harold.

It took only one look to see that Paz was dead. Jack stared down at him with a growing sense of horror. He finally looked at Harold and Marisa. "He didn't tell me where the boys were. I don't know where Mick and David are." His voice cracked once again.

A cry escaped Marisa, and she ran to Paz's car and tore open the back door. "They aren't in here." She began to cry.

"I had to shoot him. Otherwise he would have killed you," Harold said, his voice a mix of anger and fear.

The trunk. Jack stared at the car with a new sense of horror. Was it possible that Paz had put his sons into the trunk of his car?

He leaned down and fumbled in Paz's pockets until he found the car keys. As he approached the trunk the only sound was that of Marisa's sobs.

A roar resounded in his head. Would he open the trunk lid and find them curled up together, not breathing? His hand shook so violently that it took him three stabs before he managed to get the key into the lock.

He opened the trunk and wasn't sure whether to be relieved or devastated. The trunk was empty. "Call the police," he said, his voice sounding as if it came from very far away. Where were his sons? Where in the hell had Paz stashed them?

They were all seated around a large interrogation table in the Las Vegas Metropolitan Police Department. Kent had been picked up and now sat in shackles next to Officer Jeff Cookson, who was trying to make sense of a dead body behind a deserted casino and one of the wealthiest men in the country seated next to him.

Marisa and Jack sat side by side, their hands clasped in a tight grip as they listened to Cookson grill Kent for any clues that might help them locate Mick and David.

An Amber Alert had been issued but so far had

yielded nothing. Officers were out searching the area around the King's Inn casino. It was the middle of the night and David and Mick were out there someplace, alone and hopefully still alive.

Marisa felt Jack's desperation radiating through his hand. It was a desperation she shared.

"I met Patrick in a bar," Kent now said. "We got to drinking and talking, and it wasn't long before he told me how much he hated the Rothchilds and I told him how much I hated Jack."

Kent looked at Jack with narrowed eyes. "We were best friends. You could have changed my life, but you left here and never looked back."

"You could have changed your own life, Kent," Jack replied with a rough edge to his voice. "I was never responsible for you."

They had already learned that it had been Kent who had tried to break in to the ranch. He'd watched the house and had known that Marisa and Jack often stayed up late in the living room talking.

The plan had been for Kent to break in to Marisa's bedroom and steal silently across the hallway to the boys' room. If they'd awakened they wouldn't have been afraid to see Kent. Patrick had been waiting just outside the window of that room to get the boys from Kent.

When that particular plan hadn't worked, Patrick had decided to take care of getting the boys on his own. When Jack had called Kent to make arrangements to meet at Kent's house and talk about their fight, Kent had called Patrick to let him know Marisa and the boys would be alone at the ranch.

As Marisa had listened to him talking about the plot her blood had chilled, something she hadn't thought possible, as her blood was already cold enough to freeze her solid.

What had Patrick done with the boys? Where could he have put them while he went to retrieve his ransom? Were they warm enough? Were they thirsty or hungry? Were they still alive?

Her heart lurched, and she shoved that particular thought away. She had to believe that they were all right. Any thought to the contrary was too difficult to fathom.

"I've told you a million times, I don't know what he did with the boys," Kent exclaimed. "I don't know where he was living or what his exact plan was. We only met in bars or at my place. This isn't my fault. I didn't know he was dangerous."

Marisa stared at Kent in incomprehension. How could he have done this? Even if he'd hated Jack how could he have placed those two little boys in harm's way?

Jack leaned across the table, his stormy gray eyes swirling with fury. "You didn't do anything to change your life in the past, but you've definitely done something to change your future. I'll make sure you stay locked up for the rest of your miserable life."

Jack unclasped Marisa's hand, stood and stalked out of the room. Marisa went after him, and she found him leaning against the wall outside the interrogation room.

Deep sobs wrenched his body, and Marisa wrapped her arms around him and held tight. Together they wept for the lost boys, their fear palpable in the air around them.

Marisa had no idea how much time had passed before he finally straightened, leaned back against the wall and raised a hand to shield his eyes as if embarrassed by his show of emotion.

"I'm trying to be strong," he finally said, his voice weary.

"You are strong, Jack." She reached up and grabbed his hand and looked into his eyes. "It's a courageous man who walks into a deserted back lot with two suitcases full of money. It's a selfless man who goes to the person he fears most to get the money to save his boys, and it's a strong man who faces up to his fear for his children."

"Where are they, Marisa? What could he have done with them?" The torment in his eyes reflected the emotion inside her heart.

"I wish I knew." Once again he reached for her and they stood in an embrace until Officer Cookson and Harold came out of the interrogation room.

"I don't think he has any information that can help us find your kids," he said. "He's been taken back to the jail, and he'll be charged first thing Monday morning. In the meantime I need to see what we're going to do with Mr. Rothchild."

Harold said nothing. In the past hour he'd looked as if he'd aged ten years. His skin held an unhealthy pallor, and his posture was that of a defeated man.

"He saved my life," Jack said. "If he hadn't shot Paz, then I wouldn't be here right now. You can't arrest him—he killed a dangerous man."

"We're going now to meet with the district attorney and explain the whole situation to him. It's doubtful that Mr. Rothchild will face any charges," Cookson said.

Before any of them could move from their position another officer appeared. "Hey, thought you might be interested that we just got a call from the Timberline Motel. The manager called to tell us he'd found a toddler wandering around in the parking lot. He's got the kid in the office and is waiting for somebody to respond."

Jack grabbed Marisa's hand so tight she winced beneath the pressure. "The Timberline Motel? Where is it?" he asked.

"Let's go," Cookson said. "You can follow me."

Within minutes Marisa was in the passenger seat of Jack's car and Harold was in the back as they barreled down the street just behind Cookson's patrol car.

Marisa's heart beat frantically, although she was

afraid to acknowledge the tiny ray of hope that tried to emerge. It could be the child of somebody staying at the motel. It might have nothing to do with David or Mick.

Jack's knuckles were white on the steering wheel and a muscle knotted in his jaw. She wanted to tell him not to hope too much, but she saw it shining from his eyes—the need to believe that the child in the parking lot of the motel was one of his own. And even though she was afraid for him, she didn't want to be the one to take that hope away.

The Timberline Motel was located in the downtown area about ten minutes from the abandoned casino behind which Paz had been killed.

In the land of flashing, gaudy lights the one-story building was woefully inadequate, as the vacancy sign sported more than a dozen burned-out bulbs. It was obviously a low-rent operation, the kind of motel that probably rented out more by the hour than by the night.

Jack's car squealed to a halt in front of the office, and all three of them jumped out of the car and raced toward the office door.

Marisa was just behind Jack as he burst through the door. She cried out in sweet relief as she saw both David and Mick sitting on chairs in the small lobby.

"Daddy!" Mick cried, and met Jack halfway. Jack released a deep sob as he grabbed Mick to him, then rushed to David and picked him up in his arms, as well.

"Daddy, David needs time-out. He went out the window again," Mick exclaimed with a hint of indignity.

"Time-out," David said and nodded his head with a happy smile.

"We'll worry about time-out later," Jack replied through his tears.

Little David had pulled his Houdini act, climbing out the window of whatever room they had been in. Marisa gave Jack a moment to hug and kiss them, then she moved forward, needing those little-boy hugs and kisses for herself.

As the four of them had a group hug, Officer Cookson and Harold questioned the manager of the motel. "Room 121. He checked in as Martin Bale," Cookson said to Jack. "He didn't show identification and paid cash for one night. I've called in the crime-scene unit to check it all out."

"I'm taking my boys home," Jack said. He held Mick in his arms, and Marisa hugged tight to David, reveling in the warmth of his little arms around her.

"I'm sure we'll have more questions for you," Officer Cookson protested.

"Not tonight," Jack said firmly. "It's way past my boys' bedtime. I'm taking them home now so they can sleep in their own beds." He looked unflinching at the officer. "If you have any questions for me you can come to the ranch either tonight or in the morning, but right now we're going home."

"I'll stay here," Harold said. "I can tell them whatever they need to know, and then Officer Cookson can take me back to my car."

As they walked out of the motel office, a euphoric joy flowed through Marisa's heart. It was over. The danger, the drama, the terror, it was all over now and her family was safe and sound.

Her family. A fierce protectiveness surged through her. Mick and David and Jack. In a shockingly short period of time they had become her heart, her very soul. They were a unit of love she couldn't imagine not having in her life.

They had just buckled the boys into their car seats when Harold walked toward them. Instantly Marisa tensed.

In the minutes that they had driven together and followed Jack to the back lot of the King's Inn casino, Harold had talked a lot, and in that conversation Marisa had recognized him as a man who admitted the mistakes he'd made in his life, a man who had sounded as if he wanted to make amends, turn things around.

But as he approached their car every protective urge she had inside her rose to the surface. She couldn't forget that Harold was the one person on earth who could possibly take the boys from Jack.

"Jack," he called. "We need to talk."

She stepped between Jack and Harold. "Mr. Rothchild, it's late and we need to get the boys home where they belong." She emphasized the last words. "Surely whatever you have to say can wait for another day."

To her surprise Harold's mouth turned upward in a half smile. "You're a pushy little thing, aren't you? I can see what Jack sees in you. I think Jack will want to hear what I have to say."

Jack placed a hand on Marisa's shoulder and faced his father-in-law. "What is it, Harold?"

"I've made a lot of mistakes in my life, Jack. I haven't always been a good man, a righteous man."

"You came all the way out here to tell me that?" Jack asked dryly.

Harold shook his head. "I came all the way out here to tell you that I see now that taking those boys from you would be just another mistake for me. I won't fight you for custody," he said. "I see how those boys love you…how you love them. I just wanted you to know that I have no intention of causing you problems." He looked him straight in the eye. "I promise you that you don't have to worry about me anymore. I might be a lot of things, but you know that I'm a man of my word."

He held out his hand to Jack. Marisa released a tremulous sigh. She believed Harold and apparently so did Jack, for he grasped Harold's hand and they shook.

Marisa felt it in the air, the healing between the two men who both only wanted what was best for the precious little boys who were already sound asleep in their car seats.

"If you need anything for them or for yourself, you call me and I'll see that you get it," Harold said as the handshake ended.

It was only when they were in the car and headed home that the full significance of Harold's words hit Marisa and all the joy she'd felt minutes before whooshed out of her.

Jack now understood what the boys needed from him, both as a disciplinarian and as a loving parent. Harold had promised he had no intention of fighting Jack for custody.

That meant her role in Jack's life was now unnecessary. The very reason for their marriage no longer existed. She was no longer needed. She glanced over at Jack and wondered just how long it would take before he came to the same conclusion.

Chapter 13

Jack sat in the boys' room for hours after they'd come home from the police station. He'd needed to be close enough to them to hear them breathing, to smell the familiar scent of them.

When he thought of how close he'd come to losing them, his heart ached and the memory of his terror nearly froze him in place. So close—so frighteningly close.

They were safe and home where they belonged, and Harold had promised that he wouldn't try to take them away.

Jack believed him. As Harold had said, he might be many things but as he'd reminded Jack he was also a man of his word. He would cause no more anxiety as far as the boys were concerned. Jack could sleep nights knowing that Harold was no longer a threat.

It had to have been the love that Harold saw that existed among the four of them, the family unity that they'd shown must have been what had made him come to his decision to leave them alone.

Sure, there would probably be times in the future where Jack and Harold would butt heads, and certainly Jack expected Harold to be a part of the boys' lives. But the fear of losing them had eased out of Jack's heart, leaving nothing but his intense love behind.

It was near dawn when Marisa appeared in the doorway. She was clad in her little red nightgown and her long hair was tousled around her head—the very sight of her chased any memory of the terror away and he finally rose from the chair and left the boys' room.

"You need to get some sleep," she said softly.

He raked a hand through his hair and released a weary sigh. "Yeah." He smiled and reached out and traced his finger down the side of her cheek, the warmth of her skin stirring him. "Come to bed with me?"

There was a moment of hesitation as she gazed up at him. "All right," she said.

Together they walked down the hallway to his

bedroom. He stripped off his clothes as she crawled in under the sheets.

He was exhausted, both physically and emotionally, but the minute he got into bed next to her and drew her warm body against his, he wanted her.

He didn't want to talk. He didn't want to hash over what the night had held. He just wanted to make love to his wife.

She seemed to sense what he needed. She pulled off her gown and tossed it over the side of the bed, and they came together with a tenderness that was healing.

The horror of the night fell away, replaced by the heat of her lips and the comfort of her naked body against his.

There was a sense of desperation in her kiss, in the way her hands clutched his shoulders, and he guessed that she was chasing away the demons that had plagued them through the long night.

He held her tight and kissed her with all the passion, all the love that burned in his heart. This was the woman he'd been meant to marry, the woman who completed him like no other.

The winds of fate had blown her into his life. She'd needed his boys and they had needed her. The fact that Jack had fallen so deeply in love with her was just icing on the cake.

As he caressed her she cried out softly in pleasure. He loved the feel of her silky flesh, the taste of her skin as he ran his lips from one breast to the other.

He'd never felt this way with Candace. He'd never felt this need, this connection that went far beyond the physical. When he knew she was ready he moved to take her completely.

He entered her and looked down at her, her face bathed in the dawn light. Tears oozed from the corners of her eyes, tears he assumed were of relief, of pleasure.

He closed his eyes as the sweet sensations of being joined with her swept over him. He was lost in her, and being with her chased the last of the horror away, leaving him sated and at peace.

The sound of the boys awoke them just after eight. Jack released a small groan and tried to pull Marisa closer against him, but she quickly slid out of bed and pulled her nightgown over her head.

"Get some more sleep," she said. "I'll take care of them."

Jack closed his eyes as she left the room. Minutes later he heard the sound of Mick's and David's laughter, and there was no way he could stay in bed.

He wanted to be a part of that merriment. He needed to be surrounded by Mick and David and Marisa. His family, he thought with a proud, protective surge.

He got out of bed and pulled on a pair of jeans, then left the room to join the love and laughter.

* * *

"Harold won't face any charges," Rita told Jack and Marisa as they sat in the living room. She had arrived at the ranch just after lunch to check in on her niece and see how everyone was doing.

"I didn't figure he would," Jack replied. "Sure you don't want some coffee or anything?"

"Thanks, but no, I'm fine. Besides, I can only stay a few minutes. We're still sorting through this whole mess." She looked over to where Mick and David sat on the floor with their trucks. "We found some child liquid pain medication in the room. We believe Paz tried to drug the boys before he left them alone last night, but apparently he didn't give them enough to keep them asleep."

"Thank God," Jack said.

"Mick told me they had hamburgers and a drink, then he and David fell asleep on the bed," Marisa said. "They woke up sometime later and they were alone. That's when David decided it would be more fun outside the room. He couldn't manage to twist the door lock, but he could climb up on the dresser just below the window."

"This is one time I'm glad he has a fascination with going out windows," Jack exclaimed.

He gazed at his sons, his heart filling with joy. His gaze shifted to look at Marisa. She'd been quiet this morning, distant and withdrawn since the moment she'd gotten out of bed.

"If Harold hadn't killed Paz, then Paz would have spent the rest of his life behind bars. We know he killed Candace, and we have DNA evidence from Jenna Rothchild's kidnapping that will probably tie him to that, as well." Rita raised a hand to the bandage on the side of her head. "He came way too close to killing me, and it still scares me to think that Marisa might have died in that fire."

Marisa reached out and grabbed her aunt's hand. "Thank God that didn't happen."

"The good news is we located a deposit box in a bank where Paz had placed The Tears of the Quetzal. The ring is now back in police custody where it belongs," Rita said.

"And you still have your job," Marisa said teasingly. Rita had explained to them about the missing ring and how desperate she'd been to find it.

Rita grinned. "Thank goodness my supervisor has a heart. And I've promised that I'll never check out any evidence and bring it home again."

"So all's well that ends well," Jack said.

"We still don't know the extent of Paz's crimes. It might take us some time to unravel it all," Rita said.

"His hatred had years to fester," Marisa said.

"Like Kent's did." Jack frowned as he thought of the man who had once been his friend. "He was too afraid to leave here and take off on his own, too afraid to risk Los Angeles, but he hated me for having the courage to do it without him."

"He'll have a lot of time to think about it in prison," Rita said.

The three talked for a few more minutes, then Rita stood to leave. "Marisa, will you walk me out?"

Jack said goodbye to the FBI agent, then watched as Rita and Marisa left the house together. He got down on the floor between Mick and David and began to play with them.

Now perhaps they could all go back to the life they'd been living before the kidnapping. He wanted that. He wanted the comfortable routine. He wanted the boys and laughter in the daytime and Marisa and passion at night.

For the first time in forever, Jack saw his future before him and he liked what he saw, was eager to live his life—a life filled with love.

Marisa came back inside and went directly to her bedroom. Jack frowned. Her mood was making him uneasy. What was going on in her head? Today should be a day of joy, but a sense of sadness clung to Marisa, a sadness Jack didn't understand and one that worried him more than a little bit.

He thought of the tears he'd seen in her eyes when they'd made love. He'd believed at the time that they had been tears of joy, of relief after the trauma they had suffered. Had he been wrong?

His worry increased when she poked her head out

of her room and called to him. "Jack, could I speak to you for a minute?" she asked.

"I'll be right back, boys," he said as he pulled himself off the floor.

"Hurry up, Daddy. We're going to have a truck race," Mick exclaimed.

As always the word *daddy* shot sweet warmth through him. Bad Jack was gone. Even when he reprimanded them now, they still called him Daddy. Marisa had given him back his fatherhood.

Jack stepped into the guest room, which smelled like her perfume. "What's up?" he asked.

"Aunt Rita brought me something that I thought you'd want to have." She held out a white envelope toward him.

He frowned. "What's that?"

"It's the results of a paternity test for you and the boys."

He looked at her in confusion. "I didn't take a paternity test."

A flash of guilt sparked in her dark brown eyes. "I took swabs from inside the boys' mouths and a coffee cup that you had used and took them to Rita. I know it wasn't my place to do it, but I also knew that paternity was a threat that Harold was holding over your head. Anyway, Rita called in a couple of favors and got it done immediately at the FBI lab."

Jack stared at the envelope as if it were a poisonous snake. He thought of all the times Candace had hinted that she'd been unfaithful, all the times Harold had told him that there was a strong possibility that at least one of the boys wasn't his.

"It doesn't matter," he finally said. He shoved his hands into his pockets. "It doesn't matter what's written on that paper. Both those boys are mine. They're my heart, and a stupid test isn't going to change that."

"Open it, Jack. Go on. It will put an end to the question." She held the envelope closer to him.

Reluctantly he pulled his hands from his pockets and reached out for the envelope. The paper felt hot between his fingers. His mouth went dry as his heart began to beat a quickened rhythm.

He'd told her the truth. It didn't matter to him what the test revealed. Both David and Mick were his sons in every way that counted. Whether or not his blood ran through their veins wouldn't change his love for them.

Still, in knowledge was power. Even though Harold had promised not to try to take the boys, there might come a time when paternity became an issue. Wasn't it better he be armed with the truth now?

His fingers felt big and clumsy as he fumbled to open the envelope. He pulled out the paper inside and allowed the envelope to flutter to the floor at his feet.

"Go on, Jack. Look at it," Marisa said softly. Her

eyes shone overly bright and what he wanted to do was throw the paper on the floor and take her to bed. Instead he opened it and looked.

He released a small cry as he read that in the case of both boys he was their father. There was absolutely no question about it. He looked up to see Marisa's smile. "You knew," he said softly.

She nodded. "I read it before I gave it to you."

"What would you have done if the results had been different? Would you have still given it to me?"

She frowned thoughtfully. "I'm not sure. Thank goodness I didn't have to face that particular dilemma."

It was only then that Jack glanced over her shoulder and saw her suitcase open on the bed. "What are you doing?" he asked.

The smile that had lifted the corners of her luscious mouth fell and her eyes darkened. "I'm packing."

"Packing?" He looked at her in bewilderment. "Where are we going?"

"Not we—me." She averted her gaze from his and took a step backward. "You don't need me here anymore, Jack. You're doing fine with the boys, and Harold has promised he won't fight you for custody. There's really no reason for me to stay here."

A million thoughts flew through Jack's head, a million reasons that he wanted her to stay. "The boys need you," he said.

"They have all they need in you," she replied, her gaze still not meeting his.

She walked over to the closet, pulled several blouses from their hangers and laid them on the bed next to her suitcase.

A crazy sense of panic filled him. It wasn't alarm over the fact that when she left he'd have nobody to help him with Mick and David. He knew she was right. He'd be fine alone with the boys—he just didn't want to be.

The panic came from the fact that he needed her, that he loved her, but it wasn't fair for him to put that on her. She'd made it clear from the very beginning that she was here for his boys, not for him.

"I wish you'd reconsider." His words were woefully inadequate for the pain that filled his heart.

She shook her head. "It's for the best." She walked back to stand in front of him and pulled off the ring he'd given her when they'd exchanged their vows. "This is yours. I just had it out on loan."

He shoved his hands back into his pockets, unwilling to take the ring that had once belonged to his mother and now in his mind belonged to Marisa.

She shrugged and placed the ring on the top of the dresser, where the sunlight sparkled on the little diamond. "I would prefer you not tell the boys I'm leaving for good. I'll tell them I'm taking a little trip. They're young. In a couple of weeks they will forget all about me." Her voice cracked slightly.

As she began to fold the blouses and place them in her suitcase Mick yelled and Jack left her bedroom to tend to the boys.

He knew how to make music. He knew now what to do when one of the boys misbehaved. But he didn't know how to stop the woman he loved from walking away from him.

Hot tears pressed at Marisa's eyes as she sat on the edge of the bed. She tried to staunch them, but they came without volition, fast and furiously running down her cheeks.

She'd awakened that morning with the warmth of Jack's arms around her, with the scent of him lingering on her skin, and she'd known she had to leave.

It would be less painful now than it would be later. At least she was leaving of her own volition rather than being asked to leave by Jack.

Still, that didn't ease the pain that crashed through her. She'd thought she could do this. She'd believed she could marry Jack for the best interest of the boys and keep herself emotionally distant from Jack.

She'd been wrong. Jack had stirred a love and passion in her far greater than she'd ever felt before and it terrified her.

Eventually he wouldn't be satisfied being married to a woman he'd wed only in an attempt to assure his continued custody of his sons. It was better she leave now than wait until Jack's unhappiness forced her out.

She couldn't stay here knowing she had Jack's respect, his gratitude and occasionally his desire without his love. It was just too difficult.

It would have been easier to sneak out like a thief in the night without telling any of them goodbye, but she hadn't been able to stand the thought of not getting goodbye kisses and hugs.

She pulled herself up from the bed and continued her packing. She tried to ignore the noise of the boys playing in the living room, the deep melodious sound of Jack's voice as he spoke to them.

As she finished her packing she realized there had been a small part of her that had expected this moment to come. It was why she hadn't done anything about selling her house.

All too quickly she had her bags packed and was ready to leave. Once again tears pressed hot against her eyes. She didn't want to leave and yet the depth of her emotions for Jack made her want to run, to hide, before the pain got any greater.

With a weariness that weighed heavy she stood and grabbed the suitcase that she'd initially arrived with. It felt heavier than it had when she'd carried it into the house, and she knew the additional weight was the emotion she'd packed inside as she prepared to leave.

When she went into the living room Jack and the boys were in the middle of the floor, a toy truck rally taking place before them.

"M'ssa, watch!" David said as he ran a truck over a pillow and up Jack's arm. Those familiar words nearly broke her. But she refused to weep in front of the boys.

"David, Mick, come sit here with me for a minute." She sat on the sofa and patted either side of her. The boys clambered up beside her, and she put her arms around them.

The pain that cascaded through her was unbearable. For a moment she couldn't breathe. These were the children she was supposed to have, and the man seated on the floor in front of them was the man who would forever own her heart.

"I have to go away for a little while," she finally said. "I want you to be good boys for your daddy while I'm gone."

Mick stared at her. "You promised," he said, his little features screwed up in outrage. "You promised you wouldn't go anywhere."

"Yeah, you promised," David echoed. "Bad M'ssa."

She didn't know whether to laugh or to cry. She looked at Jack, but he offered her no support. He remained on the floor, his gray eyes slightly accusing.

"I know," she said. "But you don't need me

anymore. You have your daddy, who is going to take care of you forever."

"But we want you, too," Mick said.

David leaned into Marisa with his sturdy little body and eyed her angrily. "Bad M'ssa," he repeated.

They were breaking her heart. She couldn't stop the tears that escaped, and she looked at Jack for support. "Bad M'ssa," he said.

She got up from the sofa, knowing if she didn't go now she never would. The two little boys were bad enough, but the pained look in Jack's eyes was killing her.

"I'll see you soon," she said to Mick and David. She grabbed her suitcase and started for the door, which had blurred with a new mist of tears.

"Marisa, wait."

Jack got up from the floor and walked over to her. "Boys, see if you can use those blocks and build a road."

As the two went back to their play, Jack took her by the shoulders. His mesmerizing gray eyes held hers, and again her heartbreak shuddered through her.

"I can't let you leave here without telling you something," he said.

She closed her eyes for a moment, unable to look into his eyes as he told her once again how much he appreciated what she'd done here for him and his sons.

"Marisa, I love you."

Her eyes flew open, and she stared at him in stunned surprise. "I wasn't going to say anything," he continued, "because I know that loving me had nothing to do with what you've been doing here."

"You're just grateful to me," she said as thick emotion pressed hard against her chest.

"You're right, I am grateful. But that's just the beginning of what I feel for you. I love you." He reached up and placed his palm on her cheek. "You excite me, Marisa. You inspire me. I want you to be the woman who is standing beside me as the boys grow from rambunctious little boys into fine young men…and I want us to spend the rest of our lives together."

He dropped his hand from her cheek, and his eyes darkened as if in anticipation of pain. "But I don't want you to stay here because of the boys. I want it to be because you love me, and I'll understand if you have to walk away."

"Oh, Jack, I was leaving because I'm in love with you, because I couldn't stand the idea of staying here with just your gratitude." She smiled through her tears. "I love you, Jack Cortland, and I would be honored to be the woman standing next to you for the rest of our lives."

She barely got the words out of her mouth before he took possession of her lips in a kiss that broke through any fear that might have lingered in her heart, one that electrified her with passion and with the promise of a love to last a lifetime.

"Get Mommy and Daddy," Mick yelled, and grabbed Jack around the knees. Jack toppled to the floor, and pulled Marisa along with him and there was laughter and tickles and love and Marisa knew that this was where she belonged forever…with the family of her heart.

Epilogue

People milled around the front yard, where tables heavy with food stood next to a three-piece band that filled the air with good old country music.

It had been two weeks since the kidnapping, and Jack and Marisa had decided a party was in order to celebrate their life together. They had invited all the Rothchilds as well as Marisa's family.

The party had begun an hour before and was in full swing as Marisa stood on the front porch and surveyed the scene.

Her parents stood next to Harold and his second wife, Anna. The four of them chatted with animation. Probably discussing Las Vegas real estate and the current depressed situation in the market.

Harold had gone home from the police station the morning after the kidnapping and had told his trophy wife he wanted a divorce. She'd moved out with their son, and she and Harold were now hammering out the details of the breakup. In the meantime Harold had been seeing a lot of his previous wife, Anna.

Conner Rothchild, Harold's nephew, had arrived with his new wife, Vera LaRue, a sweet, sassy woman who had worked as a dancer, and standing near the food table was Natalie, Candace's twin sister, and Natalie's new husband, Matt.

"I've got more beans ready to go out," Betty said from the doorway behind Marisa. "You know the rules, I cook—but I don't serve."

Marisa smiled at Betty. "Thanks, I'll be right in to get them." Betty had worked for the past two days fixing food for this event without a complaint. She'd even begun to allow Marisa to have her morning coffee in the kitchen, and the two women had become friends.

Jenna Rothchild and her fiancé, FBI agent Lex Duncan, stood with Rita, and Marisa could only guess that they were hashing over the subject of Paz Marquez and his numerous crimes.

She went into the kitchen and grabbed the large pan of baked beans that Betty had ready to go out on the food table.

As she carried it out she saw Sam and Max standing

awkwardly together a small distance from the crowd. They no longer made her nervous. She'd come to realize that they were painfully shy. She motioned them closer as she placed the bean pan on the table.

"I hope you two plan on getting something to eat," she said. "And maybe later you'll show me how to two-step to this music."

Sam's cheeks turned a hot pink. "I don't dance, but I definitely eat."

"I might do a little two-stepping later," Max said, his gaze going to a cute blonde named Suzie who had come as a guest of one of the others.

A hand fell on Marisa's shoulder, and she turned to see Rita. "Nice party," Rita said.

"Thanks. It's nice to see all the Rothchilds playing nice together," Marisa replied.

"Did Harold tell you he got the ring back? It's now in a warehouse waiting to be catalogued. He's donated it to his touring collection of art."

"I say good riddance. That ring caused far more heartache than good," Marisa replied.

"Oh, I don't know about that. If you believe the Mayan legend, then anyone who comes into contact with the ring finds their true love."

Marisa laughed. "I think I proved the legend wrong. I was close to the ring when Patrick and I were together, but it definitely didn't work on me where he was concerned."

Rita smiled. "You must have had some of the

ring magic on you when you met Jack. From what you've told me it was love at first sight for the both of you." Rita pulled Marisa into a hug. "I've never seen you look so happy."

"I've never been so happy," Marisa said as Rita released her.

"And I hear you've started interviewing for nannies for your agency."

Marisa nodded. "I had my first interview yesterday. Within two months I hope to have the business up and running."

"Good for you," Rita exclaimed. "And now I'm going to get a plate of this delicious food."

As Marisa headed back to the front porch she noticed Anna's daughter, Silver Rothchild, in one of the lawn chairs, her handsome husband, Captain Austin Dearing, at her side.

As Marisa watched the two, Austin smiled and reached out and touched Silver's protruding stomach. It was an intimate touch between a man and the pregnant woman he loved, and it sent just a tiny wave of pain through Marisa.

She would never know the touch of a man on her pregnant tummy. She'd never experience morning sickness or the flutter of life inside her.

The pain quickly vanished as she heard David's laughter riding the hot breeze. She looked beyond the scorched ground where the barn once had stood, out to the stables in the distance.

Jack had surprised the boys with ponies, and he was now leading them on their first pony ride. Her heart filled her chest as she gazed at the man who hadn't rocked her feet with the rhythm of his drums but had definitely rocked her world with his love.

"He's become quite a man." Harold's deep voice spoke from just behind her.

Marisa smiled at the dapper older man. "Yes, he has. He's always been a good man. He just needed someone to believe in him."

"And you do."

"With all my heart," Marisa replied.

Harold's gaze swept the area and came to rest on Anna. "It's important to have somebody in your life who believes in you, somebody who loves you. I'm hoping this time I'll get it right. Anna is a good woman."

He frowned as a cell phone rang from his pocket. He pulled it out and answered. His face turned ashen, and he held the phone away from his ear and stared at Marisa. "It's June," he said, his voice a stunned whisper.

"June?" Marisa knew that was Harold's first wife. "But I thought she was dead."

"So did I," Harold ground out. He placed the phone back to his ear and wandered away.

Marisa watched him go, wondering what new drama was about to hit the lives of the Rothchilds. She returned her gaze toward the stables and saw Jack motion to her.

Her heart filled her chest as even with the distance she could feel his love reaching out to her. It would probably be rude for her to abandon their guests and run down to the stables.

She hesitated only a moment and then took off at a quick pace toward Jack and the boys. Surely everyone would recognize that she was hurrying toward the little boys who were the sons of her heart. Surely her guests would forgive her for leaving them to run toward the man she adored and the future that shone bright with the promise of laughter and love.

* * * * *

MILLS & BOON®
are proud to present a new series

nocturne™

Three dramatic and sensual tales of paranormal romance
available every month from June 2010

The excitement begins with a thrilling quartet:

TIME RAIDERS:

Only they can cross the boundaries of time; only they
have the power to save humanity.

The Seeker by Lindsay McKenna
21st May

The Slayer by Cindy Dees
21st May

The Avenger by PC Cast
4th June

The Protector by Merline Lovelace
18th June

INTRIGUE

Coming next month

2-IN-1 ANTHOLOGY

PEEK-A-BOO PROTECTOR
by Rita Herron

An abandoned baby in Samantha's care is the target of merciless kidnappers. Police chief John's sworn to protect the pair – even if he loses his heart in the bargain.

UNDERCOVER FATHER
by Ann Voss Peterson

Someone wants to harm the baby boy left aboard Reed's ship. Tenacious PI Josie can get answers. Could she also be the thing that's been missing in Reed's life?

2-IN-1 ANTHOLOGY

A VOICE IN THE DARK
by Jenna Ryan

A serial killer's brutal attack left criminal profiler Noah scarred and determined to hide from the world, until he met beautiful FBI agent Angel – the killer's next target!

TERMS OF SURRENDER
by Kylie Brant

Targeted by a revenge-obsessed criminal, hostage negotiators and ex-lovers Dace and Jolie are reunited. Yet can they heal their hearts for a second chance at love?

On sale 21st May 2010

Available at WHSmith, Tesco, ASDA, Eason and all good bookshops.
For full Mills & Boon range including eBooks visit
www.millsandboon.co.uk

® INTRIGUE

Coming next month

2-IN-1 ANTHOLOGY

TWIN TARGETS
by Jessica Andersen

Sidney would do anything to save her twin sister, even break the law. Could Special Agent John set her straight – or would both she and her sister pay the price?

DESERT ICE DADDY
by Dana Marton

When Akeem, billionaire and heir to a sheikhdom, learns that his ex Taylor's little boy has disappeared, he vows to bring her son home – and reclaim his woman!

SINGLE TITLE

HIS SECRET LIFE
by Debra Webb

Her mission is to find a hero who doesn't want to be found, but Colby Agency PI Jane always gets her man. She just didn't count on her irresistible attraction to him!

On sale 4th June 2010

2 FREE BOOKS
AND A SURPRISE GIFT

We would like to take this opportunity to thank you for reading this Mills & Boon® book by offering you the chance to take TWO more specially selected books from the Intrigue series absolutely FREE! We're also making this offer to introduce you to the benefits of the Mills & Boon® Book Club™—

- **FREE home delivery**
- **FREE gifts and competitions**
- **FREE monthly Newsletter**
- **Exclusive Mills & Boon Book Club offers**
- **Books available before they're in the shops**

Accepting these FREE books and gift places you under no obligation to buy, you may cancel at any time, even after receiving your free books. Simply complete your details below and return the entire page to the address below. You don't even need a stamp!

YES Please send me 2 free Intrigue books and a surprise gift. I understand that unless you hear from me, I will receive 5 superb new stories every month, including two 2-in-1 books priced at £4.99 each and a single book priced at £3.19, postage and packing free. I am under no obligation to purchase any books and may cancel my subscription at any time. The free books and gift will be mine to keep in any case.

Ms/Mrs/Miss/Mr _____ Initials _____

Surname _____

Address _____

_____ Postcode _____

E-mail _____

Send this whole page to: Mills & Boon Book Club, Free Book Offer, FREEPOST NAT 10298, Richmond, TW9 1BR